More Praise for *The Delicate Beast*

"In a headlong flight from history's black-winged angels, *The Delicate Beast* spirals across the globe and the twentieth century in densely sensual prose that merges the Caribbean surreal of Alejo Carpentier with the looping, philosophical conundrums of Javier Marías."
—**Esther Allen**, translator of Javier Marías's *Dark Back of Time* and Antonio di Benedetto's *Zama*

"Brilliantly written, *The Delicate Beast* is a sweeping novel of a young man's search for identity that follows him from a boyhood touched by the splendors and dangers of the 'Tropical Republic' into a new and startling international life. It is a powerful tale."
—**Peter Constantine**, author of *The Purchased Bride*

The Delicate Beast

The Delicate Beast

ROGER CELESTIN

BELLEVUE LITERARY PRESS
NEW YORK

First published in the United States in 2025
by Bellevue Literary Press, New York

For information, contact:
Bellevue Literary Press
90 Broad Street
Suite 2100
New York, NY 10004
www.blpress.org

This is a work of fiction. Characters, organizations, events, and places (even those that are actual) are either products of the author's imagination or are used fictitiously.

Library of Congress Cataloging-in-Publication Data
Names: Celestin, Roger, author.
Title: The delicate beast / Roger Celestin.
Description: First edition. | New York : Bellevue Literary Press, 2025.
Identifiers: LCCN 2024011887 | ISBN 9781954276369 (paperback ; acid-free paper) | ISBN 9781954276376 (ebook)
Subjects: LCGFT: Novels.
Classification: LCC PS3553.E47 D45 2025 | DDC 813/.54--dc23/eng/20240624
LC record available at https://lccn.loc.gov/2024011887

This publication is made possible by the New York State Council on the Arts with the support of the Office of the Governor and the New York State Legislature.

This project is supported in part by an award from the National Endowment for the Arts.

Book design and composition by Mulberry Tree Press, Inc.

Bellevue Literary Press is committed to ecological stewardship in our book production practices, working to reduce our impact on the natural environment.

♾ This book is printed on acid-free paper.

Manufactured in the United States of America.

First Edition

10 9 8 7 6 5 4 3 2 1

paperback ISBN: 978-1-954276-36-9

ebook ISBN: 978-1-954276-37-6

This novel, in part about generations,
is dedicated to three generations:
For Sonia, Cassandra, and Monsieur Homère.

The Delicate Beast

Prologue

It is my belief no man ever understands quite his own artful dodges to escape from the grim shadow of self-knowledge.

—Joseph Conrad, *Lord Jim*

SUNDAY, APRIL 23, 1995

"I am going back to Sarajevo next week."

The man has an accent, but otherwise the words come out flat, like "I'm going back to Manhattan this evening." He's sitting in the middle of a group of people in the living room of David and Carmen's Brooklyn brownstone. He looks out of place here, among these cheery people; he has the face of someone who is grieving.

It's spring, finally. The pear trees are in glorious white bloom throughout the city. The summer heat is still far away. A luminous day, an inaugural event, this Sunday gathering at David and Carmen's house in Brooklyn: For the first time since that first chilly day in autumn, that first frost so long ago, people are able to gather outside; shirtsleeves and summer dresses, already; only a few of the guests are wearing sweaters or jackets.

A buffet affair—too many people to sit down at a table. A grill has been set up in the garden. Chicken breasts are marinating in the refrigerator, soaking in a mix of olive oil, lemon juice, salt, pepper, crushed ginger, and garlic in several flat pans covered tightly with plastic wrap; on another shelf sits a large bowl of potato salad with red onions and capers in a mustard dressing. A variety of appetizers have already been laid out on the long wooden kitchen table—eggplant dip, spinach pies, nuts, olives, hummus, cheeses; breads and crackers—pita, pumpernickel, multigrain (no potato chips); fruit juices (no sugary drinks) and bottles of wine, red and white, of motley provenances—offerings from the guests, who are still arriving. It's Sunday, after all, and still early, one in the afternoon at the latest. But, already, the usual excess of people are converging in the kitchen; the ancient appeal of the hearth, still, now, here. Others have gathered on the narrow back terrace and, through a metal spiral stairway, gradually spill out into the small garden below. There are quite a few children, and they've adopted the garden as their territory; in its limited confines they've managed to work up a sweat running from one another and to nowhere in particular; once in a while, the guests inside the house hear their gleeful screams coming from below.

Outside the wide windows of David and Carmen's book-lined living room, out there beyond the promenade, on the opposite bank of the East River, the spiked promontory of skyscrapers rises at the tip of Manhattan like a postcard from the fifties: The World Trade Center towers stand out sharply against the clear blue sky, dwarfing the squatter oblongs of the surrounding buildings. On this side of the river, below David and Carmen's living room windows, people walk unhurriedly on the promenade. Some of them are still, their arms and elbows leaning on the railing, their hands cupping their faces. They gaze at the river, the massive and delicate bridges, the shimmering buildings across the wide expanse of water on this clear

April afternoon. A wiry woman in pumpkin orange shorts and a black T-shirt is attempting to push a lamppost off its base—stretching before her run. Among the others passing by are four people, a family, one can tell, even from the windows of David and Carmen's living room. It must be the way they progress, apart yet together, the man and the woman's collective gait, the inquiring bodies of the two boys scampering ahead, but their heads turned back from sudden stops and starts, seeking permission to go on. Now the four have all halted their uneven but forward progress and gathered in front of a brightly painted box on wheels, from which a diminutive man, perhaps a boy, scoops what must be ice cream—it's difficult to tell from the living room window. The father hands out cones to the two boys and pays. They continue on the boardwalk. We are all hurtling toward summer.

Back in David and Carmen's house, a few of the guests have claimed the armchairs and the couch in the living room, and remained in them since they arrived: the old-timers, the habitués, the inner circle. The airy room, bathed in early-afternoon light, is the best place to be at this time, on such a day, capacious enough to accommodate the unusual number of people.

Many academics among the guests: professors and graduate students, as well as a few writers, musicians, and journalists. Most of them seem to be from nearby, from New York City anyway, though there are some with that distinct air of having come from out of town: an affable bearing, a loose-jointed ease, the absence of the swift angularity of New Yorkers. Folding chairs, even desk chairs with wheels, have gradually been brought out from other parts of the house, from the bedrooms, from Carmen's study upstairs, David's study in the basement. The early arrivals, and those who have come into the living room from the kitchen and the garden, have all heard the man who has said he is going back to Sarajevo.

"But how *can* you go back?" This from Robert Carpentier, who knows even as he speaks that he's going against the grain, disrupting the good mirth and consensus—Banquo's ghost at Macbeth's banquet. It is already too late; everyone has already agreed that it is a good thing, the right thing, for the man from Sarajevo to go back to the besieged city.

Carpentier was among the late arrivals, but he's already had a few "rum & rum cocktails," as he calls them. He had brought the rum himself, as well as the lime and brown sugar used to make the drinks—David and Carmen, who barely drink even beer and wine, could not be counted on for such things. Even obtaining the ice had been an ordeal: a run to the corner bodega; two lefts, one right, he was told; returning by the same itinerary, but backward—he is so bad at finding his way around, he has to tell himself one left, two rights, holding on to the ice cubes tightly packed in their plastic wrapping, emptying into the sink the last dregs of a carton of orange juice, now his makeshift shaker, asking Carmen for a sharp knife to cut the lime, a large spoon to crush the ice in his palm, *all this activity* before having the first of those rum & rum cocktails. And now he's had a few of them; he's made the rounds, glass in hand; he's gone around the living room, the kitchen, the halls, and the garden, coming up against people; looking for the bathroom, he's even wandered upstairs to the bedrooms and the study.

Carpentier knows very few people at this Sunday lunch, but he loves this kind of gathering, the ease of beginning and continuing a conversation, surrounded by all these bodies and faces, strangers, but strangers of the same large tribe, brought together by friends to a house filled with people; the precautions, the self-preservation of the streets and public places vanish; the usual barriers of a great metropolis fall. As happens on a college campus or in a village, to pass by without greeting is unthinkable: no attachments, no obligations, but still the possibility of exchange. An oasis, of sorts. *Away from everything else.*

But now, in the puzzled silence, all those bodies and faces are turned or turning toward Robert Carpentier, who asks again, this time with something tighter in his voice, "How can you go back?" The man from Sarajevo has shifted his compact body in the armchair to face him and, probably, to answer Carpentier, but before he can speak, other voices rise.

"What do you mean?"

"How can you ask?"

"Of course he's going back!"

"We can't just stand by and let these people be slaughtered!"

"We have to do something!"

"You don't understand!"

"You can be such a prick."

He had driven from Manhattan with Eve. On the way to the gathering in Brooklyn, they had picked up Yann and Adelaide, mutual friends of theirs and David and Carmen's. In the car, the conversation was about the bombing in Oklahoma City, just four days before—the 168 dead, the hundreds wounded, and Bill Clinton's speech proclaiming today, April 23, 1995, a national day of mourning. Eve and Yann agreed that Clinton had done well in his eulogy, acknowledging grief, comforting, pointing the way to recovery, but staying away from being self-serving.

"He's not just another politician talking, taking advantage of this to score points," said Yann as they were crossing the Brooklyn Bridge. "Today is also Timothy McVeigh's birthday, today of all days; can you believe that, the one behind the whole thing?" Eve asked. In her corner of the backseat, Adelaide looked out the window and cried silently for the dead. Carpentier always thought she was a bit theatrical. *Why be so emotional? There's something indecent, even fake, about her behavior, pretending she's concerned by what happened to all these anonymous people.* He said nothing, and, ostensibly, focused on the driving. The explosion, the 168 dead, and the hundreds wounded in Oklahoma City seemed far away to him, even if *the attack has taken place on American soil*, as the newscasters, commentators, specialists, and experts of all kinds, and now everybody else, kept intoning. He was thinking about Eve; her comment about McVeigh seemed like an effort to join in, a break in her remoteness earlier today and these past few weeks.

He'd had to ask her several times to go with him to the Sunday meal at David and Carmen's. "What's wrong? You've always liked them. It'll look strange if I just show up without you." Since she remained silent, he continued, his irritation beginning to break through. "Do you want me to tell them you're not feeling well?" Only when he resorted to both of them not going—"Fine, we'll just stay here; I'll call Yann and Adelaide, let them know we can't pick them up anymore"—did she relent, but as if doing him a favor, which made the care she took in getting dressed all the more unexpected.

He waited while she dressed. From the living room, he heard the snap of her underwear, the rustle of her dress. He could smell her perfume. When she came out of the bedroom, he couldn't help himself and reached out to clasp the back of her neck; she knew the fierceness that lay below his apparent detachment; she had been attracted to this unexpected blend very early on, but that morning she knew that to yield, even for a few seconds, was best; she allowed his hand to remain there for a few seconds; he didn't attempt to kiss her; he removed his hand and, after finding his keys on the couch, held the door to the apartment open for her. Without a word, they walked the two blocks to the parking garage. Even past noon, the city had the muffled quality of Sunday mornings: lines of people waiting for brunch at busy diners; joggers coming back from their runs, their faces drained and beatific; there was even a church bell ringing somewhere, like something from village life, here in the midst of Manhattan. He took sidelong glances at her, taking her in; he walked more slowly, keeping her close by. *She walks in beauty, like the night . . . every raven tress*, fragments of a poem memorized in high school. She can take his breath away—even when she eats; a friend of his told him a long time ago that the one thing you can't do with people you hate is to watch them eat. He could watch Eve eat forever. Even now, seven years after their pact.

The pact he had made with Eve that day in her apartment. September 1988. They had met a month before in Greece, in early August on a pine-scented beach about half an hour outside of Athens. Afterward, they had spent almost every day and every night of that summer together. When they'd both returned to New York, not to live in the same place seemed unbearable. He was enthralled; he held on to her like a desperate man. *I will die if I'm not with her.* It was only early September, the first weekend of the month, but the weather had already shifted; the air was brisk. They made their pact. It was seven years ago; it was centuries ago.

Now, here they are; here he is in his rum daze. The people in this sun-drenched room seem shrill and unanimous, about to burst with indignant righteousness after he's blurted out his question. Unfair to think of them as a mob, but the thoughts come quickly: *Look at them, boys and girls they used to be, like their children in the garden; now they've grown older,* with *such strong opinions, safely ensconced in their lives and certainties, yet ungrateful for it, pretending they're ready to risk it all, foaming at the mouth; some have gray hair, white hair, move with difficulty; others, the majority, the younger, vigorous ones, seem even more incensed. Of all people, that sad-faced, sad-eyed, melancholy Myron, who always comes with his lute, is smiling; he's the first among them to speak out. Never did like him; always with that moronic air of knowing something you don't. A lute! A fucking lute! Every fucking time! He thinks he has to play at the end of meals, like some fucking court musician; come to think of it, he looks like the jester with the silly grin in that Frans Hals painting. Like the carmine-lipped jester holding his lute, Myron is even wearing a kind of cap, but Myron's is a thickly woven green, red, and gold wool cap! Inside the house, on a day like this!*

Must think he's some sort of white Rasta or something. I'd like to wipe that grin off his face. Fuck them all. They have no idea.

Carpentier is surprised by the violence and the possible unfairness of his thoughts. *I have to stop, I have to stop. It's useless; they don't understand. I should just get out of here or it'll get messy.* The last thing he wants. He's wondering how to leave, how to find the quickest way through all these people and out of the house, but it's too late. From his armchair across the living room, the Yugoslav speaks directly to him: "Why do you say this? I *am* going back."

He seems less awkward, the Yugoslav, less reticent than he was two weeks ago, yes, two weeks ago it was, at that *fund-raiser for Sarajevo* at one of Eve's wealthy friends' apartments, the Smythes' penthouse on Fifth Avenue. He had just arrived in New York, the Yugoslav, and he seemed almost shy in that huge living room full of people, an Upper East Side crowd not at all like the guests at this Sunday gathering in Brooklyn, where he apparently knows quite a few of the guests; he's been engaged in several conversations, whispered exchanges with David, Myron, a few others; they all seem to gravitate around him, to be paying homage, and he seems to take it as his due. Maybe this is how Robert Carpentier sees it: the Yugoslav placidly holding court at his execution. Already, in that penthouse two weeks ago, there was something about the Yugoslav that galled him, something about the man's composure even as he seemed wary and out of place.

Now, at David and Carmen's house in Brooklyn, in the book-lined living room, Carpentier feels like he's falling, unable to stop an unraveling. He looks for Eve. She stands out so clearly from all the others, but—*Oh, my love, what is this look on your face?*

He speaks to the Yugoslav across the room, and even as he speaks again, he knows it's too late; even as he speaks again, he can't bring himself to believe the other man really means what he's saying with such apparent resolve, "I am going back to Sarajevo."

A joust: two mounted knights, each warily observing the other through his visor across a field from centuries past, but no standards are fluttering in the wind here, no armor, no lances, no horses neighing, front hooves raised, ready for the gallop toward the opponent; no richly dressed nobles sitting under a dais, or commoners standing on the grass; only this group of people here and now, in summer dresses, in shirtsleeves, holding their plastic cups, their paper plates, waiting.

"If you're going back, you must know there's a good chance you won't be hurt." They seem to be the only two in the room, speaking from different realms. Again, Carpentier wishes he could leave, find a way out of what he has started, but it's too late, the public confrontation has already begun.

"That is not the point. Who can know?" The Yugoslav seems to be taking great care to pronounce each and every word.

"I mean there's actually a way to get there; you can go to the airport here, you can call for a cab, you can catch a plane here, in New York; you can find a safe way to get back into Sarajevo after you land at some other airport, I don't know which, I don't know where, even if they say it's surrounded. There has to be a doubt. You can't be certain you'll be killed, or that they won't do something to you." Like a stream contained for too long, now flooding out from him.

"That is not the point. People are dying every day in Sarajevo. I have to go back."

"No, you don't. And if you're going back, it's because there's a doubt. There's a possibility you won't be damaged."

. . .

. . .

"I think you are turning this into an intellectual conversation. This is not a question of probability."

"No; I really mean it; I mean *damaged*. They put you in a cell somewhere; they torture you; they break your teeth; they pull your nails out with pincers. And then they throw you away somewhere. If you were certain, you wouldn't go back. That's what I'm trying to say."

. . .

The Yugoslav shifts in his seat again, looking at Carpentier—at a loss, or pitying him? He seems about to continue, to add something, but, sitting on a stool in a corner of the living room, Myron now gets involved, his whiny voice rising, speaking to Carpentier even as he takes the others in. "You just don't get it, do you?" Carpentier just wants to take the few steps between himself and Myron and bash his face in. He wants to scream, "No, you don't get it, any of you. Look at this one with his wool cap and his lute; do you see him taking the next plane to Sarajevo?" Before he can make a move or say anything, the Yugoslav's words are heard by everyone, a kind of exoneration from across the room: "I know what you mean; you may be right. But I am going back to Sarajevo. People are being killed there every day."

There is nothing else to be said. The others are already

heading for the kitchen. They seem to be walking through him. He asks himself what Myron could possibly mean by "You just don't get it." *I should have bashed his face in.* He looks for Eve; she has disappeared somewhere, maybe upstairs, maybe to the garden. Maybe she's gone.

PART I

The Tropical Republic

When they begin the beguine
It brings back the sound of music so tender,
It brings back a night of tropical splendor,
It brings back a memory ever green.

I'm with you once more under the stars
And down by the shore an orchestra's playing
And even the palms seem to be swaying
When they begin the beguine.

To live it again is past all endeavor,
Except when that tune clutches my heart.

—Cole Porter, "Begin the Beguine"

The truth about that past is not that it is too brief, or too superficial, but only that we, having turned our faces so resolutely away from it, have never demanded from it what it has to give.

—James Baldwin, "A Question of Identity," in *Notes of a Native Son*

FRIDAY, APRIL 26, 1963—AND BEFORE, AND AFTER

Tropical night falling

Tropical night falling. Night falling abruptly, as it does in that part of the world. The serrated wings of bats descend on the suddenly dark water of the swimming pool in the house's main garden, swooping down to drink, their rapid, liquid dips the only sound before they swerve away and disappear in the young darkness. The boy has wondered before: Do the same ones keep coming back? Probably not, since the gardeners always find them in the morning, bats in charcoal gray clumps, poisoned by the chlorine, their velvet sheen faded, their small furry bellies distended, not too far away, on the other side of the tall hibiscus and bougainvillea hedges that border the pool on three sides.

Sometimes, an equally or even more unlucky bat—it depends on one's perspective, especially the bat's—wanders into some house and gets caught by boys, who stick a lit cigarette in its slit of a mouth, impale the cigarette onto the tiny pointed teeth; they lodge the cigarette firmly and place the bat in its favorite position, its natural position; it hangs upside down, puffs and puffs, smokes the entire cigarette like a tobacco-addled old man and then falls onto a tiled floor, or a wooden floor, or a beaten earth floor somewhere, blissful, in pain, who knows? During the day, boys in that part of the world also tie the almost invisible but solid filament tips of long grass shoots into a hangman's noose; the nooses are gently lowered and slipped onto the necks of immobile, unblinking lizards: small green ones with pale underbellies, a lighter green fading to white; or the larger ones, with a rougher, bumpy skin; the bumps on the larger ones range from light gray to a dark, almost black violet; they look like miniature iguanas. Once the filament is lowered, the noose is tightened; the shoot is straightened out just tight enough and becomes a leash; the lizards are walked around like miniature dogs. Tropical games, tropical days and nights.

Tropical is misleading for the things that happened

on that Friday in April 1963, though, the day of the whistle blow in the sun-drenched schoolyard. With their furry bellies, their ringed, shiny eyes bulging from misshapen miniature pig-wolf heads, with their toothy snouts grafted onto umbrella wings swooping down on the water in the young darkness, the bats are more fitting embodiments of the things that occurred on that particular day; but, in passing recognition of the enchantment *tropical* held for the boy and for so many others all the years before that day, in acknowledgment of what the word contained, contains still for so many, it will have to be, even if only momentarily, *tropical games, tropical days and nights*, and, for good measure, emerald green mountains, turquoise blue seas, champagne waters, pulsing music, impossibly large green fronds, orange-yellow or purple or dark green fruit hanging from branches curved by the fruits' bunched weight; dramatic, even if swift, sunsets: a rushed feast of colors before darkness descends.

For years before that day and night in late April 1963, among these colors, in this light, in this landscape where no one in the five generations of his family has died since he was born, the boy's fundamental contentment has rarely been disturbed. There are outings to the seaside or the mountains; his grandfather's stories of duels at dawn and buried treasures; the Technicolor blaze of gladiators, cowboys, and surfers in the darkness of the small movie house near the church square; his inchoate but pleasurable longings; there is his white First Communion suit, his only suit; there are the priests in their own creamy white and wine-stained robes at the Séminaire—essentially a school, in spite of its name—where he is still wearing short pants on that day in late April, not yet studying Latin and Greek, since that doesn't happen until the following year, when his classes will be taught by the priest rather than by civilians, the men and women who teach the elementary grades. Most of the priests, who run the school, are from Alsace; they have names like Schmitt, Schultz, Krieger, or Ziegler. Père Schmitt, Father Schmitt, just Schmitt to the boys among themselves, is the headmaster. Much later, the boy will have a stable image of the thin lips, pink amid the blue-gray of the shaven jaw and chin, the almost bald head, with the remaining hair cut close to the skull and brushed back stiffly on either side, the too-large nose, and the too-small eyes, a milky and malevolent pale blue behind the gold-framed glasses.

Noontime in the sun-drenched schoolyard

Today, on this Friday in late April in the early years of the decade, the boy is unable to consider such specifics. He feels only alarm, a sudden loosening in his bowels, when Schmitt's whistle blow comes piercing through the din of midday recess in the sun-drenched schoolyard where hundreds of boys are playing. Not quite a second after the whistle blow, the running, yelling boys' bodies stop and freeze in mid-motion; their thin legs quickly come to stillness on firm ground, and their arms fall rigid at their sides. Everything stops: the low, constant buzz of adolescent voices—they still have the voices of girls, these boys on the brink of manhood—frail voices that, until the whistle blow, have been repeating passages like incantations, carrying in the hot noontime air swaths of history, entire paragraphs of civics textbooks, rules of grammar, or poems and theorems to be memorized for recitation in the afternoon classes. Everything stops, even the quick and quiet games of tic-tac-toe the boys play by moving stones along finger-drawn lines on the thin films of dust made by stamping their schoolboys' boots on the black tiles of the checkerboard terrace that borders an entire side of the schoolyard.

The boys stop, the wind stops, the sun stops, and, in that awful stillness, in the noon glare, he knows very quickly that he is the designated one, the culprit who has interrupted the flow of the day, because, after the whistle blow, of the hundreds of names, it is his and none other Schmitt has called. The headmaster has raised two fingers to indicate the count. In the past, he has raised one, or two, or, very rarely, three fingers, because any more strokes of the thin, compact whip of braided bull's nerve, to be applied to the fleshy mound somewhere between a boy's buttocks and his thighs, are too sharp, too cutting, not to make welts or even draw blood as the priest's pink face turns red and purple from the quick exertion of energy.

In the noon glare and stillness, with the now silent whistle held between his teeth, index and middle finger of one hand raised above his head and pointing to the sky like a victory sign, but in fact indicating the number of strokes—two, then, this time—the solitary index finger of the other hand stiffly and horizontally pointing to his office, Schmitt stands like a semaphore, both contorted clown and righteous executioner now emerged from the shade, from where he has been watching over the hundreds of boys like a reptile.

The offense—a thrown stone, *strictement interdit*, strictly forbidden, as the regulations clearly state, along with a number of other fastidiously formulated rules: *It is strictly forbidden to throw stones; exiting the school is strictly forbidden outside of recess hours; speaking Creole is strictly forbidden inside the school*—is to be expiated after recess.

The boy is eleven. In the nearly six years he's been attending the Séminaire, this is the first time his name has been called. He is stunned, but he's witnessed the prewhipping part of the ritual so many times over the years that his body moves in spite of itself toward the hall in front of the headmaster's office. This is the rule, the expected, accurate, and unwavering response to Schmitt's pantomimed edict. He walks slowly in the dissolving silence; he walks from the sun into the shade of the hall as all the others begin to breathe and talk and move again. No commiseration is forthcoming, at least not for the moment and certainly not overtly; the other boys have too much to get back to before the end of recess: the unfinished games, the memorizations, one last chance to purchase taffy, peanuts, caramels, hard candy, shaved ice covered with multicolored syrupy toppings from street vendors posted just outside the school walls—this is the Tropics, and in the Tropical Republic, where endless summer reigns, ice is primordial and, even in the smallest towns, villages, scattered cinder-block and thatched-roof huts, the party's over when there's no more ice—one last chance to make a purchase before the weighty iron gates of the school's entrance are shut and noon recess ends. Besides, this happens almost every day, and by the time the boy reaches the shade of the hall facing Schmitt's office, the noise and movement are back to their continuous, controlled chaos. He is already alone.

He's seen many boys emerging from the headmaster's office, tears streaming down their faces. *Today, it's my turn*, he barely admits to himself as he places both feet on a single white tile in the hall, where he is to stand absolutely still until the end of recess—a single white tile, no part of his feet to stick out onto a contiguous black tile, this is the rule—with nothing to do but remain upright and think about the pain and the shaming to come. Recess will go on another half hour, followed by the lining up, class by class, in ordered rows, and then the silent procession back to classrooms for the afternoon.

And he waits. *How did this happen? I've been so careful; I've been so good; Schmitt will be coming for me soon.* He hopes recess will never end. He remembers the time he had the measles, with its fever and red patches eventually turning into flaky, itchy spots. "Don't scratch," his mother said softly to him, "if you do, you will have permanent scars." Such finality for such a small, spontaneous gesture. Or the time he jumped into the old stone basin, before the sleek turquoise pool was built on the very same spot, and the sole of his right foot landed on a jagged and cruelly sharp piece of broken glass invisible in the clear water; the searing pain, the cloud of blood billowing around him, his mother jumping into the water and embracing him, screaming, "My child, my child! Someone, help me! Help me, please!" and she not knowing where all the blood was coming from, her dress floating around her or sticking to her skin, holding him in her arms. These were heroic episodes in which he bore no blame or shame, when he emerged renewed and intact, reinstated in the wholeness of a blissful time when he saw death and its signs only through the big car's windows: satiny, mauve fabric draped over church doors, or over the doors of other people's houses; black armbands of mourning worn by other people; other people wearing white shirts, black suits, black dresses, hats and veils, their bodies bent, their faces made ugly, twisted by a pain foreign to him. He is still in that blind contentment of privileged childhood. No one in that family of so many has died since he was born; five generations live in that place and time in the compound in the hills above the straggling and crowded capital of the Tropical Republic.

This noontime in the sun-drenched yard is different from the measles or the jagged piece of glass in the basin. This time around, he's been singled out by something knowing and calculating, similar to the man who asked a few weeks before, looking directly at him, *What's he doing here, that little roach?* on that Sunday morning when he and some other boys were sitting on the lawn of a friend's house. The man's question, spat out like seeds, and his disdainful, threatening look were already the confirmation of something else, the beginning of another time. Today, in the sun-drenched yard, he thinks it's all terribly unfair; he thinks it's a mistake, or even a nightmare. *I must be having a nightmare; I'm about to wake up; this, for a small stone, a very small stone, thrown at no one in particular!* Some brownnosed Judas might have whispered to Schmitt that the stone was thrown at one of the stained-glass windows of the church that borders the schoolyard, and maybe he did throw the stone at the windows, answering a dare, proving his mettle, trying to make friends.

And now, here he is, standing on a single white tile, waiting for Schmitt and his whip. Clouds pass overhead; the light shifts ever so slightly. The thought of the pain itself is overwhelming. Some boys have pissed themselves while waiting for the headmaster to officiate, or worse: Smelling of shit, a large dark stain spreading on the back of their short pants, they've made their limping way—after requesting *permission*—to the toilets, latrines, really, at the outer end of the schoolyard and, once there, made quick, feeble, and vain attempts to clean up before returning to their single white tile in front of the headmaster's office. In his dread, the boy even attempts to make himself fall asleep, right there, standing on a single white tile in front of the headmaster's office, hoping all of this will have gone away when he wakes up. *It's a mistake. I want no part of this. It's not really happening. It doesn't have to be this way; there's another way. I want it to be the way it was. I need to get out of here.* Already, he is who he will be.

The fifties are wearing on

The boy barely manages to shut his eyes, but for a few blissful seconds, an eternity, he is lost to the world; there is no noise; all is quiet and safe; the fifties are wearing on.

He is four, five, six, seven, eight, nine, ten years old. . . . These are the long blissful years before the day in the sun-drenched yard, years of his rarely disturbed fullness. He is reading in his bed, in his bedroom in the house with the swimming pool up in the hills, where it's cool, far from the sweltering city, far from the Séminaire and Schmitt's braided whip on the day everything changed; or he is emerging from the green-tiled bathroom late one afternoon, after school, and Ada puts her ear and cheek on his belly to verify that it's no longer warm, her wily way of making sure he hasn't attempted to fool her into thinking he's taken a shower. She's looking at him; she's holding both of his arms; her face is close to his.

"You've taken your shower, you devil you?"

"Yes."

"You're sure?"

"Yes, Ada, I'm telling you." He's looking at her with as straight a face as he can manage.

"Come here."

And the game would be up. Or he was indeed telling the truth on a particular late afternoon and he had taken a shower, rather than standing outside the green-tiled stall, letting the water run while Ada remained behind the closed bathroom door, listening; he can see her bent silhouette behind the door's frosted glass. At one point, he was too old for his nanny to be in the bathroom with him; the time is gone when she would lay him across her knees to insert the weekly enema, the plant-mix potion infallible in flushing out tapeworm and other parasites. A few black sprigs had already appeared on his pubis, his armpits; the understanding that he and his younger brother were both too old to have women present at their nakedness arrived very soon after, and they both suddenly had a measure of privacy. On most afternoons, he emerged from the bathroom after a few minutes with his hands, face, crotch, and armpits washed, his hair wet from his craning his head under the cold water, and he changed into the fresh clothes laid out for him on his bed. Ada was only very rarely fooled; sometimes, she pretended to be, or the fake shower efforts were so thorough that taking one would have been the same, so she saw and felt no difference.

Why all the theatrics, then? Maybe because the water is cold on his skin, on his back, now that he and his brother have just returned from school, their bodies still warm from the heat of the day down in the sweltering city? No; really, it's a game they play, with her and against each other, who will fool her and how many times. They love Ada, the two boys; they know her warm kindness, her devotion to them, her protective surges, even against their parents. She was just a young girl when she arrived from the countryside shortly before the boy was born. Years later, well beyond the confines of the Tropical Republic, she will be with them again, following their parents *en exil*, serving the family in the clapboard and shingle house in New York, still serving the family in such different circumstances, the servant following in the wake of the employer; but Ada's own children will become nurses and doctors, while their grandfather's youngest son, the two brothers' youngest uncle, will become a doorman at the Warwick Hotel, a casualty of the frays and tears wrought by the century's migrations on the Tropical Republic's old and lineal distribution of roles.

These pretend showers are only a game the two brothers play with Ada, for they worship water. When it rains, especially in autumn—though no one uses the word; in that place of differently manifest seasons, *l'été*, summer, is the only season named—when the rains last so long, when the rains are so dense, the drops so heavy, transparent falling nuts bouncing on the tin roofs of the estate's main house and bungalows, that the sky is almost black, and the roof gutters unleash thin, freezing waterfalls; there are no people walking in the streets outside the house and beyond, no cars passing by; the nearby square is empty; the outlines of the church's red roof and steeple rising above the square have receded in sheets of rain. The world has ended. When those rains come, the boys quickly go to their room, shed their clothes, pull on bathing suits, emerge, and run outside, through the house's gardens, two young, lean animals prancing under the suddenly dark sky, in the suddenly cold air, when just before there was bright afternoon light and the air had been so warm. Now it's hailing. It's hailing in the Tropics. The two brothers are laughing, running; their ribs gleam in the rain.

"Let's go to Grand-mère's rose garden in the back!"

"No, let's go to the street!"

"They'll get too angry."

"Let's go to the pool, then."

"Yes, quickly!"

On their way to the pool, racing down the wet, slippery garden paths, the brothers make stops under the gutters; the streams of icy water splash on their bowed heads and shoulders. Now goose bumps appear on their bodies; their lips are beginning to turn blue. They're being watched from the main veranda; "Papa, you're spoiling them, letting them run around like this," as their mother says so often and says again now, while the grandfather smiles. "That's what grandfathers are for. Let them enjoy themselves. They're so young. Look how happy and healthy they are." But their grandmother, probably also thinking of the younger brother's asthma, is raising her tone: "That's enough. You're going to catch your death. Come in out of the rain."

Thunder and lightning, the sky now an ominous blue-black tinged with violet. Under the white-torn, blaring dark sky, the two boys run madly in the gardens, on the lawns, on the graveled or smoothly cemented alleys among the trees. The trees, the garden of childhood; since it is the Tropics, the plants and trees are often and suitably fragrant, large-leafed, fronded: banana, mango, soursop, custard apple, avocado, almond, guava, breadfruit, palm, coconut, and all the other trees in that warren of gardens and paths, the usually ripe mix of their smells now sucked in by the electric ozone of the storm. Lightning and then thunder again from not so far; for a second, it's as bright as on a bright sunny day, the lightning suddenly so close, and moving in, the deafening sound invading and filling ears and chests. This is precisely the moment the two boys choose to jump into the pool and to float on their backs, their faces calm, their water-filled ears muffling the sound of thunder, their eyes wide open to the dark sky, the rain and lightning. They don't hear or pretend not to hear their mother and grandmother screaming for them to get out. The artless cruelty of children, for whom dying or being mangled is unimaginable.

The boy has been told of rains lasting so long, storms so violent, winds so strong that raindrops strip the trees of their bark, houses are dislodged, trees uprooted, entire cities razed or submerged, hundreds, thousands killed before their bodies, lying at the bottom of deep, murky water, are revealed, their limbs and clothes wetly wrapped in mud and silt after the waters recede, looking like the *boat people* of a later time washing up on the golden shores of Miami; but in this place and time, in these years of blindness and contentment, he always sees himself keeping afloat, a slight, isolated, and invincible frame swimming in the rising waters, a small Tarzan diving down to the depths to retrieve chocolate bars floating up from the shelves of the Washington Grocery near the church square, Toblerone, Nestlé, foreign imports of which he never gets enough in the normal course of things. During hurricanes, sacks of rice or flour, hefty cans of butter, all stamped with squat black print, U.S. AID NOT FOR SALE, appear in the kitchens of the house. The boys don't like the orangey, slightly granular, slightly rancid butter scooped out by Ada onto their breakfast saucers, but there won't be any of the usual pale, hard sticks of butter in their silver wrapping as long as the stock of U.S. AID NOT FOR SALE lasts, well after the hurricane ends. Throughout, access to their grandfather's small copper cans of Danish butter—"Boys, taste this!"—will continue to remain a rare occurrence.

Wind and rain for days and nights and nights and days in the tropical autumn, the time of *la rentrée*, the beginning of the school year. Textbooks, either new or used by the youngest aunt and uncle, are covered once again with stiff blue wrapping paper by the boy's mother and grandmother sitting at the main dining room table; neat triangular folds, scissors, and adhesive tape; the two brothers' names are written in print on labels glued to the protective covers. The boy would prefer all new books, unmarked, clean, but he never says anything. Why create problems, why cause trouble?

This is also the time of year when the boys are taken to the city, to Chez Haddad, to have new shirts and shorts made for the school year. New high-laced boots are bought at another store in the city, not too far away, under the eighteenth-century arcades, vestiges of another bustling time. At a third shop somewhere on the outskirts of the city, the boots are fitted with heel and toe irons to delay the damages wrought by the boys' rough treatment, their running games in the schoolyard. The grandfather places the order in a shoemaker's minuscule shop, where an assemblage of corrugated-iron sheets and cinder blocks open onto what seems to be both garden and vacant patch: almond and mango trees, small piles of burning refuse, men playing dominoes in the shade of the trees, bony dogs, and, in the distance, patches of sand and sea between the trees and barbed-wire fences. The boy looks at all the shoes, completed and half made, aligned on wooden shelves or hanging in bunches from the ceiling: men's moccasins, men's two-toned laced shoes, women's sandals, women's high heels; there are also wood or cardboard patterns in a corner or leaning on a tree outside the shop. He inhales the smell of leather and looks at the smiling shoemaker, who has put down his hammer to listen to the grandfather's very specific instructions. The boy thinks Grand-père is being too detailed, too insistent; he's embarrassed and now wants to leave as quickly as possible.

During the tropical autumn, even if the season is unnamed, this time of rains and hurricanes, as preparations are made for the two brothers' return to school, beyond the estate's main house and bungalows, beyond its gardens and lawns and paths, out there on the other side of its wrought-iron gates, the flagstone-lined drainage canal that borders the main road is filled with rushing rust-colored water carrying debris, unidentifiable remains from the devastated thatched peasants' shacks in the mountains, and remnants of the corrugated-iron roofs and walls of the small shantytown houses from the hills closer above. The loosened fertile red soil of the mountains deepens the hue of the rushing water. The torrent and all it carries in its wake from the mountains and the hills reaches the end of its course in the capital city below, where some of the brown water and its debris quickly drift into the sea or remain held up for a time by shops, sidewalks, houses. In the streets and sidewalks of the city, in the shantytowns with their open sewers that border the capital, on the elegant promenade that lines the port, there will be accumulated water, mud, and ripening refuse for weeks, some of it picked up by shovels, or by hand, and taken away in wheelbarrows, some of it flattened by thousands and thousands and thousands of shoed or sandaled or shoeless feet, some of it simply blown away by winds after it all finally dries up in the sun. The rainy season will then be over.

The unloved son is showing off his arched erection and gleefully calling out to the servants

The fifties seem boundless. On this particular day in early November, the boy and his brother are at school. There is no rain, no hail, no thunder and lightning. It is the middle of a clear, still afternoon. The sun no longer pours from above, the heat's intensity has waned, and the house and its gardens are silent. Now it is one of the uncles, one of the grandfather's three sons—the youngest is out somewhere, the eldest is already in the United States, a fortunate pioneer, considering—the middle son, the unloved son, who is in the pool, by himself, floating on his back, his briefs pulled down below his knees, showing off his arched erection and gleefully calling out to the servants.

The grandfather and the grandmother are in the quiet shade of their bedroom, having their afternoon sleep, since this will be a casino night. On that hushed afternoon when the unloved son is calling from the pool, the grandfather and grandmother are sleeping, replenishing themselves for the evening. Almost all the family still living on the extensive compound is either at work or at school, or with friends somewhere: two of their four daughters, the eldest and the youngest; their youngest son; their son-in-law, their eldest daughter's husband; their grandchildren, the boy and his brother; the grandmother's grandmother. They are all out somewhere, except the middle son, the unloved son in the pool, who is very much there that afternoon, and the grandmother's grandmother, who is 103 and sits or sleeps all day, rarely coming out from her room deep in the remotest part of the main house, the high-ceilinged room that became hers after she moved in from the city to her granddaughter's house in the hills. Her long, thin hair, gray and white, with pale butter yellow streaks, is always tied up in a very tight bun; she takes her showers covered in a white batiste robe, a body with habits and customs from another time.

There is a photograph taken a decade or so before that afternoon. The house's verandas and gardens must have been filled with guests celebrating the boy's baptism. The four women in the photograph must have been ushered away from the guests and gathered in a particular generational composition under an enormous poinciana tree in the main garden. Holding in her arms the recently born boy in his baptismal dress, his great-great-grandmother stands with three other women to her right, in order of generation: her daughter, the boy's great-grandmother; next to the great-grandmother, an ample woman in a long-sleeved, outmoded outfit, stands the boy's grandmother, smiling radiantly in a moiré dress with short bouffant sleeves; last in the row, the boy's mother, wearing plain, oddly virginal attire—she looks about the same age as her mother in this photograph, more like a sister than a daughter, probably the effects of the recent birth.

Four generations of women stand next to one another, looking straight at the camera. The eldest, the one who takes her showers in a white batiste robe, is holding the fifth generation: the boy.

They have all been here for a long time: after the Taino, yes, but here in the Tropical Republic before it became the Tropical Republic, here since the first Spaniards, those men of Columbus's crew from dusty towns in Andalusia, since the French, the Breton and Norman sailors, the corsairs and buccaneers, since the Africans, the Kongo, Yoruba, Ibo, Rada, those who arrived enslaved, and all the others, all caught one way or another in the feverish thirst for gold and silver, indentured men and military men, sailors and women from poorhouses, slaves and second-born sons of aristocratic families, fortune hunters and former prostitutes, priests and adventurers, comfort women and aristocratic women, criminals and botanists. They come from all these people, the four women in the photograph, as do their husbands, absent from the photograph, as does the baby in his baptismal dress. The four women are smiling, but the great-great-grandmother's mouth is closed over her smile; she is almost entirely toothless.

On this particular afternoon, as on almost all afternoons and mornings and evenings, the boy's great-great-grandmother is in her thoughts and far away in her bedroom in the depths of the main house. She cannot hear the unloved son with his arched erection calling from the pool.

There are also several servants on the compound that afternoon. Some of them live there, and others live in their own houses, with their own families, *somewhere*. The boy has never been there. Most arrive early in the morning and leave before dark, to be relieved by those who live on the property, in quarters tenuously separated from the main house; nothing but a short alleyway, a small garden, a quick passing under a stone and cement arcade, and another world is there. Confined, intimate, with different smells.

The boy is always among the servants, sometimes along with his brother, often alone. He may be in one of the kitchens, tasting food straight from the pans before it can be laid out on serving plates and taken, garnished with carefully placed sprigs of parsley, to the family's main dining room. Or he might be playing cards in the old gardener's cramped little room, which also serves as a toolshed. "Come here, boy; let me teach you a lesson." The boy never hesitates. He enters the gardener's small room. The cards are ancient, stained, and heavy with dirt; the old man knows them by heart; sometimes, when they play for money, the boy's allowance for a day disappears into a tin box that used to contain cookies or chocolates—so little is discarded in those days—with large red flower imprints, and stored under the old man's cot with its thin, hard mattress; but the boy keeps coming back to play with him; he's also promised the old gardener that he won't tell Grand-père about his losses.

The boy is often listening to *les bonnes*, the maids, their conversations, their complaints, their gossip, while they work in the afternoon on school days, or in the morning on Saturdays and Sundays, when he is there to see them make the beds, do the wash. They use bars of caramel-colored soap cut into bulky but still manageable squares that fill their fists; they use indigo. *How do they use something so blue to turn the clothes and sheets so white?* he wonders. From ropes tied to trees or hooks, they unfasten hanging clothes, underwear, sheets, towels, all now dry and warm from the sun. They do the ironing; their irons look like torture instruments from the boy's comic books:

sturdy wooden handles, heavy, dark metal encasements filled with smoldering white coals, stood upright on the ironing table until they're hot enough to glide smoothly across starched shirts, dresses, embroidered sheets, tablecloths, and dinner napkins, all of which are then neatly folded before they are taken back to bedrooms and other parts of the house, placed in kitchen cabinets, in the drawers of mahogany dressers and armoires. "Let me help you take them in," the boy offers, and, to please him, they give him a small pile of dinner napkins or kitchen towels to carry. "Careful, don't you drop anything!"

Sometimes, he wanders into the area behind the maids' quarters, where they do the laundry, and also bathe. He once sees these women assisting one another, pouring water on one another's bodies, backs, breasts, bellies, the dark hairy place underneath; they have a large tin tub in which each kneels while another pours water on her, their skin glistening in the water and sunlight; the secret they intimate so blatantly is immense. "What are you doing here?" He's frozen on his feet; he's confused and embarrassed but attempts to assume an air of innocence and legitimacy, wants to convey somehow that he's only in this secluded part of the compound by accident, even though he knows they know he isn't. He is entirely under their spell; but when they see him just standing there, they only laugh and shoo him away. "Come back later."

He turns around, without a word. He feels he's stood his ground long enough, managed to set things right. The women have already forgotten about him. He leaves then but keeps returning; sometimes they're washing clothes, or just sitting on their low straw chairs, avatars of Taino ceremonial stools or of a later, African heritage—the boy never finds out—or reclining in their beds, talking, or ironing one another's hair, the smoky smell filling the air; sometimes, as the boy hopes, they are bathing. After the catechism lessons, after the First Communion, that *this is a sin* will only confuse him more. He keeps returning.

Now these women have left their unhurried afternoons in their own quarters, where they had been enjoying the lull that follows the serving of the noon meal, relaxed in the tacit understanding that they are not to be disturbed, that this is their own time, barring emergency or the arrival of an unexpected visitor. Now they're looking at the boys' uncle, the unloved son calling out from the swimming pool, where he's floating on his back with his arched erection. The laundress, the day cook, and the chambermaids are accompanied by a few of their friends, who have come from neighboring houses where they work; they have left those houses to spend some time elsewhere for their afternoon break, free from any immediate duties. Their aprons quickly removed, left in kitchens, bedrooms, living rooms, they walked across the square or crossed through gardens, gullies, gates; they've passed through gaps in hibiscus bushes separating the estates from the streets—there are very few high walls and no armed guards in that time when the fifties are wearing on—and settled down with their friends. They were talking—about how their sons and daughters were doing at school, about a young man and how he would be taking one to the movies soon, or about another man and how he had two other women and how he was a no-good drifter, but so handsome and so sweet—when they heard the unloved son's shouts in the still afternoon.

Marisa, the laundress, the eldest, is the only one not smiling at the scene; she must be in her late twenties or early thirties, but her seriousness and her disapproval make her seem much older. She has become a severely religious woman. Unlike most of the others, Catholics, some of them also *vodouisant*, she is a Protestant, the result of encounters with the American missionaries plying their trade throughout the Tropical Republic, either experienced returnees from China, Africa, elsewhere, or earnest young graduates of Yale or Harvard who wear polo shirts, khakis, and the local leather sandals. A few of the missionaries are also doctors. They listen, they auscultate; they dispense pills, syrups, ointments; access to them is so much easier than to the overwhelmed public hospitals and the unaffordable private clinics. They are in constant competition, these earnest young missionaries, engaged in their glorious struggle to the end with *malignant voodoo priests* and *duplicitous herbalists* and their potions, their powders *used for good* or *for evil*. The message to their recently converted flocks is repeated throughout the Tropical Republic: "We will take you on the sure and rightful path to the Lord, away from all of this backward and wicked superstition." Marisa the laundress, the former Catholic and, perhaps, former *vodouisant*, now exclusively a Protestant, goes only to these young men in their polo shirts and khakis, who have cured her of her severe migraines and who have introduced her to the pared-down rituals of another, less ceremonial faith.

Like the others, Marisa has come rushing over upon hearing the shouts, but when she sees the unloved son floating in the pool, her excitement and curiosity vanish; she averts her face and walks slowly back to the servants' quarters. The others and their friends remain. From the house's main veranda, they look over the bougainvillea and hibiscus hedges toward the pool below, lightly and repeatedly elbowing or shoving one another, the way young women who are happy to see one another after a long time do. Nothing to shock them here, nothing they haven't seen before; they shake their heads, look at the ground, hands holding chins and hiding smiles behind cupped fingers, up again at the young man in the pool, and then smile at one another once more.

"That boy won't change."

"He's a handful."

"He's gonna get it from his father."

"Yes, the Colonel will show him!"

The Colonel: The title from a previous life has endured. The grandfather had been second in command of the armed forces of the Republic. There is a picture of him, with the then president of the Tropical Republic, for whom he was chief of staff, and Dwight D. Eisenhower, the American president. The grandfather is about a decade younger in the photograph; his eyes are bright and look straight into the camera, a slight, perhaps ironic smile on his face, his arms clasped behind his back, a military man at ease. He stands slightly in the background, between the two presidents as they shake hands and smile expansively, all teeth showing; the grandfather in full uniform, kepi, decorations, the two presidents in light-colored linen or silk gabardine suits. This is a few years before the boy's name is called out by Schmitt in the sun-drenched yard that early April afternoon, but it must be autumn and not spring, summer, or winter, since the photograph was taken at the time when thanks were being given from one president to the other for help received from the Great Neighbor to the North after a recent hurricane: *I also take this opportunity to thank you, Mr. President, for the spontaneity with which you have come to our help at the time of the recent hurricane, which has caused so much damage . . . to beg you to accept our wishes for the continuing prosperity of the United States and the arrival of this era of peace . . .* and so on. Just a year before this meeting, also a *year of the era of peace*, a portrait of the same president of the Republic, the last one before The Mortician was elected president of the Republic, appeared on the cover of a famous American news weekly; he was wearing a bicorn, and his upper body was sheathed in a gold-emblazoned uniform complete with epaulettes: a glorified rendition, like those of the long-dead presidents, emperors, kings of the realm, portraits, busts, statues, and photographs of past rulers that fill the boy's history book in smaller black-and-white versions. The painting on the cover of the news weekly was of the imperial upper body of this particular president of the Republic rendered in robust browns, black, and gold against the faintest green-and-blue wash of hills, a backdrop of palm trees, a peasant riding a donkey toward the traditional huts of a traditional village: indigenous fauna and flora, people of the land, traditional dwellings, the assembled symbols of apparent pastoral peace and stability in the Tropics, destined for consumption by readers from temperate climates. Back in that time before The Mortician made his appearance, well before the day in the sun-drenched schoolyard, the fifties were wearing on and, on this hushed afternoon out of so many afternoons, the unloved son, hardly aware of the passing of time beyond his immediate surroundings, is gleefully calling out to the servants, who are beginning to worry about the Colonel's being disturbed by his son's shouts in the otherwise silent afternoon.

"What if they hear him?"

"They're sleeping; it's casino night."

"Shush . . ."

They giggle; these women are not shocked by the young man floating on his back, calling out in the still afternoon. They find the unloved son comical and hopeless. They are women with men, with husbands, with children. The boys have seldom seen their men at the house; the husbands and fiancés and boyfriends remain confined to quick, usually quiet appearances: someone in the garden being greeted by one of the gardeners or asked, "What's your business here?" Neither do the generations living at the house often see the servants' children, who are brought to the house very rarely, in their clean and starched school clothes, with their books and, sometimes, a piece of written work, a composition, an exam that has won praise from a teacher, proof that the money paid beyond their servants' salaries by the grandfather or by the boys' parents for the education of their servants' children is being well spent.

As the unloved son floats in the pool that afternoon, the gardeners nearby are also looking up from their raking or cutting tufts of grass with their machetes around tree trunks, close to the graveled alleys, where bumps emerge from the trees' roots on the smooth lawns, anywhere where the mechanical lawn mower with its blades and wheels connected to a long wooden two-handled grasp will not fit. One of them, the old gardener, the boy's card partner, takes a look at the unloved son in the pool, thoughtfully pulls on his stubby pipe, and spits on the ground; another one is just a boy himself, a gardener's helper, who will later on tell the two brothers what he has seen: their uncle in the pool, the Colonel's outburst; this boy seems not to have any particular duty, he is *around*, he *assists*; sometimes he is sent out to buy bread for the evening meal, sometimes for cigarettes or to pick up clothes from the dry cleaner's. The gardeners themselves are in fact do-everythings on the compound—watchmen, shoeshine men, barmen, even, at times, ice-cream makers (when the old gardener, a sinewy man with shoemaker muscles, as they say in that time and place, turns the crank handle of the *sorbetière*, an archaic instrument like the laundress's iron and the gardener's lawn mower, from a further-back past, a metal container fitted in a wooden barrel held by nailed metals bands; chunks of ice and handfuls of coarse salt are poured between the metal cylinder and its wood barrel casing; the old gardener turns the crank for a long time; and, in time, the liquid passion fruit or chocolate or vanilla poured into the cylinder turns into ice cream, a transubstantiation that remains a mystery for the boy, that illogical reader of comic books and fairy tales).

The boy's uncle in the pool, the unloved son, is not yet twenty, but he's already made his mark as a debauchee. He has a reputation; he flees the compound late at night to dance and *go to women*. He doesn't go to the Republic's fanciest hotels and nightclubs in the town above the hills, where men in suits or, on special occasions—for a big band's anniversary, a visiting band from Cuba or Puerto Rico, New Year's Eve, a carnival soirée, a hotel's gala evening—white tuxedo jackets ask women in their haze of perfume and their makeup and tight or flowing dresses and high heels to dance in between dinner courses, places where they all seem to know one another, one another's families. These are places where the unloved son would be immediately recognized: "Here's the Colonel's son, the one who . . . This is the Major's brother-in-law. . . . The Major married his eldest sister. . . . The X family . . . The Y family . . . The one who . . ." No, the unloved son's territory is elsewhere, in those little places, nightspots, half brothels really, in the depths of the sprawling shantytown of rough and cramped cinder-block and corrugated-iron dwellings on the other side of the gully that marks the western limit of the tree-lined town in the hills, or, if not in that area demarcated by the gully, then in other, even newer neighborhoods, with unpaved streets and no streetlights, the raw neighborhoods of an expanding town, more cinder blocks and corrugated iron in those places, those half brothels, Chez Joe or Les Papillons, whose rough wooden signs are decorated with hand-painted flowers, musical instruments, musical notes, or naked silhouettes. Outside of Chez Joe or Les Papillons, a few street vendors sit on their small wood and straw chairs, the flames of their tiny metal kerosene lamps on upturned crates glowing in the dark, their merchandise laid out in round straw trays: peanuts, cigarettes loose or by the pack, taffy, caramels, jellies, nougats wrapped in cellophane; from a cauldron blackened by the smoke and soot of countless wood fires, they spoon out chunks of pork, plantain, or yam frying in boiling oil; they can also make a sandwich of pork and hot peppers in a bun for customers entering Chez Joe or Les Papillons, passing under a ribbon of multicolored bulbs interlaced with jasmine and hibiscus; there are no drinks for sale outside except for the warmish clear tafia poured from a bottle without a label, which customers must drink immediately from the single small, quickly rinsed glass; the cold beers and sodas, the rum drinks served in large glasses with ice cubes and lime are the prerogative of the bars inside Chez Joe or Les Papillons, where music is played on a record player or by a three-man band gathered around a tiny dance floor, on which girls in tight skirts, high-heeled shoes, or shiny plastic sandals, with strong perfume and bright red lipstick, dance with one another until some man interposes himself. These are the places where the unloved son goes at night, far from the brightly lit nightclubs and hotels and the people who know him and his family, from the ritual of buttoning up one's suit jacket, walking up to a table, bending slightly at the waist, asking a mother-and-father-flanked girl to dance, the arms set just so during the merengue, except for those stealthy moments of hip against hip, groin against groin, hip against groin, if the young lady allows it and if they can be lost in the dancing crowd, not being too closely watched by the parents, the chaperone aunt, other eyes, and then taking her back to her table, again performing that slight bending at the waist to thank the young lady, resuming dinner.

Away from these carefully regulated formalities, the unloved son goes to Les Papillons or Chez Joe, to the penumbra of unrestricted close dancing and immediate intimacy. He has been followed back home late at night, past the gates, into the gardens, into the main veranda by screaming young women from these places who come to demand their due: "Pay up! Thief! What do you think? You think my pussy's a free-for-all? Who the *hell* do you think you are?" This is usually close to sunrise, when all but the old gardener, the only one trusted to be a watchman, even if just as a symbol—for what could the old man do against particularly desperate and resolute thieves, especially the ones who, some say, come naked in the night, carrying machetes, bodies smothered in oil so as to escape the grasp of would-be pursuers? It is usually this time, the time of thieves and predawn carousing, when the unloved son returns, when everyone but the old gardener is asleep, when even the grandfather and his wife have returned from the casino and are in their bedroom, close to dawn, when the bats are tracing their last muted designs over the swimming pool, and the air is fragrant, the sky and the moon and the stars so close. The young woman will not be denied, and her screaming reaches an impossible pitch. Sometimes, the old gardener pays for the unloved son, a loan, of course, which in due time will be paid back.

It's incredible that the grandfather has never witnessed these scenes played out on the edge of night, but the second-born son has already provided more than enough to feed his father's apparently boundless aversion without adding these late-night clashes. He has been seen hanging about with *the worst kind of people*; he has been seen drinking on the stone benches of the church square; he has been leading the shouting and booing at Ajoupa Ciné when the film reel has snapped, the projection is stopped, and the lights turned on; he has triggered complaints with strange but graphic notes to this or that girl, carried by a boy hired for a penny, complaints from mothers, grandmothers, aunts, complaints that have reached the Colonel at a dinner, at chance meetings at one of the stores in the city, even at the casino: "You must really ask your son to stop writing such things to my daughter" (or "my niece," "my granddaughter"), or "I'm sorry, but we can no longer receive him at the house." The Colonel has tried different methods, none involving a talk with his son, all coercive; the dislike is too strong, as if all his love and care for the males of his progeny had gone to the youngest son and to the eldest, who now lives in New York, as if the middle one is somehow beyond affection. The young debauchee's father has tried no more money, no more allowance, what little the Colonel had been giving, but the unloved son is now earning his own money going around the hot downtown streets and air-conditioned businesses selling pharmaceutical products, sweating in his gabardine trousers and beige wool jacket made for more temperate climes, not a lot of money but, still, his own. In the evenings, the Colonel has the servants hide the unloved son's shoes, all his shoes (the futile logic: He can't go out barefoot), but there is no holding back the debauchee, for when the time comes, he takes this or that gardener's broken shoes; even if the borrowed shoes give him a ballerina's tiptoed scuttling (too small) or an old man's dawdling shuffle (too large), he perseveres; he will even go out barefoot (so much for logic, then) and, somehow, along the way he will find someone, borrow other shoes, go to his pleasures. He's a bit of a simpleton, probably the result of sunstroke when he was still a boy and already running around with vagrant boys in those neighborhoods with unpaved and unnamed streets or in the labyrinthine shantytown on the other side of the gully.

On the day of the sunstroke, he'd stayed away from school; all morning they'd roamed around and later flew kites on a windy, shadeless hill, he and those boys, after making piles of the ripe almond fruits pilfered from the gardens of secluded houses throughout their morning wanderings. Here they are on the hill, oblivious to the sun beating overhead, holding on to the taut kite strings with one hand, holding an almond in the other, taking bites of the red or white almond flesh, sucking on the red or white pit, making piles of the pits to be cracked later, placed on a stone, hit with another stone for the nut inside, but the sun and the afternoon suddenly vanish in inky black for the unloved son, and he doesn't know where he is when he comes to on a straw mat in a small, cramped house, just a room really, with a corrugated-iron door and roof. He is in the warm shade of that place, sunlight still managing to seep through the cracks and the rust holes in the corrugated-iron roof; an old woman is by his side on a small low chair, carefully placing a wet bandanna on his forehead. The other boys looking in from the doorway stand aside when the Colonel arrives (who has informed the Colonel?) with the chauffeur, and the unloved son is carried back to the other side of the gully, back to the tree-lined streets, through the gates of the compound, the gardens, the main veranda, and into his bedroom in the house, where he remains in bed for many days.

When life begins again, he seems to have lost something; he is *slow in his mental faculties*, but the sunstroke and its aftermath seem to have quickened other propensities, as happens on that afternoon when the boys' great-great-grandmother is alone in her high-ceilinged room far in the depths of the house somewhere, and the Colonel and his wife are having their afternoon nap. The unloved son has just returned from the city. On his way to his room, and then to the dining room, where his meal waits for him under a screen cover to guard against flies, the unloved son stops at the pool; devoid of any deliberateness, he takes off his clothes, the gabardine pants, the shirt, the tie, the socks, the wool jacket fit only for another climate, piles them on the edge of the pool, keeps his briefs on, and jumps in. He is the unloved one, the grandfather's whipping boy; there is something in him that can only think of his stomach and what lies below it, *le ventre et le bas-ventre*, as the boy's father will tell his mother about her younger brother years later in the kitchen in New York, when they will be *en exil*, when the great house will be almost empty, and when the dissolute uncle's adventures will continue in the Bronx, Queens, Brooklyn, Manhattan. (Staten Island will always remain beyond his purview.)

Now, finally, the grandfather has been awakened by his son's shouts in the afternoon stillness and has emerged from the shade of his bedroom; he walks onto the veranda and sees the scene: the servants looking on, the brazen satyr in the turquoise pool. He begins to make his way toward his son, screaming, "*Petit salaud.* You little bastard! *Petit vicieux!* You lecherous little creep, you have no shame. Get out of there, get out of there, get *out* of there!" But the screaming man who was heading for the pool is spent by his tirade; he seems suddenly drained of all energy and slowly walks back to the bedroom.

Years later—after a lull in the killing, after *things have cooled down*, after the debauchee's father, the Colonel, the patriarch, has returned from New York to live in the deserted house again, now alone with the grandmother, after all their children have left with their husbands, their wives, their own children, most of them now living in New York, after his wife's death, when he would have a very young mistress and give her his wife's dresses (his daughters will begrudge him neither his pleasures nor his presents to the young woman, but they will draw the line at this bestowing of dresses, a kind of sacrilege against the memory of their mother), after the presents he would buy for the young mistress from the expensive shops in the city, the jewelry, perfumes, handbags, "Now that he cannot even do what he wants to do with her," as some, either envious or pitying, would say, "Why do you think she's with you, this young woman?" his niece, a still beautiful woman herself, would ask him on his last visit to New York, "Do you think it's because you're so manly?" for he's very old by then, eighty-five, eighty-six—years later, then, he would only smile at this comment made without malice but certainly with some exasperation. After his own death, one of his illegitimate children, *a child of the outside*, as they said in that place and at that time, additional evidence of the grandfather's own prurient propensities, will come forward in the United States and introduce himself to his aging half brothers and half sisters, making no legal claims, but only wanting to let them know and to share their grief for their dead father.

The unloved son, so lustful, so much like his lustful father indeed, is floating on his back in the pool that afternoon. Back in the bedroom, still seething, unable to lie down again, the Colonel paces around the spacious room where the curtains are drawn against the day's still vibrant light and heat and speaks to himself more than to his wife lying in the bed.

"He'll amount to nothing; he's hopeless. I don't know what to do anymore."

"Be patient, dear; you know how hard he's trying. He's a good boy."

"He's too old to be whipped, but that's what he deserves."

. . .

"He should leave for New York. Let's send him to New York. Let's send him to his brother."

. . .

When the boy and his brother are driven back from school in the late afternoon, the gardener's helper, who has watched the scene from entrance to exit, tells them what he's seen. The boys have dropped their schoolbags on the lawn close to one of the front gates; they listen intently to the breathless account.

"You should have seen your grandfather; he was purple. When he saw your uncle in the pool with his thing standing up and out, he started screaming. I was afraid he was going to get his gun and shoot him, yes."

"What do you mean, 'his thing standing up and out'? He was showing it to everyone? Just like that?"

"Yes; the maids were there, and friends of theirs. They left very quickly when they saw the Colonel."

. . .

The old gardener appears out of nowhere; lightly shoving his helper, he tells him, "Leave it; leave them alone," and then turns to the brothers. "Boys, don't listen to him; go take your shower." The gardener's helper leaves; the two brothers are still processing what they've been told and don't move. The old man continues, now annoyed. "Where's Ada anyway! Give me your boots" (for it is he who cleans their boots every day, wiping away the schoolyard dust with an ageless rag, then applying polish with his thumb, then leaving the boots to dry for a short while in the sun before brushing them to a shine). The boys take off their boots, hand them over to the old man; they pick up their schoolbags from the lawn and head for the house in their socks. They know their uncle is always getting into trouble with the grandfather, but this is different; this time it's different. "Can you imagine? Showing off his thing like that!" "How can he do that with everyone watching?" They wish they could have been there.

On that day, the Colonel and his wife leave the house late, not before ten in the evening, as usual; the night is very dark, but it's still a safe time, back then, a time when a fashionable woman and her husband in their sixties can drive down the road lined by poincianas to the city below, steer through small streets lit only by the flicker of street vendors' small metal lamps and a few feeble streetlights, along the coast road to the inlet where the casino's sleek pink neon sign glows against the night sky. They drive into the casino's parking lot, really just cars parked in rows on an empty patch of dirt.

There is music coming through the carved mahogany and wrought-iron doors held open by two smiling and uniformed doormen. Men in white smoking jackets, women in long dresses, men in starched guayaberas, women in short black dresses or in flowing prints are entering.

The Colonel and his wife go into the casino. They are known here. They come very often. It will be a long night at the roulette tables, until close to dawn. The grandfather used to play poker. Some of the money spent on building the house in the hills and its subsequent extensions came from his superiority at the game over his wealthy friends, his circle, even if he has never been wealthy himself. He has made himself, he is a logical man, he was trained as an engineer, he has a methodical mind, a tenacious memory, and will easily be able to help the boy do his algebra homework years later in the Bronx, in that first year of exile. "Look, read the problem carefully: If you have three dollars and twenty-five cents total, twice as many quarters as dimes and twice as many dimes as nickels, how many of each do you have? Look, it's simple: You have x nickels, y dimes, and z quarters; then if you have twice as many nickels as quarters, you can do this." He takes the gold cap off his old fountain pen and quickly jots a few equations on the sheet of grid paper.

(The boy looks at the markings just made on the sheet of paper and is chastened by the simplicity he hadn't detected.)

"So, you see . . ."

. . . And the boy does see. By the time Grand-père is finished, the veil is lifted, even if momentarily, the numbers and letters make perfect sense; the problem is solved. But he finds all this useless, needlessly opaque. For a long time before they came to the Bronx, he preferred to read fairy tales, just as he had preferred to read books from the *girls' collection* with the pink spines rather than the green ones *for boys* at the Séminaire's small lending library, stories about people and places where math and numbers had no place, but in the Bronx the grandfather would remember the theorems and formulas of his own adolescence as if he had learned them the day before.

For years, before he started to play roulette at the casino, the grandfather played poker at the most exclusive club in the Tropical Republic. At one point, his memory and his ease with numbers and probabilities were no longer enough to win systematically, his concentration and energy no longer quite what they used to be, the stamina to spend nights playing now absent, and so he gravitated to the casino's roulette tables with his wife. A game of chance, *un passe-temps*, "our *only* pastime," he liked to say, a pastime where one can win or lose, where the elegant older woman and her husband can spend those long nights into dawn among people they know and, increasingly, as the time of exile nears, people they don't know, like the mounting number of Nazi uniforms in cabaret crowds for other people, in another time and place. Here, on this evening, and on so many other evenings, waiters in short white jackets and black bow ties come and go with trays of champagne in thin coupes, whiskey and sodas, rum and Cokes in thick tumblers, delicate triangular sandwiches with the crusts of the sliced bread cut off.

When the boy sees his grandfather after one of the

casino nights, usually at breakfast if it's the weekend, or the following afternoon if it's a weekday, when he's back from school, he sometimes asks how the evening went. He only inquires when he's already certain of the answer, and only when he knows that Grand-père has won at the roulette table; otherwise, he keeps clear of the subject. He can tell the days following nights of loss from the grandfather's weary face and lethargic movements, an old man with a look of defeat about him, the seasoned gambler undone. His younger brother engages in no such deliberations, asking point-blank and every time he gets a chance, "Grand-père, did you win or lose last night?" and then either rejoicing or looking contrite at the answer, in either case impervious to any consequence. The boy wants no confrontation with preventable sorrow, no fissures in the clear surface of days and years. *Why should I ask if it will make him unhappy?* he tells himself. *Why make things unpleasant? Why cause trouble?*

The Tropical Republic had not yet acquired its baleful notoriety

Les Américains were also gone out somewhere on that afternoon when the unloved son is floating on his back with his underwear pulled down to his knees: the United Nations man; the two old couples; the young couple with their two daughters; the *pensionnaires*, as the grandfather has called the boarders, and as they are now called by everyone, these Americans who live in the various extensions to the main house built over the years with the money won at poker games.

There have been other *pensionnaires* besides the Americans over the years, but they've only ever stayed a few weeks at most: the thin young man from the French embassy who once said, with dismissive pride, "While you people were wallowing in your comfort, going to the beach with your servants and silver cocktail shakers, driving to the carnival in your obscene American cars, I was walking in the mountains, listening to the beating of the real heart of this country." The boy heard him say this to one of his aunts, wondered what the thin young man from the French embassy meant, became confused, and then forgot about it. There was the Argentinian consul and his family, with their constant drinking of maté from the wooden gourd fitted with a silver straw; to the boy, there was something unhygienic, something repulsive about all of them drinking from the same bowl, through the same straw; he could not bear to see the father's yellow teeth sharing the straw with his daughter's full pink lips. There was the young businessman from Ecuador, with whom the young aunt told her nephews she *fell in love*; then the Salvadoran cultural attaché, his wife, and their plump son, who looked Chinese to the boys because of his slanted eyes and spiky black hair; he was always too violent at games played with the boys, cowboys and Indians, or Hercules against the vampires; although he would put his hands up when caught and duly march like a prisoner in front of them, he would snatch a bunch of small, still green mangoes hanging from a low branch with his marching prisoner's raised pudgy hands and throw the fruit at the faces of his captors, hurl his plump body at them and begin to punch, roughly, to hurt, taking the brothers aback with this brutal interpretation of their games. All these people stayed only a few weeks at the compound, while waiting for permanent housing assignments from their embassies or companies. The joyous and handsome Cubans stayed only a few days, before their real purpose in the country was discovered, and it ended badly for them.

The Americans are the only ones who have stayed for a long time. The United Nations man, a *specialist of tropical agriculture*; and the two old couples, retirees who left the cold and the snow and a lifetime of work to live out the years they hoped would be long and peaceful in the Tropics. They have all been here for a few years already. The blood and terror in the Tropical Republic, bequeathed from the very beginning, had subsided for a while, then subsided for a long while, and it was during this long lull, throughout the early fifties, years before the country doctor in his homburg and thick-lensed glasses, the anonymous country doctor who looked more like a mortician than a politician, took over, years before he was about to show his other face, that these aging men and women from Michigan or New York, Maine or Connecticut came to live out the years they hoped would be long and peaceful in the Tropics.

The Tropical Republic had not yet acquired its baleful notoriety, displayed its other emblems. These aging men and women from the north had come well before the day in the sun-drenched yard, before the country doctor in his immaculate white shirts, bow ties, and dark suits showed his other face, well before his nasal pronouncements were rendered in cursive neon or in hundreds of tiny electric bulbs patterned into sentences on plywood panels erected on public squares, like guillotines of another time and place, *I am the Nation, One and Indivisible*, *The Revolution I have begun will continue for decades*, years before the display of executed bodies on the same squares, years before The Mortician became president of the Republic and unleashed his sharply dressed men in jackets and ties—hats often, dark glasses always—or his denim-garbed militia in the plains and the mountains, unleashed them all on the dwellers of stately houses in the hills above the capital, on both the owners and the servants, on the dwellers of shantytowns, on bricklayers, bankers, on the old families in the capital, in the hills above it and in the provinces, on peasants and street vendors, on members of exclusive clubs, on teachers, women of the night, carpenters, pharmacists, musicians, millionaires, and masons, on knife sharpeners, buyers and sellers of paper, bottles, and cans (so little was discarded in those years, a constituted trade emerged from what was not yet known as *recycling*), on students, fishermen, army officers, maids, businessmen, shop owners, sellers and buyers of lottery tickets, cockfight bettors, cinemagoers (there were numerous movie houses of all sizes throughout the Tropical Republic in those years before The Mortician's rule took on its other face, thirty or forty movie houses just in the capital, indoor, half covered, or drive-in, spacious and ornate or minute and minimal, with the latest equipment or just a sheet hung between two mango trees in a clearing, rows of wooden benches, celluloid rattling through an archaic projector in the starry dark), before The Mortician unleashed his sharply dressed men and denim-garbed militia on Communists, invaders, rebels, all manner of *subversives*, and another, notorious time began in the Tropical Republic. In the precarious peace of a country always on the brink, they had taken a chance, these people from Michigan or New York, Maine or Connecticut who have been coming for years now to live out their long and peaceful retirement and old age in the Tropical Republic.

The young American family arrived in the late fifties, a few years after the *specialist of tropical agriculture* and the two old couples; the father, who works at the

American embassy, is tall and slim and he stoops a bit; his hair always seems wet; a pale furrow of separation appears where his hair is combed to the side; he has very white teeth; his wife wears sunglasses that curl up at the sides; they have two daughters; one has blond hair, the other light brown hair; both have freckles.

Years later, when it will hardly matter anymore, the boy will find out that the father was not what he seemed to be—"*Il travaillait pour la CIA*," an aunt will say, or his mother, or an uncle, or the grandfather, in a definitive but still conspiratorial tone, even if it would hardly matter anymore by then.

To the boy and his brother, by the time the young family arrived at the compound, all the *pensionnaires* seemed to have emerged three-dimensional and in full Technicolor from the black-and-white American series on the large television set in its beige casing recently purchased by the grandfather: *I Love Lucy*, *Highway Patrol*, *Have Gun Will Travel*, *Sea Hunt*.

Dr. Silverstein, the UN employee, is often away, deep in the provinces, supervising an irrigation project in the plains, an anti-erosion campaign in the mountains, the introduction of new varieties of corn or rice to peasants on their small plots of land throughout the Tropical Republic. Away for weeks on end, he makes his return to the compound in his Land Rover like a hero back home after an adventure. "This place is an oasis," he would tell Grand-père and Grand-mère after each return. "It's so good to be back." Late on some evenings, he sometimes goes to the nearby square in the shadow of the church and takes back to his room one of the young women in tight dresses and plastic sandals who walk slowly around the square's fountain, among the stone benches, dark cypresses, and fragrant gardenias. Dr. Silverstein has sometimes paid for the dissolute son's pleasure debt; on some of those nights when the unloved son comes back home with a screaming young woman in his wake, loudly demanding to be paid, Dr. Silverstein emerges disheveled from his bungalow close to the pool and quickly offers to pay; the sum is paltry to him and he needs his sleep, and there is also the fact that, after all, they are of the same clientele, the middle-aged functionary stationed in the Tropics and the young debauchee. The boy has sometimes seen the American quickly walking though the garden paths, heading for his bungalow with one of those young women in tow. He feels something is amiss but doesn't know what, only that Grand-père would not approve, might even get angry, but he can't even imagine sharing these sightings with him. Problems, unnecessary trouble, he thinks; and how would he explain his own wanderings late at night in the gardens when he should be sound asleep?

Mr. and Mrs. Becker, one of the two retired couples, seem never to leave the compound. They are always sunbathing; they arrive from their bungalow at midmorning, sit in deck chairs by the pool, and almost never go into the water. The boy and his brother are then instructed by Grand-père to stay away from the pool area. "Leave it for the *pensionnaires*; you can go in when they go back to their bungalows." The two brothers often have to wait hours for the Beckers, whose skins have turned a deep reddish brown. Mrs. Becker owns many bathing suits, polka-dotted, flowered, or solid bright pastels, all one-pieces, with or without shoulder straps, some with a bow or a belt, some with a little skirt over the bottom; the boy, whose mother wears only her navy blue one-piece brought back from Miami, is amazed by Mrs. Becker's parade of swimwear. Mr. Becker only wears the same loose red plaid shorts that float around his haunches when he crawls in the water, or stick to him when he resurfaces from a quick submergence, blowing water from his nose like a large marine animal, the water trickling down his crew cut, his face, his hairy back, his hairy breasts that sag down his chest. The Beckers are always holding glasses, rum or whiskey, with ice cubes and soda; the ice bucket is refilled throughout the day by one of the servants who also sometimes take them their lunch by the pool. They eat club sandwiches made with chicken cut in small cubes, imported bacon, and mayonnaise, or bowls of spaghetti sprinkled with Parmesan, an item the cook conceals in one of the kitchen cabinets, away from the two brothers, who relish the *pensionnaire food* they seldom get to have.

The other two retirees, Mr. and Mrs. Salloway, like to spend their days reading the *Reader's Digest* and English-language newspapers on their small terrace facing away from the pool, overlooking a small garden of grass, gravel, and two cherry trees that look out of place among the mangoes, palms, and breadfruit. The Salloways like to go on outings, sometimes in the city, among other places to the National Museum, where the collection features the skull of the self-proclaimed king who shot himself—with two silver bullets, they say—early in the previous century, in those years after the revolution, followed by the declaration of independence from the French, followed a few years later by a decade-long kingdom that ended in the suicide of the former slave, cook, butcher, sailor, stableman, waiter, billiard maker, and revolutionary general turned king. In an adjoining room, remnants of the wrecks of Columbus's caravels are on display. A spare collection is exhibited in the vitrine cabinets of the dusty, resonant rooms: long and short clay pipes, stone mortars and pestles, carved wooden stools, bows and arrows or other weapons and ceremonial objects of the Taino, who were quickly acquiring the poignant charm of things about to disappear when Columbus's caravels from the other side of the ocean were entering a palm-lined bay somewhere in the north of the island that fateful year, centuries ago. On the museum's walls, washed-out murals depict the treatment of the Indians by the Spaniards, the Africans by the Spaniards, and then the Africans by the French. On one of the Salloways' trips to the museum, a guard—no uniform and hardly a salary, but trying all the same—informs the Salloways that the former king had fought at Savannah during the American Revolutionary War against the British, that he had distinguished himself in one of the bloodiest battles of the war, this in a proud whisper, and the Salloways are duly impressed; they are polite old people from New England and have grown very fond of the Tropical Republic and its people; they welcome the information as a corroboration of their attachment to the place where they have come to live out their old age away from the cold and the snow. The Salloways also go on day trips to the mountains, where the coolness, the red soil, the tangy miniature strawberries, and the low clouds that float into houses in the evenings seem incongruous in a part of the world where swaying fields of sugarcane and rice fields lie in the hot plains below. On the days when they go to the mountains, a chauffeur/tourist guide wearing a narrow-brimmed straw hat picks up the Salloways in a large and precarious American convertible; they leave for the mountains with a packed lunch prepared by one of the house's cooks, the radio blaring merengue, Frank Sinatra, French chansons. Posted at one of the wrought-iron gates, the two boys wave to them as the red convertible makes its way up the road to the mountains. "Good-bye, good-bye, have a nice day!"

Although all the *pensionnaires* have small private kitchens in their bungalows, they also have a common dining room, where they usually take their meals with the other *pensionnaires*. Their dining room used to be one of the main house's living rooms before some of the family left, before the dismemberment and extensions began. Meals are brought in by the servants from the closest of the main house's two kitchens. In spite of the years of exchange and proximity, languages find their limits, habits reclaim bodies; sometimes there are misunderstandings between the Americans and the servants. One of the women who usually serve meals to the *pensionnaires* in the living room turned dining room comes to the grandmother's rose garden screaming that Monsieur Becker has swallowed an espresso cup. "Please, madame, come see, quick; I don't know what to do!" The grandmother, who was kneeling over a rosebush, places her secateurs on the ground, stands up, takes off her gardening gloves, smooths down her skirt, leaves her rose garden, and walks to the dining room, where Mr. Becker, placid and smiling, tells her, "Look, regarday!" slipping the rim of the espresso cup in and out of his wide elastic mouth. He speaks to the grandmother in English. "I was just trying to explain to the *mam'selle* that I want a *mug* of coffee, un *mug*, madame." A whim, an atavism, an exception to the years of that strong, dark coffee served in small cups, a sudden yearning for the cups of *real American coffee* that accompanied breakfasts of pancakes, sausage, and home fries in main-street diners back home. Although he is tall, has a close-cropped crew cut, and is a jovial man, Mr. Becker looks very much like Broderick Crawford, the actor who plays the sullen, jowly, fast-talking police chief in *Highway Patrol*. Sometimes, when he walks by, the boys hum the show's screeching staccato violin and ponderous brass and drum opening theme, but seldom loud enough for Mr. Becker to hear, and then only when the boy's younger brother impatiently tells him to relax—"What's he going to do to us, the old *Américain*? Look, he's laughing; he knows we're only fooling around. Stop fretting." The boy would like to explain to Mr. Becker that he and his brother are only playing, but he doesn't; he doesn't have the nerve or the words.

The boy and his brother don't speak English. They watch the American programs on television and often have no idea what is going on unless their mother's youngest sister (the one who *fell in love* with the young Ecuadoran), who is taking English classes at her high school, translates, summarizes.

The two brothers also hear the *pensionnaires* speaking to one another; they sometimes have short conversations with them. They pucker or widen their lips, they imitate their accents, they answer their questions as accurately and succinctly as they can and try not to make any errors, especially the boy, who always wants to get it completely right, to be proper; the shorter his answers, the better he feels about their accuracy and correctness.

"How are you today?"

"I am fine, thank you."

"And how are your parents?"

"They are also fine, thank you."

"How are you doing at school?"

"Very fine, thank you. I received a nine out of ten in history."

"This is very good. Very, very good. I have something for you."

"Thank you very much."

They play with the two American girls, Debby and Caroline, and have learned a few English words and sentences from them, as well. Sometimes the two boys go through the estate's main iron gate, always left open back then. They sit on the low stone wall that lines this part of the compound where the main road curves upward toward the hills; people gather there to hitch rides or to wait for the public *camionnettes* heading for towns higher up and on to the mountains: students from the nearby schools returning home; soldiers from the barracks across the main road, on leave and heading home or to their girlfriends; peasant women who have walked down from the mountains in the early blue dawn, carrying on their heads their baskets of fruits and vegetables from their small plots—they have sold everything at the town's open market and now, their empty baskets overturned and piled in front of them, they will splurge on a motorized return home. This is the audience for the two boys' performance as they speak to each other with seemingly great seriousness in a nasal lingo, gathering in a rapid nonsensical flow all the English words they've gleaned from the aunt's translations of TV shows, from the *pensionnaires*, and from their games with Debby and Caroline. They also make up words; they don't stop; they want to seem natural, knowing. They have an innocent audience, or so they think. In fact, no one pays much attention to these two boys chattering away like madmen.

"Yeah, yeah, cuing, because the boy and the car, perter shooting, yeah!"

"Really, really? And gitting for the candy and the cowboys and kids?"

"Put up your hands, vadabard! Hands up, Johnny! Highway patrol and choclit ice cream!"

"The guitar and the girl, naw, yeah, hurry up, mister!"

"Stop here. The police! Come here; thank you!"

They know their own fraudulence, but they relish this ability to magically speak that other language all at once. They become red-cheeked American boys in jeans, wide-striped T-shirts, and baseball caps in some leafy suburb with two-car garages, flagstone paths, and green lawns where wood-paneled station wagons are parked in the driveways of flat, angular houses inhabited by pipe-smoking men in suits and ties and blond women wearing neatly tied aprons and high heels, pulling perfectly roasted, glowing turkeys out of shiny white ovens, and the weather changes from spring to summer to autumn and winter, flaming red maples to white snow. The two brothers also play the game of speaking rapid, fluent English with the servants, who mostly pretend to be taken in; they know the limits of the boys' ability, especially the servants who attend to *les Américains*.

Some could still believe the fifties would last forever

To most outsiders and to many of its more fortunate denizens during those years before The Mortician took over, the Tropical Republic seemed suspended in perpetual peace and stable hierarchy; it seemed a place where, far from the cold and the snow, one might come to live out one's retirement in the sun. The boy in his baptismal dress, later in his short pants and high laced boots, later still in his First Communion suit, the boy and the living generations of his family were living out the years when some could still believe the fifties would last forever. The accompanying article in the American news magazine bearing the portrait of the gold-emblazoned president of the Republic on its cover describes a sumptuous scene: "Cinnamon-skinned girls in Dior dresses, starchy diplomats and officers sparkling with gold braid gathered one evening last week in the majestic tile-floored great hall of the Presidential Palace. . . . The occasion: a ball in honor of Jamaica's visiting governor, Sir Hugh Foot, and Lady Foot. At ten sharp the orchestra blared out a march, and Lady Foot entered the room on the arm of a huge, kingly-looking black man resplendent in white tie, tails, and full decorations: His Excellency, president of the Republic." The fifties were wearing on.

Out there, beyond the island, throughout the territory of the Great Northern Neighbor, all manner of professionals, waiters, electricians, taxi drivers, doormen, and so many others wore the recognizable uniforms of their trades; men wore coats and hats and women wore white gloves to lunch; their sons and daughters surfed on frothy, curling waves and suddenly broke into song on the beaches of endless summers; milk was delivered in thick glass bottles left on doorsteps by milkmen—also uniformed and capped—driving shiny trucks with rounded angles that looked like oversized toys; and lynching was still a practice. The fifties were wearing on.

During those years of apparent affluence and tranquillity (for some if not for others), the grandfather, the Colonel back then, had also served as consul of the Republic in foreign cities; he had married the beautiful, elegant woman; there were children, four daughters, three sons. The Colonel himself was orphaned early on; his parents had died young. The boy will never understand, never be told, never find out why the grandfather was orphaned and adopted early on by an immensely wealthy couple, but he does know that the grandfather became the good student, unlike one of his many brothers, who in his prime, as the boy has heard so many times, *had a woman at every station*. The raffish brother had been a minor functionary in the national railroad company, whose two trains essentially transported sugarcane, coffee, and fruit from plains and mountains to factories and ships; there were perhaps twenty train stations spread out over the Tropical Republic. On his deathbed in a hospital in Brooklyn years later, the old man would ask, "Who is this good-looking woman?" about his grandnephew's wife, who had left the room for a few minutes. The grandnephew answered, quickly, briefly.

Grand-père's brother always seemed to reluctantly stay for lunch. He would arrive an hour or so before and play cards with the two boys and the young aunt, recite for them long memorized poems while dexterously shuffling the cards and squinting, pulling deeply on his cigarette—"A nasty habit," Grand-père always said, reprimanding his brother, "you really need to quit." During one of their long bouts of card playing, having shuffled around for matches in his frayed jacket and found none, he asks the boy to slip into the kitchen and light him a cigarette. "And don't let your grandfather see you." The boy has never done such a thing but just cannot deny the request. *Why is he asking me? How can I say no?* There is little chance he will be seen by anyone but the maids in the kitchen, and so, as usual, unwilling to make ripples in the clear passing of days, he does slip into the kitchen and, with the cigarette between his lips, bends his head to the stovetop flame; the coughing fit that follows is like one of his brother's asthma attacks. He's rescued by the cook, who taps his back several times until the coughing subsides, expertly lights the cigarette, and gives it back to him. "What are you trying to do? Set the place on fire? Tell your uncle not to send you back in here." He will never attempt to light or smoke a cigarette again. How can people enjoy this? Grand-père is right, *une sale habitude*, a nasty habit, like the Argentinians all drinking from the maté bowl with the same straw. He goes back to his great-uncle, and hands him the lit cigarette; in the future he will find ways to avoid the task without offending his great-uncle, a search made easier by the younger brother's willingness to take over succeeding cigarette-lighting missions.

During the quick interval between a card game and lunch, the boy's brother and the young aunt head for the dining room, and he is left alone with the raffish great-uncle. At ease with him in a way he is with no one else, the boy asks his great-uncle about his *women at every station*. "What do they all mean when they say that?" The great-uncle pulls deeply on his cigarette and smiles at him. "You'll find out one day. You see, I'm not like your grandfather. He was always a good student, and you see how he lives now? Look at me." He throws his arms up, as if relinquishing something. The boy doesn't know what to say and thinks that, even after having dared to ask, he still doesn't know what *having a woman at every station* means, exactly. The old man gently grabs his arm and leads him to the dining room, "Come. I'm starving." He obediently follows.

The good student, the boy's grandfather, went on to the Tropical Republic's military academy and then to its engineering school, and made his very respectable way in the world. Once The Mortician was in office and things became increasingly clearer, the blood erupting from behind the benign bow tie and crisp white shirt façade, the old guard left the *seats of political power*, gradually or quickly, voluntarily or not. The Colonel had already built some of the extensions, the bungalows and apartments, on the extensive property; they generated income, more substantial than the officer's salary or, later, the ex-officer's pension, more secure than the income from the poker games he was so very good at for so many years, income to supplement the pension payments that continued to arrive, incomprehensibly, miraculously, even during the worst of the slaughter. The boy's father had also been an officer in those years before the slaughter, years of fortunate continuity for his tribe's generations in this particular place and time, years of the boy's own fullness in the midst of these rooted and undying generations: first the sergeant, then the captain, and, finally, the Major.

The Major. Here, too, the title has endured. Before transferring to the military academy, the boy's father had been a medical student. The Tropical Republic's medical school was one of the very best in the Americas back then, but the young man had had to relinquish that prospect out of necessity: At the military academy he received a stipend, even before becoming an officer, allowing him to provide, partly, more or less, for his brothers and sisters, since his own father, a man who loved women and friends and amusement, often neglected or simply forgot to relinquish even a modest portion of his salary to his wife. She was a frail woman, his wife; she had married when she was still a very young woman, as was the custom in that place and time, and had given birth to seven sons and daughters—the same number of children as, but not to be confused with, the other grandfather's children, the Colonel's progeny—all in rapid succession before she became a sort of martyr, a recessive figure in dresses that were always too large for her, even though they were cut down from her older larger dresses as she grew thinner and smaller, worshipped by her children and daughters-in-law, a pitied and beloved woman who looked many years older than her early forties, beloved and pitied even more after that evening when, in a desperate and ultimate attempt at reclaiming, at reasserting *something, anything*, for herself—for there was no longer any question of sensuality or closeness or complicity or even nostalgia for a time in their youth when they had been in love, and by then there remained only the children they had had together, whom her husband seemed to think had grown by magic, since unknown to him were the used soles, the school bills, the occasionally insufficient food—that evening when the disregarded wife had left the house and taken a taxi to the Théâtre Excelsior, where her husband, accompanied by one of his young mistresses, was attending a performance of the visiting Comédie-Française troupe, that evening when the disregarded wife sat in her husband's parked Buick, and waited, but after he saw her, as the crowd spilled out from the theater after the play, among the dressed-up people, the street vendors, the passersby, the crowd, in full view of so many people she and her husband and her children and her friends and her relatives knew, and others they didn't, he briskly walked up to the parked car and opened the front passenger door, behind which she remained with her arms bravely folded across her chest, looking straight ahead to a distant point where redemption and respect, if not love and passion, were still to be reclaimed, and he, the father of her seven children, waited impassively for the very short time it took her to unfold her arms, step out of the car, and stand on the sidewalk as he drove off with the striking young woman, her hair up in an elegant bun, clutching a small handbag, a gift from the grandfather. The frail woman walked away from the onlookers and disappeared around a corner.

The boy would hear accounts of this particular event years later, like so many other stories told among those of the tribe *en exil* in New York, but during the years of his fullness, the house in the Tropical Republic where the neglected grandmother and her husband lived and slept in different rooms—he in the couple's former bedroom, she with two of her still unmarried daughters—was still crowded with her children, and everything there seemed perfect to him, filled with his other uncles and aunts. Sometimes the extravagant and unfaithful grandfather would call the boy and his brother into his bedroom, which smelled of his eau de cologne, and give each of them the gifts he had set aside for them: money, pens, pencils, coloring books, key chains, a box of Crayola crayons so large, it contained its own built-in sharpener and unheard-of colors. This last gift was forgotten on the veranda by the boy one afternoon, the sun still hot on the tiles; the abundant gradations of green, red, blue, yellow melted in streaks of individual colors into a dark puddle. The boy could not bring himself to admit it was his fault, the loss of a gift so precious in a place where so many others could not afford to buy enough notebooks, anonymous young men and women writing under streetlights with pencils sharpened to their limits, resorting to the huge pages of expired Pan Am calendars, but the grandfather's supply was endless and he didn't even notice the loss; the pens, pencils, coloring books, and much more kept coming. He would also take them to the movies in his Buick. “Films of the jungle!” the two brothers would say, Tarzan, or anything with lions, tigers, crocodiles, flamingos, giraffes, boas, lianas, and baobabs—in fact, *umbrella thorn acacia*, not a type of tree the boys could name back then, but one they instantly recognized on the screen with its flat, wide treetops, their silhouettes dark against the blazing savanna sunsets.

Sometimes the two brothers would spend weekends in that house. On those Saturdays and Sundays, they would wake up in the strangely warm mornings—they were more used to the coolness of their other grandfather’s compound in the town in the hills. This grandfather, oblivious to his wife and his sons and daughters, whom he *loved in his own way*, would call his two grandsons to the silent living room and place a record on the record player, always Mozart, the boy would find out years later. Yellow wafts of the beautiful and overwhelming music would expand in the still early air, the two boys sitting serious and rapt, the grandfather looking at them and nodding his head to the music. This grandfather would die a few weeks after the boys’ departure for New York; they visited him in the hospital before leaving, the stubble bristling and white on his dark face. “My boys are leaving, my boys are leaving,” and he knew he would not see them again: They were already enfolded in the excitement of leaving, and he was stubbornly refusing to allow any doctor to remove the kidney stones that were causing him such excruciating pain, because a fortune-teller had told him he would *die by the knife*, and so, a few months after the boys boarded the plane for New York, he died of the infection caused by the stones. For the first time, the boy would see his father cry. The Major would cry again after his mother died, not too long after her husband, speaking the name of the man who had scorned her all these years. By then, the Major was already living through his second year of exile and the boy's own life was already elsewhere: He was discovering frost, snow, dark puddles turning to ice in the streets.

Before the years of exile, the boy's father lived on the estate with the Colonel's daughter and his two boys in a house he had built on the property ceded by the Colonel, his father-in-law. The future Major has married the Colonel's eldest daughter; the Colonel had taken some time to accept him, to take him into the fold. Perhaps it was that the young officer's family was deemed unworthy of the prized daughter, or perhaps it was the age-old and vaguely incestuous attachment of certain older tribal males, or perhaps the salacious and competitive part of the Colonel's imagination—but, ultimately, as always happens, barring tragedies, there was the wedding, and the photographs: the young woman in her white dress, at once proud and dreamy and innocent, as young women of that class and time were, or were supposed to be, the Major not yet a major but wearing an officer's uniform, probably a captain's parade uniform, aiguillettes and epaulettes, the golden crossed rifles and the emblems of the Tropical Republic on his lapels, smiling, young, potent, both looking straight into the camera.

After graduating from the military academy, the boy's father was often posted away from the capital, either as second in command or, later, commanding officer in small towns, all by the sea or, later still, in the main provincial city in the north, dominated by the citadel of the king who had shot himself with two silver bullets; and she, the Colonel's daughter, the boy's newly married mother, followed her young husband to these provincial postings, coming back to the capital when it came time to give birth, first to the boy, then to his brother. Before the two boys started school in the capital, the family was always on the move.

During transfers from one small town to another, the boy and his brother are awakened in dark, purple dawns, so that the family can drive before the heat of the sun becomes too fierce. Ada's small metal suitcase and bundle are among the family's baggage; she sits at the back of the Hillman with the boys on either side of her and tells them stories in the early dawn, her voice slowing down as they fall asleep again, the sun rising red in the still cool day and then turning a pale orange, then white, and then invisible in the sky as the heat reaches its almost unbearable limit, but this is usually when they arrive at their destination.

Another posting: the family moving into another house with another garden, followed by the young officer's tour of inspection in the town and the surrounding areas, also under his jurisdiction, his office usually located in army barracks; the invitations to drinks, to dinner, to parties arriving soon after, a social life quickly taking shape. The small gardens are filled with daisies, carnations, chrysanthemums, gladiolus, and zinnias emerging from packs of seeds. "Come help me with this," their mother would say. "Make small holes here; a bit deeper; place the seed in here; no, only one, one for each hole; get some water." They would come back with small buckets filled with water, the same ones they would take to the beach to play in the sand. Those are years the boy would remember as the only ones *before exile* when his father was always present, at meals, during long days on the beach, long drives on Sunday afternoons. Friends of his father came to the house, especially Assad the Syrian, who had a small motorboat and always wore a faded blue captain's cap with an embroidered gold anchor, Assad who took them for rides on his boat and always had cold beers, Coca-Cola and 7 Up, and sandwiches in an icebox. Long and exultant days; the boys running through the small house, less often through the tall grass field near the house, days spent cutting pictures from magazines using small multicolored plastic scissors with rounded tips, leafing through comic books, listening to their mother reading books to them, usually *The Count of Monte Cristo*; they didn't understand everything, they didn't even know how to read then, but they loved it when she sat with them, one on either side of her on the couch, and the story would start again: a young sailor, his fiancée, the beautiful Mercédès, the friends who would betray him, the city of Marseille, by the sea.

"By the sea, just like this town, but much bigger, an important port with ships going in and out, carrying merchandise from all over the world; and on the sea, not too far from the coast, you could see the Château d'If, the fortress prison on the small island where Edmond Dantès would be kept in a cell for fourteen long years, all alone until the day he accidentally discovered the existence of another prisoner, old Abbot Faria. So, on that day . . ."

The two brothers are quiet and still, waiting for the story to continue; their mother's voice is clear, soothing. The flowers are about to push through in the garden or already there, tufts of bright colors tittering lightly on their stalks. The boy's contentment is unbroken. *I feel the sun on my skin. My nose is running a bit, but I won't say anything, or I won't be allowed to go swimming. I'll share the condensed milk with my brother; we'll make two holes in the can; we'll take turns and suck it out slowly.*

I'll wash myself everywhere when we come back from the beach, remove all the salt.

Assad would take the entire family to remote inlets, accessible only by boat, and there they would set up for a while, the small boat, its anchor down, unmoving on the transparent water. The boys are provided with masks and snorkels from Assad's endless reserve of equipment and tools; they can't wait to jump in, a deep, exhilarated, and atavistic yearning that leaves no room for their mother's plea, "Don't go too far, stay where I can see you." They're already jumping into the water, their mask-protected eyes wide open to the life below, the small yellow, orange, black, blue striped fish, the sea grass and coral; they swim around the boat, then under it, knocking on the small hull, casting its shadow on the white sand underneath, come close to pockmarked boulders teeming with fish, carpeted with sea urchins, use the tips of their snorkels to crack the sea urchins' spiky carapaces until sharp black spines splinter off, some floating up while others drift down, the meaty mother-of-pearl stuff inside the sea urchins now open and exposed to the world and the small fish of all colors and shapes quickly converging, nibbling on the pearly pink insides, an unexpected feast that the two boys watch motionlessly, their eyes wide open behind the masks; they could stay there forever, cracking the sea urchins, swimming among the pockmarked boulders, touching the sandy bottom with their hands, pushing up to the surface and going down again, opening up the water with their hands and arms, entranced by the colors and the different life below, swimming among the fish, themselves aquatic, only reluctantly coming back to the boat for short rests, their small bodies glistening in the sun, salt water on their skin dripping on the small boat's wooden planks.

Later, when they moved permanently from the provinces to start school and live in the shady, fragrant compound in the hills above the capital, there would be fewer outings to the sea, but they would swim almost every day, first in the old stone basin and later in the sleek turquoise swimming pool the grandfather had built on the same spot, and many of the fish they had seen on those outings, their brethren anyway, were collected for them by the grandfather in a monumental cement and glass aquarium built into the wall of the main dining room.

"You see these, the thin ones with the long filaments up front that look like mustaches, they're angelfish, *ce sont des scalares*, and the big pink ones constantly pouting, and kissing each other, these are kissing fish" (he says the last word in English: "*ce sont des kissingfish*," the three syllables breathed into one word) "and these are gourami, they have mustaches, too, see, like the angelfish, but look at the beautiful spots on them, and the transparent fins, just like lace."

And he goes on, the trained engineer, the retired Colonel who has outsmarted his circle at poker, goes on proudly and lovingly telling his grandsons about the tetras, the swordtails, and all the other fish.

"What about the ones that always stay at the bottom?"

"They're not very beautiful, are they? But very useful; look at what they do; they clean up the bottom of the aquarium; they eat everything, including the excrement of the other fish. They're called cories. . . ."

. . . (Silence and dismay from the boys, who look at each other and at him.)

"What's the matter?" (The Colonel, realizing a faux pas.)

"The *excrement?*" (The two boys, simultaneously.)

"Do you mean . . ." (The younger brother, mesmerized beyond his initial surprised disgust.)

"Yes, it's all *organic* and they don't care; they live a long time." And (now passing very quickly over the services rendered by the cories, the initial mention of *excrement* only a temporary lapse, followed by an attempt to return to a dry, scientific explanation, for he always maintains a decorum with them, a man from another time, a prude on the surface, full of rules and rectitude, who has the old gardener apologize when he himself farts during the supervision of this or that task because he could never openly admit that such filthy and intimate activity could possibly originate in his own body, and the boys, like the gardener, play the game, they comply, and once in a while, in the middle of an afternoon, when the fart is distinctly heard coming from the Colonel's body and not possibly from anywhere else, they will say together, "We're sorry, Grand-père," and look at each other with straight faces) the grandfather goes on to other aspects of the fish life in the aquarium.

The boy is glad to pretend. *Less trouble; why mess things up? He might stop telling us stories; he might give up on the aquarium.* Why not confront him with the truth? His younger brother has suggested several times, "Let's tell him we know it's him!" But the older brother wins out and the pretense goes on; the grandfather's explanations continue: "You see these swimming quickly by, the ones that look like butterflies and always swim in groups, they're called guppies."

The grandfather bought the initial batch of colorful

fish, as well as some subsequent replenishments for the aquarium, from his brother in the city, a very wealthy man who wouldn't dream of making presents of the fish to his brother or grandnephews, a man, said some mean gossips, but also his own family—so there must have been some truth to all this about the severe-looking man who never smiled and whose hair and skin were the same orangey hue—a man so avaricious, mean gossips and family members agreed, a man so avaricious that he counted the fruit on the guava and pomegranate trees in the multileveled gardens of his house, a house where since his wife's death he keeps only one servant as cook, washerwoman, ironing woman, chambermaid, and serving maid at the table, where he always eats alone. The mean gossips, and not a few family members, also say, "You know, she also goes to his bed at night, he's so miserly," something mentioned very freely by this or that aunt, leaving the boy perplexed. *What does she do for him in the middle of the night? Why would he need a maid in his room at that time?* The grandfather, logical engineer to the end, only goes to his brother for certain species, and not for those he can raise himself in a breeding tank he has built of stone and cement in back of the property, close to the place where the servants do the wash and bathe in the large tin tub.

When the two brothers moved from the provinces to live on the estate and began attending school, the grandfather would tell them all over again in his own dramatic way the story of Edmond Dantès, the young sailor who would one day become the Count of Monte Cristo and wreak terrible vengeance on those who had wronged him. In the early evening, when there are no visitors, long before the Colonel's drive to the casino with his wife, his grandsons go to him on the house's main veranda just as the sudden darkness falls and ask him to tell them one more installment of the long, fabulous story. He usually complies. The night air is cool; kerosene lamps are brought out because there will be a two-hour blackout, always at the same time. The grandfather would eventually have a generator installed, and for those two hours the kerosene lamps would be replaced by the feeble orangey light of the generator-fed bulbs. After the evening of the day Schmitt called his name, the boy would always associate the orangey light with the irruption of the men with guns and sunglasses in the gardens, and then spilling onto the veranda and into the house.

"Now, where were we? Edmond has been imprisoned in that small cell in the Château d'If for all these years. It's like a tomb, that cell, way down in the bowels of the fortress prison. Through all those years, Edmond sees no one besides the silent guards who bring him his daily rations on a tin plate. He has tried to *engager la conversation*, but they have received strict orders: No one is to speak to him. He is terribly alone; sometimes he thinks he will go mad. You understand, boys, so many years with no one to talk to?"

"Yes, yes, what happens next?"

"One day, in the middle of the afternoon, he hears three muted knocks on his cell wall. He is astounded. He stops breathing. Is this a trap? A way for the guards to test him, to drive him mad? He waits a bit more, and then . . ."

Grand-père tells the story. His voice is not deep, but it is full of nuance; he can be somber or jovial, angry or shy, a bit of a ham. The two boys are enthralled; another life is brought forth for them by that voice in the coolness and semidarkness of the veranda: the men and women in their clothes from another century, the houses and the garrets, the bustling port of Marseille, the wide boulevards of Paris, the French countryside with its wheat fields and apple orchards; their grandfather seems to have lived in that place, in that time of carriages, treasures, capes, and duels. Unlike so many of his circle who travel to that country as if to a distant origin on the other side of the ocean, the Colonel will never go to the real France of his own time; he is of the Tropical Republic; none of the yearning for that other origin for him; he wants to live nowhere but here, in this land where he and his generations have been for centuries, since the first Spaniards, those men of Columbus's crew from dusty towns in Andalusia, since the French, Breton, and Norman sailors, corsairs and buccaneers, since the Kongo, the Yoruba, the Ibo, the Rada, those who arrived enslaved, and all those others caught one way or another in the feverish thirst and what followed, when there were no more corsairs or buccaneers and the plantations were set on fire. The Colonel has made a name for himself here, has wielded power; it is his country, even after the wielding of that power is gone, his country, where he is known and respected, at the center of his clan even as the uninterrupted presence of his generations begins to fray, even as his progeny's displacement and relinquishment, forced or unforced, is already under way, even if he maintains, as much as he can, a partition between his clan and the others who now wield the power, especially after he has retired from the army—but, like so many of his circle, he loves the old performers from the other side of the ocean, whom he knows through thick 78-rpm shellac records in their glossy sleeves, Maurice Chevalier, Lucienne Delyle, Jean Sablon singing of unrequited love, voices the boys have heard so many times in the middle of the day and in the evening, especially in the early evening before the blackout, voices streaming out of the grandfather's record player encased in an acajou cabinet made by a local carpenter, and also songs and voices from a more immediate place and time, 33-rpm records brought back from Miami when the Colonel was the Tropical Republic's consul, Frank Sinatra, Nat King Cole, Perry Como. For the acutely impressionable boy, Grand-père's stories and the music he played were both faraway vestige and immediate promise: removed but beckoning, another, wider world beyond the confines of his own place and time.

Sometimes, the grandfather also tells his grandsons stories from his own place and time. In the Tropical Republic, too, there were treasures, clay urns filled with gold and silver pieces, diamonds and pearls buried in gardens by French families of another century who were fleeing their sugarcane plantations and stone mansions as the slave revolt spread across the plains. Two centuries later, in the grandfather's own time, rumors circulate: An urn has been long buried at the foot of a centenary mapou tree; two figures in the night, prudent recipients of some secret information, are digging among dilapidated walls of another age, ruins in a garden gone to seed, but after much digging no urn is found, luckily for the two diggers because, as their search is abandoned, bushes begin to change shape and move in the night; dozens of men and women carrying rakes, sickles, and machetes emerge from the darkness, where they have been lying in wait for their rightful share, or simply their share, or all of any unearthed gold, silver, and jewels yielded by the digging. For the boy, the fortunes contained in the buried, soil-encrusted urns from another time belong to the tapestry of fairy tales, comic books, and to the story of

The Count of Monte Cristo: the treasure that Edmond Dantès, the sailor escaped from his dungeon, digs up in a cave on the island of Monte Cristo, gold doubloons, pearl necklaces, ruby rings, topaz, emeralds, aquamarines, even banknotes of all colors and designations, "You cannot imagine, boys, the value of this treasure. *Un trésor inestimable, sans limites.*" And this is the treasure the sailor turned powerful count would use to carry out his devastating vengeance against those who had betrayed him, as the story continues.

Or the grandfather tells them about the time when he was a young officer himself, posted in the provinces, as their own father had been after him, driving into a small town late one afternoon and finding out that the house he was to occupy with his wife and his widowed sister, who had been traveling with them, the house on rue des Rosiers, was still being repaired. "*Je suis désolé, mon Commandant,*" said the supervising contractor, who was indeed sorry and apologetic when they arrived after hours of driving from the capital, the polite man pointing to the gaping spaces where windows and shutters would be placed, the smell of cement still fresh, the workers having already left for the day; he had stayed on just to let the commandant know, and it was unthinkable that the three of them would sleep there that night or for the next few nights.

"So, you see, there we were; we had left early and we had been traveling the whole day; Aunt Edwidge and your grandmother were getting tired. You know how Aunt Edwidge is; she was much younger then, but she was already like that, always about to make a scene. Your grandmother was composed and courteous, as usual, but I could feel she was becoming restless—you know how she stretches out her fingers and looks at her nails when it's past your bedtime and you're still up among the grown-ups?"

The two boys are used to the questions that give him time to compose—or to remember—and they nod, waiting.

"Well, she was doing that; I asked my orderly to drive around the town; he was a young private, who was also going to stay with us until the next day. So there we were with our luggage, driving around like lost people; it would get dark soon. Every time we saw someone in the streets, I asked my orderly to stop, and I would lean out the window and ask, 'Madame, monsieur, excuse us, I'm the new district officer posted here. My family and I are just now arriving and the house we were to occupy is still being worked on; we have no place to stay for the night, or for the next few days; would you know of a house that would be available?' Of course, there was no question of a hotel, you see; this was a small town, with no tourism; even people traveling on business to this place had to find a room with the locals, or drive at least an hour or two to the next town that had a hotel. The people I spoke to were very polite, but, no, there was nothing they could think of, and they themselves could not possibly put us up; their house was very small, or there was no room, what with all the family and the servants. And, you see, in my position as commanding officer, I couldn't stay just anywhere with Aunt Edwidge and your grandmother; if I had been alone, maybe, as an army man, of course I could have roughed it out for a night or two. Anyway, the situation was getting desperate; it was getting very late in the day when we saw an old woman, very respectable-looking; I'd asked the driver to stop as she was opening the gate to the garden of one of those large gingerbread houses, this one a light green with pink trimming" (a surfeit of detail from the grandfather; this is his way). "She told me that the best thing to do was to head for the restaurant on rue des Ramiers—it was only two streets over, and there someone might be able to suggest something, find a temporary solution. So on we went. We arrived in front of the restaurant; it was called Chez Paul; I asked the ladies to wait for me in the car and I went in with my orderly. It was a large room, very spacious, wooden floor, very high ceiling; two large ceiling fans were turning. It probably had been a warehouse before, when the town was thriving and ships came to collect merchandise. A few families were about to sit down to supper. You know, it was the provinces and they ate earlier there, even before it got dark; they woke up early and went to sleep early. There was a wonderful smell of fish *en sauce*; there were about twenty, twenty-five people in there, families sitting at tables, men either sitting at tables or gathered around a small bar. Music was playing, some Cuban music. A man immediately approached me; I assumed he must be the owner, Monsieur Paul; he was wearing an apron and he bent slightly to greet us. He looked at my uniform—you know, I had to wear my uniform when traveling, especially when arriving for the first time at a new posting. 'Welcome, *mon Commandant*, welcome. What can I offer you?' As I told you, we had been traveling all day and the fish *en sauce* smelled terribly good. I told Monsieur Paul I was the new commanding officer and that my wife and sister were in the car outside, that we'd like to have something to eat, if possible, and also that our house on rue des Rosiers, the house I was to occupy, was not ready for us, that we seemed to be stranded, with nowhere to go for the night or the following days. Monsieur Paul immediately sent one of the waiters to the car—'Mathieu, hurry up, go to the commandant's car and ask the ladies to come in. . . . Sit here, *mon Commandant*,' and, looking at my driver, he pointed him to another table not too far from the larger one he had proposed for us." The boys don't ask why the orderly does not sit at the same table with Grand-père, his wife, and his sister; the impossibility of this arrangement has been ingrained in them.

The night is cool. The boy can smell the scent of the pool's chlorine mingled with the fruit trees, bushes, and grass beyond the veranda. Suddenly the grounds, the house, and bungalows are all united in a single darkness; once again, as always, the power company has not forgotten the town in the hills above the capital; the blackout has started. The grandfather's voice stops, but the two boys are riveted; they won't let him stop. "Go on, go on," they say, even as they feel the story is going to take a sinister turn; the old gardener's helper brings in two kerosene lamps and leaves (this is before the Colonel had the generator installed). The old man and his grandsons continue to sit on the veranda, three figures in a yellowish breach of light carved in the unanimous night.

"The waiter returned with your grandmother and Aunt Edwidge. They sat down, bread was brought out, and Monsieur Paul asked if we would all be having the fish *en sauce*. 'Of course, Monsieur Paul,' I said, 'that would be just fine. Some lemonade for the ladies as well, if you have any, and a beer would not be unwelcome for me and my orderly, the young man at the next table.' We looked around and nodded to the diners and to the men at the bar. Even before the fish *en sauce* or the lemonade and beer were brought from the kitchen, Monsieur Paul spoke in a voice loud enough for everyone in the restaurant to hear, and explained our predicament, ending with 'So, if anyone knows of something for the commandant and his family, please tell them; let's show them our hospitality.' These people were quite kind, very nice; some of them came up to our table to commiserate, but, no, unfortunately, they didn't have anything themselves, they had nothing to suggest, and, you know, they were also reluctant, or ashamed, to propose something they thought was beneath the dignity of the new commanding officer and his family. By then, night had fallen, it was pitch-dark, and we were in the middle of our fish *en sauce*; the beer was making me feel a little better, but the problem remained unresolved: Where would we sleep? What would we do? This was the moment when the old woman who had suggested we come to the restaurant, the one who was opening the gate to the green-and-pink gingerbread house, entered the restaurant. She made her way straight to our table. I got up and asked her to sit down, but she remained standing. She was straightforward: 'I'm happy to see you are enjoying Monsieur Paul's cooking. Have you been able to find something?' When I told her that, no, unfortunately, no one had proposed anything, she looked at me, something like resignation on her face. 'Well, I didn't want to propose this to you earlier, but there is General Mortsauf's house; it's a bit out of town, but maybe it could be a temporary solution, if it can be opened for you? It's been unoccupied for some time, but someone goes in once in a while to air the house, so maybe it won't be too difficult to find some bedding and get some rooms ready for you? I see his niece is here.' The old woman turned to one of the other tables. 'Come, Mathilde, this is the new commandant and his wife and sister.' This other lady was also quite old and very respectable-looking, one of those thin provincial ladies with old-fashioned dresses that go down to their ankles; her gray hair was tied in a bun and she was wearing round horn-rimmed glasses. She wiped her mouth delicately with her dinner napkin [the grandfather mimics an old lady delicately wiping her mouth] and got up from a table, where she has been having dinner with two other ladies. She greeted us, and also remained standing. She spoke to her friend reproachfully: 'Miriam, come now, you know very well that this is not possible; the house will not do; besides, there is no electricity, and it's already dark.' This is where your grandmother intervened. You know how your grandmother is: When she speaks, she is very polite, very proper, but that tone of impatience in her voice was making its way in—you know how she is when she tells you it's time to go to bed—and we were really quite out of alternatives, so now she even sounded a little desperate, maybe even a bit rude. . . .

"'Madame, we would be very grateful if you would help us. I'm sure the house is fine, and we're not very fussy; we're quite used to being without electricity.'

"'But you see, madame, there is something wrong with the house.'

"'What could be wrong? We know it's a bit out of town, but we have a car and, as I said, we're not very fussy.'

"Madame Mathilde remained standing there, apparently considering what to do.

"'We would be very grateful; please just let us know what to do.'

"The old woman didn't seem to be able to decide."

"'Could you possibly show us to the house? After dinner, of course.'

"'There is no electricity; there is no bedding, and the

mosquito nets were taken down years ago. It's probably quite dusty.'

"'I'm sure we could find someone to take care of all that quickly enough; everyone seems so nice; quite a few people came to our table while we were having dinner.'

"'Madame, you see, this is my deceased uncle's house, General Mortsauf's house, and there have been problems. This is why no one has suggested the house to you.'

"Your grandmother just didn't know what to say, and this was when I intervened. And what did I ask?"

The boys know; they don't miss a beat: "You ask, 'What problems?'"—and they don't forget to add "madame"—"'What problems, madame?'"

At this point, knowing Grand-père's propensity for what he himself calls *the macabre*, the two boys are beginning to be quite afraid and something in them wants the story to stop, but they nevertheless make the small, quick contribution: "What problems, madame?" They also know that the grandfather may indeed decide at any moment to stop and tell them it's time for bed, or that he is tired, or that it's best to leave the rest of the story for another evening, but they cannot bear this, either. *They want to know what happened.* The grandfather continues, confident that his audience is fully engaged.

"'What can I tell you, monsieur! A few times, people from town, from here, and others, too, from the capital, they all tried to stay at the house these past few years, but they all left, the very first night, in the middle of the night; they just could not stay there.'

"'Madame, I assure you'" (this is the engineer speaking, the army officer, the man who would build the great house in the hills one day, sometimes using money won at poker games from others not as logical as he is, a pragmatic man who remembers proofs and theorems, and who knows how to build solid walls and foundations that withstand tropical storms). "'I assure you we will not have a problem; if you would just take us to the house, and help us find someone to help us settle in, we will be just fine.'

"Of course, Madame Mathilde sighs" (the grandfather, the storyteller, sighs, too; his face becomes Madame Mathilde's face; he takes on her provincial old woman's demeanor, her delicate gestures). "She looks at her friend Madame Miriam reproachfully. The thought is clear: It's all your fault; these poor people, they have no idea, and it's all your fault; and now she shakes her head from side to side."

The story continues. The two kerosene lamps hardly light the veranda in the house in the hills, surrounded by the gardens, the bungalows, the pool where the bats are sweeping down to drink. With infinitely more details from the storyteller, who describes the departure from the restaurant, leaving its fans and its yellow light, leaving the safety of families at dinner, of men at a bar, going back into the night while people look on from their tables and from the bar, saying good night to the commandant, his wife, his sister, his young orderly, accompanied by Madame Mathilde and her friend Madame Miriam, a small procession heading for the car in the dark provincial streets.

As always, the grandfather takes his time. He tells them about the coolness of the night, the dogs barking in the distance, the deserted streets of the small town, the smell of the nearby sea, Madame Miriam and Madame Mathilde knocking on doors to secure mosquito nets, bedding, and the bare essentials for a first breakfast, the church bell ringing out the late hour, the grandfather mimicking the sounds of the clock, the delicate, high-pitched and rapidly sounding *ting, ting*, followed by the mournful, plangent *donnnnngs*, one lugubrious, melancholy *dong* for each hour, nine this time; it's nine o'clock in the evening; in other stories, the ones about zombies and Erzulie, the goddess who wears four wedding bands, blue, pink, white, and gold, one for each of her husbands, or Zandolito, whose mother is a voodoo priestess and whose father a werewolf, in these other stories, it is always midnight, *the Hour.* But in this story, it's still three hours until the Hour.

Sitting on either side of him in the night, the boys just don't know what is true and what isn't. It will take years for them to decide what really happened in these stories, to determine for themselves what to keep and what to remember as the fabrications of an old man conjuring up wondrous occurrences for his two grandsons, but in that time and place, in the sheltering and isolating confines of privilege and family, they just don't know. Inevitably, they've heard things from schoolmates, from the servants, overheard conversations, yet there is no certainty. Even if the drums beating out there in the night, not too far from the limits of the compound, are dismissed as the instruments of practices foreign to their family's tradition, it is a man of that world of other instruments and practices, a thin, slightly bent man in his straw hat, sandals, patched pants and shirt, a handkerchief wrapped around his neck, who, summoned by their grandfather after their mother's plea—"Please, Papa, I will try anything. I just can't bear to see him like this; he's just skin and bones. Look at him, my poor boy"—and their grandfather's response—"Well, I will ask and have someone come"—comes to the house one day, very polite, at once respectful, well aware of the old lineal distribution of assigned places in the Tropical

Republic, but confident, sure of himself and of his own power and mastery, of the potency of his preparations and instruments, a strange man who pulls out of his straw bag a creased envelope containing the already gathered ingredients to prepare a draft for the younger brother's asthma attacks, all else having failed to prevent the debilitating choking fits that make him gasp for air, his head bent over his chest, his fists tight, his ribs showing in his thin torso, fits that leave him exhausted, missing days and weeks of school, sitting up in bed, propped up by pillows a good part of the night while the grandfather rubs his back, and his brother falls asleep. The man asks for a glass of water, into which he pours the contents of the envelope, and then for a spoon, and stirs; the viscous green-and-brown preparation looks ancient and out of place in the sparkling glass held out to the younger brother, who is gently told, "Drink it all at once; don't stop; you'll see, this will make you feel better," and the asthmatic brother, determined, courageous, swallows the mixture as the boy looks on and hides his disgust in order to accompany his brother and accomplice in the swallowing of the sluggish mixture that belongs to another world, like the stories of Zandolito and Erzulie, stories about encounters with groups of stiff and silent people carrying candles late at night on their way to ceremonies in cemeteries.

When the boy sees him entering the kitchen that day, the strange man with his straw bag and his potions, the slightly bent man in his patched pants and shirt, who looks out of place in one of the high-ceilinged, white-tiled kitchens of the great house, seems like an apparition from one of the grandfather's stories; he could have been there when the young officer arrived at that shuttered house in the provinces with his wife and sister years before, General Mortsauf's house, a witness to the opening of the wrought-iron gate (of course, it made a grating sound in the night, the grandfather's nasal imitation of groaning metal), the crossing of the garden, the opening of the main door, the smell of old wood and mold, the opening of a few windows and shutters, the lighting of lamps and candles, the distribution of bedrooms for the night, Aunt Edwidge in a bedroom down the hall from the main one (the orderly had secured something for himself somewhere else, and had left after helping with the boxes and suitcases and the quick cleaning up), the parting from the two provincial ladies, the unsuspecting trio from the capital lying down to sleep, the silence and old wood smell of the house, the three travelers asleep for a time; the strange man with his straw bag and his potions could have been there, in a corner, a witness to the words spoken to Aunt Edwidge by the man in her room, her screams in the night, the grandfather running to her bedroom, opening the door, seeing Aunt Edwidge in the large bed through the parted mosquito net, holding her throat, pointing to the man jumping over the balcony opening up onto the garden, his white cape disappearing in the darkness among the trees and bushes. Then the grandfather stops. The two brothers are terrified. Ada has to stay with them a long time before they fall asleep.

"This is terrible; your grandfather should be ashamed, telling you these stories. Yes, he should be ashamed. Look at the two of you. You have to wake up for school tomorrow. You know this is not true, don't you?"

. . . (Not a word from the two boys, who just look at her, hoping she will not leave the bedroom.)

"You know this, don't you?"

. . .

Before the boy finally falls asleep, General Mortsauf's white cape in the night mingles with Count Dracula's red-lined black cape as he had seen it at the movies, the count's bloodshot eyes are the general's, and Tante Edwidge's screams are the screams of the Technicolor Victorian ladies the vampire bends over to drain them of their blood.

The story of General Mortsauf took place years before, when the Colonel was still a young officer posted in the small provincial town by the sea. Weeks after the boys hear the story for the first time from their grandfather, Aunt Edwidge comes to the house for one of the Sunday lunches by the pool. The younger brother wants to hear the story from her again. "We'll know what really happened," he says; he has his doubts, and wants to know, even if his brother is reluctant to approach Aunt Edwidge. "Why do you want to bother her with this old story? What are you trying to do?" But the younger brother prevails and takes the boy along to the deck chair Aunt Edwidge is sitting in with a glass of Grand-père's rum punch. "It's not strong; it's a *cocktail de dames*," he informed the guests as a tray was passed around by a servant. After hearing the younger brother's request, Aunt Edwidge takes a slow sip of her drink and, speaking in a low voice, gathering the two boys in a quiet conspiracy, tells them about that night in the provincial town. She passes over the arrival and the rest very quickly and comes to the moment that had terrified them weeks before. "I was sleeping, but I couldn't breathe; I felt I was choking. I felt a presence in the room; I opened my eyes, and I saw him. I saw him standing above me, completely still, a man dressed all in white, a white uniform and white gloves, his hair and his mustache and his sideburns white; his face was like wax, and his eyes, his eyes, they were piercing, but they were dead at the same time. I could not move; I could not speak. He just stood there, looking at me; he shook his head very slowly from side to side, and then he spoke; his voice was very clear, very distinct, but very low, a voice from another time; he seemed very sad and very sorry to have to tell me what he was telling me. 'Madame, do you know where you are? Do you know where this is? *Do you know where this is? This is my house.* I am General Mortsauf and you should not be here.' And then he bent down to me. I could feel his breath; it was foul. He put his hands on my throat; they were as cold as ice, and he started pressing, choking me, his nails digging into my throat. I knew I was going to die. I could not scream, and then I screamed, I finally was able to scream, I screamed so loud, and your grandfather came into the room. . . ." They are listening to her, looking at her in the clear light of Sunday by the pool, "Look, look at my neck," and she lifts her face to them, turns the side of her neck toward them. "Look at the marks he left there, that man, General Mortsauf. Touch them!" The asthmatic brother and the boy just stare.

"Come! Touch!"

. . . (For a few seconds, they don't dare move.)

. . . (She points repeatedly at her wrinkled and spotted neck.)

The two words seem an urgent injunction, even after all the years since that night, even if Aunt Edwidge may be smiling, even if she may not be serious; the boys just don't know. An unabashed doubting Thomas, the younger brother bends down and runs his finger along the side of Tante Edwidge's wrinkled neck. The boy is shocked by the daring and the intimacy of his brother's gesture. He stands back, but he, too, wants to know.

"You see what he did to me?"

. . .

What could they say? They stand looking down at her sitting on the deck chair, her drink placed on the smooth cement floor at her side. The boy can't tell whether she is smiling or grimacing, and they quickly rejoin the activity of Sunday by the pool. The boy faster than his younger brother.

The year before his grandfather told the story of General Mortsauf in the orangey light of the veranda's kerosene lamps while the bats performed their muted dance over the great house's swimming pool, the boy's father was still stationed in the provinces and he and his brother were not yet attending school; the family lived in the army-assigned house with its garden of gladiolus, zinnias, daisies, and begonias facing an extended expanse of wild grass. There were always other boys outside the house, boys who seemed to have nothing to do but roam the streets all day, poor boys from nowhere, it seemed, ragged clothes, full of energy, with strong smells and very white teeth. The boy and his brother were not allowed to go very far from the house, but they were allowed to play with those boys. "Make sure I can see you, I want to always be able to see you, and when I call, come to the house right away," their mother often said from the garden or the living room, looking up from *The Count of Monte Cristo,* reading it one more time, that old present from the boy's father to his young wife when she was pregnant with their first child, the boy now in the tall grass and thistles, feeling another boy's hand moving inside his pants, feeling his small nestled penis unfolding like a bud and stiffening as he lies on the ground looking at the sun and the passing clouds overhead, and he puts his small hand inside the other boy's ragged short pants and does the same thing, both getting up after a while from the shady spot and running again, continuing the game of hide-and-seek they have been playing with the other boys in the not yet hot day.

In the small town by the sea that year, there were two birthday parties, one for the boy, who was turning five, and one for his brother, who was turning four. Those invited were the children from other families their parents knew, not those boys playing hide-and-seek in the thistle and tall grass; the one who lay in the shady spot with the boy had easily won all his new marbles, all bright and shiny, at least fifty of them, not a single old and chipped one among them, one of the birthday presents from his mother, given to him a few days before the party, for there would be another present from his parents at the party. His mother had been asking him where he'd put the new marbles. "I went through a lot of trouble to find these for you; you've never seen such a beautiful collection of marbles." Well before the distribution of gifts, in the full swing of the party, the boy from the tall grass and thistles and shady spot managed to catch his attention from outside the garden, where boys and girls in their starched and ironed clothes were playing and laughing while their parents drank and ate sandwiches on the veranda and in the house. "Pssst, pssst," the repeated call from outside in the dark, and the boy, knowing something was wrong, finally found a way to go over to him in an alleyway next to the house, the sounds of the party reaching them. The boy from the tall grass and thistles knew he could not come in, but he would not be denied, and he whispered sternly, stubbornly, "I want some of those sandwiches and that crunchy orange stuff you're all eating, and bring some cake, too."

. . .

"If you don't, I'll go and tell. . . ."

. . .

"Don't worry, I'll give you back your marbles."

The boy makes two trips back to the dark alleyway with paper saucers of Cheetos, cake, and, wrapped in birthday napkins, chicken, asparagus, and cheese sandwiches. The other boy eats everything right there, stands up, smiles at him. He returns the marbles in a small cloth sack. "I've added a few—from me for your birthday." "Thank you." And they part. The vagrant boy disappears in the dark; the boy goes back to the party. The boy receives many presents. They all sing "Happy Birthday" to him, in English.

At the Séminaire, where they go to school after they've moved to the grandfather's compound, there is another group of boys who hang around together, at school and outside of school. These are different boys; they and the boy know one another's families; their mothers and fathers go to one another's houses for dinners, christenings, birthdays, condolence calls, soirées, or short, spur-of-the-moment visits."Just dropping by, *ma chère*."

"It's so good to see you. What a wonderful surprise! You should stay for lunch."

"Very kind of you, but we have to get back home; lunch is waiting for us; the cook has prepared something special. Why don't you just offer us one of your lemonades, with lots of ice, and we'll be on our way?"

"André! [or Socrates, or Lejeune, or Mirna, or Rosette], please [or often without the *please*] bring us some lemonade out on the veranda! . . . So good to see you; it's been a while. Let's sit down and chat a bit. What's the news?"

After the usual "My he's grown!" or "I hear he's doing very well at school," and directly to him, "How are you?" the boy is necessarily on the periphery of these conversations between adults, old friends whose families have always known one another, with a shared past, shared concerns, politics, business, gossip, but the boy is also outside of their sons' knowing little clusters at school, this particular group led by one of his classmates, Reginald Broussard, who has two stunning sisters the boy contemplates with a longing he does not quite grasp even years after they've moved from the provinces to the town in the hills above the capital. His brother has said to their young aunt, about another of those beautiful older girls, a friend of hers, a ballet dancer who would open her own dance school years later, "Why is it when I look at Sandra I feel like peeing?" The young aunt can only laugh and repeat the story to her friends.

Gorgeous girls, four, five years older than those nine-, ten-, eleven-year-old boys, the boy's classmates who would not dream of reading books from the pink collection, the one *for girls*, as the boy does, only from the green one, *for boys*. They are trying out cigarettes; they inhale, cough, and spit but will get it in the end. They raise up their shirt collars and roll back their sleeves, like Elvis Presley or, more likely, Johnny Hallyday or Dick Rivers, the French singers with American stage names whose picture postcards are exchanged in the Tropical Republic by transistor radio–owning fans in those years that still look like the fifties, ten, eleven years old, and already strutting around on their spindly legs with the assurance of little men sure of their place in the solid world. At school they gather at recess, those boys; they smile knowingly; they pass on messages to one another in class. Most of the other boys, in the class or not, don't even notice or care, but the boy wants to belong with the determination and stubbornness of the exasperated solitary, for he and his brother are so confined and protected: "No, you cannot go to that soccer match in the city; it's too far, and how are you going to get there?" "No, we cannot go to the drive-in this evening." (This is the mythical meeting point for boys from the Séminaire at the end of the week, the Friday-night viewing followed by heated discussions of the film in the schoolyard on Monday mornings). "Why don't you go to the cinema on the square, the Sunday-morning show, as you always do?" And so for the boy and his brother, public space remains constricted; a whole city, an entire country, hundreds of thousands of people, millions of people, passing crowds, an entire world out there, one that the other boys their age seem to know, boys who have walked on their own and with their friends, with other boys their age in those streets, boys who have gathered knowledge and assurance from being out there, while the boy and his brother remain cordoned off, their isolation compensated by the tribe, the family and their friends, the two sets of grandparents and their children, all those aunts and uncles, the house and its gardens, the Americans, the house with its many guests on Sundays and on holidays, the books, the stories told by one grandfather, the endless presents from the other grandfather, the outings to the cinemas in the city with him, the Sundays at their father's farm in the plains after he's retired from the army, days spent with his brother among the mango trees, the orange trees, the sugarcane fields, the henhouses of the farm started after their father's discharge from the army, when The Mortician came to power, but those other boys represent a camaraderie he yearns for even as his intuitive dislike keeps him apart; nine, ten, eleven years old, he wants to be with other boys his age, especially since he feels their own reluctance as they've sniffed out his yearning. He doesn't want to remain alone, even with his brother; he doesn't want to remain outside; he's intrigued by those boys who know and share things he doesn't. Broussard, their leader, has devised a "Dictionary of Curse Words" assembled from medical books (Broussard's father is a doctor), scavenged from dictionaries, or magazines with photographs found in this or that uncle's or father's or grandfather's hidden stash, gleaned from overheard conversations between older brothers or cousins who are already *going to women*, as they say in that time and place, a compilation of sorts, a fragmented and elusive knowledge.

One day, during morning recess, as if relenting from their usual aloofness, Reginald Broussard and his second in command, the son of one of his mother's best friends, approach him like Roman conspirators and tell him that *he's in,* that he's one of them; access to the fraternity has been granted. The boy smiles, he acquiesces, and the results are instantaneous; no additional initiatory rites are forthcoming. The litany of definitions begins.

"Okay, what is *erection*?"

. . . (Surprise at the immediacy of access; puzzlement, silence, followed by more laconic questions, more or less precise, even clinical answers reeled off at a rapid pace; more silence, more puzzlement, more words.)

"*Erection* is when . . ." (And the simultaneously inexact and graphic definition immediately follows.) . . .

"What is *clitoris*?"

. . .

"*Clitoris* is . . ." (And the simultaneously inexact and graphic definition immediately follows.) . . .

"What is *coming*?"

"*Coming* is . . ." (And the simultaneously inexact and graphic definition immediately follows.)

. . .

The vocabulary is not completely foreign to him, even if the mechanics are unclear, the figures and body parts blurred, for he has already made inadvertent, awkward incursions into that realm.

The leaf sellers are also agents of that realm. During carnival season, among the small groups of musicians and revelers who go around the Tropical Republic's towns on Sundays, weeks before the main, frenzied three days of carnival, among the drum, maraca, bamboo trumpet, and flute players, among the devils with their black-painted bodies, their wings, pitchforks, and giant red lips (the boy knows the wings are made of cardboard, the red lips of socks filled with wood shavings or discarded fabric and attached to the men's heads with black strings or rubber bands, but his dread is nevertheless real when these men enter the gardens, ribs heaving, arms thrusting out wooden pitchforks with silver foil tips, their calloused bare feet rhythmically smacking against the smooth cement, the grass, or the gravel), among the Indians with their mirror- and bead-embroidered outfits, painted faces, feathers, and long tresses, among the wearers of gigantic papier-mâché heads that reach down to the collarbone, among all these precursory revelers, there are the leaf sellers, women who carry baskets filled with the instruments of their temporary carnival trade, wearing no disguise, just their everyday clothes, women who for a penny or two put down their baskets and use their flowers, leaves, and branches to stage graphic little vignettes. A leaf seller has been invited into the garden by one of the aunts or their visiting friends. The Colonel must be out or sleeping, for any outsiders on the property are considered intrusions, unwelcome disturbances. The woman puts down her basket on the steps of a veranda and proceeds to open a flower, slowly and dexterously pulling off a petal, extricates a pistil, says the words, performs the emphatic gestures.

"You see this is the clitoris and—"

"Oh, stop it! *Stop* it!"

The aunts and the other young ladies, their friends in their makeup, their skirts and blouses and stylish dresses, their Boussac print dresses that were so fashionable at the time, are all laughing, protesting, and beckoning at the same time, but the woman goes on, mock-serious, with a lascivious smile, eyes bright, intent on giving these proper young ladies their money's worth, as with one hand she picks up a dry elongated calabash from her basket, and with the other a large hibiscus flower, its granular, powdery yellow stamens delicately attached to the red pistil rising from its ridged petal, and begins to mimic another scene. Of course, the boys are chased away during these performances. "Don't stay here. This is not for you; this is not for your ears," they are told, but, as always, the two brothers manage to remain on the close periphery of anything that seems forbidden to them; they manage to glimpse some gestures and hear some words, echoes and fragments of which now return to the boy as Reginald and his lieutenant continue to recite from the "Dictionary."

Now that the boy has been inducted, the forced

complicity is endless, insistent: whispered questions as they go up to class in ordered rows; quickly scribbled notes passed during math or grammar lessons; or, as they sit on the bleachers, watching a soccer match between older boys during noon recess, a muttered question from one of the lieutenants: "Do you know where babies come out of?" (not "where babies come from" but "where they come out of"), followed, of course, by the answer, another lieutenant adding, as if repairing an oversight, "And sometimes the doctor has a go at her." The concrete yet nebulous, repulsive yet magnetic absurdity of these particular words hits him in the chest, a raw symptom of his escalating disbelief, disgust, and refusal, even as he also understands—but does he?—that they are making fun of him, that they are supplementing, maliciously embroidering, as the soccer match goes on, and the heat of the day is tempered by the shade of the tree branches hanging over the bleachers, where all those other boys not sitting with them remain blissfully unaware or unconcerned by these impossibilities. He cannot sift what could be true from their little men's bluster. This answer clashes with his own experience—with all the people he knows, his mother, his father, his aunts, their friends, the gardeners, the maids, with the people walking in the streets, conversations, the books he has read, the movies he has seen, the American television series, with school, the priests—nothing of what he has seen and touched conforms to what is contained in the particular words the boys are uttering: neither Caroline and Debby's smooth, pale, and delicate vulvas (he does not know that word yet, a word that has escaped both the coterie's "Dictionary" and the leaf sellers' graphic language) when, in the main garden's shady recesses, where the ferns proliferate, they have so simply and thoroughly displayed themselves to each other, as children will, nor the maids' hips, the soapy water splashing over their shoulders and breasts, the dark, grainy triangles quickly perceived when they kneel in the tin tub. None of it conforms to what he is hearing. His dislike of those boys reaches a limit, and whatever hold they once had on him through their cliquish association and supposed knowledge will soon vanish, even if they have managed to disturb something in him, to cast a dim and prurient shadow.

A week after the day when the boy is told *And sometimes the doctor has a go at her* by one of Reginald Broussard's lieutenants, his mother is driving her two sons to school in the Hillman. Her hair is gathered in a chignon; she is wearing a sleeveless pale yellow linen dress with a matching belt. The boy sits next to her as she drives the boxy little car in her high heels; he looks at her calm, lovely profile, and years later he will remember that dress, that day, that profile, he will remember that he was thinking, *She was with my father in their bedroom, all night; she looks so beautiful.* No concrete images or dispositions of bodies are associated with the thought on that early morning as they drive down to school. Dew still coats the trees and bushes; around the bends in the road, the city and the sea below appear and disappear between the flaming red of the poinciana trees; barefoot peasant women are walking down to the main market in the city with their baskets on their heads, accompanied by their little girls, smaller-scale replicas of these women, to follow in their wake for years and eventually take their place—the boy has no awareness of this implacability of his time and place's hierarchy, the great reluctance with which inherited and assigned places change in the Tropical Republic—mothers and daughters doing that elegant, nimble, and lineal walk-stumble dance, walk-stumble dance, walk-stumble dance, with their baskets on their heads, filled to the brim with cauliflower, carrots, cabbages, artichokes, beets, vegetables that grow in the hills and the mountains, not the citrus and mangoes of the plains; and walking down the road there are other children, boys and girls his age, younger, older, all walking, walking to school, not driven, bunches of them talking and laughing but always hurrying with their schoolbags strapped to their backs, ribbons in many of the little girls' hair, many wearing the red, blue, gray gingham uniforms of their various schools, the younger boys in their short pants, starched shirts, and laced boots, many of the older ones in long pants; there are also men, some walking, some hitchhiking, some just standing by the side of the road, some barefoot, some in sandals, others in shoes; the public taxis that ply the route between the town in the hills and the city are filled with passengers, those same baskets full of vegetables on the luggage racks of quite a few, since some of the peasant women have decided to spend a few of their precious coins on getting to market earlier, or are just too weary on that particular day to complete the long way down from the mountains to the city on foot. From the neighborhoods along the way, from the valley below, the pervasive and familiar smell of burning firewood drifts in the early morning, infusing the air as it always does. Looking at all this coming to life in the early morning, his lunch box on his lap, his schoolbag at his feet, turning to look at his mother's profile, her earrings, her hands holding the steering wheel, her feet pressing down on the clutch, the accelerator, the brake pedals, shifting gears in her pale yellow linen dress, in her heels, so calm and beautiful, the words he heard from the boy on the bleachers the day before seem more impossible than ever. It is settled; he will remain in his separateness. Moments like this, clear, demarcated, appear even in the callous drift of privileged childhood. His curiosity remains intact, but those boys will remain outside his accidental and artless path.

Removed as they are from the exposure that would inoculate them or at least provide them with the necessary resilience, the two brothers seem devoid of the very traits and experiences that generate factions like that of Reginald Broussard and his lieutenants. They lack the freedom of movement, the ability to make their way in a place wholly their own, as places can only belong to boys away from the confines of house, family, relatives, servants. Even if some solace can be found in that other sheltered life—the grandfather's stories, the expansiveness of the compound, its gardens, their smells and recesses, the constant coming and going of relatives, friends, and *pensionnaires* with their habits and appearance from a greater world out there, the constant passing of people on the verandas, in the gardens, around the pool, the company of the younger aunt and her friends, of the other young aunt, the other grandfather's youngest daughter and her friends, the two boys' own restricted and fraternal complicity in the midst of all this, their appetite for books, especially the older brother's, all those books and comic books (from Tintin to cookbooks from the shelves of the French Institute's lending library) and movies (so many Sunday mornings watching sepia cowboys, Technicolor Romans and surfers, black-and-white Zorros and Tarzans), the outings to the beach and to the mountains, the two brothers' particular and odd proclivity, perhaps itself a result of their isolation from cliques, for perceiving and feeling the changing of light from the yellow-green of school mornings to the sudden starry dark that follows swift orange-and-red sunsets—even if all this weaves a comforting cloak around them, there are the inevitable encounters with other nine- ten-, eleven-year-old boys, boys already strutting around on their spindly legs with the assurance of little men sure of their place in the solid world. And so the two brothers are sometimes exposed, offered up, prey.

Throughout all those years, even as the point of no return is being reached, the two brothers remain in their insulated lives, with their sometimes odd practices, so different from those of *other boys their age*. They have that habit of taking out cookbooks from the French Institute's lending library—large, heavy books with thick, glossy pages and photos of dishes from temperate climes, appetizers to desserts, *jambon en croûte*, *foie gras*, *steak au poivre*, *profiteroles*, *tartes aux fruits*, not an unfamiliar form to them, the tart, but these are covered with raspberries, blueberries, cranberries, rare and exotic fruit to them; in the glossy pages, the flowing scoops of grenadine, orange, chocolate, vanilla ice cream that emerge from the old gardener's long cranking of the ancient-looking *sorbetière* are replaced by geometrically cut slices, some even in a checkerboard pattern. The brothers sit together somewhere, on one of the verandas, or in their bedroom, or on one of the sofas around the pool. A large book lies open on both their laps; they turn the pages, smack their lips at the colorful procession of food unfolding from another world out there.

For a few months the two brothers are anemic. Intestinal parasites? A genetic proclivity? Anorexia? Instead of the sandwiches they usually carry to school in their lunch boxes, they are now fed *real meals* at home in the middle of the day, when they are picked up from school during noon recess and are driven back to the house in the hills for sautéed chicken liver, grilled meat, chopped carrots and beets. "Eat. You must get healthy and strong again," they're told. "There will be plenty of time for games in the schoolyard." In fact, throughout those months, there won't be any time for games in the schoolyard; by the time they're driven back to the Séminaire after their fortifying meals, the hundreds of boys are usually already lining up, or have even started their quiet and orderly return to the classrooms; the disciplined silence to which the two boys have returned is yet another instance of the separateness that leaves them prey to the inevitable encounters with the harshness of cliques, as on the day when the boy had to wear the Hercules outfit his godmother, his mother's sister, had a seamstress make especially for him to wear at the Belvedere afternoon carnival ball.

The carnival season had started weeks before; only those small groups of musicians and revelers were coming out so far, going from house to house in a steady musical uproar: Indians, skeletons, cowboys, the leaf sellers, the devils with their wings and tridents who strike such terror in the boy, hangers-on wearing no disguises at all, not part of the small bands and their affiliated revelers, but simple passersby with nowhere else to go, nothing else to do, hoping for a few coins themselves, gradually joining in, swinging their hips to the music, not quite surreptitiously joining those smalls groups during the weeks preceding the three days of all-out carnival. During these weeks before Mardi Gras, when bleachers are being assembled in the main square facing the resplendent white national palace in the city below, when floats are being built somewhere (the boy never knows where; they always just appear on the first day of the main carnival parade, garlanded mastodons slowly moving through the frenzied crowd), when the two major orchestras are rehearsing their official brass and percussion paeans to this particular carnival (one had to be a supporter of one or the other orchestra; there were arguments, fights even), the Tropical Republic holding its breath, it seemed, during those clear winter days (even if this season is never named) in the interval preceding the three days of all-out carnival, everyone choosing an outfit to wear for the season.

At Ajoupa Ciné, the boy has seen Hercules rescue a swooning princess by holding back her chariot, pulled dangerously close to a cliff by runaway horses; he has seen Hercules kill the Lernaean Hydra (they know such names from movies, the boy and his brother), or vanquish in single combat the champions of nefarious princes, their nefariousness evident in their rutilant robes, curlicue beards, braceleted arms, and beringed fingers; he has seen Hercules majestically walking in pine and olive tree–speckled, column-strewn landscapes, handsome and confident, his thin waist, his copper skin and sinewy muscles set off by his smoothly falling outfit, a sash over his shoulder and across his muscular chest, the rest of his outfit held up by a thick leather belt, barely covering his thighs, an outfit so simple and so different from the villains', the cruel or usurping princes; and the boy wanted that outfit to wear at the Belvedere's afternoon carnival ball.

The outfit arrives on the afternoon of the children's carnival ball, moments before they have to get in the car to be driven to the Belvedere; a hurried and alternate solution was found when it seemed the costume would not arrive in time; the boy would be going as a pirate, like his brother, mustache traced above his upper lip with burned cork, black handkerchief tied around his head, felt hat with plume, eye patch, wooden saber, but the Hercules outfit suddenly did arrive, delivered on the seamstress's outstretched arms, accompanied by a stream of apologies between gasping breaths, and taken out of its thick brown paper wrapping: it is not the earth-toned and smoothly falling folds of the garment worn by Hercules in a landscape of pines, olive trees, and columns, but a bright yellow, bouncy, and glossy satiny thing that makes the boy's heart sink as the others look on: his brother, safely contained, manly and presentable in his pirate outfit; his mother; Ada; the young aunt; his godmother, even more expectant than the others, since it is her gift. The boy is absolutely silent in his disappointment. No tears or protestations, only a passing cloud over his face. Even though wearing this outfit to the Belvedere's afternoon carnival ball seems an impossibility, he cannot bring himself to say anything, to cause even more trouble, only hoping the outfit will be too small or suddenly disappear. His mother takes him aside. "Come, let's go put it on."

She leads him by the hand and, in the closeness of his bedroom, encourages him.

"Don't look so disappointed; your godmother really wanted this gift for you. Be nice. Here, try it on. . . ."

. . .

"Here, let me help you. . . ."

. . .

They slip on the yellow outfit; the mirror in the dresser is merciless: The sash, in fact the entire upper section above the waist, clings to his small chest, perversely rounding his small belly, perversely because he is in the hard flatness and bony angularity of boyhood; the bottom part delicately and stubbornly flares out, almost a ballerina's tutu, nothing like the falling folds of the sober earth-toned material above Hercules' muscled thighs, but instead a garment that, with some adjustments, given the style worn by women in that time and place, might look becoming on one of his aunts or on his mother when leaving for a reception of an evening, on his grandmother when entering the casino, or on Brigitte Bardot, the French actress he has seen in coming attractions at Ajoupa Ciné in her tight blouse and stiletto heels clicking on the wet cobblestones of some Parisian street; but here, in this time and place, and in his mind, right now, in this moment, and for years afterward, albeit with decreasing intensity, it is a crinoline catastrophe.

"Look, if we can push down this part a bit and make it stay down, and take out this red trim [a band of sewn-on red *Roman designs* anachronistically circles the hem of the Hercules outfit], it will look much better, yes?"

. . . (He remains stubbornly silent. Helpless and defiant all at once.)

"Let me do it."

. . .

His mother calls in Ada and the seamstress, asks the first to fetch her sewing basket, then gives directions to the second. Ten minutes later, the boy is out, still looking composed, maybe even determined, even if the satiny yellow outfit is still blinding and bouncy in the afternoon sun. His mother stands back and smiles. The godmother sees the adjustments and seems relieved; she smiles. The younger brother remains diplomatically and safely silent. The pirate and Hercules get in the car with Ada, who will accompany the boys; the chauffeur takes off and the boy is hoping they will never get to the Belvedere, hoping for some providential disaster or a miracle, even if, by then, he is already too much beyond the priests' ascendancy to really believe such a thing is possible. The ride is short and eternal, fifteen minutes; outside the car windows, the boy sees carefree people who have nothing to do with this ordeal, happy children, anonymous and carefree children *who aren't going to the ball*, and then the car stops under the curved concrete awning of the Belvedere's main entrance as a doorman, in his uniform of black pants, starched white shirt, black patent-leather shoes, and black bow tie, opens the back door and the music from inside reaches the new arrivals as they disembark. Ada has to coax the boy out of the car.

"Come, come out! Don't worry, it will be fine."

. . .

As soon as he's out of the car, Ada on one side of him, the pirate brother on the other, they are confronted by at least a half dozen Zorros, complete with black capes and flat hats, whips and masks, their own maid-chaperones or parents out of sight, seemingly independent little black-garbed bodies released to wreak havoc on the world in their banded anonymity, for they cannot be recognized behind their masks, while the boy in satiny, even if now controllably flared, yellow splendor stands fully exposed in the bright afternoon light.

"Hey!" (This is followed by the boy's last name.) "Do you know who I am?"

"And how about me? Recognize me?"

"And me?"

. . . (There's nothing for it but to face them, which he does, suspended in a blind trance, again hoping that everything will disappear)

"What are you wearing?"

. . .

"What outfit is this?"

. . .

"Who are you supposed to be?"

. . .

And, more alarmingly: "What kind of getup is this?"

. . . (The boy can't be sure who is speaking, but he thinks he recognizes Reginald Broussard and some of his lieutenants.)

The miniature Zorros are closing in, hyenas around a gazelle in one of the jungle films, but a kind of miracle does occur, as a frail and timid boy from his class, the one whose sister is a newly crowned beauty queen, takes off his mask and yells out, "I recognize it! Hercules! You look great! I wish I had an outfit like that—so many Zorros, already! Let's go in!"

The outburst from this boy, normally so withdrawn, is astonishing. The other Zorros are too surprised to add anything, to prolong the baiting; the wind has been taken out of their sails by the usually quiet classmate. Ada, the brother pirate, the flouncy Hercules, and the providential miniature Zorro leave the driveway together, go up the stairs, and enter the Belvedere's ballroom. The sudden escalation of heat and light and sound and color and bodies takes them in; the music is blasting from the band on the stage; small confetti-covered bodies are moving on the circular and shiny garland-strewn dance floor.

The ordeal is over. So safe and secure to be in the crowd, away from the band of miniature Zorros' scrutiny, to be moving through the compact gathering of other bodies, making his way to one of the tables, the providential Zorro leading him, his brother, and Ada; they cut through the crowd of small dancing bodies, waiters in crisp white shirts and black bow ties also cutting through, holding their trays above the crowd, more easily than usual, since almost all the bodies are small, short; the waiters are carrying trays filled with platters of sandwiches, sodas, lemonades, orangeades; led by the providential Zorro, the boy, his brother, and Ada make their way through to one of the large round tables covered with starched tablecloths. At this table, and at all the other tables, there are maid-chaperones (many) or mothers (few, for most are at home preparing for their own ball, the evening ball), no fathers; a few boys and girls also sitting at those tables where other ones, those who are on the dance floor, have marked their places with a mask, a hat, a half-eaten sandwich on a plate.

The pirate has already asked a Calypso (flared skirt, this time appropriately so, striped shirt with puffed-up sleeves, kerchief-wrapped head and straw hat, large pendant earrings) to dance. All these bodies, small but already well versed in the mannerisms and habits of their time and clan and place, already adept at the steps and moves of merengue and *kompa* and, more rarely, cha-cha. Dancing is pervasive in the Tropical Republic, in village squares or elegant clubs, at drum-driven ceremonies or in spacious living rooms, in the small, dark half brothels with their almond trees and gravel floors frequented by the dissolute uncle or at the exclusive clubs. And dancing comes early to everyone. Here they are on the dance floor, all these miniature replicas of their parents, boys and girls from the large houses in the capital or the town above the hills; here they are on the Belvedere's dance floor, boys and girls in their Arabian princess gauze or cowboy outfits, boys and girls whose families have known one another for generations, small bodies doing dance moves, tracing patterns, as they say in that time and place, on the shiny garland and confetti–strewn dance floor of the Belvedere's annual children's carnival ball.

At some point, after much equivocation, the boy will ask a girl to dance, a painter with beret and easel, her enormous and impeccably tied bow over an artist's blouse fastened by three huge buttons, one red, one yellow, one green. Unlike the pirate brother, who has asked so many Arabian and Roman princesses and Calypsos and cowgirls and swans to dance, it takes the boy a long time to decide. The little painter is wearing ballet slippers, the result of her mother's thinking that painters and dancers belong to the same tribe of *artists*; she has been standing forever in her painter's blouse and ballet slippers and no one has asked her to dance, not a Zorro, not a devil, not a cowboy; she waits there bravely on the edge of the dance floor with her maid-chaperone while small bodies dance by in a whirl of gauze, satin, confetti, and garlands, carried by the blasting music, and it is heartbreaking, this brave waiting, the little painter's maid-chaperone anxiously looking around, and her eyes meet the boy's, with something at once supplicating and threatening, a hurt exasperation: She is so beautiful, my little painter. Why is no one asking her to dance? Why must she suffer so? Triggered out of his icy shyness, the boy walks to the two on the periphery of the dance floor and makes the gestures, the bending at the waist, says the words, "Would you like to dance?" The little painter takes his hand; they enter the crowd of other small bodies in their capes and masks and gauze and satin. The two little bodies are dancing, tracing the patterns, joining in the crowd and music; Hercules and the painter on the dance floor are safe, away from the Broussards and their cliques and lieutenants, and where babies come out of, and "What is *erection*?" and "What is *clitoris*?" Their small hands are moist and they cannot even look at each other, saved by the regularity of the beat, of the movements they make; they will dance all the remaining dances with each other.

One afternoon, a few weeks after his now pointless initiation into the clique, even the yardman's offer at Roland Montrosier's house will seem candid after the words uttered by Broussard's lieutenant. Roland is two years older than the boy, and the Montrosier house is just a few minutes' walk from the compound—out the front gate, down the main road, then very quickly the first left. The Montrosier house is not visible from the street, hidden as it is behind stone walls, bougainvillea hedges, and almond trees. This is one of the very rare places outside the compound to which the two brothers are allowed to walk alone without specific *permission* or the company of the young aunt, the young uncle, or a servant, for the Montrosiers are their closest neighbors and among their family's oldest friends. Roland's great-grandfather had been president of the Republic for two years; he hadn't made it to the end of his term, perhaps because of his politics in favor of closer ties with the United States, among other ill-advised choices for the time; admittedly, there were many other complex and extravagantly profitable business interests involved, but, for one reason or another, during the second year of Roland's great-grandfather's presidency, the politics of the Tropical Republic had fallen into the habitual escalating pattern and vicious circle of parliamentary circus, followed by vehement parliamentary opposition, followed by protests in the streets, followed by arrests, followed by barricades and spurts of armed resistance in the streets, followed by more arrests, followed, that time, by summary executions of political prisoners in the capital's main prison, followed by general insurrection, and then followed, that time, by the president of the Republic's seeking asylum in the French embassy, the ornate iron gates of the imposing house being torn apart, its gardens being trampled in the dark by a more enterprising and determined cluster dispatched by the compact crowd outside, but also galvanized by its own fury, the night lit by dozens of torches carried by these emissaries of the waiting crowd, the French ambassador barely making it through with his family and staff, the irruption of the smaller contingent into the residence, the president of the Republic, fitfully floating on outstretched hands, carried out to the streets to be delivered to the anticipating crowd. "My great-grandfather's body was torn apart and his head was paraded on a pike," said Roland in his pained pride when he told the story the boys had already heard from their own grandfather during one of the evening sessions, the story that particular time not of the Count of Monte Cristo, or of ghosts or zombies, but of that specific episode in their country's history, which the grandfather recounted with the usual suspense and drama and embroidering, even if the grandfather was only seven years old at the time those events occurred, a recounting with a surfeit of detail, a concocted eyewitness familiarity that was not in the boys' textbook, where an oval-shaped picture of Roland's great-grandfather appears somewhere in the middle of the long succession of alabaster busts, black-and-white portraits, and medallion-framed pictures of emperors, kings, and presidents surrounded by columns and paragraphs that had become History, to be learned by rote from the textbook distributed in schools throughout the Tropical Republic.

Depending on the account—the grandfather's, Roland's,

the history textbook's, or the newspapers of the time—the circumstances in which Roland's great-grandfather's head was paraded on a pike, and the reasons the U.S. Marines arrived the next day and stayed a long, long time vary. Some accounts claimed that crowds were dispatched by a spurned and jealous rival who *was in love with* the president's wife (the grandfather could not call it anything else, words like *lust* and *sexual obsession* having been deemed inappropriate for the boys); other accounts, usually from American newspapers, sometimes from the Tropical Republic's ruling class, only varied slightly: murderous bands of ignorant, illiterate peasants secretly led by foreign interests; organized bands of anarchist guerrillas with connections to foreign interests; bloodthirsty crowds reverting to savagery; an ignorant and illiterate urban populace attempting to take power (the possibility that hunger and need could propel the usually peaceable population of the Tropical Republic into the violence of that night is not one of the explanations brought forth in any of the accounts); all possibilities that spread derision, concern, fear, panic; considering the insignificant size and limited power of the Tropical Republic, the passage from derision to concern to panic might seem disproportionate, but the old story of the slave revolution that had led Thomas Jefferson to decree, "We must confine the plague to the island" lingers in many minds); *derision, concern, fear, panic* among the leaders, the Tropical Republic's ruling class overtaken by its own greed and blindness; *derision, concern, fear, panic* among the decision makers of the Great Northern Neighbor, but also, perhaps, among the simple people in the streets of Chicago, New York, or Washington, or perhaps even in the Great Plains and in small towns from coast to coast, simple people who had never heard of the Tropical Republic until the lurid and gory news was splattered on the front pages of their morning papers. And so the decision was made by the Great Northern Neighbor to send in the marines as a response to *the unacceptable and barbarous murder of a democratically elected president*, coming to the aid of a country in chaos, chaos that might even have led to a German invasion of the Tropical Republic, provided a bridgehead for the Germans, for these were the years of the Great War, dead bodies in Flanders Fields, Charleville-Mézières, Verdun, bodies strewn on plains of gray mud and barbed wire, or bloodying the river Somme, the river Meuse, the river Meurthe—although this justification seemed unlikely, this threat of German warships coming from the other side of the ocean to anchor in the placid and blue Caribbean sea. The words used to tell the different versions and justifications changed, but one event remained undisputed: This was the time when the American marines landed and remained in the Republic for a long, long time, after Roland Montrosier's great-grandfather's presidential body was torn apart and his head paraded on a pike.

This is all a lavish story for the boy, as is his history book, from the Taino and Columbus's arrival in the bay of blue sea and green hills to the point where the clean and crisp last twenty or so pages begin, free of underlining and marginalia, but not devoid of mustaches and beards and elongated ears and sunglasses added to the faces of the Tropical Republic's most recent and successive leaders, the pages the teachers of the elementary grades never reach, even by the end of the school year, a lavish story for the boy who lives blissfully, unmarked by death, rapt in the pink library and films of the jungle and Technicolor gladiators, surfers, and vampires, the changing sky, the swift sunsets, the outings to the mountains and to the seaside, all his generations intact in his time; for him, the mangled president and the Count of Monte Cristo belong to another time and place, one of galleons, gold, and far-away violence.

And now, the great-grandson of the mangled president is in his family's garden with the boy and his brother, and Macédoine and Joseph, two boys from the other side of the gully, great-grandsons, all of them, of the crowd carrying torches in the night, great-grandsons of those who were being executed in the prison cells, great-grandsons of those who were acting behind the scenes, descendants (with a few generations added) of the slaves, descendants (with a few generations added) of the masters and the slaves; sometimes they wanted the same things, the privileged and the protestors—it's difficult to tell sides in those moments of bloodletting from so long ago, even if the old story is about to be played out once again as The Mortician is establishing his power. This afternoon, these five boys are gathered in the Montrosiers' garden, boys from the sprawling estates and boys from the other side of the gully, all about the same age, and one of the Montrosiers' yardmen, a few years older, who's been holding forth on what boys, young men, *need to do*, ends his pitch with these words: "I tell you, I know she [one of the Montrosiers' young maids] works all day, but she will take a good bath and she will wash it and powder it and it will smell so sweet; so what do you say?" As if it were up to him, as if he could arrange everything, but without the malevolence the boy felt in Broussard and his lieutenants, and he feels no revulsion this time around; there's only the good-natured kidding, even if the offer of that terrible intimacy is probably real (he will not find out; for him, the discovery will occur much later, in temperate climes, at the heart of a bitterly cold winter).

"So, what do you say?"

. . . (The two brothers are taken aback; the younger brother is wondering what to do; the boy is already retreating, shaking his head.)

"No? It won't cost much; you guys have lots of money."

. . .

"All right, you're afraid or you don't have the money. Another time. But I tell you . . ." (To the last, he believes in his ability to entice.)

They all laugh, including the two from the other side of the gully, their own experience already well beyond those pampered and celibate striplings'.

At some point, Roland and the two brothers will go inside the house; Joseph and Macédoine will hang around the garden with the yardman for a while, smoke cigarettes with him, and then leave, disappearing in the labyrinth of the shantytown across the gully, where the unloved son fainted on that day of kites and almonds. Joseph and Macédoine never go into the Montrosier house, or the boys' (once again, the implacability of assigned places). Inside the Montrosiers' silent house, the furniture gleams, the tiles are cool, and a morose Saint Bernard lies in the living room. He almost never comes out; he eats lots of red meat. Every day. The boy feels sorry for the colossal and displaced animal, probably the only one of its kind in the entire Republic. The Montrosiers were also among the first families in the town in the hills to have a television in their house, a few months before the boy's grandfather ordered the set in its beige casing where Lucy and Ricky and the incredibly fast-talking police chief of *Highway Patrol* come and go. The Montrosiers have been involved in the Tropical Republic's politics, and much more, for centuries; Roland's uncle sculpted the statue of the muscular conch-blowing slave that stands in the square facing the gleaming white national palace in the city; through all the shifts and the riots, the killings in the streets or in the rooms and halls and recesses of the gleaming white palace, the factions and the elections and the blood, as well as the years of apparent order and plenty, a Montrosier was always around, behind the scenes or fully visible, as on the night when Roland's great-grandfather was torn apart by the crowd and his head was paraded on a pike.

Since it's close to the compound and is a sanctioned gathering place for the two brothers, they are often at the Montrosier house on those Sundays when they don't go to the movies after morning Mass; their Sunday allowances are then pooled with Roland's. They purchase fried plantains, thickly sliced sweet potatoes, and chunks of spicy pork from one of the street vendors around the nearby square, and sit cross-legged on the lawn under an almond tree with Macédoine, Joseph, and a few of their friends who have also come from the other side of the gully to share in the Sunday-morning feast, the food spread on the lawn in the oil-stained wrapping paper used by the vendors; the boys pick and eat until everything is gone. Sometimes, there is still time and some money left to make it to the ten o'clock show at Ajoupa Ciné; the Sunday-morning program never varies, a serialized episode followed by a feature. First the black-and-white installment: Zorro gallops on his horse through rocky landscapes, hooves hitting the ground at the speed of a sports car, pursued by soldiers, arriving at a cliff, where the horse rears up and the film stops—*To be continued next week*—or Santos the wrestler in his leather mask and his cape is about to encounter the vampires in their lair, then the abrupt stop—*To be continued next week*; the lights go on and the moans erupt from the audience of boys (no girls). "*We have to come next week to find out what happens? We have to wait?*" but the ritual indignation is suddenly cut short when the lights suddenly go out again, and the screen lights up with the drumroll, the blaring of trumpets and projectors sweeping the gigantic golden letters against the Hollywood sky, or the overpowering roar of the lion, its mane and chest resting on a garland of movie reels; the feature, *the real film*, begins with the towering red letters of the title, followed by the actors' and actresses' names against the cobalt blue sky of a Western, or it's Gidget, the American high school girl in Rome, or Hercules in a landscape of olive trees and columns under more cloudless blue skies, or the sinister organ and choir music announcing that Dracula has risen from his grave, and it is almost always night, and the days in the film are always waning too quickly for the boys cowering in their seats until they emerge in the full light of Sunday noon and head back home, where, for the boy and his brother, the gathering of family and friends around the pool will begin.

Who is God?

Before the feast on Roland's lawn or the cool darkness of Ajoupa Ciné, Sunday-morning Mass beckons, an obligation since the boy's First Communion a few years back, when he turned seven. Catechism at the Séminaire had started long before that ceremony: days and weeks and months of preparation, of learning the consecrated stances and gestures, of memorizing, metabolizing another knowledge.

Who is God?

God is a spirit, perfect, creator and master of all

things. He is our Father, a Father filled with love, who loves all that exists.

Why do we say that God is a spirit?

We say that God is a spirit because he has no body.

Days, weeks, and months of the boy's encounter with the melodious somberness of Latin, *Credo in unum Deum, Patrem omnipotentem, factorem caeli et terrae, visibilium omnium et invisibilium*, or his memorizing of *Pater Noster.*

Pater noster, qui es in caelis, sanctificetur nomen tuum.
Adveniat regnum tuum.
Fiat voluntas tua, sicut in caelo et in terra.
Panem nostrum quotidianum da nobis hodie, et dimitte nobis debita nostra sicut et nos dimittimus debitoribus nostris.
Et ne nos inducas in tentationem, sed libera nos a malo.
Amen.

Questions, answers, prayers to be learned by heart, recited like rules of grammar, poems, or pages of history.

That year at the Séminaire, for a few months on Friday afternoons, religious instruction slide shows have replaced music class, the last class of the day on the last day of the week, when the boys are restless, on the brink of freedom. During the week, in any class, in any grade at the Séminaire, they are all tightly contained in the strict schedule and parceled-out activities, seldom breaking the rules that govern their classes, small kingdoms overseen by civilians (the priests teach the upper grades), classes taught by stern or less stern men and women of modest means in the Tropical Republic's inexorable distribution of roles, but confident in their acquired knowledge in a place and at a time where education is so prized and coveted, and so unevenly parceled out. Most of the time, in the Séminaire's long tradition of officially sanctioned rituals of reward and punishment, these men and women of modest means are immune from parental reproach or wrangling ("Why did you hit my son?" "Why did my son have to stay after school?" "Why did you give my son such a low grade for his beautifully written composition?"). The distribution of report cards is among the most dreaded of these rituals. Sitting behind her desk or standing in front of the class, the teacher calls out the names and the ranks like verdicts and hands out the *carnets de notes*, the bimonthly report cards, the highest average first, the lowest last, public accolades, public shame, new seats assigned to match the new ranking, the highest average in the last seat in the back to the left, the lowest, the first seat in the front to the right, the better to keep watch on those mediocre miscreants. Apprehension and frozen faces of the last few as the roll call continues, boys coming up to the front, holding all their belongings, receiving their report cards, and walking back to their new seats if their place in the ranking has changed, the others, the ones already anonymous again in their assigned rankings and seats looking on, waiting, no one among the remaining half dozen wanting to be *le dernier de la classe*, the last in the class, the very worst student; some remnant of pride always remains for even the penultimate.

The boy, the voracious reader, was always among *les premiers de la classe*; he was less adept at math but managed quite well throughout the basic operations and into the almost literary beauty of geometry, until the pitfalls of algebra later on, after the time of exile had started.

Throughout those years at the Séminaire, he always managed to avoid public punishment, public pain, unless we count Mademoiselle Marie, his first-grade teacher, when he had just started school at the Séminaire, pulling him by the ear, pinching the inside of his ear with her nails, the cuts made by her finely filed nails making scabs after a few days, and his crying out in pain during his bath one afternoon, Ada asking, "What's wrong? Why are you crying?" her increasingly more alarmed questions met by his silent refusal to say anything, his mother's insistence when called by Ada, "Tell me, What's the matter?" his tearful confession (she would have found out anyway during the weekly cleaning with cotton swabs and alcohol of her two boys' ears, a task she performs herself, just as she attends to cutting their nails herself, attending personally to those well-cared-for little bodies), and what followed the next day: the other grandfather, not the Colonel, but the cinemagoer, the dispenser of Crayola boxes and other gifts, driving to the Séminaire, not bothering to stop at the office, quickly climbing the steps leading to the boy's classroom, opening the door and interrupting Mademoiselle Marie's class, asking her to please step out onto the terrace outside her classroom. He faces her there, as the boy and all his classmates watch the confrontation through the classroom's translucent louvered glass windows. He tells her his name, as if he were at a cocktail party, or making a social call, tells her his grandson's name, informs her why he is there, and tells her she knows full well what she did, without his having to "linger on the details."

. . . (Mademoiselle Marie calculates that the best option is to remain silent, to hope that the man's mounting fury will spend itself.)

"Do you know how long we've been coming here? My

father, his father, his father's father, and before that, and way back before that went to school here! From the first grade you teach now to the very last class taught by *les pères*, the priests across the yard, from first grade to last, all of us, you understand?"

. . . (What can Mademoiselle Marie possibly reply?)

The morning is quiet, the sky not yet white from the sun at its height; a breeze blows on the terrace, the still cool late morning breeze before the heat begins. The boy's classmates are now alone in the classroom, freed by the break in the routine, unfettered from Mademoiselle Marie's control, at least for now; they have all left their desks and crowded at the louvered glass windows, all eyes on the shadow play being performed on the other side of the glass louvers by the tall, thin man in his white suit and their teacher, all eyes on the terrace and all ears trying to catch any word at all, but the boy is afraid this dramatic break in the course of things will leave him exposed and helpless when his grandfather is gone, that he will be alone with Mademoiselle Marie again, back in her jurisdiction, defenseless. Nor can he bear this public display, this breach of decorum; he would prefer to suffer, and he is relieved that the other boys don't seem to know this is his grandfather, the man out there on the terrace in his white suit, holding his panama hat, berating the feared Mademoiselle Marie, for it's obvious, even if the words cannot be heard clearly from behind the glass slats, that this is not a friendly exchange.

"You're just an employee. You're no one."

. . .

"You can be replaced anytime."

. . .

"But, monsieur!" (The standoff could not have lasted

any longer without some sort of reaction from Mademoiselle Marie, some words of denial or protest.)

"If you ever lay a hand on that boy again, I will come to the school and I will shoot you like a dog!"

And he leaves, emptied by this last utterance, relieved to relinquish the role he had taken on because his rage and indignation at the healing but still painful nail marks in his grandson's ear had led him to that classroom door and then to the terrace to engage in the vehement exchange with Mademoiselle Marie, for, of course, he would never be able to do such a thing, *to shoot Mademoiselle Marie like a dog*, even to contemplate such a thing, even in the Tropical Republic's old and lineal distribution of places and roles. The threat made on the still cool terrace is all bluster from that man who loves the company of his grandsons, friends, and mistresses, and neglects to provide for his seven sons and daughters, even if similar and worse things will soon happen in the Tropical Republic, in the other time soon to begin, and other more strange and extreme scenes will play out, like the man shot for a parking space by one of The Mortician's newly empowered local despots, spitting out terrible words, "I asked you to move once, why didn't you listen right away? Now you're dead, and I've still got power to the tips of my nipples," as he stops his car in the middle of the street, leaves the driver's side door open, and goes into a grocery store to buy cigarettes, while the other man lies in a crooked and unleveled position, half on the sidewalk and half on the street, no one daring to approach, to touch, to check, to examine or cover the inert body, even as a shiny red trickle is emerging from under the head and quickly turning dark in the sun. Compared to that impending time, the grandfather's tirade on the terrace seems amusing, even benign, for the grandfather who loves the company of friends and mistresses is all bluster, and his boys are precious to him, this first son of his first son in particular, it seems, although he has never shown any ostentatious preference.

The fiery grandfather will not be able to intervene on the day when the men in sunglasses irrupt into the house in the hills, the day the boy will see a dead body for the first time in his life, the day when Schmitt's whistle blow will pierce through the sun-drenched yard, ferreting the boy out of the peace and protection of being a good student and of not having broken any of the major rules all those years.

For generations of boys, the ritual distribution of report cards is only one of the officially sanctioned array of punishments: a boy standing absolutely still in front of the class while the lesson goes on in the warm afternoon, books held out in both hands, arms outstretched, the number and weight of the books depending on the seriousness of the offense, the particular teacher's sense of proportion, his whim, his disposition, his thin ruler not missing a boy's arms if they are lowered, even slightly; the short, stinging blows of a ruler on outstretched fingers; the hundreds of lines to be written out, endlessly replicating the same sentence in the schoolboy's ornate and awkward handwriting, *I will not call out in class* or *I will not come to class unprepared*, written out *in all the modes of the indicative, the conditional, the subjunctive, and the imperative* (often, brothers, sisters, and friends are enlisted over the weekend to help write out those hundreds of lines to be returned on Monday morning, or else); and, for the most serious offenses, the headmaster's office, Schmitt's whip of braided bull's nerve.

During the week, in all these classes, from *douzième*

to *sixième*, first to sixth grade, those boys' bodies are attentive; they learn, prodigiously, and they learn how to learn; the famous Jesuit maxim "Give me a child for his first seven years and I'll give you a man"; they had the boy for five years, not in the exact and consecrated time span, but they had him even if, ultimately, the Tropics and the boy's own disposition provided a constant counterpoint, a corrective that would leave him intact, or at least open, ready to receive other knowledge more in tune with his own temperament.

The music lesson is an exception to the ordered unrolling of days at the Séminaire. The little man who teaches music in his starched white suit is a break in the routine, outside permanent staff, outside tradition, unauthorized to mete out punishment. He arrives on Friday afternoons, on the last day of the week for the last class of the day, the spot that would be taken over at one point by the religious instruction slide shows. The music teacher arrives at a time when parents and servants are already beginning to gather outside the gates to pick up this or that boy. He sets his metronome on the desk, plays a few notes on his violin, begging the boys to stop their heckling, all those boys, over thirty of them in the classroom, their small bodies and their heads moving in unison, from side to side, imitating the metronome, clucking, jeering, the music teacher helpless, begging, "Stop, boys. I really need this job, boys. Please, stop!" So many of those boys, who will become businessmen, politicians, *men of substance and power*, will not even have a clear memory of this little man; in most cases, their appreciation of the kind of music that he teaches will remain limited to their daughters or their wives playing the piano upon polite requests at tea afternoons or rum evenings. The boy would like to learn the notation system, he would like to learn how to play the violin or the piano, but he goes along with the others. Why go against the grain, the general flow? Why stand out? Why make trouble?

In the boy's class, during the last few months of that year of his First Communion, the little man has been replaced by Father Anders, the smiling, lenient, and ruddy (French wine and tropical sun) priest from Norway, "the country of Santa Claus," as he has told the boys, his voice mild in the dark, for the classroom's curtains have been drawn and the carousel of colorful slides is unrolling on the small screen: Moses has sent scouts into the Promised Land; they come back with a bunch of white grapes so large that two men have to carry it on their shoulders, "Truly the land of milk and honey after the flight from Egypt" and the long wandering in the desert, "but, *mes enfants*, Moses will not enter the Promised Land, for he has doubted God" (the boy always thought it was unfair of Yahweh to do this to Moses); Samson wreaking bloody havoc with a donkey's jawbone in the tight and ordered ranks of the infamous Philistine idolaters; for a while, the boy thought *Hosanna* was a beautiful woman, like Ruth, or Bathsheba, the one King David saw, desired, and took from one of the officers he had sent to his death; or Father Anders tells them the story of Absalom, King David's handsome son, with his long hair caught in the branches of a tree, hanging there, a dangling and helpless prey for his enemies to savage with spears and swords. The slide shows continue; the colors are bright, the blood shiny red, the tunics a brilliant blue, the weapons steely gray; this is as violent and astounding as Grand-père's stories, the history of the Tropical Republic, or the films at Ajoupa Ciné. In the dark, many of the boys are quietly munching on peanuts and sticks of rolled taffy, the play of salt and sugar, salt then sugar, salt then sugar again on their tongues.

Closer to the time of the First Communion, Father Anders has left the heroic and bloody feats behind and reached Jesus and the miracles, the birth in the stable, the unctuous Pharisees' betrayal of the lean Jesus of Nazareth with his bright eyes and his beard and long hair, the long night of utter solitude on Gethsemane, his arrest by the Romans, Pilate washing his hands of all this, Golgotha hill, the whipping, the great thirst and the Roman soldier's vile offer of water that turned out to be vinegar, the nailing of Jesus' wrists and ankles to the cross; "Actually," the boys are informed in the penumbral projection room, "a single piece was carried to Golgotha and then nailed to the other piece that was already standing vertical." When they reach the stories of the martyrs, the boy is baffled by their willingness to be mauled and killed by wild beasts, bloody paws and bloody teeth digging into their bodies while thousands of spectators look on and applaud from Colosseum bleachers. At first, he refuses to accept the validation of such sacrifice—*Why don't they just pretend and save themselves from all this suffering? Why don't they practice their faith in secret?*—but the weeks and months of catechism lull him into a deep submission; his doubts and reservations are gradually submerged.

His back to the bright colors on the screen, his face and body swathed in the projected images, Father Anders continues in his mild, earnest voice: "All that suffering, boys, Jesus sent by his Father for all of us; he took on all our sins so that one day we will all be reunited in Heaven if we live the life of good Christians." The boy is enthralled as he goes through the year, even as he, too, is chewing on taffy and then adding a few peanuts in his mouth, one bite of taffy, a few peanuts, sweet, salty; the slides pass by on the screen, Father Anders's voice so soothing as the astounding events unroll. The boy has no doubt that this mystery is real; he is eager to understand. He memorizes, he fasts, he prays, and he learns about the sacraments.

The boy is kneeling on a prie-dieu set on the terrace that borders the classroom, a priest on a chair close to him while the other boys are doing math problems or conjugating verbs on the other side of the louvered windows.

"Forgive me, Father, for I have sinned."

"What sins have you committed, my son?"

. . . (The hesitation is only a result of his inexperience; in the months before First Communion, there is nothing yet he cannot say in the preparations for confession. The priest's head is leaning toward him, confidentially; the boy looks at his ear, the hair growing inside his ear; in the background, beyond the priest's leaning head, the wide-open space beyond the terrace, palm trees against a sky of passing clouds, white at noon and tinged with purple in the late afternoon.)

During these practice confessions, leading up to the final, real one before First Communion, his list of sins is met with quick replies, sometimes only one word, sometimes silence from the priest.

"I've lied."

"Yes . . ."

"I've been disobedient."

. . .

"I've said bad words."

. . .

"Is there any more? Is this all?"

The memory of the boy in the tall grass and thistle,

that day in the town by the sea where his father had been posted, has receded, as have the maids' glistening skin and the secret they intimate so blatantly, or the games played with Debby and Caroline where the ferns proliferate in the shadiest recesses of the garden; all of this is buried somewhere, to return later, when he will be disconnecting and severing from the meticulously acquired knowledge, its prayers and rituals, the months of memorization; by then, he will use, knowingly this time, the established phrases of the sacrament in answer to the priest's insistence: "I have had bad thoughts; I have done bad things," nothing more specific, only the ritual's safe and sanctioned formulations; by then, he won't tell the man on the other side of the latticed window anything more.

But throughout the time preceding the First Communion, and for a few months afterward, the boy has no doubt. He is enchanted, whole. He accepts and metabolizes the conundrum of the Trinity like a sacred and unsolvable geometry theorem. Days and weeks go by, the rains of the return to school are replaced by radiant winter days (even if they never say *winter* or *autumn* or *spring* in that time and place, even if the manifestly changing seasons are for elsewhere), days of fasting, of singing hymns, boys' voices rising to the church vault, and then one day the swarms of small yellow-green butterflies appear everywhere; it's April. He is taken to the tailor for the white suit; measurements are taken. The tailor's gestures are precise, the measuring tape swiftly rolled around his waist, then down from groin to ankle. "Is this length fine? Do we want a cuff for the pants? Will you also be needing a shirt? A bow tie? Socks? Handkerchiefs?" His mother is smiling at him. Everything is purchased, everything white, like the beads of the rosary he holds in prayer in his hands in the picture taken the day before the whole family drives to the Séminaire's church in the city; his hair is newly cut, his skin flawless, his mouth full like a girl's, his eyes looking slightly upward after the directives from the photographer in his studio.

"Look up a bit more."

. . .

"No, a bit less. Keep your hands clasped together, with the rosary around your fingers."

. . .

"Yes, like that; don't move."

On the Sunday of the First Communion, he is driven with the family to the Séminaire's church in the city. He's light-headed; he's been fasting since Friday afternoon, since that most important of confessions, the real confession, no longer an exercise like those of all the weeks and months of preparation before, but a real one, the one that has readied him to receive the body of Christ, to accept the wafer to be delicately placed on the quivering tongue, to dissolve there—"Never bite," he had been told. "This is the body of Christ." He's heard stories about blood trickling through the mouths of imprudent, forgetful, or sacrilegious boys. Years later, when all this will have passed, and the hold on him of religion not released, but simply faded and gone, through lassitude and boredom rather than resistance or revolt, his brother will tell that joke to their friends gathered around Cokes and pizza or burgers in some diner in New York, the joke about the boy who chewed and chewed and chewed and, unable to get the better of the recalcitrant wafer, said, "I must've stumbled on the Nazarene's foreskin," and all that laughter following. But in the dim light of the confessional, that first real time, hearing the priest's breath and the rustle of his robe on the other side of the lattice, the boy had gone as deeply as he could into the sins he had committed, until there was nothing left to divulge. What he did not tell was simply what he had suppressed and forgotten, a transitorily vanished knowledge. There was no holding back; there was simply no more to be told. He was emptied of impurity; ready, in a trance, apart.

On the morning of the First Communion, there is a silent deference toward him, as to a medieval princeling, with his missal, his medals, and his rosary. In a secret rush, two of the maids have given him, the boy now invested with seraphic potency, small gold and silver medals of their own, precious belongings to be placed in the pockets of his white jacket, to be thus blessed in the recesses of his clothing and returned to them after the ceremony, sanctified; the boy is their intercessor, still a child but so apart today that even his brother looks at him differently; the games they've played together in the days and weeks and months before seem like sins themselves, the raucous rituals of pagans.

He is next to his brother in the car, the grandfather and the grandmother sit on either side of them, and the young aunt sits in front with the chauffeur. The boy's mother and father are going down to the city in another car, for the grandfather has insisted—this is his first grandson; he has been helping him memorize the Latin prayers all throughout the year, trying to explain the unexplainable, trying nevertheless—he wants to "accompany the boy on this day," as he puts it. "Please, allow me the privilege." The boy's father readily says yes; he is not made for that sort of thing, although his own faith has already lasted and will last well beyond the boy's; he still goes on retreats with the priests, days without speech, vows of silence.

It's a Sunday in April. There are fewer people on the poinciana-lined road, no women going to market with their vegetable- or fruit-laden baskets, no clusters of schoolchildren walking to school; the air is cooler; the swarms of small yellow-green butterflies have come out. The boy looks through the car window, beyond Grand-mère's clothes and hat and perfume; he sees the people walking down the road and, at a bend in the road, the posters for movies playing on that Sunday; the colorful posters, like his games with his brother, are of another world, emptied of meaning for now; he is on his way to something else, ensconced in his silence.

When they arrive at the Séminaire, the car stops at the main gate; he leaves the family to join the other boys, the other first-time communicants gathered on the tiled terrace that borders the yard, quiet and still on this day; the others are also wearing all white, the shirts, the socks, the small ties or bow ties, even the shoes. One of the boys is wearing a suit and even a vest, a dandy already; his rosary is placed in the vest pocket like a watch chain. A few other boys are only wearing shirts, with a tie, but short pants—their families probably could not afford the new suit; all are quiet. They hold their missals; they wait, over a hundred of them gathered there, all silent; even Reginald Broussard and his lieutenants seem reverent and muted on that Sunday. And then the procession begins. The boys are led through the school's gates and into the city streets by Father Anders, the Norwegian, in order to enter the church from the main doors; the procession winds around the school, in the streets where all those people, outsiders to the ritual, are stopping to look at those boys slowly walking in hushed double rows. They must be quite a sight to the street vendors and the men and women running their

Sunday errands, those boys in white holding their missals and rosaries, heading for the celebration of ancient sacrifice. The boy wishes they had entered the church directly from the school; he feels exposed and slightly ridiculous in the Sunday streets, being watched not only by grown-ups but also by boys his own age stopping to watch the procession go by; he wishes he could just be heading for a movie or even to school, on a normal day, not making a spectacle of himself, an intrusion in the usual unrolling of the day, exposed—*What must they think? We look so strange.* But this only lasts a moment before he's enfolded once again, carried by the quiet momentum as they reach the church entrance.

The bells of the Séminaire's church are ringing, the procession enters the church vestibule, and, as the first boys pass by the baptismal font, music suddenly fills the church, completely. The choir and the organ, like the yellow wafts of Mozart at the other grandfather's house; the procession of boys in white, their rosaries folded around their fingers; the people in the pews, all these parents of his friends, all these women in their dresses and hats and gloves and mantillas, the men in their suits, standing in the blocks of pews, watching their boys go down the aisle to the first benches: All this is a fragrant blur to the boy held upright and moving only by a determination not to stumble, to go through the steps and not be noticed, propelled by his deep cowardice or, more kindly, his deep-seated allegiance to order and decorum, to an undisturbed passing of time, above all determined not to bite the wafer, to let it slowly dissolve on his tongue. There are roses everywhere, ornate bunches on either side of the altar, smaller bouquets attached to the end of each pew in the main aisle, fresh petals spread on the main aisle, on the pews, darkened petals between the pages of his missal. The smell of roses, the smell of incense, mixed with the sound of the music, enter him and, above all else on that day, mark the moment in his body.

And then they drive back up to the house in the hills for an early lunch, earlier than usual, so that the boy can break his fast with all the guests gathered in their deck chairs or sitting around tables set up around the pool. The release from all the months of memorizing and fasting, from the entry into the mysteries, begins almost immediately: He wants to swim with the other boys and girls who've been invited, cousins, friends, his brother, all already shouting and splashing in the pool, their bodies gleaming in the sun, but the grandfather says something startling: "Your body is sacred, pure; you cannot display it like this, not so quickly, not so soon after . . ." The boy looks at Grand-père; this seems extraneous, one sacrifice too many, and so he decides he will not comply, already accepting the consequences; an extraordinary moment of defiance from him, but, already, his mother is gently chiding and cajoling Grand-père, solicitous but determined.

"Come, Papa, let him enjoy himself with the others. He has done it; there's no need for this old-fashioned stuff. He's a child; let him enjoy himself. . . ."

. . .

The grandfather himself must not have been taking his own admonition seriously, for he quickly relents, smiles, and sends the boy off to change.

The swim is already the beginning of the relinquishing. The final severing will take place later, on an afternoon during his convalescence from the measles, when he makes his first and last attempt to communicate directly with God, to give himself over, on that afternoon toward the end of his illness, when the flakes have already dried and fallen off, his skin back to its boyish smoothness. He lies in bed and waits in his cleaned, starched, and ironed pajamas; he has just had a bath. He had been to Communion right before the onset of red spots, not a single impure thought since, no opportunity, no room to commit even a venial sin in the interlude of fever and clear broths, unbuttered slices of bread; he could never be so clean, so unsullied, and he says the words in his mind and out loud. He hears himself say them: "Come now, show yourself to me," but there is nothing, no burning bush, no disembodied voice, no shadow, not even a quick and furtive crease in the sheets, not a sound in the ordered stillness of his room.

After that afternoon, things just follow their course. Months and years, the differently manifest seasons passing one after the other. For a while, the confessions continue at regular intervals: the boy entering into the darkness of the church on the square of the town in the hills on Saturday afternoons, entering the confessional's cubicle, followed by the opening and shutting of the latticed divider, the rustling of a priest he never sees, a voice, first his, then the priest's, the murmured and sequestered exchange between a boy in his short pants and a man in his robes.

"Forgive me, Father, for I have sinned."

"When was your last confession, my son?"

"One week." (Or one month, or two months, and then sometimes not telling the body on the other side the accurate interval, which, in time, would become unmentionable. Prepared lists of sins; even with the knowledge that none of them was unforgivable, he can never bring himself to say everything, taking refuge in the feeble and periphrastic constructions of a boy who has learned the formulations well.)

"Tell me."

"I've had bad thoughts," or "I've done bad things." *"J'ai eu de mauvaises pensées"; "J'ai fait de mauvaises choses."*

"What kind? Alone, or with others, my son?"

. . .

He's puzzled; he feels cornered. Alone or with others? The priest must be referring to *doing* bad things. Either way, he can think of nothing he wants to tell; increasingly, his sins belong to him alone; increasingly, some thoughts and deeds will not be conveyed to this man on the other side of the small latticed window. Sometimes he lies to the priest on the other side of the lattice. He invents; he embroiders. There are just not enough real and avowable sins to make the confession credible, but he will not tell about some of the thoughts still unformed in him and attendant to the maids' baths in the sunlight among the hibiscus, their skin and the dripping water or, later, about Debby and Caroline's pale vulvas; as for that time with the boy in the tall grass and thistles, he will only remember these moments concretely much later, when it will no longer matter.

And so the game of hide-and-seek between the two bodies in the latticed light goes on, always ending with the established penance, varying only in length: ten Hail Marys, ten Our Fathers, or five, or sometimes fewer, never more. Only once was there an added admonition from the other side of the small window: "You know these are wicked deeds; you know these are bad thoughts; you have confessed and you have been absolved, but I want you to make an effort not to repeat these offenses. I know you are able to do this, my son; now go." The boy can't even determine what provoked the additional words; fortunately, it's quick and anonymous (he doesn't know this priest, who doesn't belong to the same order as Schmitt, Anders, and the others from the Séminaire) and takes place in the latticed penumbra, where there are no eyes looking into other eyes; it lasts just a few seconds, this encounter between ephemeral shame (his) and formulaic forbearance (the priest's), for the boy is in a hurry to pay the debt, make the penance, acknowledge what remains of his adherence to all this, the Hail Marys, the Our Fathers, and quickly, as quickly as possible, leave. He makes his way out of the confessional and kneels at the first available bench, but one far enough away from the stall into which another small body has just disappeared; like swiftly and efficiently pulling off an adhesive bandage from a wound, the rapid and automatic recitation of the exonerating prayers is an exercise in speed, for outside another world is waiting, his brother, other boys, the sun and the air and the smells beyond the church's adumbral confines. He emerges in the clear light. Free once more. Intact.

A few years later, Sunday-morning Mass, celebrated in the church with its pointy red steeple soaring toward the clear blue sky, has become a routine imposition on his pleasures; he and his brother have whittled down the ritual to its consecrated and mandatory minimum. As soon as the small bell rings the benediction, they scurry down a side aisle; before the Mass lingers on like the credits after a film has ended at Ajoupa Ciné, they are already rushing out, even before the priest's "Go in peace" signals the official end of Mass. They are always the first outside the church, and Sunday stretches out before them as they head for the morning show: Zorro, Hercules, Tarzan, Dracula, Gidget, Joselito—the little Spaniard boy with the golden voice.

Sometimes they go to the afternoon show instead, with the young aunt, her favorite cousin, and their friends, young women confronting in their own way the distribution of assigned places and the codes of condoned behavior, fraying in those years of the late fifties and the first years of the early sixties, which still look like the fifties. They enter Ajoupa Ciné in the still strong light of afternoon and emerge into the dark, when the street vendors have already lit their metal lamps.

On most Sunday afternoons, the two girls walk to the church square in their Boussac dresses and their stylish rectangular purses and flat shoes, one's hair in a ponytail, the other's in the trendy teased bouffant, punctured by a strategically placed little bow; both wear pale pink lipstick, verging on white, also the rage among girls their age in that place and in that time. Between them, whispered conversations about boys and actors and actresses, fiery longings, forlorn regrets, heartrending breakups.

On the square, boys are buying girls ice cream and sending billets-doux through intermediaries, the boy and his brother sometimes used as strategic go-betweens by these older boys, these young men who look longingly at the young aunt and her cousin, two girls seemingly aloof in their shielding companionship, returning most messages with cold disdain, but sometimes accepting a piece of paper folded into intricate triangular patterns, inscribed with an ardent declaration or proposing a rendezvous: performances of courtly love from another, faraway time and place being played out in the Tropics. The square's gardens are fragrant with gardenias, frangipani, freshly cut grass; the pathways are filled with the Sunday crowd in its Sunday best: men, women, children, couples, families, the anonymous crowd; the sellers of sweets and peanuts, chewing gum and cigarettes sitting on their low chairs; ice-cream vendors ringing the bells of their metal carts; pastry vendors carrying flat wooden cases on their heads, bending down to open their cases for buyers in one smooth movement; vendors of patties, beef, or codfish in crusty dough, carrying their baskets in the crooks of their arms and coming to a standstill when beckoned, opening their baskets, letting the warm mingled smell of meat, codfish, and baked dough rise from beneath layers of paper, taking coins and delicately handing out patties small and large like offerings; women crouching in front of their dark-sided pots of boiling oil, selling spicy chunks of pork and slices of fried plantain; shoeshine men busy brushing shoes or inserting pieces of cardboard between ankles and socks before applying polish; others swiftly scraping rhombuses of compact shaved ice from a hefty block resting among bottles in their wooden carts; a flavor is chosen and the rhombus is covered in green, orange, red, or purple syrup and handed out to a customer, a few drops of liquid color dripping. Coins are exchanged. It is still too early for the young women in their tight skirts, heavy perfume, and high heels to come out on the square.

The boy and his brother sit on one of the stone benches, still warm from the sun even though the day is quickly waning, night about to fall. Sometimes, in the quickly disappearing light, they are asked in whispers by the two older girls to take a short walk. "*Va te promener avec ton frère.*" "Go take a walk with your brother, come back in five minutes, and don't go too far," adding, "We must be able to see you at all times," a breach of the agreement these girls have with their parents, who count on close, constant, and mutual surveillance, the boys as chaperones and the older girls as guardians, ensuring the boys' safety in that public space, in that anonymous crowd, away from the sheltering house and its gardens, but the boys do take those short walks, turning to see from a distance the young aunt and her cousin as two or three young men lean in to speak in passionate and coded phrases.

The young aunt has already *fallen in love.* "Twice," as she has confided to the boy and his brother; first with the young Ecuadoran businessman who stayed for a few months in one of the compound's bungalows—"We kissed so many times, my first real kisses," a short-lived outburst, a closely guarded secret, at least from her parents, the Colonel and his wife, the Colonel especially—and now she is in love with the young man who is buying her ice cream on this fragrant afternoon.

The young aunt has been reading a book many other young women from the town in the hills are reading, handed from one to the other, *On Becoming a Woman.* "This is just a loan; make sure you return it," or "Read that part on page twenty-three carefully," or "Wait till you read what it says about kissing," a hushed passing-on and unofficially sanctioned rite, for the mothers are aware of the book but seem to trust the comely young woman looking out to the reader from the cover, with her high-collared white blouse, blue sweater, and medium-length hair; the mothers trust her to convey her apparent wisdom and knowledge to their daughters. "A beautiful and wholesome young woman; *une belle jeune fille, et une jeune fille bien*," the mothers agree; she seems to be serenely ignoring the two young men smiling widely in the background of the cover photo, young men in their jackets, ties, and two-tone shoes, peripheral but looming presences, boys turning into young men, the wolves who will come around one day "if one is not careful."

Several times, the boy manages to have access to the book, left unguarded on the young aunt's night table or on one of the deck chairs by the pool; he's attempted to read some of the supposedly revelatory passages but given up every time, stopped by the opaque, circuitous language and lacking enough time to find what he's looking for, rapidly turning the pages. *I can't understand what they find in this book. Why do they make such a fuss?* To him, the young woman in the foreground and the widely smiling young men in the background all look like the Technicolor people in the movies he sees at Ajoupa Ciné, or the American series he watches on television: people from another world. He is perplexed when he hears dreamily or excitedly whispered scraps as he lingers around the young aunt and her friends, poised as he is on the tortured periphery of another vocabulary, the cryptic locutions of another world, whose secret he is eager to discover, *the life of the body before marriage, to give oneself to someone.*

His quest is unending; he is relentless, as he was the time he and his brother insisted on knowing what Ada, sent on an errand by the young aunt one evening, was going to buy. They followed her into the gardens, unmoved by her repeated dismissals. The boys' persistence, Ada's repeated and apparently obstinate refusals, Ada at the gate, stopped by the brothers' pleading; their cajoling, more insistence, until, exasperated, she uttered that strange new word, *Kotex*, which still meant nothing to them, a conundrum, not an answer, until Ada, in her forgiving wisdom, tells them, "It's for girls, for women at their time of the month. This is not for you."

. . . (Neither brother knows what to say to that. They just look at each other.)

"Now let me be."

. . . (They look at each other again.)

"That's enough! Go do your homework!"

Ada closed the gate behind her and headed into the night to run her errand.

The boys don't quite know how to face the young aunt when they see her quietly waiting for them, sitting on a couch in front of the television, where once again and as always she will translate, but now invested with the new mystery carried by the word *Kotex*. The two brothers sit on either side of her, the show begins, and, once again, they all hope whoever pulls the switch at the power company somewhere in the city below will forget them and the town in the hills, and they will not have to imagine what happens next in the suddenly interrupted episode as they wait out the end of the blackout in the pale glow of oil lamps or the yellowish light of bulbs powered by the feeble generator. The young aunt is quiet this evening because Grand-père has told her in the afternoon that, after all, she cannot have that party around the pool.

"But Papa, everyone's already invited! How can you do this! No!"

"I've told you, it's not possible."

"But you told me it was fine, and I've already invited everyone!"

. . . (Confident in his authority, he knows he doesn't have to say anything.)

"Everyone's already invited! All my friends! We've worked so hard! This is just not possible!"

The Colonel has indeed given his permission, and the preparations for the party around the pool have been going on for some time: "Tell this one to come, tell that one to come." "Of course, it's okay if she comes with her brother and his friends." "Let's just make sure this one or that one doesn't come; I can't stand her; I can't stand him," and the winnowing has gone on among the young aunt and her friends, with the excitement of an extraordinary gathering at its heart. There has never been such a party at the compound; only the young aunt and her friends will be there, no older sisters or brothers, unless they happen to be friends of her friends, and no mothers or fathers, only young people with young people, a new generation recognizable in the Tropical Republic as it has become recognizable out there in the world.

A friend of the young aunt has asked the lead singer of Les Rockers to come play at the party and "He's accepted! He's accepted! He said 'Yes'!" and he will be there at 2:00 P.M. sharp on the day to set up with the band, electric guitars, drums, the bass, the lead singer of Les Rockers singing the latest hits by Johnny Hallyday, Richard Anthony, Dick Rivers, the pompadoured and leather-jacketed singers from France with American-sounding names whose hits are often remakes of the American hits, remakes of remakes by Les Rockers of the Tropical Republic, who will also play their renditions of songs by Elvis Presley, Ray Charles, and Chubby Checker (rock and roll and the twist are melding in these years), as well as their own interpretations of the traditional merengues and boleros of the Tropical Republic's big bands; Les Rockers will play the full range of music heard on the Tropical Republic's radio stations, on transistor radios, and on portable record players. They are famous in the Tropical Republic and, like the French and American performers, they have a fan club, postcards, color photographs of the five of them passed around, so it's quite something, it's miraculous that they will be playing at the young aunt's party. Friends will bring food and drinks, platters of sandwiches and lemonade made with the help of cooks; glass bottles of soft drinks will be delivered in wooden cases, while amber bottles of rum will be secreted under jackets or in brown paper bags; lime, sugar, and lots of ice. Young people in flared or pleated skirts, tight jeans, T-shirts (their sleeves rolled up), blouses, and shirts (unbuttoned as far down as possible if the adults are not around) will dance around the pool; music will clang through the usually silent gardens and paths, reaching into the recesses of the estate, where the old woman with her hair in a tight bun takes her showers covered in a batiste gown in the depths of the main house. Now none of this will take place.

. . ."What do you mean it's not possible? I've just told you the party is canceled. I've thought about it: too many people, too much noise, all these people will disturb the *pensionnaires*. It's just too much trouble. No and no."

"But . . ."

"Please don't insist."

. . .

"This is so unfair. You want me just to be here and not have friends. This is so unjust."

. . .

"You want me to be an old maid, that's what you want. One day you'll be sorry." She dares not go further. She leaves; she will cry.

Later that day, the boy overhears a conversation between his mother and Grand-père. She's attempting to intercede one more time, but, at one point, the Colonel, who has run out of arguments, conclusively declares, "All men are lecherous; even *I* am lecherous," words that put an end to his eldest daughter's mediation. The eavesdropping boy understands that the pronouncement has to do with the young men who would have come to the party around the pool, the party that will not take place after all, and he also understands that the grandfather shares something with these young men and with his own son, the one who was beckoning the maids to marvel at his arched erection while he floated in the pool.

The boy's allegiance is split.

First, there is Grand-père. Grand-père who tells him and his brother those long stories in the evenings; softly rubs his brother's bony back for hours during asthma attacks in the middle of the night; prepares a sturdy base for the Christmas tree with the two boys and the old gardener, cinder blocks covered with brown wrapping paper on which a band of shiny silver sand is sprinkled to replicate the road to Bethlehem, the winding road sometimes disappearing around a bend between tiny plastic villages and pine forests; Grand-père who decorates the Christmas tree with them and asks, "Who will place the star at the top of the tree this year? Who will help with the garlands?"; Grand-père who helps the boys place the brightly painted plaster figurines in the manger and, throughout the season, reminds them to move the Three Kings along the road to Bethlehem, Melchior, Gaspard, and Balthazar bearing their gold, frankincense, and myrrh; Grand-père who initiates the two boys, his grandsons, to the pleasures of butter and wine, a tiny amount in their glass of water barely turned pink by the addition, lots of sugar.

During the season of pines cut down and carried from the red-soiled mountains to the town in the hills and the city below, the Colonel sometimes buys his grandsons lantern churches and cathedrals made by the same boys who trade in kites during the days of Lent; the lantern sellers go through the compound's gates and approach the main veranda, holding up their delicately detailed replicas (like carnival, the Christmas season allows for freer access to the estate), boys holding up their intricately laced churches and cathedrals made of cartons and thin strips of wood; used shoe boxes, used cardboard boxes, used ice-cream and Popsicle sticks (so little is discarded in those years) transformed into tiny arches, flying buttresses, columns and towers, rose windows covered in translucent kite paper glowing in the dark of the garden, the candles flickering inside the miniature churches and cathedrals, projecting trembling yellow, blue, red, green shapes onto the steps of the veranda and the dark tree trunks in the garden. This is also the one time of the year when the boys are taken to a restaurant in the city below, an exceptional event, and here again the grandfather officiates, a smiling and benevolent magus presiding over the territory of their known pleasures.

And then there is the young aunt. The young aunt and her friends, their laughter and hushed secrets, the music they listen to, the card games they play with the boys, the Sunday-afternoon *chassé-croisés* between these young woman and the young men who send them intricately folded notes through emissaries, the young aunt who has fallen in love, twice, as she told them, all part of a deeper mystery she and her friends share with the maids, who take their baths in the open, the sun pouring down on them as they kneel in one of the large tin tubs they also use to do the wash. As the young aunt translates for the boy and his brother that evening, after her father had broken his promise of a party around the pool, yet another enigma has been added by Ada's exasperated and cryptic pronouncement, "It's for girls, for women in their time of the month. This is not for you."

As the time when The Mortician will show his true face nears, the young aunt is the only unmarried daughter living on the estate—unmarried but fifteen, sixteen, seventeen years old. The Colonel's three other daughters, the young aunt's older sisters, are married by then. The eldest, the boy's mother, who lives in a separate house on the estate with her husband, the Major. The second daughter, the boy's godmother, who now lives with her husband, a quiet, affable man who works as an accountant in a construction supply company in the city, a man who loves Chopin and says he will never leave the Tropical Republic, no matter what turn politics may take—"Where would I go?" The boy's godmother has a temper and wanted some distance from the Colonel's dominion; there was an argument one day; the Colonel had really been too insistent, too overbearing that time around, and his frustrated and angry daughter could only cry out, "I want to be an adult under my own roof!" and so she had left with her two daughters and her Chopin-loving husband to live in her own house, even if only a short drive away in the town in the hills. The third daughter, the most recently married one, the one who was courted, as they said in that time and place, by the medical student, is living in the city below with her husband, now a doctor. The doctor's wife looked like the Italian actress Sophia Loren and had tea parties for her friends, chic young women, with their husbands or fiancés, all of them sitting out on the lawns, playing badminton, playing cards, having come to their friend's gathering on the compound's grounds when she was not yet married or engaged, still abiding by the rules you abide by, or seem to abide by, until the proposal and the marriage and the young man and the young woman leave for that first night together after the ceremony in the church on the square and the reception in the mountains, where the air is cool and the earth turns red and the clouds come into houses in the evenings. Before she left in her turn with her husband, the aunt who looked like Sophia Loren had also had to bend to the ancient bond between parents and daughters, especially between inflexible fathers and their ardent daughters.

The boy would see the medical student arrive in the early evening after dinner; the courted aunt would welcome him at one of the gates and take him inside the house, where he would be greeted by the Colonel and his wife. Maybe the boy's mother and father would also be there, or other visitors, or, usually, the young aunt, as she was almost always home in the evenings. Often, the aunt who looked like Sophia Loren would sit on one of the verandas or by the pool with the medical student, who would become her husband; sent by the Colonel, one of the servants would walk up to them and offer lemonade or coffee. Night would fall; the bats would come out and dance their silhouetted and muted dance over the pool; sometimes the power would be cut and the orangey light of the small generator-powered bulbs by the pool produced barely enough light for the daughter and the medical student's bodies to be clearly seen from the house, at which point the Colonel would send a servant out again, with additional lamps, or send out the young aunt, or the boy and his brother. "Go sit with them. They don't want to just be alone there all by themselves; it's impolite." Later, well into the years of exile in some living room in New York, the boy, now in his late teens, will hear the aunt, who will still look like Sophia Loren, say to other young women and to older ladies sitting apart while the men *talk politics*, holding out for the end of The Mortician's rule, as they will for years, "We always found a way, and we didn't just kiss, you know; sometimes his hand was under my dress, his fingers . . . So much fussing and hiding, but I couldn't care less about what Papa had to say. He was just too much, such an old-fashioned man. Those were different times; you kids are lucky today, sex everywhere, all those drugs, communes, and all that." The fifties will truly have ended by then.

In the early years of the sixties, things were changing quickly in the Tropical Republic, just as they were in the world out there beyond the island, and things were changing for the Colonel as well, but for the inflexible old man used to giving orders and to being obeyed, yet finding himself by accident in that particular position and in that particular time when the long generational succession in one unchanging place was finally coming to an end, each break in the established pattern must have seemed like an irreparable crumbling, each small concession, like the party by the pool his daughter wanted, a crack announcing the end of his own time, a breach in the unbroken passing of years and decades.

The Canadian women who came to the Tropical Republic from their frozen north in the middle of their country's winter were also and in their own way creating disturbances in the Colonel's place and time. At first, when parts of the main house had just been reconfigured, swaths of former living rooms turned into bedrooms, verandas into kitchens, when bungalows had been added where there had once only been trees and grass and plants, new dwellings in which paying outsiders would live for a few days or a few weeks or, sometimes, for years, there were, among the businessmen, retirees, embassy officials, and UN personnel, a few young and not so young *Canadiennes* staying at the reconfigured ancestral home for a week, or sometimes two. They came with their hairdos and pants and shorts and skirts and bathing suits and pale skins from the Canadian winter. That particular procession of *pensionnaires* from the frozen north ended abruptly, though, one February dawn when the grandfather had the watchman escort the two *Canadiennes* and their quickly packed luggage out the main gate. Returning with his wife from the casino, as they were making their way through the still dark paths of the grounds, the Colonel saw two of his gardeners, thin silhouettes against the dark blue early dawn, quietly leave Mademoiselle Gagnon and Mademoiselle Gauthier's bungalow, and his reaction was as heated as on the day he had seen the unloved son floating in the pool, displaying his arched erection. The *Canadiennes* had to leave immediately.

"But where will they go at this time of day?" (His wife's entreaty.)

"I don't care where they go; I don't care if it's very early; they'll be fine."

"But at least wait a bit."

"No! They will leave now! Let them go to the Kayona!" (The Kayona was a hotel, not at all like his *pension de famille*, as he called the rented part of the compound, but a hotel as most hotels usually looked at that time in the Tropics: geometrical rows of rooms, manicured lawns, white-jacketed staff, thatched bungalows, kidney-shaped turquoise swimming pool, long mahogany bar.) "They take in anyone there! Let them go and sit on the square with the others! They're the same!" (He meant the young ladies from the other side of the gully who had sometimes come to loudly demand their due from the dissolute son.)

. . . (His wife understood that insisting was useless.)

And so, in the dark blue early dawn, Mademoiselle Gagnon and Mademoiselle Gauthier were escorted to the gate by the old gardener, who was carrying their suitcases.

It was not meant to end like this. The grandfather had

attempted to prevent this denouement. The reservation had arrived by mail, confirmed by telegram; Mademoiselle Gagnon and Mademoiselle Gauthier duly arrived on the appointed day (there were no appointed times back then in the Tropical Republic, or in many other places; the movement of bodies, their conveyance from country to country, continent to continent had not reached their later precision and regularity; the day of arrival, not the hour, was all that could be determined; waiting all day, even into night sometimes was usual procedure in the Tropical Republic and in many other places like it). Already familiar with the habits and propensities of these young women from the frozen north, a familiarity acquired through a succession of other Mademoiselle Gagnons and Mademoiselle Gauthiers who had stayed at the compound, since outings to the Tropical Republic had become established destinations among these young and sometimes not so young women from Canada, the grandfather, in a last attempt at accepting *their type of clientele* at the compound, explained to them, in the very first few minutes of the very first day of their stay, even as he was writing down their names with his fountain pen in the thick-leafed register and smiling at them, thinking of previous misunderstandings with other Mademoiselle Gagnons and Mademoiselle Gauthiers, patiently and politely explained to them the limits of their interactions and exchanges with *the help*: that they had to understand this was a different place with different customs, different rules of conduct, *différentes manières de se conduire*, that they should keep a distance from the help, that they certainly should not go for walks with the help, nor go to the movies with the help, that the staff, *le personnel*, was there to serve in its official and professional capacity, nothing more.

All of this preamble was perhaps understandable coming from the proprietor of what was, after all, not exclusively a commercial arrangement—*This is not a hotel, but our home*, as he also informed the two Canadian women signing the register. However, beyond the fact that generations of his family lived there, beyond the rules of this place, our home, and not a hotel, and his request for understanding, adaptation, and decorum, there was the Colonel's own particular, conscious lust and, still beyond this propensity, there was at the core of his explanations to Mademoiselle Gagnon and Mademoiselle Gauthier, sedimented by years and habits and now crystalized in the Colonel, the ancient and conditioned inability to countenance the sight or even the thought of these young women from their frozen north engaging with these particular young men of the Tropical Republic in anything outside of their most bounded and bridled activities: to serve meals and drinks, cut lawns, clean shoes, watch the bungalows, nothing more—even if, among the forebears of these two gardeners, just like the Colonel's, and this is the point, *just like the Colonel's*, there had been not only slaves, fieldworkers, peasants, and servants but also emperors and kings, generals and presidents. Even if, here and now, among the relatives—distant or not—of these two gardeners, there were men whom the grandfather had once served as army officer and as consul, there remained, both in the Colonel's own mind and in his private life in the compound, the thought and the practice: "I have served, I am of here, we have been here forever, but I am not of your clan," even if they were all of the Tropical Republic, progenies of the same long and violent drift.

The Colonel's entrenched and crippling flaw, his inability to countenance the sight or even the thought of these young women from their frozen north *consorting* with the two gardeners, had taken root and grown from generation to generation, over the spread of centuries, beginning with the Taino and their poignant charm of things about to disappear as Columbus and his crews entered a blue bay in caravels, in search of gold and silver, the docking quickly followed by the slaughter and the dying, first in mines and then in fields, the vast and repeated and repeated and repeated replenishing of the quickly dying Taino with all those other bodies from Africa, the terrible and intimate hierarchy of all those bodies, masters, slaves, drifters, indentured servants, shopkeepers, second-born sons of depleted aristocracies seeking their fortune in the New World, priests and soldiers, poor, rich, all of them in opulent and bloody proximity, the jewels and dresses imported from the other side of the ocean or the whippings and the lopping off of limbs, the languorous afternoons in ornate and shady houses or the heat of the day in fields and outhouses, the dancing to orchestras in embroidered and chandeliered living rooms or to drums in courtyards lit by the flames of open fires, the prayers and hymns in chapels and cathedrals or the ceremonial sacrificing of roosters and pigs, the uprisings, at first quelled by banded planters, then by soldiers and man-eating dogs, followed by more lopping off of limbs, burnings at the stake, the repeated attempts by the few to deny the many what could not be denied, and then the Revolution and the new order that followed the Revolution, the continued proximity of bodies even in a new hierarchy, with the new rulers, the rightful rulers, as they saw it, the *authentic* ones, who looked like those two gardeners, in this new proximity with the others, who looked more like the Colonel and his progeny, those who, in the aftermath of the Revolution in which they had also fought, were dismissed as less than authentic, mere remains and residue of the former rulers and owners who had left or been exterminated.

For a long time since, and into this time of the Colonel and his own descendants, in those years on the cusp of The Mortician's rule, a rift has endured between the two: on one side those whom the Colonel considers his clan and lineage, and, on the other, the *authentics*, yet all of them, on both sides, sharing the tenacious, festering inheritance, then and now, all of them players in the timeworn chronicle encountered abstractly by the boy in his history textbook and more intimately through the small and daily refractions in his privileged childhood, such as the time he invited a boy from school to spend the day at the compound and when the two boys were splashing around in the pool, the Colonel, observing his grandson and the other boy from the main veranda, called his grandson, as if to ask him what time the meal should be served by the side of the pool for him and his friend, or some question about schoolwork, but instead, in that voice the boy loved, but now tinged with a cold and unfamiliar urgency the boy would detect when things had become pressing and brutal under The Mortician, asked him something else.

"Who is this boy?"

"He's a friend from the Séminaire; he's the one I told you about; he's spending the day with me."

. . .

. . . ?

"You see, I know he's a nice boy but I don't think you should bring him here anymore."

"Why not?"

"He is not one of us."

. . . ?

"I'm sorry; he's here and he will spend the day with you; but there is a word you have to learn: *authentic*; he is an *authentic*."

. . . ?

. . . (Only a continued and unusually severe look from Grand-père. No further explanation forthcoming.)

"So, I can't bring him here anymore?"

"No; it's better like that. Now go, go be with him."

. . .

Depending on their fluctuating proximity to his gravitational pull and the accidents and determinations of their own individual stories, the members of the Colonel's clan have lived and continued to live their own lives well before and well after those visitors from the frozen north, swerving from his obsessive preservation, casting that part of him aside, or more or less diligently following in his wake, bending to the crippling and archaic malformation that afflicts him and that he feeds with increasingly strident determination as his power and his time are waning. They are all affected, some more, others less, and in different ways, all those generations preceding the Colonel, and all those living generations still in the throes of the debilitating pattern steadily shaped in that old drift of history and honed to an insistent but increasingly nugatory sharpness by the Colonel, as the Mademoiselle Gagnons and Mademoiselle Gauthiers had learned in that dark blue early dawn. Well before and well after these visitors from the frozen north, the members of Colonel's clan have made and continue to make their own lives and patterns, swerving more or less from his gravitational pull and obsessive preservation. There is the boy's father, who remains autonomous and whole and unaffected in spite of living with his two boys and his wife on the Colonel's property, in a house he has built on a part of the compound ceded to the Colonel's eldest daughter; there is the Colonel's eldest daughter, the boy's mother, with her kindness and innocence and openness, who silently bemoans that crippling propensity in her father; there is the youngest daughter's exasperation and defiance (she does not heed her father's directive to stay out of the sun, and lounges for hours by the pool); there is the eldest son, already abroad, the fortunate pioneer; and there are the other married daughters, living in their own houses in the Tropical Republic; there is the unloved son, the dissolute son whose own defiance is unknowing, involuntary as his individual lust takes him beyond the official bounds created by the debilitating pattern when he goes to those cramped cinder-block and corrugated-iron dwellings on the other side of the gully; and there is the youngest son, the one the Colonel has taken out of school and who drives him around, his boy, his handsome boy with his thick head of hair, not a dissolute like the other one, even if he, too, has gone to women, as is said in that place and time—all of them, the Colonel's clan, depending on their proximity to his gravitational pull and the accidents and determinations of their own individual stories, all of them, casting that part of him aside, ignoring him, or following in his wake.

The old pattern is blindly perpetuated by some, dealt out with an insouciance revolting to the slighted, among others the young man who, one evening at one of the balls at the Belvedere, smooths down and buttons up the short white jacket of his navy cadet's gala uniform and approaches the table where the aunt who will marry the young doctor is sitting with her set; as the young man in his navy cadet's gala uniform begins to bend slightly at the waist, about to ask her to dance, the aunt looks up at him and says, "Nothing for us, thank you; we've already ordered." Emperors, kings, presidents, senators, navy cadets, and officers but, also, at least in the way they look without their gala uniforms or senators' linen suits, as opposed to the Colonel's clan, whose difference and privilege remain indelible regardless of raiment, this young man and those like him could be vendors of shaved ice covered with multicolored syrupy toppings, gardeners and watchmen, sellers of lottery tickets, peasants, one of so many in those anonymously crowded streets, all those people walking, hurrying bodies and blurred faces the boy sees from the big car's windows. The young man in the short white jacket of his navy cadet's gala uniform turns around, takes a few quick steps toward the dance floor, and is lost in the crowd, amid the confetti and music and dancing bodies in organdy dresses, gala uniforms, and linen suits.

The boy will hear this story and many others years later, in the years of exile, when the aunt, who will still look like Sophia Loren, though less and less so, smiling wistfully, a bit ashamed now, a bit contrite, says, "I had no idea who that man was; I thought he was a waiter."

The situation was upended when the Colonel was consul of the Tropical Republic in Miami, Florida, USA—*the South*—where signs proclaimed prohibitions even more blatantly, where water fountains and lunch counters were for some and not others, and sitting in buses had a peculiar but prescribed geometry, the Colonel and his family looking different from these some and these others in those years of bouffant blondness and conking, bobby socks and lynchings, uniformed taxi drivers, women wearing gloves to lunch, men wearing suits and hats to work, the family looking different, but the Colonel's children also being a foreign diplomat's children, even if not quite looking like some or others, the young aunt and her brother attended the ornate brick school with manicured lawns and all that blondness and freckles and bobby socks and crew cuts and striped T-shirts. The fifties were wearing on.

Reaching the point of no return

The situation would be upended yet again as The Mortician's campaign against those not deemed authentic or authentic enough was reaching the point of no return. There were signs. On one Sunday morning the harbinger is a lean young man glaring at the boy; he singles him out at a gathering in the Montrosiers' garden, one of those Sunday mornings when the boy hasn't gone to the movies after Mass and is instead sitting on the lawn with other boys, all of them eating chunks of pork, fried plantains with their hands; the man looks straight at the boy among the others and asks, "What's he doing here, that little roach?" The query ends with a word the boy has heard a few times before as the Tropical Republic nears the point of no return, a harsh syllable, the now consecrated name for those perceived to be against The Mortician, a name for people who previously have often, but not always, been the ones deemed not authentic enough, a label applied to the old guard being brought to heel, in particular to the army officers from the old guard being asked to retire, or being retired, or sometimes worse. As the point of no return approaches, the name extends to everyone not deemed enthusiastic enough, everyone becoming a suspect, not only the dwellers of stately houses in the hills above the capital (both owners and servants) but the dwellers of shantytowns, too, bricklayers, bankers, street vendors, members of exclusive clubs, teachers, women of the night, carpenters, pharmacists, musicians, millionaires, knife sharpeners, students, fishermen, businessmen, shop owners, sellers and buyers of lottery tickets, bettors on cockfights, readers of *subversive literature*, shoemakers and priests, all targeted by the new order taking shape.

The lean man asking the question is the outsider at this Sunday gathering of boys; he is still a young man, but years older than all the boys sitting on the Montrosiers' lawn, neither an acquaintance of the Montrosiers nor of the boys gathered there, the privileged saplings and their less fortunate friends from the other side of the gully who have come to share in the feast as they have so many times before and expecting this time to be like other times, but on this particular Sunday morning the lean man is in the garden, insistent and speaking directly to the boy. Roland has seen him around; maybe he's a servant's fiancé, maybe a friend of one of the gardeners, maybe a soldier in civilian clothes, in his Sunday best, most probably one of the denim-garbed men and women of The Mortician's militia who have started appearing everywhere recently, this one having shed the denim uniform for a white cotton shirt and white gabardine pants that seem to flow around his thin frame. Roland says a few words to try to placate the lean man, to bring back the mirth and complicity of boys eating food with their hands on this Sunday morning.

"He's a good friend; he's okay."

. . . (The man, malevolent, and appearing malevolent to the boy.)

. . . (The boy, suddenly drained of all joy, frightened and feeling exposed, and appearing exposed and frightened to the man.)

"Come on, let's all have some more food." (Roland, pursuing his diplomacy.)

. . . (The man, his eyes on the boy and on the boy only.)

. . . (Roland smiling. The boy not smiling. The other boys not smiling.)

. . . (The man, his eyes still and hard on the boy.)

The lean man spits noisily on the lawn and walks away.

The portents have become increasingly unambiguous in the preceding year, and this man with his malevolent look, singling out the boy and spitting noisily on the lawn, is already an announcement of the end.

For years before that Sunday on the Montrosiers' lawn, for years before the day in the sun-drenched yard and Schmitt's office that closely followed that Sunday, there had already been interferences, remote but gradually intruding static in the boy's blind contentment. Like advancing clouds from far away, there had already been what happened to the Cubans who had briefly stayed at the compound, and, further from the boy's own time and place, there had been the black-and-white photos in that magazine on the day he was told by his infirm aunt, his father's sister—the cross-eyed one with a bowlegged walk from polio contracted as a child—when his face rose from the black-and-white photos he'd come upon while leafing through the pages of *Historia* and seen photos of those crookedly standing bodies with curved backs and bent knees, black-and-white and sometimes fuzzy photos of piles of emaciated dead bodies that were hardly bodies anymore, when he could not understand what he was seeing, when he saw their nakedness and their ribs and bony arms and legs and heads, their closed or open eyes, she said to him, "You see this? *Ça c'est Himmler.* This is Himmler; this is Eichmann; this is what they did to those people, *les Juifs*." The seven-, eight-year-old boy's reply, "But why? What had they done, *les Juifs*?" contained all his rawness and refusal, and his still indefinite awareness that he was encountering something incompatible with his contentment. His aunt's answer was without appeal. "*C'était des assassins, ces gens-là, les Nazis, des a-ssa-ssins.*" She said it with a finality that allowed for no argument of any kind. "They were assassins, these people, the Nazis, a-ssa-ssins."

This was the first time the boy heard the word, with its ominous clashing of heavy *a* and sharp *z*, *Nazi*. The ensuing explanation was accurate, detailed even, for the infirm aunt was remarkably well read—they called her *l'intellectuelle*—and her information was always dependable and precise. Years later, her younger sister, by then a former beauty pageant contestant, would bemoan the fact that her crippled sister had died a virgin at eighty-one after terrible suffering from the cancer that also decimated her siblings. "She didn't deserve this final suffering; she had such a difficult life. It's an injustice." When the boy would learn again about these people and these events, *Hitler* (*Hit-lair*) and *Himmler (Himm-lair*) and *camps de concentration* and *les Nazis* and *les GIs*, this time in English, at school in New York, when he would learn about World War II well beyond what he had seen when his father took him and his brother to the movies of an evening in the Tropical Republic, Technicolor young men with square jaws and crew cuts and three-day beards on the screen, young men in olive green uniforms and helmets, carrying rifles and machine guns, soldiers aboard jeeps and aircraft carriers, landings on beaches, walking through ruined remnants of bombarded cities far away, what would remain, clear and focused even in their imprecise, gray, and blurry quality, would be those black-and-white photos in the magazine, crooked standing bodies looking through barbed-wire fences, the piles of dead bodies, their arms dangling from carts or in piles in a ditch from not too long before his own time, just a few years before, but far away, in Europe.

In the boy's own time and place, other black-and-white photos appeared when he leafed through the pages of *Bohemia*, photos of those men, the *barbudos*, of their dead bodies, sometimes their severed heads, the *barbudos* killed by Batista, *le dictateur Batista*, whose name had become a curse in the fragrant compound, especially after the playful and handsome Cubans had lived there a few days and one of them, with some of his friends sitting on the steps of one of the bungalows, looking on, had taught the boy his first sentence in Spanish—"*Voy a las montañas con los barbudos de Fidel Castro*"—and another one did a charcoal drawing of Jesus he gave as a present to the boy's grandmother, who had intervened with her husband to let these men stay at the compound, for the Colonel's wife, whom he sometimes called his *cubana*, had ancestors from that other island you could see from the Tropical Republic on a clear day, and this probably played into her decision to fool her husband, but could the Colonel really be fooled? He must have wanted to do this anyway, since what could these young and vital men, not tourists, not diplomats, not United Nations personnel, not retirees from Michigan or New York or Maine or Connecticut, what could they be doing here, at the compound? What could they be doing but preparing to join the others in the hills of Cuba before descending into Havana and, for better or for worse, entering History on foot, in oxcarts, trucks, and jeeps, in Chevrolets, Fords, and Buicks? Before the descent into Havana, there were the photos of so many of those *barbudos*, caught by the government troops, the coagulated blood dark gray and black in the photos, bodies with their eyes sometimes open, sometimes closed, unexplainable marks on those bodies, unexplainable to the boy because *torture* was something theatrical done to bodies in the movies he saw at Ajoupa Ciné, something done to muscular heroes chained in dungeons, questioned by usurping and cruel princes in rutilant robes, with curlicue beards, braceleted arms, and beringed fingers, not something done to real bodies, so real, lying there with those dark stains on them, their eyes open or closed, their mouths and teeth open to the sky, while the Cubans who had stayed at the compound that winter were very much alive and the boy was captivated by their language and long hair and beards and laughter and playfulness.

The Cubans stayed in two of the bungalows and spilled out onto the gardens, drinking rum and lemonade, smoking and talking; the Colonel's *cubana* would sit and speak with them in Spanish, always about family and professions and interests, never about what she well knew they were doing here, in the compound on that December filled with the smell of pine trees cut down for the upcoming holidays. They would also try out a few French sentences, with an accent, answering the questions, making conversation, always polite and grateful for the lull in the compound's bungalows and alleys and gardens before they would have to be on their way.

This lasted for close to two weeks, until, one day, two of them, the one who had taught the boy his first Spanish sentence, and another, the shortest one, the only short one in the group, were caught and badly beaten by The Mortician's men, paraded through the streets of the city below, displayed for journalists, and then, already looking like those photos of bodies from *Bohemia*, taken to who knows where. The entire group had left the compound in the middle of the night two days before; there was a boat waiting, and all of them, except for the unfortunate two, got away, making it to the hills of Cuba. On the day the unfortunate two were caught, a friend of the family came to the house to report what she had seen.

The grandfather and his wife were sitting with this old friend on the main veranda; the boy and his brother were not allowed to be present, but, hiding amid the hibiscus and bougainvillea beneath the veranda, they could hear. The three adults waited until the lemonade had been served and Marisa, the severely religious laundress, who was replacing one of the usual servants, had gone back to the kitchen with the empty tray. The friend drank quickly from her glass, wiped her forehead with her small embroidered handkerchief, and began by telling them where and at what time the two Cubans had been caught, while they listened silently, intent on her words; she took a deep breath before continuing.

"You're both so lucky; no one seems to know they were staying here; make sure you don't tell anyone; make sure. This could be very bad."

. . . (The Colonel and his wife were shocked and, looking at their friend, they could only beckon her to continue. From beneath the veranda, the boy heard no reply from Grand-père and Grand-mère.)

"You should have seen them, with their hands tied; their eyelids were swollen; their teeth were broken; they could hardly walk; they were barefoot, pushed along like thieves, like criminals. . . . Their clothes were torn. . . ."

. . . (Continued silence from Grand-père and

Grand-mère, but, from their hiding place beneath the veranda, the two boys heard their grandmother sobbing.)

"It was horrible."

We will rid the world of the scourge of subversives with your help

A few weeks later, a letter of thanks addressed to the grandmother arrived, signed by all the Cubans who had gotten away and were now basking in the first flush of victory, *con la euforia del triunfo*, a letter signed with their warm regards, *y un abrazo* for the Colonel and many thanks again for their kindness and for their family's kindness, and a special greeting to the boy who had learned his first sentence in Spanish with one of them. "Tell him we are no longer fighting in the mountains and that we have won." They regretted the presence of their two friends never heard from again, their comrades who had become sacrificial and public offerings from The Mortician to the Great Northern Neighbor, for in those years at the height of the Cold War, and well beyond those years, when a simple band of armed and determined men could change the fate of countries (*ragtag army* was a term favored by the press), it was an easy strategy for the kepi-wearing (see their heads), thickly medaled (see their chests) rulers of the south with their shoes or boots shined to a blinding sheen (see their feet) or for their civilian counterparts in their linen suits and white smoking jackets to elbow or slither their way into the good graces of the Great Northern Neighbor. All that was required was dutiful, even if only cosmetic, justification of the beating back of their protesting populations with sticks, water jets, rubber bullets, all that was required to vindicate the dead-of-night disappearances, the blindingly lit torture chambers installed in army barracks and prisons or in the basements of isolated country homes, the killings, accidental or not, in these same chambers, but also everywhere, even in the streets, in clear daylight, all that was required of these uniformed or suited leaders was to apply particular labels to their activities, labels that screamed, *We will fight the subversives with you! We will obliterate the subversives with you! We are with you in your crusade to rid the world of this scourge*, for money and weapons and advisers and training to come pouring in.

Only months before the Cubans' stay at the compound, The Mortician had withstood a landing of thirteen men (a sheer coincidence, this fateful number), a small group of men disembarking on a moonlit beach just a few miles from the capital, a ragtag army that almost succeeded in toppling him but, instead, as a result of terrible luck and some careless behavior, ended up shot by denim- or khaki-wearing men or cut to pieces by peasants' machetes. The Mortician quickly became adept at the game of *We will rid the world of the scourge of subversives with your help*, while whispered, always whispered, conversations about subsequent landings, real, imagined, or fabricated, spread like village gossip at the compound in the town in the hills and everywhere else in the Tropical Republic. Barriers and checkpoints sprang up. The boy's and his brother's lunch boxes with their decals of Zorro or the Musketeers were clumsily opened by men in denim or khaki when on the way to school the car would have to stop at one of the checkpoints set up between the town in the hills and the city below and throughout the roads of the Tropical Republic, a generalized shakedown disguised as *state of emergency measures*, money to be remitted forthwith in exchange for paper passes while cars were erratically searched, primarily for guns and then for *suspect material*, books by certain authors, certain issues of certain foreign magazines, tracts dropped from planes, any trace of being a *subversive*, any link to those who were challenging The Mortician's tight, relentless, and bloody meshwork fallen over the Tropical Republic.

The most dazzling beauty contest ever to have been organized in the Tropical Republic

It was not always like this, The Mortician's rule, even if the time of whispering and being afraid of the dark came quickly, the anxious waiting in the yellow light of kerosene lamps for the return of electricity after the nightly blackout, hoping the jeeps and the cars would not stop at this or that gate. It was not like this at the beginning of his rule: In the first flush of his own unexpected and forceful electoral victory, there was a period of apparent tranquillity after the ransacking of newspaper offices and radio studios, intimidations (and worse), bombs, beatings (and worse)—though, to be fair, these activities were carried out by some of the other candidates as well. In the relatively peaceful period following the election, The Mortician savored the capacity to bring them to heel, these arrogant people, these so-called *elites* in their homes and their gardens and their clubs, with their sons and, much more rarely, their daughters sent to universities in Paris, Berlin, and, increasingly more as the fifties were becoming the sixties, New York, Chicago, Boston.

These sons and daughters of the ruling class would be among the favorite targets of the new regime. For example, this widely smiling prodigal son who after two whole years of study in a foreign capital emerged from a just-landed plane and, standing at the top of the deplaning stairs like a movie star, brandished a diploma in ballroom dancing (with a specialization in tango) for his friends who had gathered at the airport to celebrate his return. This returnee took his place in the family business just a few days later. Most other sons and daughters of the elite came back with more substantial results, but still usually joined the family business, or became bankers (often, another family business), engineers, doctors, lawyers, and, less often as The Mortician's time came and lasted, politicians. Other young men, some from less wealthy families, but of the same extended clan to be brought to heel, attended the Tropical Republic's medical school, one of the very best in the Americas back then, or entered the military academy, continuing a long tradition of officers from the extended clan. It was these people, those who were perceived as remnants of the former plantation-owning rulers, those who, for better or for worse, held the true reins of power even when they seemed sidelined, who were going to be brought to heel, at first in that public and flashy ritual, the beauty contest.

"Your daughters will participate, those young ladies with their bouffant hairdos, Boussac dresses, and insolent smiles." Even if the edict was never so bluntly and specifically stated, it was understood that Madame Ducasse, the wife of one of The Mortician's closest advisers, the smiling (with her mouth only, the eyes and their immediate surroundings remaining absolutely still) and expensively dressed lady who came to your door of an early evening, driven in a maroon Chevrolet convertible by a sharply dressed man in civilian clothes wearing a hat and sunglasses, was someone whose polite prattle about *the need for amusement after such a difficult time* (Madame Ducasse meant the recent campaign and the elections), the need to begin getting Véronique or Evelyne or Lisa ready for the most dazzling beauty contest ever to have been organized in the Tropical Republic, should be taken very seriously. The Mortician himself had entrusted Madame Ducasse with a mission to select a dozen of the most beautiful young women who would represent the Tropical Republic, and Madame Ducasse was taken most seriously indeed; she was taken seriously by all, with not a single exception, including the hot-tempered grandfather who had gone to the Séminaire and threatened to shoot Mademoiselle Marie like a dog if she ever laid a hand on the boy again, for his youngest daughter had been selected, *had been honored by being selected* by the Ministry of Tourism to participate, as that youngest daughter recounted years later to the boy: "I must admit, all modesty aside, that I was among the most beautiful young women of my age; I was eighteen then! I would never have thought of entering this beauty contest that they announced with great fanfare, over and over again, in all the newspapers and on radio stations in the capital and in all the towns in all the provinces; they were looking to select the young beauty who would represent the country at the Miss Sugarcane Contest to be held in Cali, Colombia. Our country had been proud to see one of ours, Albertine Blanchard, crowned Sugarcane Queen out of thirty other international contestants two years before . . . the president" (in this account, The Mortician is simply referred to as the president) "dreamed of seeing us win the prize a second time. So, one evening, my father had the visit from Madame Ducasse, and here I was, the shy one, the unsociable one, who would run away and hide when visitors came to the house, here I was propelled onto the stage, exposed to audiences, to the lights and the projectors. . . ."

Of course, the Ministry of Tourism, the official organizer of festivities and purveyor of pageantry, would not be the one to disburse funds for attire becoming of beauty pageant contestants; the forced expense was part of the bringing to heel of the very wealthy families, as well as the not so wealthy ones, and those who were not wealthy at all, but belonged to a rarefied circle through their common and more or less vestigial affinity with the decimated former rulers of the time before the Revolution. The Ministry of Tourism would not be the one to pay, yet someone had to, for there were all the outfits required to attend the countless lunches, dinners, cocktail parties, and there were the bathing suits and the high-heeled shoes, and, most important, most costly, there were the sumptuous *robes de soirée*, diaphanous, gauzy, and frothy, or velvety, satiny, and dense. And so different attires and accessories were gathered by the designated families, bought directly from Paris and New York by the wealthy, while among the less affluent help was enlisted from local couturieres and seamstresses; patterns were bought, or copied from magazines from Paris and New York; aunts sewed, friends sewed, brothers raged (silently), contributions were made (the hot-tempered grandfather who loved the company of friends and mistresses and neglected to provide for his seven sons and daughters could not be counted on, especially for this particular endeavor, and for once his refusal—or his forgetting—to contribute was understood and, for once, even approved by his family), but the shy young woman, his youngest daughter (eighteen!), walked and marched and paraded in her high heels and bathing suit and her hairdos and *robes de soirée* around the kidney-shaped swimming pools of the capital's luxury hotels, lit up in the night, under the star-studded sky, with the moon so close. The hot-tempered grandfather's youngest daughter attended the countless lunches and dinners and cocktail parties with all of the other young women driven in convertibles throughout the capital, speeding through in raucous caravans, honking horns dispersing anonymous and opaque crowds throughout the capital's streets, music blaring like a halo around these young women ferried to yet another event, displayed but untouchable even as they were being displayed, for *interfering* with them was not within the realm of possibility, bathed as they were in the aura of immunity granted by the very fact that they represented the Tropical Republic, by the very fact, which was already the same fact, that they represented The Mortician himself, since the fusion between The Mortician and the Tropical Republic was already far advanced. Soon, the ancient merging of ruler and realm would no longer be merely assumed, but proclaimed in brightly shaped signs made of hundreds of small electric bulbs or in cursive neon patterned into sentences on wooden panels erected in public squares like guillotines of another time and place, *I am the Nation, One and Indivisible.* The ancient fusion between ruler and rule had already begun here again, in the very early period of The Mortician's reign; the most lavish and flamboyant beauty contest ever to have been organized in the Tropical Republic was only the first, still unclear and still bloodless sign, an ostensibly harmless portent of what was to come, like the lean man in the Montrosiers' garden who had called the boy a *roach.*

The point of no return was imperceptible in the brilliant lights of the projectors' red, yellow, blue, and green rays combining in a bright vaporous white, or in the softer glow of lanterns set up around the kidney-shaped swimming pools, hanging off trees under the stars and the moon so close, the gardens fragrant in the tropical night, while an anonymous crowd gathered outside, beyond the manicured lawns, peering through the wrought-iron gates, trying to catch a glimpse, wondering about the unusual display of light or, more likely, attending to the business of surviving or enjoying themselves in their own modest pleasures, walking through the night, buying chunks of spicy pork or fried plantains, gulping down shots of rum by the light of small metal lamps while, around the turquoise pools, in a life far from theirs, these young women were being announced one by one by the master of ceremonies in his white smoking jacket, a small band playing out the latest merengue or standards from the Tropical Republic's prolific tradition. The rapt audience was made up of new officials and members of the new contingent rising in the wake of The Mortician's victory, and, of course increasingly more numerous, these young women's families, who gradually or conveniently forgot Madame Ducasse's ominous early-evening visit—"Your daughters will attend. You will attend"—mothers, fathers, aunts, grandfathers, grandmothers, entire families and generations forgetting the veiled threat, or too afraid to remember the threat, or afraid and not forgetting the threat but surrendering anyway to the soft glow of the lanterns, abandoning themselves to the pleasures of the balmy tropical evenings.

Both their father and grandfather, the Major and the Colonel, having given their permission, the boy and his brother, the beauty contestant's cherished nephews, dressed in their white shirts and long pants, were taken along one evening by friends of their eighteen-year-old aunt, while their parents and grandparents remained at home, away from the lights and the music, knowing, or at least not having forgotten, unlike so many others of their extended clan, what their attendance meant but unable to resist the young aunt's entreaty: "You know I don't want to do this; I know you can't come, but at least let the boys come. They'll be safe; they'll make me feel better."

So the boys were picked up in the early evening by friends of their aunt and driven in a haze of cologne and perfume to a beachside hotel with a long palm-lined driveway. They sat upright around linen-covered round tables set up around a turquoise swimming pool while the young women in their evening dresses and the young men in their suits and jackets and starched guayaberas ordered scotch and sodas, rum and Cokes, soft drinks for the boys, and sandwiches during the interlude before the contestants were announced and started their parade on the walkway built in a semicircle at one end of the pool. The boys were allowed into their aunt's dressing room during the interlude, their pubescence a badge granting entry to the maze of rooms requisitioned by the Ministry of Tourism for the most lavish and flamboyant beauty contest ever to have been organized in the Tropical Republic. Along the way to their aunt's dressing room, led by one of her friends, as beautiful and baffling to the boy as all the other young women selected for the pageant, the two brothers made lefts and rights through halls and rooms, caught glimpses of lightbulb-ringed mirrors and dressing tables, rows of high heels, dresses hanging in makeshift freestanding closets, young women being fitted into a *robe de soirée* or stepping into a pair of high heels. Some of them recognized the boys, saying, "Come, give me a kiss" or "You're so sweet to come see us," and the boy's heart was beating fast, his brother so much more at ease in the midst of all this, blithely kissing and hugging, while he, the older brother, could barely answer the questions and was close to fainting in the perfumed embraces and kisses, the crisp crush of tulle or the glossy gleam of satin.

The Mortician never attended any of these affairs. He remained an absent, overseeing specter, represented by his partisans, who were at first ill at ease in their new surroundings, around pools, at lunches, dinners, cocktail parties, at the Club, at certain exclusive restaurants, at the Belvedere, only just beginning to take the measure of their recently acquired power, glancing and, as time went by, staring and, as time went by, sneering at the old guard, whose daughters were strolling on the walkway and on the stage, offered up yet immune, protected for now by the fusion between The Mortician and this pageantry and, beyond it, the Republic itself, a fusion already potent but whose fulfillment the absent yet present Mortician was methodically preparing far from the vaporous white light, far from the coupes of champagne, the perfume, the whiskey sodas, the music, the *robes de soirée*, the bathing suits worn with high heels, far from the glow of the display under the stars.

Beyond the luxurious hotels and palm-lined driveways, people who had never set foot on the shiny tiled floors of compounds surrounded by fragrant gardens had been summoned to The Mortician's gleaming white presidential palace and taken through its gates in jeeps and cars driven by men wearing sunglasses day and night, people like the thin, slightly bent man in his straw hat and sandals and patched pants and shirt, a handkerchief wrapped around his neck, the man of that world of other instruments and practices whose help the boy's grandfather had requested for the younger brother's asthma. The

Mortician was intent on establishing his claim to being the authentic representative of the authentic people, rather than the so-called elite, whose daughters were parading in the most lavish and flamboyant beauty contest ever to have been organized in the Tropical Republic. In time, many of those men being driven through the gates, the men in straw hats and sandals and patched pants and shirts, would also begin to wear the sunglasses and the denim uniforms and the suits and hats, and they, too, would carry guns in the holsters of their denim uniforms or tucked in the belts of their fancy trousers.

As the point of no return was being reached, as the swarms in khaki and denim and fancy clothes were being unleashed throughout the Tropical Republic, on the dwellers of stately houses and on the dwellers of shantytowns, they would also be unleashed in the countryside, on the men and women who had tilled their own small plots of land since the Revolution. There would be a visit one late afternoon, after the peasants have come back from their fields. After the initial and traditional salutations are exchanged, after the tiller of land and the man in uniform sit on the low straw chairs outside the hut, after the offering of coffee or rum, after the silence, as the first stars are beginning to appear, the well-fed voice enfolded in the immunity afforded by his denim uniform would speak.

"This is a fine piece of land."

. . . (The peasant pulls on his pipe and gazes outward toward the black mass of hills and mountains beyond the plain, buying time, buying a few seconds against the inevitable.)

"Yes, indeed, this is a fine piece of land. . . ."

. . . (The few seconds, barely, have come and gone;

the peasant continues to gaze out at some point in the darkness.)

"I like this piece of land; it will do just fine."

. . . (The tiller of fields continues to look out in the dark distance; to look directly at the man sitting across from him would be to acknowledge, to accept.)

"This is a fine daughter you have; she's certainly grown into a fine figure of a woman; how old is Annaïsse this year? Fourteen? Fifteen?"

. . . (There is nothing more to be said, by him or by the other man now getting up from his chair and slowly walking into the night without looking back, his steps, his hips taking the extra time and space assumed by those certain of their power.)

And the land would be left to others who didn't know how to work it, the former authentic driven away from their land by the newly consecrated authentic. The exodus to the capital would begin. The peasants from the mountains and the plains, untried in the ways of the city, perhaps with a relative in the capital already, if they were lucky, would come to swell the shantytowns, the crowds in the streets, the teeming marketplaces, the squares; men and women leaving their land, refusing to work for the men in denim uniforms, sharp clothes, hats, and sunglasses, refusing to feed their robust appetites, all the more robust for having been kept for so long from what they had coveted for so long, now taking the measure of their newly acquired power everywhere: like the man who shot another man dead for a parking spot that day in the town in the hills; or those others who got carried away by the action and the rousing score of *The Magnificent Seven* at a sold-out showing at the Excelsior, and, in imitation of Yul Brynner dressed in black from hat to boots or slender

Steve McQueen in his blue jeans and leather chaps shooting it out with the bad guys, pulled out their own guns in the dark of the theater and enthusiastically shot several rounds at the ornate ceiling while the panicked crowd rushed for the exits.

This would happen at every showing of *The Magnificent Seven* in this particular grand old theater before spreading everywhere. At one point, in a vain, a valiant, even a foolhardy attempt, considering the circumstances, in an effort at putting a stop to this *dangerous extravagance*, a notice was posted at the Excelsior's entrance, a notice like those posted at the swinging doors of saloons in Technicolor Westerns: "The management requests that all weapons be left at the door with the attendant." But who would enforce this, who would dare challenge those men in the throes of their newly found power? No one but those they considered to be their commanders, and even then, in the new and vague hierarchy and the mounting frenzy toward the point of no return, who would ensure that their compliance would last? They could not be contained. And so the crowds deserted the movie houses when Westerns were showing. Or war movies. Or gangster movies. Or even sword-and-sandals. Or even swashbuckling movies. Until the only movies safe to see were the Technicolor musicals and comedies, *Gidget Goes to Rome* or some other city, or blond surfers on golden California beaches, or the trials and tribulations of Joselito, the little Spaniard with the golden voice.

Not too long before, it had been quite safe to see movies of any kind at the Excelsior, or at any other movie house. On a Sunday afternoon, after a long day at the beach, the boy and his brother are taken to the Excelsior for a private showing of *Modern Times*. They're accompanied by the young aunt and friends of hers from the French Institute who know the Excelsior's manager. The theater is just down the street from the Séminaire; the street, teeming with people on weekdays, is now silent and desolate in the still, hot air. The anguishing hush of certain Sunday afternoons. The Séminaire's gates are closed, and the boy feels a tightening in his chest when he thinks of Monday morning, tomorrow morning. *I haven't memorized those pages for history yet; I won't be able to do it tonight; maybe I'll have time during recess, or maybe he won't call on me. Please, let him not call on me.* Once inside the Excelsior's air-conditioned lobby, he breathes freely again. As the small group starts going up the steps to the theater's balcony, he looks up at the large posters behind their wood-framed glass announcing upcoming films: The faces of Jeff Chandler, Silvana Mangano, Kurt Jurgens, Audrey Hepburn, Rossano Brazzi, Richard Widmark, Vittorio Gassman either look out onto the silent lobby or their full bodies are busy loving or killing each other in gaudily painted scenes: surfer-studded beaches, cowboy-filled barrooms, neon-lit streets. The usually ubiquitous Brigitte Bardot is not among the faces or the bodies today. The young aunt, the two cherished nephews, the French cultural attaché, his family, and a few friends of theirs sit in the balcony's front row and the movie immediately begins; they watch a mustachioed little man in his striped workman's overalls grow manic at an assembly line before being swallowed up by cogwheels, and, in another scene, they watch the same little man roller-skate with such elegance and abandon, so perilously close to the edge of the toy section of a deserted department store. The boy has never seen a Charlie Chaplin movie before and he's mesmerized; no words are spoken; the jaunty piano tune accompanying the Little Tramp's adventures reverberates in the empty Excelsior, the figures suddenly speeding up, then slowing down, and speeding up again, the flow only quickly interrupted by frames containing the words that can only be mouthed by the Little Tramp in the bowler and the other figures on the screen. It's like a comic book, but so much better; the boy wishes it would never end.

Besides empty theaters, stately houses, and churches, quiet, uncrowded places are rare in the capital, or near it; as The Mortician's reign advances, they recede even more, the crowds becoming denser as the countryside hemorrhages. Even before so many of the peasants from throughout the Tropical Republic permanently left their land, the ones who were not too far in the mountains and the plains were brought to the capital in hundreds of truckloads for rallies and celebrations: the very recent anniversaries of The Mortician's reign, visits of foreign dignitaries. Thousands of small flags are distributed to the peasants and to their fellow citizens who live in the shantytowns around the capital; commands are barked out: "You must wave them when you see Him, even from far away." "You must scream as loud as you can and say 'Long Live Our Leader!' when you see Him, even from far away!"

The boy hears the exchanges between the grandfather and others, his father, his mother, aunts, uncles, their wives and husbands, visitors in the warren of trees and paths in the house in the hills.

"There will be another rally this weekend."

"Those wretched people are given a dollar and a bowl of cornmeal and herring and then they'll be trucked back to their villages the next day."

"Where do they wash?"

"Where do they sleep?"

One Friday afternoon, close to the day of the whistle blow in the sun-drenched yard, as the boy and his brother are being driven back from school unusually late, the car is forced to stop at an intersection; unsmiling behind their sunglasses even as the sun has already set, men in khaki or denim are standing in the middle of the avenue, blocking their way and waving on a caravan of flatbed trucks carrying tightly packed people, many leaning out from the wooden racks. Throughout the encounter the boy and his brother remain still, looking through the windows at the trucks filled with people and at the men in their sunglasses and uniforms holding machine guns against their chests or, more nonchalantly, holding them by their leather straps or their handles, hanging loosely by their sides. The driver is as meek as he can be; both of his hands rest on the steering wheel, his head slightly bent down. When the passing of trucks has ended, two of the men imperiously wave the car on.

On some Monday mornings, the boy and his brother see traces of the crowds' passage at their school; the Séminaire's usually spotless yard is strewn with torn food wrappings and crunched-up sheets of shit-smeared newspaper; the trucks had come later than anticipated to pick up the hundreds of men and women who had been left there for the night, and the priests had not been able to have their help work fast enough before the boys arrived for morning classes. On those Mondays, none of the boys would even think of going near the toilets, latrines really, at the outer end of the schoolyard.

The throngs of people are returned to their villages and shantytowns in the same trucks that had come for them, until the next rally, the next celebration of an anniversary, the next visit of a foreign dignitary. Such visits are more and more scarce as The Mortician's reign advances, and, as the point of no return is being reached, when the visits of foreign dignitaries have stopped completely, the crowds are gathered increasingly more often to celebrate the capture and the execution of *rebels*.

Among the new authentics, the denim-garbed, the sharp-suited, the khaki-uniformed, men *close to the palace* or men in the countryside speaking in their well-fed voices to peasants in the hills and the plains about their land and their daughters, men who come to claim their due in the shops and restaurants of the capital, or men who come to make their demands in the small hotels and cinemas of the provinces, to claim their due from even fishermen and ladies of the night, among those new authentics, there are competing factions, clashes over the sharing of power and spoils. At one point, The Mortician himself is defied by his closest confederate, the commander of his militia. A faithful and ruthless ally from the days when The Mortician was still an anonymous country doctor, the commander of the militia now wants *more*, more power, more of the spoils, but The Mortician prevails and the commander takes his mutiny to the hills, leading quick attacks on isolated army barracks in the provinces, and sometimes even in the capital, in an odd replay of the *barbudos'* tactics on that other island not so long before, at a time when a simple band of armed and determined men could change the fate of countries. This is the time when the first checkpoints appear; The Mortician's grip over the Tropical Republic, his relentless and bloody meshwork, tightens even more. The days of the most dazzling beauty contest ever to have been organized in the Tropical Republic recede into what now seems a distant past, where people in towns could go see Westerns and war movies without misgivings, and peasants could survive on land that had belonged to their families for generations.

Like the peasants, and unlike the peasants, was the Major. The boy's father owned a piece of land in the plains near the capital, not unlike the plots so many former slaves had inherited long ago from the redistribution after the end of the great plantations, but much larger, and purchased just a few years before the whistle blow in the sun-drenched yard, while he was still an officer, both a precautionary step, since he probably knew his time in the army wouldn't last, and a logical choice, given his old passion for land and farming. After his dismissal from the army, as The Mortician's rule was still in the glow of the most dazzling beauty contest ever to have been organized in the Tropical Republic, the Major had started this second career, so much closer to his own inclination than the army, closer even to the inclination that had taken him to the medical studies he'd been forced to relinquish because of his forgetful, extravagant, and irresponsible father, who loved the company of his grandsons, friends, and mistresses but neglected to provide for his seven sons and daughters.

Even when he was still a commanding officer in the provincial towns by the sea, the Major had already started reading about this other trade: breeds of egg-laying chickens, breeds of cows, varieties of fruit trees, irrigation techniques; he'd even had quite a few conversations with Dr. Silverstein, the UN man. By the time of his discharge from the army, the small farm was producing the milk, eggs, and cream (an unstable and coveted delicacy in the hot Tropics) whose sale would in time generously replace the officer's pay. At first, before they could afford to hire a driver, the boy's mother herself drove around in the Hillman throughout the capital and the town in the hills, making stops at imposing houses, or compounds like the one she lived in with her husband, while the young man the Major had hired to help filled a basket with the milk, eggs, and cream and took it through wrought-iron gates into yards and gardens to deliver the products to waiting cooks, maids, gardeners, whoever was on hand. On some Saturdays the boy would accompany his mother on those rounds, sitting in the front seat with her, turning to look at her profile, her earrings, her hands holding the steering wheel, shifting gears, her feet pressing down on the clutch, the accelerator, the brake pedals, in a pale yellow linen dress, or in another dress, always so elegant in her heels, so beautiful.

For months before the point of no return, the family continues to spend some Sundays at the farm in the plains. They pile into the Hillman after breakfast and drive the hour or so to the property. Near the only other building on the land besides the low-roofed chicken coop, the Major has added a cement structure used as an irrigation cistern for the farming, or a swimming basin for the boys, who call it a basin because *pool* is only used for the sleek turquoise structure in the gardens of the compound in the hills. The basin at the farm is a much larger and rougher thing, made of smoothed-out cement, but left unpainted, squat and devoid of a filtering device, its water free of the chlorine used in *the Grand-père pool*, as the boys call it. The basin is usually empty when the family arrives; the Major honks the Hillman's horn three times as they make a sharp left from the main road and reach the small wooden gate; the foreman in his wide-brimmed straw hat waves to them as he opens the two sides of the gate to let the car through, and then catches up and joins them as they unpack in the shade of the farmhouse.

"How are things, Alcindor?"

"Things are what they are, Major. We had a good harvest of oranges last week. That young sow is big-bellied again."

. . .

"I know you asked me to keep her isolated: I kept her in the enclosure out back, but one of them got to her anyway."

. . .

"I know, Major, I know; but I figured it out when I saw her raising her butt and pressing it right up against the enclosure to one of the young pigs hanging around. . . . You bet he didn't refuse the offer. . . . Begging your respect, Madame Major."

. . . (The boy's mother can barely contain her laughter and looks around to see whether her two boys are listening, but they're already out exploring among the orange trees, the mango trees, and in the sugarcane and sisal fields beyond the property.)

"Things will have their way, Major, Madame Major."

"Don't go too far; stay where I can hear you!" (At the farm, the mother's words are not taken as seriously as elsewhere. Her boys are safe among the trees, cows, and chickens. This is the countryside, the sheltered and hallowed parcel of land in the countryside.)

"That Mr. and Mrs. you sent out last week, they sure seem to be very fond of each other."

. . . (The Major has no idea whom Alcindor is referring to.)

"He means Lionel and Evelyne; remember, we told them they could come out anytime?"

"Yes indeed, like flies to horse shit they took to each other, those two," Alcindor continues. "No daylight between them, that I could see."

"Well, Alcindor, you seem to have had your hands full this past week."

"Yes, Major."

By the time the boys return from their exploration, the basin is almost full; Alcindor has turned on the pump and a thick jet of water gushes out steadily from an oversized pipe laid out over the basin. The boy is riveted by the speed of quickly rising water even as he prepares to go in; the first jump in the basin's cold water is always the best. He dives in and comes out and dives in again and again while his brother floats in the basin, legs and arms dangling from the inflated inner tube of a truck tire, his back in the water, his head resting on the tube, his eyes closed to the sky and sun. Soon they are joined by the Major and his wife. Alcindor treats them all to coconuts and sugarcane. He holds out a stalk obliquely and brings the machete down in precise arcs; the sugarcane's flesh appears in sudden straight white strips as the bark is peeled off by the sharp blade. Alcindor makes different cuts on the coconuts. First he lops off a small section of the green husk to expose the shell beneath, and then, using the machete's pointed tip, carves out a small hole and hands out the coconut, the first one to the mother, who tilts it and begins to drink, then more coconuts to the others, and as the empty coconuts are returned to him, Alcindor places them on a flat rock and cuts them in half with a single swing; the machete then cuts off perfectly shaped makeshift spoons from the husk that are used to scoop out and eat the soft, juicy flesh. After the family leaves, he will release the basin's water among the rows of orange and mango trees.

They drive back in the deepening blue of the late-afternoon sky, the swift, vibrant sunset; by the time they've returned to the fragrant compound in the hills, it will be dark and the bats will have started their mute dancing over the pool. Sundays and Sundays of this. They seem infinite even as they are coming to an end.

The farm may be the Major's property, but Alcindor has the presence and authority of a sovereign on the land, advancing between the rows of orange trees, smoking his pipe, cutting dry hanging branches with a swing of his machete, overseeing the picking of fruit or the weighing of eggs by boys and girls from nearby employed for these tasks for a few hours, as needed. Alcindor has never been away from this particular part of the Tropical Republic's plains for more than a few days. He has several sons and daughters; the number of wives and *acquaintances* has never been clear.

One of his daughters will become a nurse in New York, yet another break in the old pattern of peasants becoming peasants and servants becoming servants in the slow and relentless unfolding of the decades and centuries. After the Major had to flee the Tropical Republic and was living in New York, he went to visit his former foreman in a cramped apartment in Brooklyn, early on in the years of exile. It was a very cold winter day. Alcindor now seemed shrunken and gray and feeble; he bemoaned his decision to comply with his daughter's request for him to leave the village and the land, get aboard that thing, the airplane, and spend the long hours sitting still, first in the daytime and then in the dark as the sun set outside the airplane's round windows, not knowing where he was, but always managing to seem calm, hold steady even as he was trembling inside, being taken to a place far from the wide sky overhead, far from the rows of orange trees and the fields of sugarcane quickly changing color in the suddenly setting sun or glistening blue under the low moon, leaving all this, as he told the Major, for that cramped place where people live on top of one another, leaving all this to care for his recently born grandchild. The tall, regal man had become his grandchild's babysitter. "All day in that *a-part-ment*, Major, all the time in that *a-part-ment*, where my feet can't feel soil and grass, hardly ever getting to walk in the streets even, and the cold, Major, the cold! I just can't take it here. I love that little baby, but I'll go crazy if I stay here. I'll go crazy."

The Major himself could not go back, but Alcindor could. A few weeks after his visit to the Brooklyn apartment, the boy's father received a letter written on Alcindor's behalf by one of the public scribes who sat at small wobbly desks in the shade of mango trees between thatch huts and one-room pink-and-blue mud or cinder-block houses. In his letter, Alcindor thanked the Major for his visit, informing him that he had left his daughter's Brooklyn apartment, that he was back home in the plains. "I should never have listened to her. She's very kind, she loves her old father, she sends me money every month, but I'm back and I should never have left; I know it's difficult for you, Major, in the land of foreigners, and I wish you well. The farm is being well taken care of by this new owner; I see what's going on from my plot. I won't say anymore, and I have nothing more to do with it. I hug the boys very tight. Please give my regards to Madame Major, Alcindor."

Before either Alcindor or the Major left the Tropical

Republic, one for a few months, the other forever, the days of visits to the farm and the outings to the beach continued, as did the Sundays around the pool, as did the Masses cut short by the boy's calculated and abating adherence to the ritual, as did the movies in the dark of Ajoupa Ciné, the boy emerging in the clear light of Sunday, the day still so new and promising; all this continued, until it ended abruptly.

Days of sedition and checkpoints and fear

Days of sedition and checkpoints and fear, everywhere, whispered conversations about *rebels* and *landings*, real or not. On a Sunday—after the Mass reduced to its bare requisites—and after the movie at Ajoupa Ciné, the two boys join the young aunt to visit one of her friends from the high school, Cécile, whose younger brother's unsmiling face and seriousness, as well as the things he tells the boy and his brother, make him seem strange and much older, though he's only a year older than the boy. He also seems slightly deranged. His father was among the very first ones taken away one night by the denim-garbed men with their sunglasses, waving their guns and machine guns in the dark. "He disappeared, my father, he just disappeared; they came in the middle of the night and they took him away."

The days after he was taken away, the man's wife and daughter went to the army barracks near the church square to ask about him, to implore, to find out something, anything. They went several times the next day, and then the next few days and weeks. The last time they went there, after they passed by the now familiar sentinels posted at the entrance and walked through the interior gardens—even in army barracks, the ubiquitous bougainvillea and hibiscus obscured the blood and the fear—after they walked through the grimy halls and stepped into the office they were beginning to know quite well, the man in khaki behind the desk took a long look at Cécile and then smiled at the other men milling around, men in khaki, men in denim, and two or three of the sharp-suited ones. The man behind the desk smiled like someone eyeing a meal, and Cécile's mother understood she would no longer be going to make inquiries with her daughter. After that day when the men had looked so insistently at Cécile, the despondent woman only asked her son and daughter to be very careful, and to hope. She walked alone to the army barracks to ask about her missing husband.

The young aunt is sitting on the house's small veranda with Cécile and her mother, who has come out from her bedroom for a while to bask in the Sunday-morning light, to bask in the banter of these young women, soon joined by other friends. They all wear small bows in their bouffant hair. They're drinking lemonade. They may soon go for a walk to the church square in their Boussac dresses. Even Cécile is smiling; she forgets, for a while. There are moments of relief when friends come to visit on Sunday mornings, talking and even laughing in the shade of the veranda; they all know what's happened.

The two brothers are sitting in the garden, staring at Cécile's brother as he talks about what they've only ever heard adults talk about, but unlike adults, the strange boy isn't whispering and seems not to care at all about being overheard. The boys have seen all those around them at the compound lower their voices to carefully gauged whispers whenever they *talked politics*. Here, in the clear light of Sunday, sitting in the unfamiliar garden with this strange boy speaking so loudly, they feel exposed; they are afraid; they are riveted.

"I'm telling you, he's invincible. He can't be killed; they'll never catch him." (The strange, fearless boy is referring to the former commander of The Mortician's militia, who has risen against his former boss.)

. . .

"Yesterday he led his men again and they attacked the army's headquarters, just around the corner from the palace; they killed at least fifty soldiers and they all got away."

. . .

"He can turn himself into a black dog whenever he wants; they just can't get to him. Why do you think The Mortician is having all black dogs shot on sight?"

. . .

The boy is thinking that this sounds like one of Grand-père's stories, but, here again, he can't quite make out what to believe. His brother looks just as uncertain.

Only a week after the Sunday at Cécile's house, the former commander of the militia is reported captured by The Mortician's men during a house-to-house search on the outskirts of the capital. *The traitor has been apprehended by the heroic Volunteers of National Security. The traitor has been executed.* His body is to be exhibited at one of the capital's main roundabouts. The news is broadcast every hour on the hour on all radio stations and methodically shouted at all hours through megaphones by soldiers standing on speeding jeeps. Leaflets are thrown from jeeps and dark-windowed cars, distributed in marketplaces, at checkpoints, on street corners by the denim-garbed men and the sharp-suited men; piles of leaflets are left in stores and movie houses, at lottery kiosks, on church pews.

The Sunday following the announced capture and execution, the boys are in that garden again, listening to Cécile's strange younger brother.

"I'm telling you, this is propaganda. This isn't true; they're lying."

. . . (*Propaganda* sounds baffling and vaguely threatening to the two brothers; they've only ever overheard the word during the carefully whispered conversations; to them, the four syllables marshal a mixture of the repulsive and alarming.)

"He was just shot at during a clash with The Mortician's men; he was definitely not captured in some stupid house-to-house search. They shot so many bullets at him and he just laughed and wiped the bullets off his chest and threw them to the ground. Bullets can't hurt him; he's protected. He's invincible. They just ran away, these cowards, and now they're pretending they've caught him, that they've killed him."

. . .

"They'll never catch him. Never."

The boy who reads fairy tales and books from the pink collection, who has listened for endless hours to his grandfather's stories of a general's ashen ghost dressed all in white disappearing in the provincial night, stories of zombies and Erzulie, the goddess who wears four wedding bands, blue, pink, white, and gold, one for each of her husbands, stories of Zandolito, whose mother is a voodoo priestess and whose father is a werewolf, stories about encounters in cemeteries at night and stories about buried urns in the gardens of long-vanished plantations, the boy knows that the story now being told by the strange new friend whose father has been taken away in the night by the denim-garbed men is a different kind of story, but he also knows that the words are said out of desperation and anger and grief, and he sees now that tears have appeared in the corners of the strange and reckless new friend's eyes as he continues to speak, loudly, telling the boy and his brother that "bullets can't hurt that man. He is protected; he is invincible. They just ran away, these cowards, and now they're pretending they've killed him." He is repeating himself, his words now a hopeless yet defiant lament.

It will be a long time before they see Cécile's brother again. The following day, a Monday, the former commander's body is exposed at a roundabout near the airport, splayed on a high-backed wooden chair tilted and leaning against the metal pole jutting out from the roundabout's center. "He was shot days ago," the gardener's helper, the one who had told the boys about the unloved son floating in the pool, tells them when they get home from school that Monday.

"There were flies all over him and you could smell him from far away, right through the crowd."

"How did you get there?"

"How did you get to see it?"

"They came with a truck in my neighborhood this morning, you know, those trucks that carry rocks and gravel from the mountains; they made a bunch of us get on and took us down there to the city. Some of us told them we had to get to work, but they started hitting us. . . . We were all crunched up in the truck. . . ."

"Did you get hit?"

"Did they hurt you?"

"No. I went into the truck right away. There were so many people in there; we were packed in. They gave us little flags and people were singing and dancing; they were giving out bottles of rum; it was early, but so many people were drinking and singing. It stank in there. At one point I managed to get away; there were so many people, they couldn't keep all of us there. . . . I walked back to the house."

"*You walked all the way back?*"

"Yes. What do you think? I would spend my money on a *camionnette*? You think I'm rich like you?" (He sucked on his teeth.) "I got here late, but I told the Colonel what happened and he just told me to get back to work and not to worry about it."

"*There were flies all over him?* What did he look like? Did they beat him up?"

"Yeah, they beat him up all right; I think they beat him up before and after they shot him; they wanted to make sure."

. . .

The boy has never seen a dead body. He thinks of Cécile's brother and his tears, how passionately he had told the boys that the former commander was invincible, that he just laughed at the bullets and wiped them off his chest. The boy wondered whether Cécile's brother would ever go see for himself the former commander's body exposed at a roundabout, splayed on a tilted high-backed wooden chair.

Three weeks later, the bodies of two young men are displayed at the same roundabout. Another landing has taken place. Everyone knows that these young men, and the twenty or so others who landed with them in a small bay somewhere in the north of the island, had been promised help by *les Américains*, help that never came; everyone knew that they'd been left there in the mountains where they had retreated, coming down like starved dogs foraging for food in the villages below. Only these two young men survived, *to be publicly executed* near the capital's main cemetery and then splayed on two high-backed wooden chairs like the former militia commander whose troops they had fought. This time the crowds are even denser than they were for the public display of the dead commander. In addition to people from the capital and its outskirts packed onto trucks, all civil servants, professors, teachers, and their students are *invited to attend*, just like the young women who were invited by the smiling Madame Ducasse to participate in the most dazzling beauty contest ever to have been organized in the Tropical Republic. *All who attend primary schools, high schools, universities, and kindergartens are invited to attend this ceremony.* The program includes singing again; rum and food are distributed, ice cones and taffy for the young ones and the very young ones.

A photograph of the two young men shows them immediately before the execution. Their arms are tied back with rope to square wooden posts planted in the ground. There is no apparent fear in the two young men; they both look calm, inquisitive even; they look untouched, unbeaten, *untortured*, for The Mortician has invited the diplomatic corps to witness the execution of *Communist rebels, subversives who wanted to overthrow a legally elected president.* They have to be presentable; they are not disheveled or dirty. One looks to the right of the photograph, at something else, away from the camera, maybe at someone in the crowd being prevented by one of the soldiers in khaki from getting closer, perhaps to spit at the man about to be executed, or even to scratch or hit him. There is something knowing in the other young man in the foreground; he even has a slight, barely discernible smile, reminiscent of the beatific smile of the slightly mad, or the mentally deficient who sweep dishes off tables, spill water, break plates and glasses, or piss themselves but seem to know what they are doing, spiting those around them. This situation is different: This young man, who is going to be shot by a firing squad in a few minutes, is smiling the tranquil smile of the brave, with no regrets or apologies.

Decades later, when *time of exile* will have almost become just words, ludicrous even, when that event will be a faraway and muddled memory from which the boy thinks he has been released, the man he has become will see a grainy film of the execution on his computer, the two young men being tied to poles, facing the firing squad, the shots fired but emitting no sound, for the film is silent, the coup de grâce coldly and efficiently administered by a brawny soldier in khaki fatigues holding an oddly large gun, like a gun in a dream, the soldier keeping his legs efficiently apart, standing over each of them in turn and firing, the two young men's knees folding one last time, their bodies shuddering, then abruptly slumping to the ground, legs bent, head and chest forward, arms held up behind their backs by the loosely tied rope, and the man staring at the grainy film of an execution so long ago will be filled with a sorrow he did not know he had been bearing all those years. For the first time, this particular event will be real to him, undeniable, and he will sob. But it will be too late. He will have built a life where such things are kept far away and deeply buried.

The two bodies are displayed at the roundabout, decomposing in the heat day after day on two tilted high-backed chairs. A week later, when several groups of schoolchildren are taken there before their first morning class, the roundabout is bare; the two bodies and the chairs have been removed during the night. Shortly after, traffic is back to its usual madness, but as soon as it gets dark, the usually busy area is deserted. Only cars with darkened windows, their headlights turned off, or jeeps filled with soldiers pass by.

The day in the sun-drenched schoolyard

The yellow-green butterflies have come out, clouds of them expanding and contracting against the perfectly blue sky. It's been spring for some time now, somewhere in the meridian of that unnamed season in the Tropical Republic, on the day of the whistle blow in the sun-drenched yard. The boy is standing alone in front of the headmaster's office in the still, quiet afternoon. All the other boys are already in the classrooms; the priests are at their midday meal or teaching in classrooms on the other side of the schoolyard, empty at this hour. The boy opens his eyes to the silent afternoon. He is standing still, alone on one of the white tiles facing the headmaster's office, but he dares to turn his head from time to time, a solitary figure observing a deserted cityscape during a bombing alert after the screaming sirens have stopped.

The lull doesn't last. The afternoon classes have just started after the midday break, but, barely heard at first, and then inescapable, an unusual hum of gathered voices is rising on the other side of the Séminaire's tall entrance gates. Standing on his white tile in front of the headmaster's office, near the gates, the boy can hear this. The headmaster's assistant, a gangly man always dressed in a white suit that seems made of chalk powder, is the first to come out into the bright early afternoon; he opens one of the small doors built into the gates and people begin streaming in, some still diffident, others already frantic, servants and parents, uncles, aunts, family friends, their presence odd at this time of the day, for there are still hours remaining before the end-of-day bell.

"I've come to pick up my son."

"I've come to pick up André Lafontant!"

"I've come to pick up Max Du Plessix!"

"I've come to pick up the Dousset brothers!"

"Please, I'm here for my son!"

"For the love of God, let the children out now!"

The headmaster's assistant seems to be holding back an increasingly packed wave, contained but gathering on the cemented part of the yard where boys usually meet those who pick them up after school. No panic yet; there is still time, probably, perhaps. Schmitt is walking across the dusty yard, quickly—out of character for him, this haste, as he wipes his mouth with a white napkin. He is followed by several other priests, their cassocks white and folding in quick shadowed creases as they make their way across the yard to the unusual cluster of people gathering in the cemented part of the yard. The cassocks are now among the civilians; the exchanges are quick; the reason why they are all here so unusually early, the servants, parents, uncles, older cousins, aunts, family friends, must have been conveyed quickly and efficiently to the headmaster, because only a minute after the cassocks have mingled with the small crowd, Schmidtt blows his whistle three times, the emergency signal that the school day is over and that all instructors are to *initiate end-of-day dismissal immediately.*

Grand-père is suddenly there among the people who have come so unusually early; he leaves the cemented part of the yard and walks quickly to the boy, who is still standing in front of the headmaster's office. "Go upstairs;

go quickly to your classroom and get your things. Hurry up," he tells his grandson, his voice now tinged with the cold and unfamiliar urgency the boy had heard when he was told about *authentics* and would hear again when he would be asked a few days later to use his small hands to place bullets wrapped in a plastic bag in the underside of a bidet in fear of a search by The Mortician's men; the Colonel's gun would be hidden elsewhere.

One by one, the boys are taken away by those who have come to pick them up; only a very few remain among the priests and teachers as the boy leaves with his grandfather through the now fully opened gates. They drive through a muted city. The boy sits in the front seat with his grandfather; the old man is now mumbling to himself, his eyes fixed on the road. What the Colonel is saying to himself isn't clear, but he is intent on driving carefully, slowly, as he makes his way through the silent sun-drenched streets being crossed hurriedly by rare pedestrians and patrolled by militia, soldier-filled jeeps, dark-windowed cars. The first dead body the boy sees from the car, the first corpse he has ever seen, is lying in the middle of the main road that leads from the city to the house in the hills, just as they approach the last major intersection, the last traffic light before the road begins its climb toward the hills.

The car is halted by denim-garbed men standing around the body. They approach the car with a bored, leisurely walk. One bends to the window on the driver's side; others lean their faces down to the boy's window. He is certain they are about to rip open the car doors, and he squeezes his schoolbag to his chest. The Colonel smiles; there is only meekness in that smile, subservience. Seconds later, illogically, against all odds on that day and at that time, the old man and the boy are waved on but ordered off the main road, directed toward smaller streets. Several more bodies are lying on sidewalks or in the middle of streets; the tar is blacker and shinier in patches and streaks near the bodies. The grandfather continues to mumble to himself as he drives slowly through the silent streets of a neighborhood unfamiliar to the boy: houses barely visible behind nineteenth-century brick walls, hedges of hibiscus and bougainvillea, wrought-iron gates, and, everywhere, the men in denim, the men in sharp clothes and hats and sunglasses, and, sometimes, soldiers.

How are the boy and his grandfather not stopped that day? How are those two in the large car not stopped as they slowly drive through what is being played out? Years later the boy will still not fully understand. *Maybe they were too busy doing what they were doing in the houses and their gardens to pay attention to us?* This is one of his explanations to himself; he will accept anything but that *it was a miracle*. Years later, especially, the boy who simply became bored with the sacraments and the mystery, the boy who had pared down Sunday Mass to its bare, sinless essentials could not accept anything that would explain away their escape that day with such pronouncements, their getting through that late morning unscathed. He would hear such an explanation, though, in the story of that day told by a relative. "It was a miracle; they were in the car, driving very slowly; they were invisible that day; it was a miracle. The Mortician's men were everywhere; they were inside those houses. Others were left standing on the walls between the houses and the streets, keeping watch; many others were posted in the streets, holding their rifles and machine guns, stopping cars. I'm telling you, it was a miracle they got away that day."

They came later to the house in the hills for the Major

and his wife. They went there in the evening because they had *missed* the Major and his wife during the day. They had gone to the farm, where they would have *shot them like dogs*, or worse. Their leader knew the boy's parents always went there on Fridays because he himself had gone there several times recently in repeated efforts to purchase the farm, at a price he himself had set; he seemed to have particular need of that piece of land. The compound in the hills, the grandfather's property, had not provoked such specific and informed attentiveness; maybe the Colonel's age and his regular presence at the casino during those long nights into dawn had turned him into an ornamental figure, not to be feared or suspected. He was simply not on the List.

On that day, the story would begin so many times in living rooms in New York, *so many things happened*. There were different versions, differently remembered, differently told accounts, but they all converged, they all verified one another, more or less, over the years. Decades later, the boy's mother would *write that day down* for him, and mail him a letter to where he had traveled. "My very dear son, as you asked me, I'm writing these few lines to tell you about the terrible moments your father and I went through during that time." He read the long letter like an offering from another time. "It was a beautiful spring day," her letter continued; by then, the many years in temperate climes had made the naming of all seasons ordinary; like all the others living away from the Tropical Republic, his mother had lost the habit of naming only summer. "On that day, April 26, 1963, I was supposed to take you and your brother to school. Your brother had spent a terrible night; an asthma attack had left him so very feeble. In the morning, your father and I decided to take him to your uncle, our family doctor, who lived in the city. I must remind you that your father was supposed to go to the small farm we owned back then." He already knew most of this, but his mother found it necessary to repeat what was already known in order to tell him about what he might not already know. Her letter took on the quality of a testimony; she had taken her son's request seriously. "Your father always went there on Fridays, the day when the bulk of the week's deliveries of milk, eggs, and fruit took place, and he was in charge of those deliveries. I was supposed to have lunch with my cousin's wife at their house in the city, so I had the boy who helped with the deliveries go over and tell her I might be late because of your brother's asthma attack. The boy didn't return, but my cousin's husband came to the clinic not too long after. I was with your brother and your uncle in his examining room; your father was sitting on the clinic's terrace with some friends. You know how my cousin is, always very dramatic; but on that day you can imagine how quiet and serious he was when he rushed to the clinic to warn us."

Much of what happened on that sun-drenched day was in his mother's letter, but he gleaned the rest from other accounts and conversations over the next few days in the Tropical Republic and then over months and years in New York, *afterward*, especially during dinners where the recent exiles gathered in the daze and discovery of the cold, even before they saw snow for the first time, most of them, still in the daze and discovery of buildings, streets, fruit, people they had only seen at the movies or on television, accounts and conversations only whispered at first, even in the warm safety of a fifth-floor apartment in the Bronx or of a house on a tree-lined street in Queens, exchanges only whispered, even in the safety of distance, of being far from there, whispered because there were the friends and relatives still back there to think of, for who knew how far The Mortician could reach and listen, who knew what could still be done to those friends and relatives left behind? Accounts of that day and night *back there* were given more freely as the months went by, released by time and distance, all the accounts of that day completing what the boy himself saw and heard and felt on that day, and before, and after.

"On that day, April 26, 1963," his mother's letter states, like a memory repeated for a final record, the boy's mother is in the waiting room of the family doctor's clinic with the asthmatic brother; the boy's father is on the clinic's terrace, almost at street level, on a busy corner of the capital; he is talking with other men, some of them friends who have accompanied their wives or children sitting in the waiting room. The Major is on the open terrace, in the clear light of the busy day, exposed and unknowing as cars and people pass by, the street teeming with pedestrians on their errands, beggars, street vendors in this neighborhood not too far from the city center, where the attempted kidnapping of The Mortician's son has just taken place. No one seems to know yet in this neighborhood; information does not circulate very fast in that time and place when a phone call to someone overseas is an event, a time and place when, after things happen, the accounts of their occurrence spread slowly, one body to another, before gathering pace, other bodies becoming informed and aware, joining the ranks of those who know, and then fleeing to safety with the new knowledge, as they should, as they must.

The Major is talking with friends as his wife's cousin quickly comes up the few steps that lead from the street to the terrace, an out-of-breath harbinger of the end, on that day. If a particular day must be designated, it would have to be this one, the end of decades and centuries of settled generations. His words are directed at the Major, but everyone on the terrace can hear. "Don't you know what's going on? There's been an attempt to kidnap The Mortician's son; shots were fired. They're hunting down former officers, and others, too; they're going into houses; they're killing everywhere." The cousin is always a bit too dramatic, even at moments like these that seem to call for his words and tone. Since the Major doesn't quite seem to understand, he hisses in his ear, "You need to leave quickly. You need to hide; you need to get out of here now!"

The frenzied rush to hide, to disappear from the clear light of day: The Major and his wife leave the boy's younger brother, now able to breathe normally once again, with the grandfather's brother, the retired minor functionary in the railroad company, who proceeds to take the younger brother to the house in the hills, to the safety, they all think, of the house in the hills, while the Major and his wife each rush to a different hiding place. The long night follows, the men in denim and sharp clothes and hats and sunglasses going about, doing what they are doing, the long night of people huddling inside their houses, hoping, many praying, others attempting to run through a garden, to use some back alley, to run *somewhere safe*, hoping that the sound of the brakes of jeeps and cars out there in the dark street or in the noon light is an illusion, a mistake, that they are stopping for another house across the street or just a bit farther down, bodies wanting to meld and disappear into the walls, to *not be there* as the long night of irruptions into houses continues, as The Mortician's men continue doing what they are doing, the boy's father spending the miraculous or lucky night on the corrugated-iron roof of a garage adjacent to his brother-in-law's house, since it's unsafe to be inside the house during the night, as there may be searches, the mother somewhere else, safety in separation—"At least one of us should come out alive."

The following evening, the clearest option is *seeking asylum* in an embassy, which means getting past the men, cars, and jeeps posted at embassy entrances, finding a way into ambassadors' residences. Help comes from the aunt, who only months before walked in the most dazzling beauty contest ever to have been organized in the Tropical Republic; her French friends arrange for her brother, the Major, and his wife to be driven through the militia-filled streets to the Ecuadoran embassy in the French embassy's official car prominently bearing the French flag. Years later, the Major himself will be able to smile as he remembers the shaving off of his cherished mustache, the powdering of his hair, the eyeglasses and the pipe his brother-in-law, the doctor, had lent him. "I looked like some ambassador myself or some old professor as we drove through the embassy gates. I was sitting in the back with the French ambassador; your mother was hiding in the car trunk. The driver was told to just drive through, slowly. I had my gun, the weapon I'd kept after relinquishing my service revolver. I was holding it through my jacket pocket; I knew I wouldn't let them take me alive, if it came to that." Turning to his wife, who is sitting next to him in the living room of their house on a tree-lined street in Queens, he smiles and adds, "The things we went through, the things we went through back then, darling." She smiles back, says, "It's a long time ago; we were lucky."

Back then, on that day, April 26, 1963, and during the

days and weeks and months that followed, the boy was puzzled by the *diplomatic immunity of embassy grounds* in that place and time, not the miracle of it, but the logical improbability of men *busy doing what they were doing* on the other side of the hibiscus and bougainvillea bushes, inside those houses, filled with appetites and frustration, yet also kept in check by the ordered abstraction of conventions such as the *diplomatic immunity of embassy grounds*. During those days and nights, he was terrified and baffled. How could they kill in the streets and in people's houses and still be kept away from those embassies by just a gate and some bougainvillea bushes? What was keeping them out? Only later would he understand that when it came to embassies, there were limits to be respected, that unnecessarily ostentatious displays were to be kept in check. Only later would he understand that appearances had to be saved, even on that day and the days and years that followed, that there were countermanding powers at work: "If you enter our embassy, it will be considered an act of war" (this from the smaller republics to the south), or "If you do this, we will no longer be able to continue to provide you with aid, with money, with training, in our fight against the subversives; we will no longer be able to support you" (this from the Great Neighbor to the North).

Still, an unpredictable margin of error, a wordless understanding made it possible to respect the *diplomatic immunity of embassies* and yet proceed with the killing and the rest everywhere else, as long as the appearance and pretext of hunting down *subversives attempting to overthrow a legally elected president* could be maintained. Orders were officially given, but with the understanding that they were not to be obeyed to the letter, in any case not immediately, since directives could be delayed in the chain of command, such as it was, or jumbled in the bureaucratic maze of seals and signatures. The bloody momentum of unleashed frustration and individual appetites could remain unimpeded in the common knowledge that information did not circulate very fast in that time and place, when a phone call to someone overseas was an event. And so, throughout that day and afterward, no soldiers or denim-garbed men entered the embassies, no embassy gardens were trampled in the dark night by more enterprising and determined emissaries of crowds waiting outside, no bodies were torn apart by awaiting crowds as happened in the time when Roland Montrosier's great-grandfather was president, and no marines from the Great Neighbor to the North disembarked on the Tropical Republic's shores or landed at its minuscule airport. Once it was understood that there were official lines not to be publicly crossed, or else, the denim-garbed men and the men in sharp clothes could continue doing what they were doing. As long as the tacit rules were publicly respected in that time when the subversives had to be contained and eliminated, as long as the son of a bitch was our son of a bitch, as one president of the Great Neighbor to the North had proclaimed about a notorious strongman of the South, the people of the Tropical Republic were left alone with The Mortician and his men. Hiding somewhere, anywhere, or finding asylum on immune embassy grounds were the only options left, followed by departure, and then only when permission was granted, *safe conducts* issued. Some of the hunted people left days later, others months or years later, others never.

The compound was not protected by *diplomatic immunity*, but how could all those living there go into hiding? And where would they go? *Maybe they won't come here*, the boy thought. After all, the Colonel had made it through the checkpoints after he'd picked up the boy from the Séminaire; his name was apparently not on the List. The boy's younger brother had also arrived safely at the compound, accompanied by the raffish great-uncle. Why would The Mortician's men come here?

They came to the compound that evening. They had *missed* the Major and his wife at the farm during the day, so they came to look for them at the compound. The boy recalls, or assembles from different accounts, the day of the sun-drenched yard and the evening and night that followed, the exact words and gestures, the lights and shadows, the temperature and the sounds of that day, the grain of people's skin, the glint of nonchalantly held or coldly pointed machine guns and rifles, the casualness of the voice answering the grandfather that evening, as Grand-père rose from the couch, where he had been telling the boys yet another installment of *The Count of Monte Cristo*, pretending all would be fine, that they would all be fine, that the men wouldn't come there.

The first three or four materialized on the veranda, wearing their sunglasses in the yellowish light of generator-powered bulbs, holding or pointing their rifles and machine guns, irruptions from a nightmare, out of place and yet so tangible, stubbornly refusing to disappear. Grand-père tucked in his shirt and raised his waistband as he rose from the couch, smoothed down the tufts of hair on either side of his bald head, and addressed the one who seemed in command of the denim-garbed men now all over the gardens in the dark. "Gentlemen," he began, the old military reflex, the retired officer's attempt at establishing a rapport between men of similar institutions, "what is going on? Is there a thief on the grounds?" Others were already spreading throughout the house, opening doors, opening windows, looking under beds, inside armoires. Some of them were now gathered on the veranda, reporting to their leader, "They're not here. We've looked everywhere." A few of them approached the young aunt, a sniffing pack about to take her away; among them the boy recognized the lean man from the Montrosiers' garden that Sunday morning, the one who had called him a roach, no longer in his Sunday best, now wearing the denim uniform and the sunglasses. The boy remembered the voice quite well when the lean man spoke. "No, that's not her; that's the sister." Since they had not found the Major, they were going to take his wife, but this young woman was not the wife. There was no order to take anyone else for now; the Colonel would be enough, even if he was not on the List. They had come for the Major and his wife, but they would take away the Colonel—something concrete to be presented to irate superiors. And maybe he *should* be on the List. Why not?

"What's going on? Is there a thief on the grounds?" was followed by the simple and laconic answer, "No, Colonel, we've come for you," or perhaps "You're the one we've come for." After the search was completed, the leader of this particular band made the decision with a sigh of regret. "Let's go; let's just take him," and, addressing the grandfather, "Colonel, you will come with us." Grand-père was escorted out. "Remain calm, dear; just stay inside with the boys. I will be fine," he told Grand-mère. His arms were up in the air; the two boys were holding on to him, to his legs as he was being escorted toward the gate. Grand-mère was keeping up with them, asking, screaming, "Where are you taking my husband?"

There was no shoving of the lower back, no pushing of the shoulder with a rifle butt, no invective; instead, a silent and surprising awkwardness among the denim-garbed men in the garden cortège even as they determinedly continued doing what they were doing.

After The Mortician's men suddenly and impossibly materialized in the compound in the hills, after Grand-père was led out to the point near the main gate where he and the men around him could no longer be distinguished in the darkness, Grand-mère walked back onto the main veranda with the two boys and sat on a couch with them. She looked around her. Two of her children were also there, the young aunt and the dissolute uncle. The great-great-grandmother was in her room deep in the remotest part of the main house; she was sleeping; she would know nothing of this and would die peacefully a year later. The servants who were at the house that evening had also gathered on the main veranda. Ada was carrying sandwiches for the boys; Marisa, the severely religious laundress, was crying and praying; the old gardener sat on the steps and pulled on his pipe. Only the youngest uncle, the one with the thick head of hair, was not there, and this was what Grand-mère focused on now, a way of getting through this hour and the next.

"Where is he? Where is my son?"

"Madame Colonel, he went out just before dark. I'm sure he's fine; he'll be back."

. . . (Grand-mère looked for a long time at the old gardener who had just spoken.)

"Yes, he went next door to George's; he'll be right back," offered the young aunt, who was still thinking of the sniffing pack gathered around her just a few minutes before.

All of the *pensionnaires* were now arriving on the veranda. It was a cool night; Debbie and Cynthia were wearing sweaters; the young American family, Mr. and Mrs. Salloway, Mr. and Mrs. Becker, and Dr. Silverstein looked odd in this part of the compound, where they were almost never seen, and never seen all at once; they looked like guests at a cocktail party in some wood-paneled stone house in the suburbs of Connecticut. Mr. and Mrs. Salloway's suntans glowed in the yellowish light; Debbie and Cynthia's father spoke to the grandmother in his accented French and asked about what had happened. Grand-mère's voice was a thousand years old.

"They just took him away. Who knows where they're taking him."

"I'm sorry; there was nothing we could do. Did they say where they were taking him?"

"I don't know; I just don't know."

"*Je suis désolé, madame, vraiment désolé.* I'm sorry; I'm so sorry."

. . .

"Do you have any idea where they've taken him?"

. . .

The Colonel's wife remained absolutely silent. Not saying the name of the place was a way of holding out hope. Those who had been taken to that place were never seen again, and if they were seen again, it was always too late, so the grandfather could not possibly have been taken there. He must have been taken to another one of the jails or army barracks, to another place; maybe they would understand an error had been made and would release him even before they arrived anywhere.

The youngest uncle had just returned; he sat next to his mother, rested his elbows on his thighs, his hands cupping his face, and looked down at his knees. His mother did not question him; she only looked at him, her relief was so great. This was about the time when the *pensionnaires* all left; there was something awkward now, indecent even, about their presence on the veranda with the family; the first to leave were Debbie, Cynthia, and their parents, then the two retired couples, followed by Dr. Silverstein; Ada remained with the family, the two boys now sitting on either side of her on a small sofa. Among the servants, only the old gardener remained, sitting on the steps leading to the veranda, a valiant and futile sentinel.

After that day and that night, everything became clear

After that day and that night, everything became clear, even to people like the boy's uncle, the accountant in a construction supply company in the city, the one who loved Chopin and always said he would never leave, no matter what turn politics might take. "Where would I go?" he had asked when they were still in the bright lights of the most dazzling beauty contest ever to have been organized in the Tropical Republic. He still would not leave now, not even after that day and that night, but everything had become quite clear to him.

After that day and that night, it became clear to everyone that the time of the most dazzling beauty contest ever to have been organized in the Tropical Republic had only been a reprieve, even if the signs had still been there for anyone who wanted to see them. The occasional shootings had already begun, the sporadic disappearances, the killing of that man by another man with power to the tips of his nipples for a parking spot, the disappearance of Cécile's father because he was a distant relative of one of those *subversives* who had landed on a moonlit coast in an attempt to overthrow The Mortician's *rightful, duly elected government*. The yearning for pleasure and permanence was so strong in that time and place, as it is in all times and places, that the end was still not clear under the bright multicolored lights shining on beautiful young women in evening gowns and high heels, or bathing suits and high heels, parading around kidney-shaped swimming pools in the fragrant night, while the denim-garbed men, so lean in their ancient, now exacerbated appetites, and the sharply dressed men, with their well-fed voices, were already talking to peasants about their fine plots of land and their now grown daughters, or entering shops in the city to ask for their due; it was still not clear back then, which suddenly seemed so long ago, that a day would come when there would be no going back, that reaching the haven of foreign embassy grounds or hiding somewhere, anywhere, would be the only way out as the real unleashing began.

Curfew has been declared. *Curfew*, another strange word to the boy. At the compound there is enough food stored for normal meals; breakfast, lunch, and dinner are served at the usual appointed times. A bakery has remained open, where the boy gardener is sent for fresh bread early in the morning, before the day's supply runs out. Schools are closed; the boys would not have been sent anyway, lambs to slaughter. Should they hide them as the men in denim continue doing what they are doing in those days and nights? Where would they hide? Perhaps simply send them somewhere else? Maybe to the Major's father in the city below? A friend's? An uncle's, or an aunt's?

That first night, a night when for the first time in his life the boy cannot fall asleep, his younger brother breathes heavily and regularly on the other bed, exhausted by his recent asthma attack. For a long time, the boy thinks he hears car doors closing, or footsteps in the garden, coming up the stairs to the veranda, until he finally falls asleep.

In the already clear light of the following day, the boy and his brother sit at the breakfast table with their grandmother, their young aunt, their youngest uncle, and their dissolute middle uncle. Coffee is poured; bread is buttered. No decision is made. It becomes clear that they will not venture beyond the wrought-iron gates, out there where the streets are empty but for the cars and jeeps passing by, or the odd truck ferrying rocks, gravel, and sand from the quarry in the mountains above. Each time, every single time, they all hope neither car nor jeep will stop. No peasant women come through to take their baskets off their heads and spread their tomatoes or oranges for sale. No decision is made at the breakfast table. As safe or as exposed here, it seems, as anywhere else. And how to get anywhere else, in any case? They will just wait.

"Eat. You need to eat." The grandmother is speaking to her children; her two grandsons are already eating. Even during those three days and nights when no one in the house knows what is really happening beyond the gates, the pleasure of butter on warm bread remains. The boys eat with the eager appetite of children, even if they know that everything has changed.

The blurry passing of those three days and nights, whether recollected or assembled. Some things stand out. On the first day, the servants, who would not be immediately noticed and stopped, are the only ones to take a chance on going outside; they come back with encouraging reports from an aunt about the Major and his wife, "They said to tell you that they made it to the Ecuadoran embassy." The youngest uncle's thick head of hair is shaved off; he has asked his friend from next door to do it, staunch and dependable George, who has come to the house to be with his friend, whose father has been taken away by the men in denim; George has complied with the youngest uncle's request and also shaved off his own hair. The two young men look diminished, sullen and defiant; their skulls are a dark green-gray. They walk through the gardens together in their loose short-sleeved shirts; there is something medieval about them, or even older, martyrs from biblical times. The boy looks at them and remembers those black-and-white pictures, the emaciated bodies from the concentration camps in *Historia.*

On the second day, the aunt who lives not too far away with her Chopin-loving husband comes with him to the compound. She has always been the willful one. Her decision had been made and she communicated it in one quick flow to her husband. "Come, let's go see my mother. Let's go see them. They're all alone over there. We'll speak to those people at the roadblocks; we'll get through. We'll leave the girls with the maids; they'll be fine." Her husband, as always, listened and obeyed, and he drove their small Renault through the almost deserted streets of the town in the hills, past the church square and up the road leading to the mountains, and they did get through to the compound. They all hug one another; no one cries. Grand-mère explains in her measured way, in very few words, that the servants have been going out, that they've come back with news; the men in denim are everywhere. Her daughter interrupts her. "We had to stop at three roadblocks; they searched the car each time." Grand-mère continues: No news of the Colonel has reached them; the boys' mother and father have made it to an embassy, the Ecuadoran embassy; they're safe.

They all sit down to eat. They talk about when schools will open their doors again; they talk about the unusually cool weather, about anything but what is being done out there beyond the wrought-iron gates. "We must hope for the best. We'll see." These words keep being said. The boy's grandmother remains quiet; she stretches out her fingers in that elegant feline and feminine way and looks at her fingernails, at the ring with its dark aquamarine stone surrounded by small diamonds and the wedding band on her fingers; she sighs a deep and neutral sigh. The boys look at each other and at the others around them, who seem ravaged by some disease that leaves no discernible marks; they all seem depleted. *Something has ended*, even if no one at that moment, sitting around the long mahogany table with its embroidered tablecloth set for any such meal on any such day, even if no one around that table in that exact place and time can think such encompassing thoughts.

Immediately after the meal, the willful aunt and her Chopin-loving husband get into their car for the short drive back to their house before it gets dark. The others remain in the compound with its gardens and trees, and its pool, where the Beckers are now collecting their towels after hours in the sun. The day is waning, and then the sun sets, abruptly, as it does in that part of the world.

The evenings do seem much cooler than usual; even the days seem cooler. Lucy and Ricky, the cowboys and the police cars have vanished from the television set; they are now replaced by the Tropical Republic's flag endlessly ruffling against a background of a blue sky and the national anthem. As it gets dark, the boys and the others gather on the large veranda and put on one of the Colonel's records. They listen to Lucienne Delyle, one of his favorites, sing songs from long ago and from the other side of the Atlantic, songs about broken hearts, longing lovers, deceitful lovers. The accordion and the violins accompany a husky woman's voice singing about the quays of Paris in the fog, a fog the boy imagines is similar to the fog that enters houses up in the mountains above, "*J'attendrai*," "I Will Wait," an old song from decades before, or another song about passionate lovers, as the needle makes its scratchy path along the grooves, "I Was Drunk on His Kisses," followed by another song played over and over again during those nights as the bats perform their mute dance over the pool, "Darling, in your embrace I want to hold you tighter, I want to feel the imprint and the warmth of your body, darling, lost in your arms I already feel that your embrace is lying," and the reader of fairy tales and books from the pink collection is lost in those songs already becoming part of the indelible sound track of those days and nights when the news is so uncertain as they all wait for the waiting to break.

On the third day, in the early morning, the grandfather unexpectedly appears in the compound's main alley in soiled trousers and a shirt much too large for him, and no laces on shoes also much too large for him. The former colonel, the former second in command of the armed forces of the Republic, the former consul of the Tropical Republic in Miami, looks wan and gray, unwashed, unshaven; this is what the boy notices most: the soiled, unfamiliar clothes, the broken shoes, the unshaven face, the gray-and-white bristles that give the storyteller, the initiator into the pleasures of wine and butter, a sinister, slightly repulsive look.

"Don't touch me; let me take a shower. Let me just go in." (This in a weary voice to his wife, who has come rushing to embrace him in the same hibiscus-bordered alley at the end of which he had vanished in the dark three nights before.)

. . . (His wife, who wants to embrace him, is perplexed.)

"I'm fine; let me go in; let me just go take a shower."

The boys, the servants, the unloved son, the favored son (his gray-and-green skull a strange relic of the past few days), the young aunt, and a few of the *pensionnaires* have gathered around the Colonel and his wife, silent onlookers, relieved, eager to hear, eager to know. "I'm fine. Thank you, all of you; I'm fine." And he goes up the stairs leading to the main veranda, followed by his wife, into the hallway, and into their bedroom.

In the dining room, where he sits to eat an omelette prepared by Ada, Grand-père has shaved and is wearing fresh clothes. He seems to have lost weight; he looks like a patient just out of the hospital, with the fragile bearing of those who have been through a serious illness, or an amputation. The grandmother has prepared a bundle and asked the old gardener to burn the soiled clothes and the shoes. "Make sure you burn them; don't give these things away to anyone." The Colonel eats with appetite and smiles at the boys. Still, he tells them all nothing. When his empty plate has been picked up and taken to the kitchen, alone with his family, he tells them about the caravan of jeeps and cars filled with the denim-garbed men, the sharply dressed men wearing hats and sunglasses, the several stops made in the night, the entry into other gardens and other houses while he sits between two of the denim-garbed men in the parked car, and then with two additional prisoners ("What else can I call them?"), all of them taken to the prison fort in the city below, near the airport, to the place where they had all hoped he would not be taken. He tells them about the stripping to their underwear and socks, the piling into cells, no one daring to speak.

"The one man who spoke was hit with a rifle butt; his jaw was broken. He was taken to another cell; I never saw him again. We were about twenty in my cell; only four could lie down to sleep at one time, so we took turns; there was only one small window too far up to be reached; fresh air came in through that window, but at one point one of the others in the cell said, 'The night train is coming,' and a swarm of mosquitoes came through the window."

. . .

"There was a bucket for us to do our business in; the mosquitoes went straight for the corner where it was kept; it didn't smell good in that cell; some of the other prisoners had been there for a few days already. We were all waiting. I recognized Pierre Dougé there and Philippe Keller; we looked at one another, but we said nothing."

. . .

"A uniformed guard brought us some food at dawn, and again when it got dark—a thin soup for breakfast and for dinner, nothing in the middle of the day. We all had to use the two spoons we had in the cell. I resisted for the first two days, but then I was too hungry and I ate my share."

. . .

"This morning, when it was still dark, they came for us, for all of those in my cell. Some of the others from other cells were asking the guards where we were being taken; the guards didn't hit anyone, but no one answered. We were led out of the cell and started to go through a door; I could see a large courtyard on the other side of the door; we could hear commands, and shots being fired. A man stopped me, not one of the ones in uniform or one of the men in denim; he was wearing a jacket and tie and a hat. He took me aside; he said to me, 'Colonel, what are you doing here? This is not a place for you; come with me.' We walked through some dark hallways, cells on either side, and he said to me, 'You don't remember me?'"

Years back, the man had been all but a beggar. As a last resort, he had gone to the commanding officer of the provincial town—not to his office, but to his home. There had been something desperate about this man, the look of those who would die soon. Grand-mère had the cook serve him a hot meal, polenta and herring, and gave him some of her husband's old clothes. They sat, the three of them, the officer, his wife, and the desperate man, now fed, and drinking one of the officer's rum drinks; they sat on the front veranda of the small house where the young officer was stationed, and they talked. The man left with some money and a letter for one of the officer's friends in the capital, and they never heard from him again.

At the breakfast table, the grandfather didn't tell them about something else that had occurred during his days in the prison fort. The boy would only hear in New York about the small, brightly lit room with the bloodstained walls, dark blood coagulating on the already dirty floor and walls, or still bright red from the recent session, the grandfather sitting on a stool, two men standing over him. "The short one came very close, screaming in my face. He smelled of sweat and rum and he kept blowing smoke in my face; he slapped me once, without asking any questions. The other one made a fist and was about to continue, but another man came into the room; he made them stop and asked me to leave with him."

Only the first version, censoring the part in the bloody cell, is recounted at the breakfast table on the morning the grandfather comes back from the fort prison on the outskirts of the capital. The versions have something in common: The man who provided the Colonel with the stained pants and shirt and the too-large shoes and told him to leave quickly was only "someone I helped a long time ago; without him, I would not be here."

Yet another version would make its way into conversations in New York, in the time of exile. It was not a man the Colonel and his wife had helped a long time before that early dawn in the fort prison; it was not thanks to him the Colonel had made his way back, walking through the capital's deserted streets, crouching behind parked cars or hiding under arcades when he saw the large American cars or the jeeps trundling through the still dark streets, finally finding an early *camionnette* to take him to the town in the hills—"I will pay you all the fares; don't stop for anyone else. Just take me there"—it was, instead, Debbie and Cynthia's father, "*un agent de la CIA*," who had intervened.

Debbie and Cynthia's father had gone straight to one of The Mortician's closest advisers and explained, forcefully, that the Colonel was not involved in politics, that there would be *repercussions at the highest level* if he or any member of his family was harmed in any way. He also explained that the message should be conveyed to The Mortician himself.

The American with the hair that always seemed wet, a pale furrow of separation where it was combed to the side, his wife, who wore sunglasses that curled up at the sides, and their two blond and freckled daughters would all leave the Tropical Republic a year later. They were never heard from again and it would never be clear to the boy whether it was the man who had gone in desperation to the Colonel when he was only a young officer in a provincial town so many years before or the man who was rumored to *work for the CIA* who had made it possible for his grandfather to come back home alive.

Two days after his return from the prison fort, Grandpère sits with the two boys on the veranda in the yellow glow of the generator-powered bulbs and tells them about the streets of New York, where *fine grains of glass are mixed into the cement of the sidewalks and eat up the soles of shoes.* He also tells them about the size of that city, how one can ride an underground train, *le subway*, for a whole hour, and still be in the city. He tells them once again about the time he was consul in Florida and about manicured green lawns and *Automat* restaurants, where you insert coins and lift small glass windows to get to cheeseburgers and hot dogs, and he tells them about that street in Manhattan where twenty cinemas stand next to one another or face one another, *all on the same street.*

For the first time since the day in the sun-drenched yard and the night that the men in denim and suits and sunglasses materialized like a nightmare on the veranda, the boy sleeps through the night and opens his eyes in the clear light of day, his brother still sleeping, breathing regularly in the bed next to him. When the two boys sit down at breakfast, the grandfather, the grandmother, the youngest aunt, the youngest son, and the unloved son are all already there.

"Your parents will be leaving for New York the day after tomorrow. They received permission; it's called *a safe conduct.* I have a safe conduct, too, but only to take you to see them at the embassy."

"Where's the embassy? Are they waiting for us?"

"Are we leaving with them?"

"I will take you myself this morning."

"But are we leaving with them?"

"Finish your breakfast and go get ready. Ada, go help them get ready. Come on, let's get started."

. . .

The two boys attempt no tricks behind the closed bathroom door that morning; the games of evading their showers belong to another time. They come out of their bedroom well scrubbed and combed, wearing Sunday clothes. Their grandfather drives them to the Ecuadoran embassy; they sit next to him in the front. This is the first time they have gone beyond the compound's gates since *that day*. They pass the church square, the steeple red and clearly delineated against the blue morning sky. The streets are still empty—only a few street vendors, no schoolchildren. The car is stopped at several checkpoints—from afar, full bodies standing on both sides of wood or metal barriers, then parts of bending bodies, shoulders and faces at the car windows; the sunglasses, the rifles, the machine guns, the guns up close. The safe conduct is produced several times, examined several times, followed several times by the swift and imperious wave of a hand. *Go ahead. You're good for now, but just you wait. Another time; we'll see.*

About halfway down to the city below, Grand-père turns off the main road; he drives through the still, quiet streets of yet another neighborhood where the boy and his brother have never been. He stops the car at the gate of a house they can't see from the street. Some men in denim, some in uniforms, and some others in jackets and pants, hats and sunglasses stand at the house's gate and throughout the quiet, narrow street, where a few cars and jeeps are parked. The creased safe conduct with its stamp and signature (violet ink, thick letters, curlicues) is produced by the grandfather, and then unfolded once more, this time by one of the men in civilian clothes, who takes his time, looking up at the sky as if watching the flight of passing birds, pausing several times in his reading of the two or three lines before handing the refolded safe conduct back to the grandfather, whose hands have remained on the steering wheel throughout. After the inspection comes the almost whispered pronouncement in a voice at once certain of its power and annoyed at the obligation to abide by the written directive; a contained desire to do harm, curbed by another authority, but still imperious where it can be. As he hands back the folded piece of paper, the man says in an even voice, "You can't go in; those two can; you will wait here for them." The grandfather knows there can be no question, no additional words, or the man will find in any word a reason, some justification for a slap, a punch, a gun butt, in spite of the official safe conduct. "Get going."

The boy opens the car door and goes through the house's wrought-iron gates with his brother; they walk through the garden, a long alley of grass and cobblestones, bougainvillea and hibiscus bushes, several palm trees and almond trees, bunches of yellowing fruit hanging from tall mango trees. At the end of the alley, a large gingerbread house stands, bordered by two sets of stone stairs leading up to either side of the front veranda; a servant opens the main door. After the ride in the car and the walk through the garden, the two brothers enter the sudden coolness and shade of the house. A smiling South American man is in the vestibule, at the bottom of a flight of shiny wooden stairs. He must be the ambassador; he seems at ease, at home. “Come in, boys, come in,” he offers. Their mother and father stand behind him, the two of them in borrowed clothes, their father looking even odder without his mustache; their mother quickly kneels down to take both of them in her arms, holds her two boys tightly, kissing them and murmuring, “We’re fine, we’re fine. How are you both? I’m so happy to see you.” The Major and the South American man stand aside with two other people: a tall, imposing man with a thin mustache like the one the boy’s father had until a few days ago, and a striking woman, not quite as tall as the man. They both look so terribly sad; they look spent; they, too, seem dressed in borrowed clothes. They smile wanly at the two boys; they look like they’ve been scooped out from within. The boy is looking at them through his mother’s hair as she tightly embraces him.

The embrace is over; their mother turns to the man and the woman.

“This is Colonel Brierre, and his wife, Madame Brierre; say hello to them.”

. . . (They shake hands with the man and kiss the lady.)

“They also had to leave home; they’ve been staying here these past few days, too; their room is upstairs. We’re all leaving for New York tomorrow.”

. . .

No one knows what to say. The ambassador calls the boys’ mother and father by their first names, his voice a signal of the return to time passing. “Maybe you want to be alone with them? Why don’t you use the office? I’m sorry, boys, but we have very little time. You’ll have to leave very soon; this is all we have time for.” The ambassador’s office seems cramped; rows of books line one of the walls, a fan hangs from the high ceiling, a big desk has been pushed against one of the walls, and next to it two mattresses have been placed on cases of champagne and whiskey. The Major and his wife have been sleeping there for the past four nights. The Major's voice is unusually mild.

"The ambassador has been very kind; he's been taking good care of us. He'll be driving us to the airport tomorrow."

"Can't we leave with you?"

"Why can't we all just leave? Why?"

. . . (Their father has no words and looks to the boys' mother for help.)

"It is not possible for now; you will stay with Grand-père and Grand-mère at the house. You need to finish out the school year; we have to get your papers ready. Grand-père will take care of this; don't worry. You will join us later. Don't worry. We'll be fine."

. . . (They already knew they wouldn't be leaving with their parents; Grand-père had explained this in the car, on their way to the embassy, but it seems impossible to them that they won't all be leaving together, even though they know that everything has changed. Still, both of them had to ask, to be sure.)

"You have to be strong." (The Major appealing to the old bond between men.)

"You look strange without your mustache." (The boy wanting to respond to that appeal by sounding like he doesn't care.)

"I know, but don't worry, it will grow back."

Their mother tells them that the Brierres *have lost everything; they've suffered terribly.*

The four of them are in the room with its desk and

cases of champagne and whiskey and shelves of books for just a few more minutes, just a moment, and then they walk out of the ambassador's office. They hold and kiss one another one last time. The boys leave with a servant, who leads them through the garden but stops at the gate. The grandfather is waiting in the car, his hands still on the wheel; he watches the gate open, smiles at the two boys, and leans over to open the car door for them while the man in civilian clothes and the ones in denim look on. Grand-père drives away, slowly.

At the time, no one tells the boys what happened to the Brierres, to the tall, imposing man and his striking wife, why *they have lost everything and suffered terribly.* They're able to gather the story in increments from listening to *les conversations des adultes* over the following days and weeks, as the schools open again, as the street vendors and the crowds of people reappear. They put the story together from accounts and conversations after they have left the Tropical Republic, whispered, even in the warm safety of the fifth floor of some building in the Bronx or of a house on a tree-lined street in Queens, in the safety of distance, of being far from there.

Old enough to bleed, old enough to be slaughtered

Brierre had been a classmate of their father at the military academy; his wife was an old friend of their mother; they had all attended many of the same gatherings over the years. On the day of the whistle blow in the sun-drenched schoolyard, the jeeps and the cars stop in front of the Brierre house in one of the old neighborhoods of the capital. They have come to this particular house, at this particular time, for this particular family; there is no error. Some of the men are posted in the street; others are told to stand guard on the old stone walls, armed and bristling shadows against the bright sky; the rest enter the garden and head for the house. Like so many others, Brierre and his wife are in hiding that day; they, too, like the boy's father, have been told, "What are you doing here? Don't you know what's going on? They're going into houses; they're killing everywhere. You need to leave now!" The Brierres quickly left wherever they were, like so many former officers of the army of the Tropical Republic.

Two maids and a gardener are shot down by the first men to come through the wrought-iron gate of the Brierre house; the men then spread quickly and slowly, like figures in a dream; they are now beyond the veranda and inside the house; Brierre's father is picked up in his wheelchair and thrown out of one of the bedroom windows on the house's second floor; he lies still and broken on flagstones among almonds and leaves brought down by his fall through the trees below. Downstairs, the Brierres' newborn baby is wrenched from his grandmother's tight embrace, the old woman's feeble arms unfastened by other quick and sinewy arms and hands; she's told to join her husband; she's taken upstairs and pushed out the same window. The boys would hear stories about the Brierre baby never being seen again, about strange and violent rituals in the white presidential palace. Withdrawing his finger from the undressed adolescent daughter whose throat has been slit, one of the sharply dressed men says, "Gentlemen, she was a virgin!" Another one adds, "Old enough to bleed, old enough to be slaughtered." The house is burned down. They leave. They continue their rounds. They continue doing what they are doing.

For the boy, beyond everything else that happened and could have happened on that day, what happened at the

Brierre house would be more encompassing, more tenacious than everything else he has witnessed or assembled, even if throughout the years that followed he would keep the men's *visit* to the Brierre house, like all the other *visits* to all these other houses, deeply buried, and, decades later, when *time of exile* will have almost become just words, ludicrous even, when what happened at the Brierre house on that day of the whistle blow in the sun-drenched yard, when the things these men had done in that house, to the people in that house, to the old man, his wife, to the young woman who was found *old enough to bleed and old enough to be slaughtered*, what had been done especially to her but also to the gardener and the two maids who were the first victims as these men were entering the house's garden, to the baby whose disappearance was never explained, when what happened in that particular house on that particular day will be a faraway and muddled memory from which he thinks he has been released, when the man he has become will have built a life where such things are kept far away and deeply buried, what occurred in the Brierre house that day would rise like a lone figure in a deserted landscape, appearing once again above all the brutal but leveled memories of that day.

The boy's mother did not mention the Brierres in the letter requested by her son years later. She had spoken about them several times before then, either prompted by a coincidence, the mention of someone's name from that time, or answering her son's direct questions about the man and the woman from those few days at the Ecuadoran embassy. On those occasions, she remembered all the details quite well, but this letter, sent decades later, was devoid of slaughter; it was written with the restraint and formulaic quality time provides, the quality of memories smoothed down by time and words. "Four days after going into hiding, we left; we went into exile. We were so sad to leave our country, our children; we had to leave everything. We were taken to the airport in the ambassador's car with a safe conduct. On the plane taking us to New York, two agents of the CIA came to speak with your father [when reading the letter, her son couldn't ask her how she knew the two men were *des agents de la CIA*]; I advised him not to speak with them, for fear anyone would harm my children and my family." CIA agents on a plane talking to political refugees on their way to the United States: It was that kind of time, a time when a simple band of armed and determined men could change the fate of countries. The Great Neighbor to the North had to keep a watchful eye on all parties concerned, on all factions, those who seemed in power, those who seemed to be challenging those in power, which side they were on, to what extent they could be counted on, how to keep track of them, when to support one or the other, when to make a promise, when not to keep it, even at the last minute, the eternal juggling of interests from the time of old empires, from the very beginning. The boy's mother did not think of such things; her agony was simpler, more intimate. "You can imagine how we felt, having to leave you behind, at such a time, with everything that was happening then."

From the exiled couple's first year in New York, a photograph shows the boy's mother in a pale green dress; she is wearing heels and holding a handbag; her husband stands next to her in a dark suit and a hat. It must be winter, or a very cold autumn day; they're both wearing gloves and hats, but their coats are slightly open, probably for the picture: a couple of the early sixties that still looked like the fifties, standing on a street corner in temperate climes where the seasons change. "Your mother had lost so much weight while waiting for the two of you to join her and your father in New York, she looked like a model," said the aunt, who was looking through the photo album with him in the living room of the house on a tree-lined street in Queens, years after the boy's own arrival in New York.

Good-bye, everybody

It would be seventeen long months—April to September, and then an entire year to the following September—before the boy and his brother could leave the Tropical Republic and join their parents in New York. After three weeks of school closings and curfews, stores started to open at regular hours; once again, peasant women from the mountains would stop and come into the compound to sell their fruit and vegetables; Lucy and Ricky, Ethel and Fred, the cowboys and the policemen regained their place on the television screen, replacing the flag and the national anthem. A few visitors came by, always before nightfall. It seemed as if the family that remained at the compound had been forgotten or neglected by the blood and the unsated appetites, but the boy's dread of the braking jeeps and cars would not relent.

After schools reopened, there was the strange, awkward reencounter with other boys. Sides were more clearly drawn now. There were the families that had been put on the List, those who had been targeted, visited by the men in denim and sunglasses (two of the seats in the boy's classroom were empty); there were those who just wanted to be left out of everything, to be left in peace (the delusion of that time); and there were those whose families belonged, or probably belonged, to the new order. The boys all shared the same routine but were now wary of what could be said and what should be kept quiet in the aftermath of those days and nights when *they had done what they had done.*

The routine of the Séminaire's days now seemed useless to the boy, living as he was in the anticipation of departure, of leaving everything behind. The boy, who had always been one of *the first in the class* when report cards were distributed, who had always been assigned one of the seats in the last row of the classroom reserved for the very best students, quickly found himself sitting somewhere in the middle. *Why should I learn all this? Why should I care about the memorizing and the exams?* Even the panoply of punishments was now emptied of any potency. Still, he maintained a semblance of respect for the routine and the rules, just enough to remain inconspicuous, to avoid punishment, to avoid confrontation. *Just pretend; it's about to end.*

But it took seventeen months. There was the tail end of the school year, the long summer, followed by school in the unnamed seasons. Throughout that time and until he and his brother stepped on the boarding stairs of the plane bound for Miami and then onward to New York, until the smiling stewardess in her uniform and jaunty little cap that looked like a soldier's, but in pale blue, took them to their seats, until that day, their first time on a plane, until the cabin door was closed, the smell of air-conditioned coolness and airplane fuel replacing the smell of the warm air and burning firewood and overripe fruit, until the plane started taxiing, vibrating as it accelerated, until the whole countryside—the fields of sugarcane, mango trees, palm trees, coconut trees, and peasants' huts—was turned into a passing haze by the plane's unleashed speed, followed a few seconds later by the lurch of being lifted from the ground, until the horizontal multicolored blur outside the cabin windows turned into the tilted sea as the plane's ascent continued, until the sails of small fishermen's boats became no more than dots in the turquoise blue of the bay and the darker blue beyond the bay, until the brown eroded mountains speckled with rare clumps of trees below suddenly became whole and visible in all their vastness, until then, until he was sure they would not be returning to the airport, until then, the boy dreaded the jeeps and cars and the men they contained, the jeeps and cars that would not just keep passing but, instead, would once again stop at the compound's gates, not another house, but this house, coming for you and no one else, no mistake.

Whenever it looked as if the things that had happened on the day of the whistle blow in the sun-drenched yard would start all over again, the two boys would be driven to the other grandfather's house in the city, *quickly and quietly*—"Ada, pack a few clothes together for the boys; we're leaving now; don't say anything to anyone!"—or driven to a friend's house in the town in the hills, or to an aunt's summer house in the mountains, where the red soil, the cold evenings, and the clouds that entered though the balcony made it feel like another, faraway country, Switzerland perhaps.

In the interlude between the day of the whistle blow in the sun-drenched yard and their departure, the two boys' movements are even more regulated than before; the two frail and privileged boys' bodies are even more sheltered and cherished. "You have to understand; we want to make sure you're safe," or "No, you cannot go to the square on your own or even with your aunt, or your uncle; it's already getting dark; go tomorrow, another day. Yes, you can spend the day at Paul's, but I myself will drive you and I'll pick you up at four; no, you cannot walk back on your own," or "Your parents are counting on us; think of your parents." The two boys usually comply; besides, they are already living in the expectancy of a place where red-cheeked boys in jeans, wide-striped T-shirts, and baseball caps live in leafy suburbs with flagstone paths and green lawns, where wood-paneled station wagons are parked in the driveways of flat, angular houses, with their blond women wearing high heels and neatly tied aprons, pull glowing, perfectly roasted brown turkeys out of shiny white ovens, and the weather changes from spring to summer to autumn to winter, flaming red maples in the fall, snow in winter.

The boy and his brother are propelled by the preparations for another life, the boy more so than his brother. The grandfather is determined to get them ready for that other life. On Saturdays, for an hour or so, they sit at a desk on one of the smaller verandas, where English lessons are dispensed by Grand-père, beginning with the basic infinitives, "to have" and "to be," about which he tells the boys that "*thou art*" is hardly ever used. Among the other preparations, *les préparatifs du départ*, the brothers are taken to the dentist, their first visit, "because you can't imagine what dentists cost over there"; besides, it's also a condition for obtaining the required medical certificate. Bodies being readied for the necessities of another climate, another realm, to be pricked with the polio shot, another requirement, the minute puncture turning into a purulent sore only a few days later, even if the two brothers had obeyed and had not gotten it wet, had not gone swimming in the pool, had kept the arm out when they took showers, the sore turning into a scab, the scab taking weeks to fall off, a raised round scar replacing it on each boy's thin arm.

Closer to the day of departure, they are taken to the photographer's studio, the same one who had photographed the boy for his First Communion; this time it's for the passport photos, and since they are still young enough, a single passport for both boys, their photos glued next to each other on the same page of the passport with the multicolored cover, black and red, with a green palm tree flanked by other, more martial and Mortician-specific emblems of the Tropical Republic, the upper blue strip of the old flag now replaced by the upper black strip of "*the Revolution I have started*." Late in the second summer, the two brothers are taken to their appointment with the American consular officer, who speaks to them in French but sounds like Mr. Becker, or Broderick Crawford, the police chief from *Highway Patrol*. And then they are ready.

For the grandfather, it is a given; it is a consecrated truth that he will be the one to accompany the boys on the journey, that they will all leave together, the two boys, Grand-père, Grand-mère, the young aunt, the youngest uncle, and the dissolute son.

"I want to return you to your parents. I want to say to them in New York, 'Here they are! Safe! Mission accomplished!'" (The old military reflex surfacing, but also the theatrical and sometimes sappy storyteller.)

"Yes. And you'll take us to the Bronx Zoo and to Macy's, *the world's largest department store*." (Knowledge accumulated from the English lessons dispensed during the Colonel's class of two on the main veranda.)

"And let's not forget the Automat on Forty-second Street."

"Absolutely."

But there are delays for the Colonel and his family; their visas will not be ready until a few months after the two brothers' departure in early September. It is at about that time that the rumors of another landing start; yet another group of determined young men has disembarked somewhere on the shores of the Tropical Republic, making yet another attempt at overthrowing The Mortician. Years later, well before she sent him the letter he had asked for, the boy's mother would say, "You can imagine how we felt, so far from you; and everyone knew they were about to start again, that the children of ex-officers were in danger, that the whole thing would start again. And you two were ready to travel, ready to leave, and he was sulking! He wanted to be the one to bring you here! There was no way. And he knew it, but you know your grandfather; he had to sulk; he likes to have his own way." The Colonel, the logical man trained as an engineer, the one who has built and extended the family compound over the years, who can systematically win at poker games until dawn and explicate algebra problems for his grandson, is also a sentimental man blinded by the joyful spectacle he has anticipated.

On the morning of their departure, the boys go to Grand-père's bedroom in their long pants, starched white shirts, and shiny Sunday shoes. They are going to be accompanied by their father's brother, who can travel freely despite such a close relationship to their father, who had been put on the List, who had taken refuge in a foreign embassy, and had ultimately fled the Tropical Republic. This uncle has inherited his father's fiery temper; he has refused to pay the tributes; he has thrown out of his store a man in frayed but impeccably ironed gabardine pants and jacket, a man wearing the ubiquitous hat and sunglasses that signal his affiliation with the new order, who has been making hushed but pressing demands on one of the cashiers: "I'll take that television set now; I'll come back to pay next week," or perhaps "I've come to collect the new tax." The uncle has pushed him through the opened door and into the street, adding a few words about the man's mother in the process. Such behavior is impossible, *a death warrant* in the time of The Mortician's rule, but a former friend of this uncle is now highly placed in the recently established hierarchy; like so many others, this man has joined the new faction; he, too, is sharing in the spoils and has taken to wearing the fancy clothes and sunglasses, but he has continued to protect the unpredictable and reckless man he still considers a friend from afar. The uncle will be replacing the grandfather in accompanying the two boys to New York to reunite them with their parents.

Sitting up in the large bed, propped up by pillows like a convalescent, with the curtains drawn, Grand-père refuses to come out of his bedroom to see the boys off. The Colonel is capable of the most dramaturgical behavior, small but cunningly constructed tableaux, arranged with the same care he applies every year to the Three Kings' itinerary below the Christmas tree. The two boys go through the scene of farewell in the half-light, reassuring him that they will soon go to the Bronx Zoo, to Macy's, *the world's largest department store*, and to the Forty-second Street Automat together. And they mean it; they sympathize with the old man even if they know he's wrong, as he knows he's wrong, as much as he wants to take them to New York himself, a kind of homage paid to his efforts, his dedication to his eldest daughter's two sons.

Even during this farewell, the boy is rehearsing in his mind what he knows of that place where the chief of police of *Highway Patrol*, the righter of wrongs of *Have Gun Will Travel*, where Lucy, Ricky, Fred, and Ethel have come from like fruit spilling out of a horn of plenty, and also Mr. and Mrs. Becker, the Salloways, most of the *pensionnaires* throughout the years, Debby and Caroline and their parents, the square-jawed and unshaven GIs making their way through ruins in the European countryside in war films seen with his father, where all those men and women in their coats, hats, and gloves live, as well as the city fifty times larger than the Tropical Republic's capital, New York, where the world's largest department store is, the grandiose city where fine grains of glass are mixed into the cement of the sidewalks and eat up the soles of shoes, Manhattan, where there are twenty cinemas next to one another, facing one another *on the same street*. He is already there and has gladly relinquished the life he and the generations before him have known, a life coming to an end in the time between the whistle blow in the sun-drenched yard and the day of departure: The interlude that began in slaughter and ended in the cool air and the kerosene smell of the departing airplane has severed him from the generational pull of his time in the Tropical Republic. He feels sorry for the grandfather, but he also feels the future in the instant and would not have stayed another minute in the darkened room or anywhere else in the Tropical Republic. Standing there in the bedroom with its drawn curtains, going through the ceremony of farewell, he has already left. During that time, in the excitement of leaving, nothing remains of the bliss of all the years that preceded the slaughter.

The two brothers also say good-bye to their other grandfather, who is lying in a hospital bed, the stubble bristling and white on his dark, unshaven face. "My boys are leaving, my boys are leaving," he murmurs as they bend down to kiss him, knowing he will not see them again. They are already enfolded in the excitement of leaving, and he is stubbornly refusing to have the kidney stones that cause him such excruciating pain removed because a fortune-teller had told him, "You will die by the knife." A few months after the boys board the plane for New York, he will die of the infection caused by the stones, the first to die of the generations the boy has known in his own time. His wife will remain in the city with their youngest son and youngest daughter, in the house where he had slept apart from her for so many years. The boys also visited her there before leaving. She, too, will die after the two brothers leave the Tropical Republic, less than a year after the husband who had forsaken her.

The boys say good-bye to all the servants and gardeners; they say good-bye to aunts and uncles—handshakes, kisses, and embraces. They're taken to the airport by their grandmother and Ada; the chauffeur drives. Their grandfather, listless in the shade of his bedroom, is not there; his solitary mise-en-scène continues while, at the airport, the small group is met by the young aunt who once paraded in the most dazzling beauty contest ever to have been organized in the Tropical Republic, and by her older sister, the cross-eyed aunt who walked that bowlegged walk because of the polio she had as a child, the brilliant one who told the boy, "*C'était des assassins, ces gens-là, les Nazis.*" Her eyes cannot be seen behind her sunglasses and, as she often does, she takes over; she organizes the small group's movements through the different stages that precede departure. She tells the chauffeur where to take the suitcases; she tells her nephews that the time has come to join their uncle in the line for registration and passport control.

It is a time when the movement of bodies at airports is far from the carefully controlled and obsessive choreography to come in later years. Those who are saying goodbye to travelers can still get very far, beyond bag check, beyond passport control, and, sometimes, even quite close to the tarmac, smelling the same airplane fuel smelled by the travelers and the ground crew, kissing and hugging one last time or waving handkerchiefs from concrete terraces open under the sky and the weighty white clouds, where they can watch the travelers make that final crossing in the sun, amid the smell of airplane fuel mingled with that of overripe fruit and hot, moist air.

The two boys dutifully follow the uncle; stiff and proper, they cross the tarmac in the already hot day; they start climbing the grated metal steps to the airplane; the propellers are already turning; they follow the smiling stewardess into the coolness of the cabin.

The same story of arrival told countless times

At the end of that day, the boy sees the great city's lights from far above, a treasure chest of countless white and orange points glittering in the dark. The same story of arrival told countless times, this time with the variations of his own time and place: getting out of the plane—"Don't forget anything, boys"; waiting in a vast neon-lit hall, the uncle—this time it's an uncle—opening and handing over passports once again to men in dark trousers and white shirts sitting behind glass panels; the uncle and the two nephews picking up their suitcases and emerging into yet another hall packed with a waiting crowd, finding among all these people the familiar faces they haven't seen in so long, their mother's tight embrace, then their father's, the four of them looking at one another, their mother's tears as she says, "My sons, my sons . . . You see, I told you we would be fine; we're so happy to see you, my boys; come, come! Let me kiss you again," their father, composing himself, saying, "Let's keep moving; let's go to the car"; the hundreds of cars lined in neat rows in the well-lit parking lot, the drive through the night on the well-lit highways, the reassurance and the words between them and their parents, the uncle remaining silent, the well-lit streets after the well-lit highways, the car stopping in front of a five-story building in the Bronx. "Does the whole thing belong to us?" the younger brother asks. "No, many other families live here." The group climbs the five flights of steps with the suitcases. The door to the apartment is open. The apartment is filled with friends and relatives who've come to celebrate the two boys' arrival, all of these friends and relatives, including the Colonel's eldest son, the fortunate pioneer who left the Tropical Republic years before, all of them gathered in that apartment on the fifth floor of a building somewhere in a place called the Bronx. The boy immediately notices the bowl of fruit filled with peaches, grapes, plums, summer fruit in that part of the world, rare and exotic fruit to the new arrivals. A meal follows; everyone is seated around the dining room table and at individual folding metal tables so completely new to the boy, still so common at the time in New York, already relics from the fifties.

At some point, the friends and relatives leave; it's already late, close to midnight. The boys have rarely ever been awake at this time. The difficulty of falling asleep—"Let's stay awake the whole night"—but then they're overtaken by sleep anyway. In the morning, their father has already left for work; their mother has asked her employer for the day off to be with her sons. They unpack together; they tell her about their time after she left; she asks about Grand-père, Grand-mère, the others, when they will be coming. Later, she takes them to the movies to see *A Hard Day's Night*, playing in a double feature with *The Island of the Blue Dolphins* at the De Luxe Theatre on Tremont Avenue. Even if he understands almost nothing of what was being said in either film, the boy will never forget the long strumming guitar note and the screams of running girls that trigger *A Hard Day's Night*'s breathless black-and-white rush and flow—the Beatles have landed in America; the fifties are finally ending. Intermission: Their mother buys them popcorn, "and anything else you want." After the second feature in the dark theater, the mother and the two sons she hasn't seen in so long emerge into the full light of day on the crowded avenue as the boys' first day in this immense new city continues.

Even if the surprise and the excitement remain intact for a long time, the humbling awkwardness of the first few months is unavoidable. The apprenticeship of living in a new country takes its course: The language remains strange at first, in spite of the grandfather's efforts on the veranda back in the Tropical Republic—"thou art" is indeed very seldom used (never, in fact), but there is so much else the boys don't know. The void at first, and then only the gaps of all the words not understood. The gaps are quickly filled during the first weeks and months, even as the exciting strangeness continues: their new school; the absence of priests in their wine-stained robes, and the perplexing presence of girls sitting next to them in class; the teachers and those boys and girls looking like people from the magazines the two brothers have leafed through and the television shows and films they have seen; the two of them, right hand on chest, mouthing, "I pledge allegiance to the flag of the United States of America, and to the republic for which it stands," not understanding much of it at first, only wanting to be like all the other boys and girls.

On the first day of school, just two weeks after his arrival, the boy's class is deployed in the schoolyard for gym. Two teams are formed by the already enterprising and dominant boys; he is given a strange and unwieldy leather implement that looks like a gladiator's weapon and is told where to stand, "out there." He goes through the motions of a game he knows nothing about, *softball*; boys standing, boys moving; he imitates them, crouching, shoulders bent, looking alert and ready, his small fist punching the inside of the implement fitted to his other hand, as he's seen the others do, and he does manage to fool everyone for a good while. A ball is thrown repeatedly at a player from the other team until he hits it with a wooden club; other players on his team keep still, run, throw, while he safely remains in his part of the field, understanding nothing of what is going on. For a while, the ball never comes to him, until, fatally, it does, and he knows enough to run to it and grab it as he's seen the others do, but then he can only watch as a player from the other team runs and keeps running; other boys on his team are screaming at him, and he finally throws the ball to one of them, to any one of them, anything to get rid of this ball now lying heavy in his hand, but it's too late, as the exultant boys from the opposing team gather in one group, jumping up and down, and the gym teacher walks over to him, shaking his head, sympathetic, not screaming, not reprimanding, but asking him to "go sit over there, okay?"

In the first weeks and months, there is the first outing to Manhattan, thousands of people walking up and down Fifth Avenue and all the intersecting streets and all the other avenues; there is the discovery of *strawberry blond* hair worn in the bouffant so common at the time, and the discovery of puddles turned to solid ice in the streets, snow falling from the sky and muffling all sound. For the first time in the two boys' lives, they experience the thrill of moving unaccompanied through the crowds and streets of a city, of being unnoticed.

In the apartment on the top floor of the five-floor building the younger brother thought belonged exclusively to their family, a new life begins. When the younger brother asks where the parents go all day, the boys are told about the *factory* where the mother sews two halves of skirts together and the other *factory*, where the father sews labels onto shirt collars. "*You know how to sew?*" the younger brother asks the first time the boys are told about factories. "Well, I didn't," their father replies, "but you learn very fast; anyway, it's only for a while." Walking to school, a short distance away, coming back to an empty apartment, the strangeness of watching their mother cook when she comes back from work, of their bedroom being so close to their parents'. A new life, a closeness they have never known before; meals taken together at regular times around the Formica table in the kitchen; the two boys and their father going to the supermarket on Saturday mornings and then to the greengrocer's. During the first few months, they are told to choose whatever they want. By Monday or, sometimes, Tuesday, the boys have consumed everything new to them: the small boxes of cereal, twelve of them in a single pack, each one with a different kind of cereal—press along the perforations with your thumb, pull up the flap, and pour the milk right into the small box; the incredible variety of candy; the mounds of apples, grapes, pears, those exotic fruits. Their parents look on; sometimes, in the middle of the week, after work, they go back to the supermarket and the greengrocer's and replenish the supplies.

New arrivals, new exiles from the Tropical Republic come to visit after that first night, increasingly more of them as The Mortician's men continue doing what they are doing. The conversations about this or that landing are whispered in those early days, for who knows what could still happen to those left behind, and when the boy's mother and father go to the movie house on Tremont Avenue with a few friends to see the film starring a glamorous Hollywood couple playing star-crossed lovers against the bloody backdrop of the quite recognizable Mortician's Tropical Republic, now so well known, now so notorious after being confused for years with some paradisaic island in the Pacific, the boy's mother and father and their friends wear hats and sunglasses or even masks to hide their faces. Among the exiles there is the knowledge, perhaps just the paranoid rumor, that The Mortician's men, posted somewhere near the theater entrance, are writing down the names of those who are coming to watch that insulting, unpatriotic, malicious, and calumnious piece of garbage financed by Communist sympathizers, subversives who, even from abroad, are attempting to overthrow the legally elected president; their families and friends who are still in the Tropical Republic will *suffer the consequences.*

The Romanian doctor who removes the boy's tonsils during his first winter in New York, and subsequently becomes a friend of his family, thinks his parents and the other exiles from the Tropical Republic are right to wear hats and sunglasses, or even masks, to go see the film. "These people, where you come from and where I come from, they are capable of anything; you are right to take precautions; we were lucky to be able to leave, and so were you," he tells the boy's parents. With some luck, with some connections and duly displayed regret and humility, he himself would have been allowed the privilege of being a window washer back in Bucharest or perhaps a sanitation worker in a small village in the countryside. "In my country, too, these things have been happening for years. They're happening now; it's getting worse." There are others who arrived, from Hungary and from Czechoslovakia, months before, years before; now they are brought by the Romanian doctor to the apartment in the Bronx for a drink, for a meal with counterparts from the other side of the world, all of them, the ones from Eastern Europe and the ones from the Tropics, bemused, once they have exchanged stories, by the blind callousness of the strategy of "He may be a son of a bitch, but he's our son of a bitch" or baffled by what they consider the foolhardy or romantic or privileged or simply idiotic and cruel blindness of some of the people in this rich country who still believe in the promise of a workers' paradise back there on the other side of Europe, in the gray ancestral landscapes these exiles left, that they had to leave behind. Exiles, refugees, immigrants in the apartment in the Bronx exchanging stories, old stories, of leaving and arriving and of the time it takes to be whole once again in the place of arrival, as if this were ever really possible.

Three years later, after the family has left the fifth-floor apartment in the building in the Bronx, his mother is no longer taking the subway in the early morning to the factory to sew together two halves of skirts, and his father is no longer sewing labels onto shirt collars and has bought a new car, the family moves to a house on a tree-lined street in Queens. People and things still look like they have been pulled from a Norman Rockwell painting or have emerged fully formed and in Technicolor from the grandfather's large television set in its beige casing: Mrs. Murphy, an old Irish neighbor with blue hair, plaid pants, and a manicured French poodle; Mr. Masini, the Korean War veteran, his crew cut and jazz record collection; the cars still large and girded in chrome; the trees with yellow and flame orange leaves in autumn; frozen ponds in winter. He has not been to Sunday Mass for as long as he can remember, and passing by the reputed butcher shop on Parsons Boulevard, the teenager sees the last president of the Tropical Republic before The Mortician's arrival, the military man who appeared a decade before on the front cover of the famous newsweekly wearing a bicorn, his upper body sheathed in a gold-emblazoned uniform complete with epaulettes, his imperial upper body rendered in robust browns, black, and gold against a background of the faintest green-and-blue wash of hills, now an old man buying his Thanksgiving turkey in his new country, a gray and shrunken figure wearing a thick dark blue winter coat, a lustrous gray hat, and heavy gold-framed glasses, reduced and fragile but cosseted in his expensive coat, nonchalantly handing one of the butcher's assistants a five-dollar bill for carrying out his just-bought turkey to his chauffeured car, butcher boy and former leader emerging onto the sunny, busy boulevard as autumn is turning into winter on this late November in the heart of Queens, New York, USA.

PART II

The World Out There

A second chance—that's the delusion. There never was to be but one.

—Henry James, "The Middle Years"

Friday, December 15, 1972—and before, and after

On this cold and gray December morning, Robert Carpentier is on a train on his way to Meerlo, a village in Holland. The last mushroom-colored buildings of Paris are quickly replaced by the small stone *pavillons* of the suburbs with their red tile roofs and fenced-in gardens. Then come the fields of the countryside, sprinkled with an unusual early coating of snow. Carpentier hasn't seen snow since the previous winter in New York. He must be twenty-one, twenty-two years old, not much more, and this is his first year in Europe. In Paris, in this city he already knows but has never seen, where he knows no one, he goes to encounter the reality of people and things previously experienced only in books and films, taking him further away from the determination of birth, blood, place, and time; away from the past. A second chance.

The jeeps and cars come to a standstill in front of the main gate of the house in the hills right after nightfall, but the sun seems to still be shining brightly in the sky, round

and white and malevolent. Men in denim or shirts and pants, or suits, all wearing sunglasses, all carrying rifles, pistols, machine guns, emerge from the cars and jeeps.

He has left Paris for a few days during the winter recess, and he's on this train from the Gare du Nord to visit Margrit van der Berg, gray-eyed and thick-haired Margrit van der Berg of Meerlo. They had met in the early fall, before classes started. They found themselves the only ones standing in front of Chardin's *The Ray* in the closeness of a recess in one of the Louvre's long and resonant wood-floored halls.

Robert Carpentier can't take his eyes away from the insides of the ray exposed in their creamy mix of white, red, and pink rawness; he's oblivious to everything else in

the painting: the scattered oyster shells, the snarling cat, the jug of water, the bunched table linen, even to what seems to be the ray's thick-lipped and beatific smile. As if in a trance, he speaks to the young woman who is also looking at the painting, the only other person here with him in front of this strange, radiant, and shadowy assemblage of things from another time. "Doesn't it remind you of Soutine's carcasses?" he volunteers. He doesn't mean to alarm her, he doesn't want her to think he's *trying anything*, but he just had to say something. She turns from the painting and looks at him as if his face and body were one. She smiles, and answers him as if they'd been speaking for hours, in a living room or a bedroom or a café; she seems so sure of herself, even a bit arrogant, maybe challenging him to something, "Yes, I see what you mean, but, you see, given where I'm from"—she offers this like a riddle—"I prefer to think he continues the best of what the Flemish painters did, people like Abraham van Beijeren or Jan Davidszoon de Heem. . . ."

The French sentences are spoken with almost no accent. The corners of her gray eyes are crinkling; she continues to smile as she speaks in her challenging way. The throaty Dutch names, the way she switches from French to that language Carpentier hears for the first time in his life, what she is saying, her confident and playful tone, all of this moves him and he forgets about Chardin and the ray, the oysters, the hissing cat; he would like to continue to speak with her for days and also to take off those thick black stockings she is wearing, and the plaid skirt and black turtleneck that make her look like a schoolgirl.

"We met under the sign of Chardin," he would say to her when they were in bed in his room at the student residence later in the afternoon. Robert Carpentier came late to sex; his experience was quite limited for someone of his place and time, an outsider, an aberration even, in the crowds of feasting bodies released from the confines of the fifties and the sixties when they still looked like the fifties, so that the words he first speaks and continues to speak to the young woman standing alone with him in front of Chardin's strange painting come not from familiarity or calculation but from a more potent muddle of inexperience and desire.

"From Holland, then." He knows there can be no other place, as she continues to smile and look at him. He can say no more. His heart is pounding and fills his chest. And then he manages some words, adding, "Well, we can stay with your people *and* with Soutine, too; think of *your* Rembrandt's *Carcass of Beef*; it's also here at the Louvre. So we have French Chardin *and* Soutine *and* those others. . . . I won't even try to repeat their names." Her eyes continue to smile and she looks at him as he looks at her; they take each other in completely, eyes and bodies and mouths speaking words. "Would you like me to show you some of the paintings from *my* people? Would you like to see?" "Yes," he replies.

And so he follows her through one of the great halls, to another section of the Louvre, almost empty on this Sunday afternoon in the first years of the seventies, while the thousands and thousands of people walking about in the afternoon light of Paris in autumn forgo the museum and enjoy the last fine days before the sky settles in its low winter gray and the drizzly rains begin. They prefer to be outside under the still bright sky, those people sitting on the metal chairs of the Luxembourg Garden, their faces turned to the still warm sun, thousands and thousands of them strolling on the avenues or on the banks of the Seine, so many of them who have already been countless times to the museum being discovered by the new and untried arrivals in Paris, Robert Carpentier and Margrit van der Berg.

He follows her in the nearly empty museum; she leads and ushers him into *her* sixteenth century, into *her* seventeenth century, as she says; they go together to see *her* people, to see, one by one, *Still Life with Lemon*, *Still Life with Carps*, *Still Life with Ham*, *Still Life with Candlestick*; they can't stop laughing and, at one point in what they are now calling "The Still Life Tour," he proposes "*Still Life with Baguette*!" and she says, "Why not! There's often bread in these paintings; and why not *Still Life with Cockatiel*, or *Still Life with* whatever you want . . . Or even this, look, *Two Monkeys Stealing Fruit from a Fruit Basket*." She also tells him about the death and decay beneath the color and opulence and about other signs and meanings buried in the passing of three, four centuries, but he remains fixated on the plush colors and ornate arrangements of cheeses, lobsters, oysters, hams, flowers, and fruit gathered on the thick folds of tablecloths. Although he clearly hears her, he won't allow himself to see beyond the brilliant surfaces; in his impairment, even the heads of dead deer and the bodies of hanging pheasants remain merely rich adornment, detached from any violence, part of the pageantry of a world that is not at all his, and this is how he wants it to remain. Then the tour is over, and they go back to the Chardin in the alcove, to the ray with its beatific smile and its insides spilling out.

As they both stand in front of the painting once again, he asks her, not turning to look at her, "Have you ever read Proust?" He vaguely realizes his question can sound ludicrous, pedantic, but he means it in earnest; all of this is new to him. He himself started to read the long novel the previous year and is only now reaching the third volume; the passage he's thinking of at this moment is about *The Ray*, from a shorter work, something Marcel Proust had written about painting and that one of Carpentier's professors in New York had told him to look up. On his very first walk in Paris, he'd stumbled on the short book at the top of a pile in one of the stalls by the Seine, and he'd come to find *The Ray* at the Louvre on this early fall Sunday. "Yes, of course I've read Proust," she replies. He feels a bit chastised, but his heart is no longer pounding; he feels as if he's entering a house where he's never been. Then there is no going back, and he asks, "Would you like to go with me to my room and I'll read something to you, something he's written about this painting?" Her answer is simple, immediate; she seems suddenly emptied of any guile. "Yes."

On the way, they have the wisdom and the restraint—the luck and acumen of their age?—to stop for whatever food and wine they can find on a Sunday afternoon, when Paris becomes a provincial town; not quite the closed shutters and Sunday Mass of a village, but it seems all stores are closed, people left to their own devices, unfastened from work and the daily tasks of survival. In his room, afterward, he reads the passage to her; he reads to her about "this strange monster . . . the beauty of its vast and delicate structure, tinted with red blood, blue nerves, and white muscles, like the nave of a polychrome cathedral." After reading the passage, he asks her to speak to him in Dutch. And she does, her head resting on his arm; he understands nothing; maybe she's reciting a passage from a book herself, maybe just whatever comes to her mind. Then they find each other again on his narrow bed as the long, early fall day finally shifts into night.

Margrit is only in Paris for a month; she's come for an

intensive course at the École Camondo and will return to Holland in October. "I'm studying architecture, like my father," she tells him. They talk about what he's doing in Paris, the Dutch school system, the École Camondo, Soutine, Chardin, especially *The Ray*, and the Dutch painters again. They agree that he will go visit her in Holland during the winter break.

In his compartment on the train from Paris to Meerlo, there's only one other passenger, a young man a few years older than he is, glowing in his suntan in late December, who looks up with interest as Carpentier inserts his travel bag in the metal rack above the seats. The young man immediately proceeds to tell Carpentier that he's from Lebanon, then asks, "Where are you from?" Carpentier sits by the window, across from the young man, who seems intent on talking. Carpentier welcomes the company; this is his first trip on a train, a real train going from one country to another. He answers the young man's questions, tells him about his scholarship to study in Paris. "I'm good for at least three years."

The young Lebanese speaks breathlessly, as if he, too, needs the comfort of conversation. "You know, Lebanon is beautiful. Beirut is the Paris of the Middle East," he says with a chuckle, adding, "I know, it sounds like advertising, but I'm sure you've heard this somewhere: *You can be swimming in the Mediterranean in the morning and be up in the mountains and go skiing just a few hours later.*" "No, I didn't know; I'm sure it must be beautiful. Where are you going in Holland?" "Getting off in Amsterdam—end of the line; I'm selling vacation packages to Lebanon. After Holland, I'm heading for Belgium; these people in the north just can't wait to have some sun and sea after their crappy winters."

As they continue talking with the abandon of people new to a place, seeking company, seeking comfort, the young man opens a leather-bound binder filled with articles in French, in English, in German, and glossy color photographs of golden beaches, olive groves, blue skies, farmers in wide-brimmed straw hats holding out bunches of grapes or enormous peaches; there are also bell towers and minarets and crowded nightclubs where men and women in elegant evening clothes are crouching, kneeling, clapping their hands around belly dancers on shiny dance floors.

A few years later, Carpentier would wonder about what happened to him after the killing started, what happened to the young Lebanese guy in his striped bell-bottoms and longish hair and sideburns, carrying his thick binder of golden beaches and snowcapped mountains—"*You can be swimming in the Mediterranean in the morning and be up in the mountains and go skiing just a few hours later*"—what happened to him in the bloodshed that followed, two, maybe three years after they'd met on the train from Paris to Amsterdam, when the soldiers and the militia and the snipers became unavoidable in his imploding country and, in their wake, as always, the fleeing civilians, the flaming buildings, the ruined cities and devastated villages.

Meeting the young man on that train, Carpentier's *first real train trip*, was an opening onto wider, unknown vistas unrolling before him as the past receded into flawless memories of childhood, outings to the mountains, outings to the sea, incredible stories of faraway places recounted in the coolness of recent nightfall before the sudden irruption of brutality. The images contained in the young man's binder, Mediterranean summers of elegant men and women at nightclubs, farmers tilling a fertile land and holding up the richly hued fruits of their labor, were confirmations that the flawless past of childhood could perdure elsewhere, that its kingdom could be never ending, as long as one kept going forward, sloughing off a particular part of the past. Even after the killing started in the young man's country of olive groves, snowcapped mountains, and sandy beaches two or three years after the meeting on that train Carpentier had taken to see Margrit of Meerlo, he would maintain his blind surge forward. Only many years later, sitting at a meal among people he had avoided for so long, people he loved, as much as he was capable of this, but people he had tried to leave behind because of their own affinities with the damaged past, would he finally understand.

Before his departure for Paris, there had already been that other bloodbath, that *quagmire in the Indochinese Peninsula*, a conflict so much closer to Carpentier's own concerns, even if it definitely had nothing to do with his presence in Paris, since, there again, he'd refused to see, since he'd been entirely unable to acknowledge the implications for him of the war raging on the other side of the world, even as a lottery was put in place by the government of his adopted country to determine *who would go next*. There were 366 blue plastic capsules containing the birth dates to be drawn in the country's first draft lottery, 366 rather than 365, the extra one to account for the variations of leap years; therefore February 29 had its own blue capsule, thus 366 blue plastic capsules, and according to the supposedly random and impartial system, it so happened that Carpentier and the other young men who shared the same birthday would be if not among the very first, then quite close to the first of successive waves of young men to be introduced to the ways of warfare at Fort Polk, Camp Lejeune, or Parris Island, or elsewhere, and then, not too long after, sent to fight and kill or be killed on the other side of the world.

At first, and true to form, Carpentier refused to see how close to the first wave he was, until the conversation with his father in the kitchen of their house sometime after the start of the draft lottery, his father, who did not want to see him go "over there," almost imploring in the kitchen, an uncommon—in fact, an unprecedented—tone for him. He was determined to have a conversation with his elder son, who was about to leave New York for Paris and seemed blithely unaware of his place in the lottery. The lottery results were what they were. Carpentier didn't care; his time hadn't come yet, but his father wanted him to acknowledge how close his spot was in the rotation. He had never heard his father speak like this. "I don't want one of my two sons to die in some rice paddy or some jungle out there. Why go all the way out there to fight people who've never done us any harm? This isn't like the Nazis," he offered, like evidence in a legal argument, a fact that couldn't be denied. Unlike this elder son, Carpentier's father had understood and taken notice and watched with increasing but concealed anguish as the war continued in spite of the protests, the marches and confrontations across the country, the days of tear gas, days of rage and bombs, cracked heads and worse, in spite of shots fired on a campus in the heartland, four college students killed by the National Guard, body bags returning from the other side of the world, while his son's birthday and age brought him closer to that moment when it would become impossible to pretend, to not see.

The words didn't come easily to the diffident father, who found it hard to speak to the two sons he cherished but with whom he could not have more than brief exchanges. The fondness and esteem they all felt were always kept in check; this was the way it had been with them since the boys became adolescents and then young men, his wife always the emissary, the go-between, but this evening, as they were about to drive to the airport, he could not avoid a conversation with his elder son, who was leaving for Paris. The exchange in the kitchen began with an innocuous remark about the weight of his son's suitcase, his son's reassurance that it was fine, exactly the allowed weight, followed by another comment about whether he had enough money or not, the son's continued and terse reassurance before the older man blurted out what lay at the heart of his uncharacteristic outpouring of words, words he could only say as if he were being rude or impatient, all the love and concern cloaked in apparent gruffness.

"What are you going to do if you're called? Maybe it would be better if you didn't come back?"

. . .

"This is something you have to think about; you know that, don't you?"

. . .

"I know," Carpentier replied after a moment. He was already not thinking of this at all, but of leaving, of the night crossing over the Atlantic, of leaving New York and of arriving in the city he already knew but had never seen, Paris, where he would know no one, where he would be alone; the decision to go *die in some rice paddy or some jungle out there* or not was relegated to some indefinite future. He would not face either the new violence brought up by his father or the past violence that had led to his family's presence in New York.

They did embrace at the airport, the embrace of a

reserved older man and his distant firstborn, both unaccustomed to such displays, but this was a moment and a contact they couldn't avoid this evening, as the elder son was leaving for who knew how long. His brother was also at the airport to see him off, an aunt and uncle had also come, and his mother, too, bravely smiling. Years later, she would tell him how heartbroken she was. "You can't understand; you will only understand when you have your own children one day. When we took you to the airport that evening, I said to myself, Here we are, separating again." But now, her face close to his, on the evening of departure, she said only, "Write to us. Call us. Call us as soon as you get there if you can."

As he was leaving home and during his first few days in Paris, Carpentier believed it was quite possible he'd never see any of them again, that he was leaving them forever in his wake, leaving everything behind, the determination of blood and clan, and the past. He was like a thief, stealing away from a depleted house and unsuspecting innocents.

They are all tall and lean; some of them have wings that unfold and shed a few feathers as they emerge from the cars and jeeps; some are also holding silver tridents; some are smoking cigarettes whose orange tips glimmer in the weird dusk. The smell of cigarette smoke, incense, and rose petals fills the bright darkness. From the gate the house looks like a lantern filled with the glow of candles, like the churches and cathedrals built during the Christmas season by the same boys who build kites during the windy weeks of Lent.

Away from tribe and place, away from home and friends

Away from tribe and place, away from home and friends. Paris is the second departure, the second severing, but here, this time around, on this entire continent, he knows no one from where he was born. Once again, he goes through the intact and substantiating ritual; he goes to meet the reality of things and people experienced only in books and films before. He is basking in the encounter.

On this first trip out of Paris since his arrival, his first trip by train, he feels unbounded. The winter fields and villages of Europe pass by: tree-lined roads in the mist; gray steeples towering over the clustered houses of ancient villages in the hills; children either going to school or already returning—it's late morning, so who knows? He takes it all in; the conversation with the young Lebanese guy on his way to Amsterdam has intensified his exhilaration. To meet him here, in a train compartment, with his catalog, on his way to sell golden beaches and olive groves to people of northern cities who yearn for the sun during their gray winters, to meet him and have this conversation with him seems like more tangible proof of a greater world out there that he can only go to encounter alone, far from tribe and place, just as he had met Margrit in the Louvre's resounding halls, Margrit of Meerlo, the girl he is going to visit in her village in the south of Holland. Clan and place, family and home are left behind, obliterated.

At the small train station in Meerlo, he's surprised to be met not only by Margrit but also by her mother, father, and younger brother—the family, again, but under a different guise this time, not his family and thus new and thrilling and unscathed. All four have bicycles; Margrit is holding on to the handlebars of an extra bicycle for Carpentier.

The air smells like the countryside; a few cows are grazing in a field right next to the station; smooth cement, tar, and concrete, and then, suddenly, dark furrowed soil. Another Europe, different from Paris, this provincial train station in Holland. The encounter with Margrit at the Louvre comes back to him, their romp through centuries of her people's paintings; here, as he steps off the train and walks toward the Dutch family, there is no framed heap of fruit, there are no grapes and peaches, plums and cherries strewn about, defying the laws of gravity, no stately pinkish ham, no dead pheasants hanging upside down, no cluttering oysters, no wine-filled glasses and silverware or the sanguine orange of a lobster's carapace, all laid out on the rich folds of a tablecloth, but, in his daze, Carpentier feels he is at the core of something that he alone is the first of his tribe to encounter as he walks toward Margrit and her family, the four of them, half sitting, half standing on their bicycles, one foot on the ground, inheritors of the burnished colors and pageantry of an opulent tradition, its founding violence so removed as to be invisible, buried; all of Europe here, ensconced in its peace and wealth, gathered on the platform of this provincial train station in Holland.

Once the introductions are made, in English, for they all speak English—"This is a friend from Paris, Robert Carpentier; he's studying art history at the Sorbonne"—after Carpentier's small travel bag is secured to the back of his bicycle by Margrit's brother, they all ride to the van der Berg house, on the periphery of Meerlo, somewhere between countryside and suburb. It's a modern house, angular, with a smooth concrete façade and large rectilinear glass panes; it seems out of place in this lush countryside hemmed by fields that smell of manure.

They all sit around a rectangular table of light wood and thin metal legs in the expansive kitchen; they have tea and coffee; they spread butter and an assortment of jams on thickly sliced dark bread. They are polite; they smile; the father asks about his studies; the mother, who now speaks to him in French, asks him about "his past." As he begins to answer, she interrupts him, quite politely, almost gently: "Before Paris, before the United States." As he continues, she seems to have found something she was looking for, confirming something she suspected, but of which she was not quite sure.

She glances at her husband just as Margrit is asking Carpentier whether he would like to go for a walk, and the father immediately suggests that the younger brother accompany them, "so he can also benefit from the Parisian's presence," as he puts it with a smile. After a walk around the village, Carpentier, Margrit, and the younger brother return; they pass through the kitchen and then the living room. "We're back; Robert and I are going to go upstairs," Margrit calls out to her parents in English; the parents are both sitting on a gray leather couch in front of a slate fireplace; they smile, and the father suggests Robert might want to play a few games of ping-pong in the playroom; the younger brother can go upstairs with them. "He'll show you where the balls and rackets are; you never know where they are, Margrit." After the younger brother hands them rackets and balls from a wooden chest in a corner of the room, Margrit and Carpentier play several games of ping-pong in a large sunny playroom with a skylight. The portly Dutch clouds pass overhead; the light begins to fade. The younger brother shows no sign of leaving them alone for even a minute, and, a few moments later, Carpentier, who is not invited to stay overnight, is taken by car to the train station; he will catch the last train going back to France that evening. Carpentier and Margrit will write to each other for a few months, but they won't ever see each other again.

A week after he returns from the trip to Meerlo, the long winter break is still on; classes won't resume for another two weeks. Having left Paris once again in the early morning, Carpentier is now driving straight through Germany in a borrowed clunky Renault that the previous owner, a student, will eventually tell him to keep because he can no longer afford the gas and constant repairs. Carpentier is driving with two friends—Nikos, who arrived in Paris in early November, even though he had been admitted to the prestigious Athens Polytechnic, and Claire, Nikos's girlfriend, an English student in Paris for the year. Nikos has met her only recently, at the very English pub set up in the basement of the Collège Franco-Britannique, the student residence where Claire lives. The Collège Franco-Britannique is a very short walk from the Maison du Maroc, where Carpentier and Nikos have their rooms at the student residence campus in the south of Paris, an extensive garden-filled agglomeration of dorms, dining halls, playing fields, even tennis courts and a theater. Carpentier thinks Claire speaks like Miss Jean Brodie, a teacher at a boarding school in the film with that English actress, Maggie Smith. Claire could easily afford her own apartment, closer to the center of Paris, but, she tells them, the residential campus was her choice. "I wanted to see what it's like; Mum and Dad were quite angry." After Claire had told her mother on the phone about the boy she was seeing in Paris, her mother gasped, "A Greek! Really, dear, next time, someone white, please?" Claire tells them this while they're having lunch in the main dining hall. It has remained with Carpentier, this crisp little sentence somewhere between appeal and injunction from the upper-crust English mother to her daughter in Paris, doing God knows what with this Greek. Nikos has light brown hair and a mustache the same color. *Does he have to be pink*, Carpentier wonders, *and have red or blond hair to qualify?* At his residence hall, where most of the students are from Morocco, they usually speak to Carpentier in Arabic and are always surprised when he tells them, in French, that he doesn't understand; at first, before they knew him, before a few of them became his friends, they looked at him, puzzled, some walking away shaking their heads. Carpentier wonders what Claire's mother would make of his indeterminate appearance.

The walls of the Maison du Maroc's large lobby are decorated with arabesque motifs in wood, stucco, and tilework. At either end of the lobby there are small painted tables, a few stools, and armchairs inlaid with mother-of-pearl. A common room adjoins the lobby, with a large television set, where a regular group of residents gathers to watch soccer matches or the news; the students who use it seem to smoke endlessly. Carpentier never enters that room. Announcements are taped on the wall near the heavy brass doors of the exit: "Books for sale," "Slightly used desk and two chairs," "Cheap train tickets"; in a corner across from these announcements, several freestanding bulletin boards display photos and articles, with headlines in French and Arabic, neatly cut from newspapers and magazines. Whenever he goes into or out of the residence, Carpentier quickly passes in front of the pictures of dead bodies and bandaged people, men, women, children, people in tents, people bleeding, their faces screaming. One day, talk of a rent strike begins to circulate among the residents of the Maison du Maroc. "The king [they mean, of course, the king of Morocco, His Highness Hassan II] is an accomplice of the imperialists." "Solidarity with our Palestinian brothers." Carpentier hopes he won't have to move out. It was complicated to get a room here.

After what happened at the Athens Polytechnic, after the tanks and the soldiers crashed through the gates, Nikos came to Paris, where he met Carpentier at the Maison du Maroc. Nikos was arriving with his suitcase to move into the room next to his, the last room left in the entire residence, and they met in the hall. Carpentier was surprised to see someone move into a room so late in the school year—it was already November, already quite late for students to be arriving—but Nikos had *special circumstances*, though these were not the words he used to tell Carpentier about what had happened and how he ended up in Paris that fall.

"You can't imagine what they did. This may be normal for places like your country, or Africa, or South America, but we haven't seen this sort of thing since the end of the war, since the civil war. The tanks crashed right through the gates of the school while students were still hanging on; they crashed right through them, and then they went inside; so many were killed; so many were taken away."

. . .

Very quickly, something of a bond is established between those two young men, foreigners in the city where they've met, where they're talking as loudly as they want, walking in the streets, taking the metro and the bus, sitting in lecture halls, having coffees and beers at café terraces in the still warm late fall.

Nikos and Carpentier have arrived in Paris a few years

too late for the flaming barricades of May '68 and the clashes with the police, the iron bars, the slingshots and paving stones, the polycarbonate shields, the sticks and the tear gas; to them, especially to Carpentier, this is a city at peace, a city of splendor, with its river and monuments, its curving streets and wide avenues bearing the names of epic battles and famous men. Aftershocks of the recent upheaval are still discernible, Paris like a landscape after the battle: riot police vans permanently stationed in *strategic areas*, posted there to prevent a sudden recurrence of *the events*; leaflets distributed by this or that *radical faction*; the lingering and irrational uneasiness that a *takeover by radicals* could still occur—"They want to take us into chaos!"—or that Soviet tanks could roll down the Champs-Élysées the way German tanks had done a short three decades before—"It's a good thing we don't depend on the American nuclear umbrella!"

The seventies have barely started, and in these early years of the decade, Nikos and Carpentier, especially Carpentier, feel far from the killing out there, on the other side of the world or, sometimes, closer, even in some places in Europe, as Nikos's own presence in Paris clearly indicates.

There's a silent confederacy between Nikos and Carpentier when they encounter one of those intense Parisian students who want to enlist them in this party or that faction. Nikos is still too close to the *special circumstances* that have brought him to Paris, too distrustful; as for Carpentier, as he was made, as he had grown, his own experience of killing and slaughter, such as it was, has been buffered and eclipsed by the years in New York, his encounter with dead bodies is located in a more distant place and time, and he remains intent on his own getaway and attendant discovery, fixated on the grand itinerary he sees himself tracing, a solitary pilgrim unable even to recognize the soundness of these requests made by other young men and women, busy as he is with the obliteration of his past, blindly surging forward, while these others, his age or slightly older or slightly younger, in the same time and place, in this Europe of the early part of the decade, are still holding out for a revolution that has not occurred but that they think could still happen, even if temporarily it has to take the shape of a violence that seems foreign to the wealth and opulence surrounding them, *because*, many of them think, and try to explain to him, *because* of the wealth and abundance surrounding them, which they see as the real violence, the centuries-old injustice they mean to redress.

Carpentier's high school and college years in New York were haunted by the words of a famous, now aging philosopher. Back from his visit to some of those believers who opted for violently addressing the violence, believers who are now in a German prison, this philosopher has been invited to speak about his journey by the residents of the Maison du Japon, another student residence on the campus. The philosopher speaks about what he calls *un devoir de violence*, a duty to do violence, and it's strange for Carpentier, sitting in the spacious but now crowded room with its traditional Japanese bamboo and rice paper panels in the fading autumn light, strange to see so close to him, here on the small stage, the man who haunted his adolescence and beyond speak about his visit to a high-security German prison, a short, pudgy man in a buttoned wool vest over his turtleneck, his eyes magnified by his glasses' thick lenses, placidly smoking his pipe and in his clear, educated voice talking about the emaciated prisoners of the German state, their solitary confinement, their hunger strike, and the *duty to do violence.*

Carpentier can't make the connection between the dense disquisitions he plodded through in high school and college and what the short, pudgy man is now saying; there is a breach between what fascinated him in the philosopher's books and what he's hearing in the crowded room with its traditional Japanese bamboo and rice paper panels in the fading autumn light, a breach between idealized encounter—for he has always hoped that he would one day meet the philosopher—and this, here, now. It's as if the philosopher has completely changed, as if this man he's met only through his writings is now attempting to force him, Carpentier and none other, even if he is sitting anonymously among these other students on this sunset afternoon in the south of Paris, to force him into a reckoning. Carpentier quickly dismisses the thought. *He's not talking to me.*

On this winter afternoon, as he drives through Germany, Carpentier has no desire to visit or go anywhere near the prison. He's vaguely aware of the bombs, the kidnappings and killings, more aware after the talk at the Japanese House, but the *duty to do violence* is not for him; it is swept aside and left behind like his tribe on the other side of the Atlantic.

As they approach, the armed men, the winged men can see silhouettes moving about inside the vast lantern; music is playing in there, a woman's voice accompanied by a full orchestra and an accordion; the men move impossibly slowly and impossibly quickly through the gate and fan out into the gardens, some flying between the trees, others

walking, and, as they all reach the main veranda at the same time, the silhouettes in the wedge of light inside the house take on sudden density and color.

Carpentier has no desire to visit the prison or even go near it.

He had left Paris in the early morning with Claire and Nikos, and they are driving right through Germany; they want to make the last ferry of the day from Germany to Denmark. Dusseldorf, Essen, Dortmund pass by in a gray blur on either side of the highway while BMWs, Mercedes, and other big cars insistently flash their yellow beams inches behind the already shaking Renault; the little car is hardly managing to reach the minimum speed limit. *Is there even a speed limit?* Carpentier wonders about this, but he is so trained in the ways of a regulated American cautiousness that he remains quiet, taking in the country they're driving through. So this is it, the Ruhr Valley; this is the industrial heartland, then and now, the steelworks that fed the powerful war machine; these people are now at peace, shopping, traveling, going on vacations, unfastened from the violence, living, working, and sleeping in peaceful and opulent cities and villages, far from the killing and the rest of it. Or so he chooses to believe.

They make it to Puttgarden in plenty of time. The ferry crosses the narrow strait between Germany and Denmark in the late afternoon. The winter sun sets early; it's already getting dark when they disembark at Rødby and start on the drive to Copenhagen. A friend from Paris has called a friend who lives here: "You'll see, Stefan will be very happy to put you Parisians up for a couple of days."

Indeed, they're heartily welcomed. It's now three in

the morning; Claire, Nikos, and Carpentier have been in Stefan's apartment, on a cobblestone street somewhere in the center of the city, for several hours. Quite a few other young people have been arriving, taking off caps, gloves, and coats, rubbing their hands, exchanging a few words with *the Parisians*, quickly finding a place to sit; they are now a dozen or so in the apartment, sitting on cushions, on the couch, or on the floor, talking, drinking, smoking. Stefan is watching over a slowly bubbling sauce in the tiny kitchen and has insisted that they keep the music quite loud as he cooks. Carpentier, always worried, always apprehensive about the knock on the door and what would follow, keeps quiet, but there are apparently no neighbors to worry about, no intruders waiting in the halls, in the dark. "We don't care about the commercials; we'll talk louder when they come on."

"We'll at least try to make sense during the breaks."

"He was so young, you know, so young." (One of the guys says this about Jimi Hendrix, who died two or three years earlier.)

. . . (Carpentier finds nothing to reply to this.)

The large radio is also blasting songs by the Who, the Rolling Stones, Pink Floyd, Crosby, Stills, Nash & Young, and, sometimes, something European, a German band perhaps, or Danish—Carpentier can't tell; of the DJ's words, he understands only the names of the English or American bands and the few odd words spoken in English. The DJ's commentary and the music are sometimes interrupted by a commercial; Carpentier can't tell the difference between what the radio host is saying about the music and the commercials he sometimes reads out himself. The music dominates, most of it American, or English, transposed here, relished by these young people who seem more familiar with the lyrics than he will ever be, shaking their heads to the beat, mouthing the words. At one point, as if struck by a communal lethargy, they seem to relent as the first few bars of a song Carpentier has often danced to at parties in New York fill the room; the languid organ music, then, among the first few words he could never entirely distinguish, never truly understand: *Fandango? Cartwheels?* We skip a light and then go? Some of the others have gotten up to dance. A girl takes him by the hand; they dance very slowly, hardly moving, holding on tightly to each other; he doesn't even know her name, or he's forgotten her name. He is in Europe beyond Europe, the icy outer reaches of the continent, even further from the killing *and the rest of it* than he was in Paris. Carpentier holds the girl holding him, both hardly moving to the song whose words he's never completely understood, even if some of the words are quite clear. The song continues to play for a long time; he holds on tightly to the girl.

The song takes him back to the night in New York in that park, site of the old New York World's Fair, with its millions of visitors a few years before, now filled with the Friday-night parade of young people, the crowds in public places of the late sixties all around him, the pungent smell of grass filling the night, when he forgot that it had all started with the small square of blotter paper he'd swallowed with his meal of fried chicken and orange soda not long before in the fast-food place, his feet slowly getting larger as the evening wore on, his limbs becoming longer, rubbery, voices gathering symphonic quality, the whoosh and swish of movement slowly spreading out in color gradations, his *peaking*, as was said in that time and place, his cresting in that park, with its central metal sphere dedicated to "Man's Achievements on a Shrinking Globe in an Expanding Universe," planted among the futuristic buildings left to rust in the years that followed the fair, peaking in that crowd-filled park, later finding a secluded corner and becoming God himself, it seemed, galaxies on his fingernails, and the grandiose solitude, his creating other people so that he would feel less lonely in the vast, unending universe he'd seen in the past few hours, from primordial soup to cave dwellers and beyond, up to the point where he was now in the early gray dawn, the energy and elation waning, beginning to understand that he had not read all the books, and the depressing descent began, but he did manage to emerge, and after that night, after that hollowed-out dawn, the few other times he'd done it again would never be like that first night, from which he'd emerged victorious, free of everything: family, country, the past.

After a while, the music stops, the DJ begins to speak again, and the dancers let go of one another; beckoned by Stefan, some of them head for the kitchen.

"Come help me. The sauce is ready; the noodles are going to get soft." (He says *noodles*, not *pasta* or *spaghetti*; his English is dainty, each word carefully articulated.)

"What would you like me to do?"

"Take some plates from over there. Nikos, bring out some wine and open the bottles."

"What about me? What can I take?"

"Could you slice some bread and put it in that basket over there?"

"I'll bring the salad." They're all hungry, those who were dancing and those who were talking, all now finding places at the low table in the middle of the room, or a corner of the couch, most of them sitting on the floor, eating with the appetite of young people who can eat boundlessly. They're speaking English and Danish, a few are trying out their French, switching from one to the other, as they speak to Claire, Nikos, and Carpentier, or to one another. Stefan lowered the volume on the radio while they were all settling down, and now, sitting close to the radio, Carpentier hears the broadcaster and can distinguish a single word, *Vietnam*, and again, *Vietnam*, *Vietnam*, and some other words that get lost in the announcer's uninterrupted output; he turns to the girl he'd been dancing with, now sitting on the floor next to him. "What did he say? What is he saying?" he asks as some of the others alerted by what they hear in his voice also listen to the DJ, paying close attention now, suddenly serious, at the very least puzzled by the interruption of the feast, forks held in midair, forks put back on their plates, glasses placed back on the low table or on the floor, and the girl he had been dancing with turns to him, smiling, beaming; he will remember that face, that smile for years, beatific, carnal, and ironic. "He says the war is over, Robert. He says Vietnam is over." For just a moment, the DJ's voice is replaced by a voice Carpentier has heard before, and the words are in English. "Good evening. I have asked for this radio and television time tonight for the purpose of announcing that we today have concluded an agreement to end the war and bring peace with honor in Vietnam and in Southeast Asia." Then the DJ's voice returns and the girl kisses Carpentier, ceremonially, on both cheeks, and then on the mouth; he tastes the pasta sauce in the long, warm kiss. The others are cheering and kissing and hugging. Claire and Nikos come to embrace him. They all start eating and drinking again. *Vietnam*, *Vietnam* is repeated again and again in exchanges in English, in French, in Danish.

On the way back to Paris in the early morning two days later, Nikos, Claire, and Carpentier stop for gas at the only station they find open in the still gray streets of Copenhagen. Once again, they board the ferry to cross the narrow channel. During the drive back across Germany, they leave the German highway only once—to exchange money at a bank; Nikos leaves the bank with a thick glass ashtray he's picked up and hidden under his coat. "It will look royal in my room," he says.

During one of their conversations between stints of sleep, as they take turns driving once again through German and French villages, through dark fields and the distant aura of city lights, Claire, the upper-crust English girl whose mother had crisply said, "Really dear, next time, someone white, please?" asks Carpentier about the *situation in Ireland*. "Could you explain it to me? It's hopelessly complicated, you know." She's asked him because he's also attending classes at the Institute of Political Studies, and Claire thinks he would know, but his attention and energy are focused on his classes in art history at the Sorbonne, on Jean-Baptiste-Siméon Chardin's compositions and colors, baskets of peaches and jars of olives, wine-filled glass flasks, dead rabbits and pheasants, boys in frock coats and wigs blowing soap bubbles, holding violins, or playing with tops, and the ray, *this strange monster . . . the beauty of its vast and delicate structure, tinted with red blood, blue nerves, and white muscles, like the nave of a polychrome cathedral.* He has also looked closely at one of Chardin's self-portraits many times, the face of a man at once peaceful and perceptive; the spectacles give him the air of a scholar; the odd turban and bow on his head make him look like a woman, a face far from dying in the mud on the other side of the world, far from the troubles in Ireland. Carpentier wonders why some Europeans are still at one another's throats today. He tells Claire, "It's all about religion and land and tradition, and the old colonial thing, these troubles in Ireland." He does know more; he's had to read not only about the IRA and the violence in Northern Ireland but the ETA and the Basque separatists in Spain, as well as national liberation movements in Angola, in South Africa; he's had to make a presentation in one of his seminars at the Institute, comparing the Red Brigades in Italy to the Weathermen in the USA. "You, the American, this looks like a good topic for you, *non*?" the professor at the Institute had said to him. He could say more to Claire about the complicated situation in Ireland, but he would prefer not to. In any case, she doesn't insist and falls back asleep.

More driving, night falls; they reach Paris as dawn is beginning to break; the campus's lawns are light blue with frost. Nikos and Claire go to Nikos's room, Carpentier, in a daze, to his room, where he barely manages to take off his coat before falling asleep on the narrow bed.

The three of them wake up in the early evening, replenished and famished; Nikos comes to knock on his door. "Want to get some food with us somewhere?" They leave the car parked where they'd left it what seems like centuries ago; they can't bear to get into it again and instead take the metro to Saint-Germain. It must be the weekend; the neighborhood is even more crowded than usual. They go into an Italian place Claire knows; they eat pizza with forks and knives, the plump individual and formal pizzas one orders in Parisian restaurants, not the familiar slices Carpentier is used to eating while walking in the streets of New York, but, for the first time since he's arrived, he feels this is home, this city to which he's returned after the trip to see Margrit van der Berg in Holland, after the trip to Denmark, the ferry crossing, the long drive across Germany and France, this city where he lives and knows no one from where he was born. Copenhagen seems provincial, far away, and, to him, peaceful and privileged in splendid isolation. After the Danish DJ's announcement that night at Stefan's, the question of whether or not to return to New York because of the war and his place in the lottery has receded even further; he won't have to decide, not that he ever gave it a serious thought. His conversation with his father in the kitchen on the evening he left for Paris seems like a dream from a long time ago.

What are you going to do if you're called?

. . .

This is something you have to think about.

. . .

After the long winter break, after the trips to Holland and to Denmark, the spring semester finally begins. Carpentier attends classes as sparingly as he can at the Institute of Political Studies, storing as much time and energy as possible for the art history classes at the Sorbonne, since some cursory reading and memorization get him through the courses at the Institute, the famed Institute, with its young men and women in their green loden coats, the young men in navy blue blazers and gray pants, the young women in flat shoes with buckles, their hair in buns and ponytails, lightly made up, all dutifully purchasing *Le Monde*'s first edition in the early afternoon, all being prepped for *positions of power and responsibility*, as are the first Africans he has seen in his life, young men with their expensive suits (most of them) and tribal scars (some of them), those about whom a girl from Alsace he meets at the residential campus says, "They have no problem, these Africans; they'll return home and rule and make lots of money; they'll lord it over their people, while the Marie-Christines and Jean-Pierres" (she means the ones in the lodens, blazers, and flat shoes with buckles) "are being set up to rule here, over people like me, the proles and peasants of our great egalitarian republic, all these fuckers, these *phallocrats*" (a common appellation for males in those days, in the rarefied theoretical writings and in the streets). She spoke like that, the girl from Alsace, in whose bed he learned how to say *to come* in French, *jouir*, a word he only knew in English until the moment when, infuriated, she said to him "*Tu as jouis?*" and he didn't understand what she meant, and when he did understand, he offered to start all over again, immediately, such as one can when one is twenty-one, twenty-two years old, not much older.

"*Tu es drôle, toi*, you're funny."

. . .

"You're at the Institute, but you're different, not like those snobby fuckers. *Un drôle d'Américain* . . . But then again, you're not really an American. . . ."

. . .

She says nothing. She seems to be making up her mind.

"All right, then, yes, let's start again . . . since you say so," she says after a few seconds, as if this is something she doesn't really want to do, a concession to his lack of experience. She pushes his head down and tells him exactly what to do. He wants to please her, and it is quite a long time before she grabs his head again, this time to bring his face to hers, and they kiss, and he is above the entire length of her, her legs around him when they both begin to *jouir*. . . . "Well, here he is, finally!" (Assertively, mockingly, contentedly, as if referring to a friend she's been waiting impatiently for at a café and who's just shown up rather late.)

He goes to bed with the girl from Alsace several times that first year in Paris, and with others: the Turkish medical student who lives on the residential campus, Claire's Irish friend who comes to visit her for a week, a Senegalese girl at the Institute, one of the very few African women studying over there, and, beginning and ending early on in the fall, Margrit van der Berg. Young women who don't deprive themselves of other young men, or of other young women, even if the pretty Moroccan student in the same computer science program as Nikos and who also lives in their residence hall has made it an unbreakable rule that the guys she brings to her room must "only do it *that way* because I have to go back home *intacte*; *tu comprends, intacte*? Otherwise, it will be impossible for me over there." Adding, "You don't seem to dislike it anyway."

He understands her reasons. *Maybe, yes, for her, if not for me, to go back home, one day. But why would she want to go back at all if this is the way it is over there? Why doesn't she just stay here? Away from them, from those who would despise her or hurt her?* He himself can only go blindly forward, neither with the elegant

Africans with their governmental futures nor the girl from Alsace with her very uncertain future, neither the Marie-Christines and Jean-Pierres being primed *for positions of power and responsibility* nor the acquaintances who have either openly or indirectly beckoned him and Nikos to join "*notre groupe Maoïste*," or "*notre groupe Trotskiste*," or, even "*le PCF*," the French Communist Party, or some other party, some other faction, some other cell. Those committed to *the duty to violence* and *l'action violente révolutionnaire*, on the other hand, seem to have avoided or given up on him and Nikos, and some of them will end up dead, shot on a street corner or in a supermarket in Berlin, Rome, or Madrid, or alive but wasting away in hunger strikes, or grimly eating the anonymous food pushed through rectangular slits in the metal doors of their single cells, defiantly awaiting trial in high-security German or Italian or French or Spanish prisons, awaiting their upcoming public trials, biding their time for yet another opportunity to scream out their hatred of the System that will crumble and their allegiance to the Cause that will never be lost. *Political action*, violent or not, is not for Nikos or Carpentier. Nikos is too fresh from what had happened in Athens, too skittish, and too intent on getting through his computer science curriculum and going back home to make a living one day, hopefully soon; and not for Carpentier, the interloper, who will not go back home and can only rush headlong toward an ever-shifting, ever-receding point.

End of November. The gray and grayer sky settled over Paris weeks ago. Carpentier remembers very clearly when the luminous days of his first year in Paris ended: He was coming out of a café with Nikos and Paul, a Parisian student they've met at the dining hall, when, looking up at the low sky, Paul said, "*Merde*, that's it; it's taken up its winter quarters over the city."

Through Nikos, he met several other Greek students in the fall of that first year in Paris; all, like Nikos, were a few years older than he was, all were living in rooms on the residential campus, and, because of that proximity rather than any particular affinity, it was mostly with them that he would have his meals at the campus's dining halls, walk through the well-tended grounds after dinner, sit at the terrace of the Fleurus Café across the boulevard, especially as spring came around and the days grew longer, Carpentier luxuriating in the length of days as May turned to June, the sun still shedding light on the city at ten, even at eleven on those clear late spring, early summer evenings when the sky took infinitely long to turn from a light blue to a dark violet blue and then to black.

He finds a kind of anchorage in Nikos and his friends, a camaraderie that takes him in like a mascot. There is Konstantinos, with his tight jeans, long hair, and eyes of a Byzantine icon, who seems to be with a different girl or a different boy every week; there is Dimitri, who seems to spend his days at the Fleurus displaying his mastery of the café's two pinball machines; and there is also red-haired, red-bearded Yannis, who has a marked preference for green clothes, pants, shirts, sweaters, jackets, all shades of green; Nikos calls him "the best-dressed anarchist of the entire campus." Yannis is noticeably older than the others; he had to leave Greece very quickly a few years earlier, as the colonels' hunt for *subversives* was gathering steam.

Yannis approaches women at the residence's dining halls, at the Fleurus, in the gardens, or as they are crossing the boulevard to or from the metro station; his territory is restricted to the campus and its immediate surroundings; he apparently goes to central Paris only for classes. "*Bonjour, vous voulez prendre un café—ou un verre—avec moi?*" he would begin, and, often, the young woman would have that coffee, or that beer, or that glass of wine with the red-haired, red-bearded Greek and they would walk and talk with him and, sometimes, they would follow him to his room, or take him to theirs.

One early evening that first spring in Paris, with Carpentier in tow, Yannis makes the formulaic invitation: "*Bonsoir, voulez-vous prendre un café avec nous?*" The young woman seems amused by the offer, an amusement already beyond the obvious craftiness of an invitation for a coffee, since the dining halls are about to open their doors for dinner; she takes off her glasses and tilts her head to the side, looking first at the one who's spoken, then at the one standing next to him. The three are smiling. They smile throughout. As Yannis has informed the Greek coterie and Carpentier, "*C'est le moment délicat*"; everything hinges on the first few seconds, the first words, the first reply.

. . .

"What kind of accent is that?"

"Greek. What kind of accent is yours?"

"Why don't you guess? How about him? Where is he from?" Before Carpentier can speak for himself, Yannis delivers the information, but she understands *Tahiti*.

"Really? I saw pictures—coconut trees, blue lagoons, sunsets, rainbows. I never thought someone could actually be from there. I thought it was a place where people went on vacation."

. . .

Then Carpentier explains, clears up the slight consonant error, and ends with a question of his own.

"Swedish?"

. . . (She understands he means to pursue her own story, not his.)

"Farther south." (She's really beginning to enjoy herself.)

"Danish." (Yannis now offering his own guesses.)

. . .

"Hungarian."

. . .

"Polish."

. . .

"Dutch."

"No, no."

"Russian."

"Now you *are* getting lost. You're both useless. Even if you're getting warmer. Here's a clue to help you: I'm from a divided city in a divided country."

. . .

Then Yannis and Carpentier finally understand. As they begin and then continue to talk about Berlin with her, they walk together to the Fleurus. They sit at a table outside, their three heads close together against the whir of passing traffic on the boulevard, but she is doing most of the talking, intent on finding out more about Carpentier; Yannis and his more recent troubles are apparently not compelling enough, already known, already within the realm of her experience. Instead, she wants to know what brought Carpentier to Paris, how he ended up here, why he speaks English so well. After their conversation, after the trio crosses the boulevard and enters the residential campus grounds, it is Carpentier alone she invites to her room, the one suffused by the aura of bygone violence—even if he has emerged *intact.*

Later, at the dining hall where they usually meet for dinner, Yannis has already given his account of what happened; Carpentier is greeted raucously at the table. "Look at him, look at our boy!" "Come tell us!" He is ill at ease; his soul frets in the shadow of their exchanges, their sharing of stories about the women or the men they've been with, but these young men, his friends, have embraced him, the only non-Greek of the group, with such immediacy and generosity that he cannot bring himself to protest. Even if the recurring focus of their conversation is usually the women or the men they've been to bed with rather than anything else they could talk about, he doesn't try to extricate himself from the anchorage he finds in the Greek group, in spite of whatever misgivings he may have. *Why make them feel bad? Why spoil the mood at the table?* He dismisses his own doubts as anachronistic prudery, inexperience, or his own deficiency in the ways of young people of his generation.

At the table this evening, he tells them that he stayed only a short time in the Berliner's room; he offers no details. They don't insist; they know his reticence. Besides, Yannis is already busy with the story of another recent encounter. He is showing them Polaroids of a fleshly, dark-haired young woman, sitting at his desk, and then lying on his bed at the Fondation Héllénique, at first in a dress and heels, a rarity in those years of jeans and T-shirts and blouses and sandals; then naked on the bed, her breasts, her lush pubis offered up, an assertive glint in her wide-open eyes. The Polaroids are gradually spread out by Yannis between their food trays in a haphazard arrangement at the center of the table. *Crouching hounds circling a cornered deer,*

Carpentier tells himself. As they bend over the photos on the table, Yannis speaks like a man pronouncing a verdict, "*La voilà, la nouvelle bourgeoisie grecque!*" He says it in French because Carpentier is here with them; he usually speaks with the others in Greek. "And she so enjoyed it," he adds, spitting out the words, certainly thinking of those who had profited from the colonels' dictatorship, *ridden the ruling junta's khaki coattails*, a phrase he's used many times before, certainly thinking of the events that had led him to Paris a few years before, the best-dressed anarchist of the entire residential campus, an early victim of the hunt for subversives now finding an unwitting outlet for retribution in that voluptuous young woman in dress and high heels, offered up naked on his bed.

Silence and embarrassed laughter at the table. Disapproval? Acquiescence? It's not clear. Carpentier himself feels targeted by the terse pronouncement, because Yannis looked fiercely and directly at him when he uttered those words, *La voilà, la nouvelle bourgeoisie grecque.* Yannis has made comments in the past, derisive, cutting, even if in the friendly or ironic tone of one who doesn't really mean what he is saying, alluding to what he considers Carpentier's affiliation with that quickly disappearing *class category*. Maybe, Carpentier thinks, this is a kind of personal, even if indirect, reprisal on Yannis's part, payback for the young woman from Berlin taking Carpentier to her room instead of him. Could it also be that Yannis, the escapee from a military dictatorship, the exile, the best-dressed anarchist of the entire campus, resents Carpentier's ability to go to Greece that summer, even if nothing is quite certain yet, his being able to go to Greece with Nikos during the colonels' continued rule, while Yannis cannot go home? Robert Carpentier doesn't process these possibilities immediately and, even when he does, he will not understand how *going back home* could be so compelling for anyone.

The young aunt, sitting in a wheelchair, is playing cards with her two nephews in a corner while, in another corner, the grandfather, his wife, his eldest daughter and her husband, his two sons, and several gardeners and maids are sitting and talking at a table that could also be the desk where the grandfather registers new arrivals; the people at the table are playing cards and having an animated conversation about the water in the pool, whether it is too chlorinated and whether the thick layer of rose petals covering the water should be cleared; they're being served club sandwiches and champagne by a servant wearing black pants, a white shirt, and a black bow tie.

Yannis's words are lingering in the dining hall chatter while his display of photographs lies on the table. Carpentier feels a slight queasiness; something has been breached, even if no one says anything as Yannis quickly gathers his Polaroids like a blackjack croupier while looking at his friends. Yannis's face remains blank, confronting their silence and embarrassed laughter with confidence, not asking for any complicity or approval, certain of his own righteousness and of his friends' having been aroused by the scenes framed in his photographs. He may be right about the others, but, to Carpentier, the pronouncement *La voilà, la nouvelle bourgeoisie grecque* and the photograph of the naked young woman have only and momentarily managed to unearth a more violent scene devoid of any capacity to provoke desire.

They all leave the dining hall together. On the way to their rooms or to the Fleurus or to take an evening walk in the campus's gardens, Nikos says to him, "Don't worry about him, Robert, but do watch out; he can be weird."

The invitation to Greece comes late that first spring

The invitation to Greece comes late that first spring in Paris. The gray sky has retracted like a stage dome. Once again people are sitting in the parks, on the café terraces; the campus grounds smell of freshly cut grass; the residents linger in the gardens' alleys well after dark, later every day. Nikos is restless, looking forward to going back home for the summer in spite of what happened at the Polytechnic in the fall, the tanks crashing through the university's gates, the arrests, the killings. He wasn't affiliated with any group identified by the military; it is safe enough for him to go home again, and he is already eager to leave. "You have to come to Greece; you'll see how beautiful it is," he tells Carpentier. At first, Carpentier doesn't know how to answer; he remembers their conversations from the fall, when Nikos had just arrived, still shocked by what had happened, and the fact that the colonels were still very much in power. But Nikos seems intent on going back; there is no doubt that he is spending the summer in Greece. "I've been away for too long. I have to walk around Athens again, see my mother, take her to the village; it's time to go home." Again, this strange, perplexing desire *to go home again*.

Carpentier has enough money to make it through the summer, until his scholarship payments start again in September. The long summer truce lies ahead; returning to New York is impossible. He won't go back; he will stay away as long as he can. Forever. But the thought of remaining in Paris for the summer depresses him; everyone will be leaving; the student residences will be closed most of the time; Paris will be deserted. *Traveling in France in the summer* was an abstraction, a story he told himself during the winter months of thin, relentless rain, falling from the low sky, puddles in the streets never drying up, cigarette smoke sticking to the glass fronts of cafés, the Paris cold nowhere near the cold of New York winters, but somehow more invasive, chilling him to the bone. "Paris is in a basin," he was told, "it's the humidity." In the Sorbonne's drafty library or in his room at the Maison du Maroc, he would go back to a book on Chardin or to photocopied notes on the common market or the history of fascism. Nikos's stories of young people boarding ferryboats for rocky brown-and-gold islands in the blue Aegean appealed to him, a desire for that particular landscape, the longing for yet another place beyond, yet another remove from tribe and past. Nikos's insistence convinces him. "I'll put you up. I live with my mother, very near the center, but I'm sure you won't stay long in Athens and you'll head for the islands very quickly after you arrive."

It is Abderrahmane, however, one of the "Africans going back home," as the girl from Alsace would have said, thin, austere Abderrahmane, who is in the passenger seat as Carpentier drives to Greece in the clunky Renault that first summer in Europe. Abderrahmane is now at the end of his studies in Paris; he is a few years older than Carpentier and looks quite serious in his round tortoiseshell glasses and his goatee, his uniform of black trousers, gray jacket, spotless starched white shirt buttoned at the collar.

Carpentier had seen him quite often at the main dining

hall of the campus, sitting at one of the tables for eight but always placed in such a way as to be the center of successive meals with other, deferent African students intent on his words, young men and women different from their Pierre Cardin–suited brethren attending the Institute of Political Studies. It is thin, quiet Abderrahmane, who looks like a figure from another time, the ill-fated Lumumba perhaps, someone absolutely unconcerned with Chardin's peaches, dead pheasants, and boys in frock coats, who is in the passenger seat. It was supposed to be Nikos, or Dimitri, the pinball wizard, but Nikos had bought into a capacious third- or fourth-hand Peugeot with a group of fellow Greeks and would be waiting for him in Athens, while Dimitri had decided at the last minute to meet some friends in Spain. Abderrahmane had seen Carpentier's last-minute notices pinned to the bulletin boards of the dining halls—"Traveling by car to Athens on July 5th. Share gas and tolls"—and proposed that they go together. Their brief predeparture meeting took place in the main dining hall, where Abderrahmane immediately agreed to all conditions, told Carpentier he was going to spend less than a week in Greece, to see a girl he'd met two summers before in Paris, and would be leaving for Nouakchott immediately afterward. They left Paris a few days later. Carpentier is relieved not to have to make the journey alone, even if he is slightly apprehensive about traveling with the Mauritanian, who seems so serious, so austere.

Abderrahmane turns out to be an affable and generous traveling companion. After two days of driving through France's vineyards, wheat fields, and villages, then crossing into Italy and going down the Adriatic coast, as they are approaching the outskirts of Brindisi to catch the ferryboat bound for Patras, he answers Carpentier's "Aren't you going to feel isolated when you go back to Mauritania?" in such a way that in the Mauritanian's reply Carpentier perceives, even if indistinctly, something of the strangeness, something of the limits, perhaps, of his own undertaking, an inkling, perhaps, of the blindness of his own enterprise, as Abderrahmane, a bit taken aback by his question, but not at all insulted or annoyed or belligerent, in fact with a chuckle and only some mild surprise that the question could even be formulated, that it could have some sort of rational basis, replies, "Isolated? But I'm going back home and I'll be in the center of Africa!" In the very next instant, at slightly different speeds, two thoughts occur to Robert Carpentier: the first, which he keeps to himself, recognizing its futility and irrelevance, even its pettiness in ferreting out a supposed geographical inexactitude: *Mauritania is not in the center of Africa*, a thought that displays his willful misreading of an earnestly and metaphorically stated proposition by his traveling companion. Carpentier knows but cannot fully admit in that instant that this thought is perhaps a halfhearted justification on his part, a bid at alleviating some indefinable guilt. The second thought unfolds slightly more slowly: Like his Pierre Cardin–suited brethren who walk the halls of the Institute of Political Studies, Abderrahmane could become an ambassador, a cabinet member, maybe even president one day, following the traditional and foreordained path to power for those who have *returned home*, the new men of power, the ones who would lord it over their people, as the girl from Alsace would have said, although something about Abderrahmane's leanness and keen intelligence, his seriousness and earnest dedication to *his people*, his statements about *eradicating corruption* signals that the quiet Mauritanian might meet with scorn, rejection, and probably worse when back home, that something might turn out badly for him. Even as he respects and admires Abderrahmane's quiet and unquestioned resolve, Carpentier doesn't envy the Mauritanian's return home and even pities his determination, his bypassing or denying or just not even seeing the accidental quality of birth and place.

The serious passenger heading for home and the driver adrift are heading for an Italian port to board the ferryboat bound for a Greek port, for one the gateway to briefly seeing a girl met two summers before, an ultimate stop before *returning home definitively*, for the other the entry to yet another territory where he will know no one from where he was born, opting once more for yet another encounter with the imagined possibility of an unfettered life.

During the four days it takes for them to get from Paris to the Italian port, and later on the way to Athens, they talk about the economic situation in Mauritania, how fast Carpentier drives, the Parisians and their hospitality or inhospitality, the budding centrality of computers in advanced industrial economies and the now obvious presence and importance of multinationals, their (the multinationals) entering a much more evident field of perception, the quality of food at the dining halls, how one of them likes to swim and the other not, the French countryside, the Italian countryside, the connection between Africa (West and North) and France (the "Hexagon"), the connection between West Africa, the Soviet Union, and China, the competition for raw material between the planet's dominant economies (which leads to some conclusive comments—Abderrahmane's—and some vague musings—Carpentier's), what Carpentier will do after his studies (which lead to nothing conclusive at all), where Abderrahmane had met the Greek girl he is on his way to see again in Athens, the very high cost of gas in France and Italy compared to the United States, the United States and Vietnam, the United States and Africa (they both have very little to say about this), Carpentier's life in New York, the two travelers' respective childhoods, the amazingly long days in Paris in June, and a number of other things, but never again, either in passing or at length, never again, at all, does either one allude to why it could be considered funny or odd or both that Carpentier would ask Abderrahmane whether he would feel isolated once he was back in Mauritania, once he was *back home*.

Dusk. The ferry slowly docks at the port of Patras. Throughout the clamorous disembarkation of cars and people, and then during the drive from Patras to Athens, Carpentier is in a trance. *I'm far from home; I'm home again*. Absolute and thrilling novelty, but also the recognition of a past time, the immediate affinity with something at once outmoded, unfinished, and thriving all around him: the carefully maintained, if sometimes dented, cars from previous decades, the sixties, the fifties, even earlier, the constant honking, the small cups of dark coffee and glasses of water carried on a stainless steel tray by an aproned boy waiter from a café to a small shop a few doors down, the direct and unhurried gaze of passersby, people dressed in light summer clothes, the steel of reinforced-concrete columns jutting from the temporary roofs of half-finished constructions, the smell of grilled meat in the open air, street vendors, a man's loud and nasal voice coming from a megaphone as he sells watermelons from the back of a small truck, an old man holding a wooden stick bristling with lottery tickets, walking from café to small shop to café. Then, on the drive to Athens, the scrawny oleander and yellowing weeds by the side of the road, where two lanes are turned to three by unflappable or seething drivers, seething or unflappable, but all determined to get to wherever they're going as quickly as they can; people and things, movements out of step with the regimented and burnished quality of what he has experienced in France this year, in New York the previous years, a whiff of the place of childhood before the brutality, even as the newness and difference of Greece enfold him.

After a two-hour drive to Athens, Carpentier drops off Abderrahmane on a street corner. They shake hands; something stoic lingers in their final exchange, a reluctance to admit they will never see each other again. "*Merci, et bonne chance, Robert.*" "You, too, Abderrahmane; thank you and good luck."

Abderrahmane has disappeared around the corner. Carpentier feels the abrupt thrill of being alone in an unfamiliar place. Then, of course, he gets lost in Athens. He doesn't mind. After an hour of persevering through wrong turns, deciphering street names, enthusiastic but ineffectual English- and French-laced exchanges with pedestrians gladly stopping their progress on sidewalks and bending to the Renault's windows, heads and chests of other drivers leaning out of other cars at traffic lights, he parks near a kiosk and uses its oversize red phone to call the number Nikos had given him; he receives additional directions, but in the end Nikos has to come to retrieve him from the neon and traffic of the square, as night has now fallen and it does not look like Carpentier will be able to find his way to the apartment at number 15 Dorileou Street, just two blocks from the American embassy.

While waiting for Nikos, he stands outside the car; he looks up at the sky, now a deep, dark blue illuminated from below by the square's bright streetlights and neon.

He observes the people passing by, the crowd of a summer evening; he looks up at the billboards on top of the buildings around the square: a woman with long blond hair holding a bottle of a yellow soft drink the same color as her bathing suit; a red pack of Santé cigarettes, the only lettering he can read without effort; another blond on the pack, this time with the darkened eyelids, red lips, and curled hair of an earlier decade. All around the square people are sitting at outdoor restaurants and cafés; a warm breeze is blowing; it's early summer in a large urban square *somewhere on the Mediterranean coast.* The Med-i-ter-ra-nean; nothing more specific for now; he prefers to let the scene remain as foreign to him as possible; he could stay standing there for hours. Nikos's partly owned Peugeot is suddenly parked behind the Renault; Nikos quickly emerges from the car. "Welcome, welcome, sorry about the directions. You must be tired, Robert. Just get back in your car and follow me. It's just a few minutes away; I'll drive slowly." At 15 Dorileou Street, Nikos takes his suitcase. "Let's just walk up; it's only the second floor." Nikos's mother opens the door to the apartment, holds out her hand, and then kisses him on both cheeks as they communicate in the language of repeated, emphatically articulated words and phrases understood in context, gestures, and smiles; Nikos also translates. A meal is laid out in the small dining room. Sliding doors open onto a terrace. On his first evening in this country, knowing no one from where he was born, the feeling persists of something already encountered in another place and time. *I'm far from home; I'm home again.*

Nikos has taken some time off from his summer job as a waiter in his uncle's restaurant to be free in Athens with Carpentier, who is now, the day after his arrival, walking in the streets of the city with his friend, deciphering the signs on storefronts, the lettering of posters, newspaper headlines. Under Nikos's solicitous but necessarily irregular supervision, he had already learned a few phrases of Greek in their rooms in Paris, conjugated the two basic infinitives, *to be, to have, Ego ime, esi ise, Ego exo, esi exis, emis exoume*, Carpentier then and now chafing at the capriciousness of gender: *Sun* is masculine, *junta* is feminine, like *spoon*, and *moon* is neuter; Carpentier despairs at the mystery of declensions as he walks in the streets of this city, new and yet familiar to him.

In these early years of the seventies, it seems only the Greeks speak Greek. When Carpentier successfully buys a pack of chewing gum on his own, saying the just-learned phrase, evidently without a hint of an accent, since the man in the kiosk does not even hesitate, does not display any surprise in acknowledging the request, and hands back change and chewing gum, he rejoices in his small victory and feels that here, among these people and things, he could just be sitting in this or that bus, or anywhere else, a café terrace, a library, or a restaurant, or walking in the streets, that he could just be anonymous, that he could just be buying some bread or be waiting in line for a film, someone in a crowd in a city somewhere, *without the rest of it.*

Though Carpentier does notice the omnipresent silhouette of a helmeted soldier, a bayoneted rifle over his shoulder, standing against the backdrop of a phoenix rising from flames, he needs Nikos's help to translate the lettering on the poster: *April 21, 1967 lives!* The curt celebration of the military coup's anniversary, and, crowning the composition, more lettering: *Hellas, Greece.* No one uses the word *dictatorship* out loud, but its winged emblem is there for everyone to see; the posters are taped on storefronts, lampposts, on the sides of kiosks that sell everything from newspapers and magazines to plastic toys, candy, maps, and milk. The silhouetted soldier and the phoenix are everywhere, even on matchboxes, and Carpentier can't resist commenting.

"You know, that plump bird looks like it's roasting on the red flame, screaming in the flames, not being born again. . . . It looks like it wants out of there: *Somebody, help me! I'm roasting! I'm burning!*"

"Shhhh." (Nikos quickly raising a finger to his lips.)

. . . (Carpentier puzzled, only for a second; only for a second because he knows how quick and vicious certain consequences can be.)

. . . (Nikos looking at him, unsmiling.)

"Yes, I know; I'm sorry."

Carpentier knows; Carpentier is sorry; he has known the indiscriminate anxiety, the contained violence always on the brink of being released, but his contrition is only a fleeting moment in his exuberant and blissful encounter with this place and these people. *I'm far from home; I'm home again*, even if the energizing newness and the soothing recognition also carry in their wake the memory of a brutality played out long before, before Paris, before New York, dormant all those years. Carpentier understands, Carpentier knows, but he will not forgo his pleasure or restrain his appetite. He will go on alone, beyond the gravitational pull of tribe and place, tinged as they are with the old brutality and with *everything else*. His obstinate refusal to acknowledge any obstacle in his blind surge forward lies behind the silliness of his comment about the colonels' bird emblem; besides, there are no threatening uniforms around on this clear summer day, unless you count that gesticulating traffic guard at the intersection;

there are no sinister civilian agents mixed into the summer crowd, as far as he can tell; and anyway, dazed by the sun, he is already in motion, walking up the hill to the Acropolis with Nikos.

In the short time he has been in Athens, it has not been the viciousness his friend has recounted that's moved him, the threatening beast crouching behind the summer sun, but the fruits stalls, the tourist trinkets, the leather shops, the carefree people having meals outdoors, drinking iced coffees, pedestrians finding the shaded side of the streets, the ubiquity and coolness of marble in the most unlikely places, not only the columns of ancient structures, statues, whole or dismembered, Cycladic figurines in the dusty vitrines of the museum they visited in the morning, remnants of a glorious past where one expects to find marble, but also covering the stairwells of modest apartment buildings, the stuff of sidewalks, the floors of kitchens and living rooms, bars, shops, restaurants, cafés with their tables and chairs in the open air set for the summer days and nights. "What will they do when it rains?" he asks Nikos.

"It doesn't rain."

"At all?"

"Not in the summer, no; almost never does. Maybe once, a long time ago, there were a few drops during the summer. I can't even remember."

. . .

"It's not the Tropics, Robert."

. . .

A few days later, Nikos takes him to a seaside town, a short drive from Athens. "Let's get away from the heat; let's go have a beer, or an ice cream." There is no traffic at all on the road, no moon above, and stars fill the sky as the two of them leave the lights of the city behind, the evening quickly becoming cooler as they approach and start smelling the sea. Then a small town takes shape, the first of a string of summer resorts along the coast sweeping out of Athens, this one with a marina, stone houses set behind gardens of pines, olive trees, fig trees, bougainvillea, pomegranate; among them, newer apartment buildings, their terraces filled with potted plants, lavender and geranium. The streets are lined with eucalyptus trees; the town center is just a few cafés and restaurants, an outdoor movie theater; a place devoted to simple pleasures. A creamy yellow round-domed church sits in the middle of an empty square; Nikos tells him there's a golf course nearby.

They walk up one of the streets; the strings of lightbulbs in front of its bars and clubs cut a bright strip in the otherwise dimly lit and quiet town: bars, clubs, restaurants side by side, with shadowy interiors; speakers set outside blast American rock or country; the only language heard is English, as almost all the customers are American: soldiers with crew cuts in civilian clothes or mixed apparel—fatigue pants and Hawaiian shirts, olive T-shirts and light summer pants. They are all paying in dollars; some of them are quite drunk. There is an American base nearby, and the U.S. Sixth Fleet is stationed off the coast of an ancient town just a few kilometers away, where, thousands of years ago, the cult of Demeter and her lost daughter, Persephone, were celebrated.

Nikos and Carpentier walk up and down the small street, spectators in a zone apart, before heading for a café on the seafront.

"You know, you could come swim here during the day, or even a little farther along the coast; you've been in Greece for three days already and you haven't gone for a swim yet!"

. . .

"Unacceptable, especially after what you've told me about you and the sea"—and, lowering his voice, he adds, "It's not our responsibility to kick out the colonels. The Americans brought them in; the Americans should get rid of them."

. . .

"The colonels are still here because the Americans want them here; these guys in their Hawaiian shirts are as guilty as the colonels and their gang."

. . . (Carpentier knows, but he will not engage; the summer night, the summer night, let nothing else intrude.)

"Okay, let's get that beer, or an ice cream if you prefer, Robert; but I'm paying."

The next day, Nikos is back at work and it is Konstantinos of the Byzantine-icon eyes and not yet anachronistic hippie ponytail who sits by Carpentier and gives him directions as they drive to another town with another beach a bit farther up the coast. When they turn off the main road, the smell of pine becomes intense, mixed with the salt air and the dust of the unpaved road they take down to a beach of white sand and smooth pebbles. Clusters of pines and tamarisks, and a few umbrellas dot the beach; the blue-and-turquoise water is just barely rippled by a slight breeze.

They spread their towels on the pebbled sand. Soon after, they are racing, laughing, splashing as their feet first hit the water, and then they swim out so far that the beach becomes a thin ribbon unfurled between sea and sky. Carpentier has never swum out so far in his life. It's been such a long time since the sea has given him such bliss; after a long while he stops swimming, not even out of breath. He can see far down through the deep transparency of the water; he floats on his back, the water filling his ears, his eyes open to the blue sky, squinting against the sun. Unmoored from everything.

Konstantinos taps his shoulder, and they swim back to the beach, this time in regular, unhurried strokes. They walk back to their towels, next to a group of workers from a nearby construction site, a half-finished villa set back from the beach in a thick cluster of pine trees. "Taking a break, taking a dip before going back," one of the workers says. Konstantinos is speaking to them; they light cigarettes. There are also two or three families, couples, or mothers alone with children, and several groups of young men and women, either in the shade of the pine trees or under beach umbrellas. Several old men and women are bobbing in the water; multicolored plastic flowers are plastered on one woman's bathing cap. Gathered in couples or circles, the old people don't swim; they float for hours, talking as if they were in their living rooms. Konstantinos explains to Carpentier that they compare and energetically argue about the number of swims they've had so far in a given summer, storing the sea's energy and health for the winter.

Carpentier's childhood trips to the beach were often complicated, carefully prepared outings to private beaches, the ceremony of cocktail shakers and ironed tablecloths, coolers and picnic baskets, a servant; later, there were the teeming beaches of New York summers with high school friends, catching the bus, spending the whole day there, from late morning to sunset, the waves of the foamy green-and-brown Atlantic, the compact crowds of bathers, the transistor radios and the smell of suntan lotion, lifeguards with their orange bathing suits, their noses covered in white cream, their silver whistles around their necks, the boardwalks and numbered jetties, the sand-encrusted cheese and liverwurst sandwiches of those summers. All of that, the beaches of childhood and those of adolescence, is eradicated here and now in the sudden rush to the unbroken Aegean, swimming out with Konstantinos, followed by the conversation with the construction workers, *taking a break, taking a dip before going back*. Here, too, a new life could begin, unencumbered by the past.

Neither Nikos nor Konstantinos can be with Carpentier that evening; they're both working at the uncle's restaurant, but Nikos bought a ticket to *Agamemnon* for his friend. "The theater is right under the Parthenon; you'll see, people will be waiting in line outside the theater, it's called the Herodion," Nikos told him.

A few days after his arrival, he's become familiar with certain areas of Athens; he's been to the Acropolis, to the tourist shops nearby, the leather-goods market, all a few minutes from the theater, and he easily finds his way from Dorileou Street to the Herodion. He's given himself plenty of time; he walks slowly. The heat of the day is gone; an old man in pajamas, freshly up from his long afternoon siesta, is watering rows of potted plants on his second-floor terrace; the streets are filling up. Once again, it will be a clear evening.

When he gets to the theater, he has to wait in line. There are quite a few tourists, their skin reddish from the sun; quite a few young Greeks; all of them, locals and strangers from all over Europe and beyond, waiting to enter the theater for a performance of ancient murder and sacrifice. Only a few cars are passing on the avenue, but more and more taxis are now stopping to drop off passengers. The line moves quickly. Once inside, he is overwhelmed and then taken in by the amphitheater's ascending stone bleachers, which reach for the sky above; thousands of people, the undertow of voices. Before beginning the climb to his seat, he looks over at the empty stage, already lit and waiting. About halfway up he finds the right section, then his row, toward the middle, and settles in amid the assembled crowd's low, continuous hum. In the first row, down there, sitting a few feet from the stage, dignitaries wearing suits, their wives in formal dresses; uniformed army officers, a few policemen in their gray uniforms and caps are standing in the aisles, their arms loosely held behind their backs. Beyond the empty stage and the theater, the sun has just set; the clusters of pine and cypress are already dark against the hills, silhouetted against the pink and blue of the early-evening sky.

Ushers are briskly taking the last arrivals to their seats; this final rush is followed by complete and sudden silence as the lone watchman who has been on the ramparts waiting for news of the distant war in Troy enters the circle of light and speaks, his voice incredibly loud and clear in the deepening darkness. Carpentier distinguishes a rare few words, *Atreus*, *Agamemnon*, *Ilion*—he knows Ilion is Troy, hence the *Illiad*; he knows the story of Agamemnon's return, and he's read the notes in English in the program, but, content and anonymous among the thousands of others, he won't turn to those around him to ask for an explanation. None of the story's details matters to him; he won't break the spell. He's able to follow the major shifts, the lit beacon in the night announcing the fall of Troy, the end of the watchman's long soliloquy. . . . Then he is abruptly shaken out of his trance: A small man somewhere in the first few rows is standing alone and applauding; he can be seen clearly in spite of the darkness. He's wearing a white shirt and white trousers; he's almost bald; he's wearing glasses. He's standing quite straight and applauding loudly, uncontrollably. Thousands of faces are turned toward him. Two policemen converge on him from either end of his row, but the man makes no attempt at escaping; he continues to applaud even faster as the two policemen reach him, pull his hands down, and take him away. Carpentier turns to his neighbors; one of them, with his index finger on his lips, signals for him to be quiet; another one tells him in a hurried hush, "The messenger has said, 'Our king is coming back!' . . . and that man was making applause." He offers no other explanation and turns his head back to the stage. Carpentier does the same. The actors onstage haven't stopped. The play continues. The chorus enters, old men leaning on their staffs, intoning, chanting, slowly moving across the stage while Clytemnestra, Agamemnon's queen, appears in the background, lighting incense on an altar. . . .

Later, Nikos explains to Carpentier why the man was taken away. "It's the colonels again. That poor man was reacting to 'Our king is coming back,' you see?" Carpentier doesn't see; he has no idea why the man was taken away. "They couldn't just let him make a fuss, applauding and disrupting the performance, right?" he asks. Nikos is patient and continues his explanation, now taking his time. "The king of Greece, Constantine? He left years ago, after the colonels took over, and they're preparing a referendum to get rid of him forever; haven't you seen the word *NAI* all over Athens? It means 'YES,' yes to the colonels, yes to their remaining in power. That man you saw at the Herodion is probably in jail now." Carpentier sees the scene again, the night sky above the open theater; the thousands of people, the actors on the lit stage, the chorus of old men and the imposing queen in the background, the little man being carried off by the two policemen. "Do you think they hurt him?" he asks. Nikos answers very quickly, almost interrupting him. "Yes, I'm sure, the poor guy; they want to make sure the referendum goes well; they won't tolerate any protest." Carpentier says nothing for a few seconds, and then suggests they get something to eat. "I left Dorileou hours ago; I'm starving." Later on, when they meet Konstantinos at a bar, Carpentier asks, "Can you make it to the beach again tomorrow? I could pick you up." The summer nights, the summer days, let nothing else intrude.

Now that he has been told about the colonels' ubiquitous phoenix and also knows about the referendum, Carpentier can't avoid seeing the word *NAI* and knowing what it means. Signs of the referendum are everywhere: posters, flyers, the front pages of newspapers. The three colossal letters are even mounted on scaffolding affixed to the side of Lycabettus hill, one of the city's two highest points; at night, the *NAI* on the hill glows from the white light of projectors from below. They can be seen quite clearly from a good swath of Athens, even during the day.

There's a small church at the very top of Lycabettus and, just below the church, a café. One unusually warm evening, a few days after the performance, Carpentier walks up the hill with James and Alana, two Scottish students he's met at the beach. It's cooler up there, on top of the hill. They have ice cream at the café; the three massive letters can't be seen from there. *A respite*, Carpentier thinks—*I'm tired of seeing those letters.*

By the time the referendum takes place, he's already left Athens for the Peloponnese with James and Alana; they've persuaded him to forgo the islands and to drive around the peninsula instead. They were planning on hitchhiking, but they've offered to share the cost of driving with him in the Renault. "This is what you need to see, not just Athens and the Acropolis. And the Peloponnese is full of beaches," Alana tells him that evening while they're having ice cream on Lycabettus. James just nods, his eyes on both of them.

They stay in the cheapest places. They rent rooms; they sleep on beaches, on rented rooftops; it never rains. They often camp; James and Alana have all the equipment they need. The small car is filled with suitcases, sleeping bags, a tent; there's even a frying pan. They drive to the ancient sites: Epidaurus, Mycenae, as far as Olympus. Carpentier relies on having read the *Odyssey*, parts of the *Iliad*, and a few tragedies. His knowledge is tenuous, but it's all he needs to remain in his bliss. The dusty olive trees and the sea, the clear skies, the two people he's traveling with, two people from yet another place far from the violence *out there*, the newness of this kind of summer is more vital to him than the temples, monuments, and citadels, backdrops to an ancient civilization's stories of lineal blood and crime. As for the colonels and the referendum, they are left behind with the giant letters mounted on scaffolding on a hill in Athens.

James knows quite a bit about ancient Greece, but he seems almost reluctant to speak out; his explanations are quickly given, hushed offerings about when an amphitheater was built, a statue sculpted, sacrificial rites, daily life in classical Athens. Carpentier sometimes struggles to understand his English. "He won't make an effort, the laddie," Alana tells him, but it's obvious she approves; James only smiles at this. On their first night camping, they eat ham sandwiches and drink two bottles of white wine still warm from the sun. In the middle of the night,

Alana comes to get Carpentier from the sleeping bag he's borrowed from them and leads him by the hand to the tent she shares with James, who is wide awake. Carpentier returns to his sleeping bag at dawn. During the day the three are reserved and move around one another delicately. Their nights are spent like moments in a separate life. Their trip through the Peloponnese lasts two weeks.

At Mycenae, they visit the ruins of Agamemnon's palace. Carpentier thinks of telling Alana and James about his evening at the theater in Athens, the messenger announcing Agamemnon's return to his palace, and the little man standing straight up, furiously applauding, then being taken away by the police. He decides not to.

The last few days and nights in Athens go by very quickly. Late August, and Carpentier has just enough money left to drive back to Paris, if the ride is shared. Alana and James have to return to Scotland, so they leave with him.

They drive across northern Italy: Verona, Brescia, Milan; Carpentier recognizes places, roads driven through in the early summer with Abderrahmane. *He must be in the heart of Africa now, back home; maybe he's doing just fine.* Signs for Geneva. "Make sure you don't go into Switzerland. Keep to the right," James tells him; he has become their navigator. Afternoon turns into night as they drive through France; they reach Paris in the early morning. Carpentier has to wait for the Maison du Maroc office to open to pick up the key to his new room and gather a few things left in the residence's storage over the summer. He takes Alana and James to the Fleurus, where they order several rounds of coffee, croissants. The waiter remembers Carpentier. "Where are all your Greek friends?" he asks. "They're still over there; they'll be back." Once again, Paris feels like home. The same way he'd felt after the trip to Copenhagen last winter. This is where he will remain; there's nowhere else for now. Greece was a fantasy—quickly glimpsed, now gone. Another harbor, far away from the past, but out of his reach.

Alana and James stay in his room for a few days; he takes them around what has become his city. On their last day, Carpentier drives them to the train station; they're off to London, and then there will be the long train ride back to Scotland. They hug one another at the Gare du Nord. The people around them are pale and hurried. They promise to see one another again.

No one Carpentier knows is back in Paris yet. The campus is almost empty. He walks through the streets for hours. It's still warm enough to go swimming at the Piscine Deligny, an outdoor pool floating on the bank of the Seine. Old men in tiny, tight bathing suits play ping pong on the upper deck. The days are still incredibly long.

Soon the city begins to fill up again. Families returning from their summer vacation, unloading their cars in front of their buildings; crowded stationery stores, school-supply shops; mothers with children in tow, buying books, fountain pens, pencil boxes, erasers; students returning from the French provinces, or from farther away, Bucharest, Dakar, Tokyo. Nikos and Konstantinos come back in late September. Classes resume. He is home now.

Two or three years after his encounter with the young man on the train to Holland

Two or three years after his arrival in Paris, two or three years after his encounter with the young man on the train to Holland, on his way to gray European capitals to sell golden beaches and endless sun, the killing started in

Lebanon, and that was also the time when Carpentier met the Lebanese group of friends in Paris through Bertrand, whom he'd met through one of the Greeks. By then, Chardin's work had become the subject of his doctoral research and his attention was held even more tenaciously by the painter's brilliant surfaces and opulent arrangements. Still and yet again basking in the encounter of things and people he'd seen only in books and films before, Robert Carpentier did not at first understand, perhaps did not want to understand, and perhaps never acknowledged the link between the running civilians, the burning buildings, the devastated cities, the ruined villages in Lebanon and the presence in Paris of the stylish, sophisticated, often erudite group composed of Michel, Selim, Justine, Henri, Nadine, and especially Nabil, whom he had met during his first few months in Paris, earlier than the others.

After he's been with the Lebanese many times in student rooms, in apartments and cafés, lecture halls and movie houses, there is a particularly memorable evening that lasts until dawn at Nadine's small studio near place Clichy, where he also meets Albert, that burly friend of Nadine's, a businessman—whatever that means—buying and selling who knows what, still living in Beirut in spite of the war, but passing through Paris on his way to London, Albert, who spills out a pile of cocaine from a plastic bag onto Nadine's glass-topped table, proceeds to noisily sniff two neatly separated rails with a rolled 500-franc bill he has taken out of a wallet from the jacket of his light brown, white-striped Pierre Cardin suit in a room where just about everyone else is wearing jeans and shirts or the assorted student attires of the time, and then grandly beckons the others sitting on the couch or on the floor around the low table, this at a time when Carpentier has a bit more money to spare than during his first two or three years in Paris, when he had to depend essentially on his scholarship, but, still, the rolled bill represents a substantial portion of his monthly budget these days.

Albert's gesture is princely; his world of commerce, first-class flights, expensive hotels and restaurants is far from the life of those students gathered in Nadine's studio, even though most of them seem to have enough money to afford studios and apartments, unlike Carpentier, who still lives in a room at the student residence in the south of Paris. Carpentier now goes through the unfamiliar gestures of separating two thick lines from the white pile with Pierre's credit card, mimics Pierre's motions, rolls the 500-franc note very tightly before lowering his head to the low table and sniffing the crystalline powder, followed by the others. The talking continues, about Virginia Woolf this time, and, as is always the case when Nabil is with them, about films. "Now that's what I call love, this young woman holding her boyfriend's arm while he pees against a wall; Hitchcock saw this from a train compartment window; he told someone about this in an interview. . . ." Nabil pauses, knowing he's got their full attention.

. . .

"Go on, then. . . ."

And Nabil goes on, unstoppable, charming, his head and neck delicately poised as he speaks. An oracular burnt-sienna scribe reclining on a couple of pillows on the floor, he goes through a swath of Hitchcock's films and then takes his friends sitting on the floor and couch back to Virginia Woolf and *Mrs. Dalloway*, to how much Lucrezia loves her shell-shocked husband, back from the trenches of World War I, her despair at seeing him a listless stranger in the world while all those pedestrians are going on about their business in the streets and parks and stores of London on that sunny day when Clarissa Dalloway is walking through the city before the evening of her dinner party. Then Nabil takes them back to Hitchcock observing the young couple from his train window, the young woman holding her young man's arm as he pees. "That's what I call love; old Hitchcock is right, so precise, so wonderfully perverse. . . . Remember the very last scene in *North by Northwest*, when the train enters the tunnel . . ."

Bertrand is also there, quiet for now, listening, a heavy-lidded, long-lashed Buddha sitting cross-legged on the floor, sprinkling crumbs of hash with two fingers of one hand onto a small heap of tobacco held in his other cupped hand; the mixing, rolling, and licking completed, he passes the tightly rolled joint to whoever is sitting next to him, an offering to the assembly, and he will now roll another, a special one just for Carpentier, who does not smoke tobacco. "It's only hashish and grass, no tobacco. This is for Robert, who has never smoked a cigarette in his life; can you believe it, *no tobacco*? Talk about *perversity*! What do you expect from an American, even that kind of American." As he hands over the joint with its rolled yellow metro ticket filter tip to Carpentier, Bertrand is already picking up from where Nabil left off, and brings in Ozu, the apparent simplicity of the Japanese director's wonderful frames, the jubilation his films arouse, but he's soon cut off by Gustavo, short, wiry, pugnacious Gustavo of Madrid, the only one among them standing as he talks, Gustavo, who brings *Gillès Délèze* and *Jakès Lakannn* into the conversation, as he always does, the French philosopher and the French psychoanalyst becoming Spaniards in Gustavo's quick, heavily accented, and nasal delivery. The Madrilenian suddenly pauses, slyly, dramatically, considering a comment made by Nadine, and replies, "You know that suicide has always been a serious matter among us," looking at all of them, smiling, his small eyes squinting with irony. The others don't quite understand how he got from Nadine's comment to suicide, but they know better than to ask. Not a comment from anyone; they know how cutting he can be.

. . .

Albert, who was bending down over the white pile on the glass table during Gustavo's soliloquy, looks up at the wiry little Madrilenian, smiles, shakes his big head from side to side, murmurs longingly, mockingly, "*Oh, un in-tel-lec-tuel,*" and placidly continues to parcel out another two rails from the pile; Carpentier dreads what might be about to happen and is relieved when he sees Nadine bring out a bottle of Haig Pinch whiskey. "*Il paraît que c'est excellent; on va l'essayer,*" she says to no one in particular as she sets the bottle and a few glasses on the table and begins to pour while Albert is still bent over the pile, meticulously straightening out the two rails with his credit card. Gustavo, who remains standing, looks like a punk, as Bertrand says about him; he also looks like a skinhead in his boots, black jeans, and shirt, his paleness and closely shaved blondness topped by a slightly raised tuft. It isn't that Albert's size dissuades him from pushing the large man's head into the white pile, crashing through the glass table, but only that he's intent on what he's in the process of saying; Albert is irrelevant in his burliness and his Pierre Cardin suit. Gustavo may not even have heard him, and indeed continues, impervious, talking fast; he has so much to say, to convey, as if his life depends on it, until Bertrand, his hands busy yet again with the rolling paper and the piece of hash and the tobacco, intervenes. "This suicide thing is getting old; we're somewhere else now, *non*?" Acknowledging the tribe they constitute, after all, a tribe with its affinities and aspirations, these young people, here, on this night, who have come to this gathering, born in Paris or in some provincial town in France, or other cities and countries, brought together in the sheltered chiaroscuro of the small studio where no men in plainclothes or in uniforms will knock at the door, unless some neighbor complains about too much noise—"Just too much walking around at this ungodly hour!" or "It's three in the morning, for the love of God! Have you no consideration?" or "We have to go to work in the morning! Have you no decency?"—and then they would have to disband, quietly go down the flights of steps and make their way back to their own rooms and studios and apartments in the still, dark streets. There is no indignant neighbor tonight, though, and they continue well after dawn, until the first metro.

As he did with the Greeks, Carpentier is finding precarious anchorage in the company of the Lebanese group and brilliant Bertrand, who can also prepare and roll a joint with a single hand, or with Gustavo, who turns French philosophers and psychoanalysts into Spaniards in his rapid histrionic and heavily accented delivery. With them, not the Greeks, he spends the long nights into dawn, with them the lectures, not at the Institute or the Sorbonne, but at the new university hurriedly built in the woods adjoining Paris by the authorities in the aftermath of barricades and paving stones; with them the metro and then the bus and then the walk through the woods to reach those drab, quickly erected buildings where the long-nailed, chain-smoking philosopher lectures in a smoke-filled classroom obviously too small for the purpose, that classroom where you have to arrive early lest you be left out of the weekly seminar and the sharing of something that is already making its mark on the world out there.

Much remains impenetrable for Carpentier in the philosopher's ostensibly nonchalant delivery and the rare questions and comments from the rapt listeners, but, carried in the wake of Bertrand, Nabil, and the others, carried by their momentum and by his own fascination and curiosity, he soldiers on in the smoke-filled room. Sometimes he snatches fragments of such clarity that they seem to have come transformed into completion from his own store of vaguely formulated notions. At one of the sessions he thinks he recognizes something he once grandiosely referred to as *getting beyond already traced channels* when he was vehemently holding forth in a conversation with the dubious and even mocking father of one of his high school friends in New York during an afternoon when an apocalyptic snowstorm had grouped them in unusual proximity, a notion now taking shape like realized predictions in the smoke-filled room. Although Jean-Baptiste-Siméon Chardin is never once mentioned in the philosopher's ostensibly offhand delivery—indeed, Chardin's corseted women, wigged boys, and radiant fruit seem as far removed as could be from the *war machines*, *striated spaces*, and *bodies without organs* of that fall's lectures—it is in that room, while listening and taking notes in a blinding and revealing trance, that Carpentier comes upon what he sees as validation of his own attempt at cutting loose and making his way in the world alone. *Away from it all.*

He continued to attend the philosopher's lectures at the university in the woods on Tuesday mornings with Bertrand, Nabil, and the others. Their own seriousness, their vehemence even, about small things, things others neglected or disdained, things far from *current events* and political violence in the world out there, continued to sustain him. They would often gather at Nabil's studio in the Marais. During one of those gatherings, after Selim suggested they should "talk about something else," Nabil asked, "What do you want us to talk about? *Politics in China? The civil war in Lebanon?* We already know everything there is to be known about that one; no matter where, it's always the poor people who end up paying, paying for the damage, the mess, all of it. We know all this; let's go on to something else, *please*." Carpentier was grateful to him.

Another evening, at Bertrand's place, there was a long argument about what the tiny figures of two women in Vermeer's *View of Delft* could possibly be telling each other, standing there on the bank of the dark, gleaming river, the stately clouds looming overhead. Nabil, Nadine, Robert, Justine, and Bertrand were all looking

at a reproduction of the painting taped to a wall in the living room. Standing on the gold strip of the riverbank in their starched white bonnets, collars, and ample dresses, the two women seemed so tranquil and sturdy, and yet so intent on their conversation; Nadine, Robert, Justine, and Bertrand even disagreed about who they were and what they were carrying in their baskets. “It has to be personal belongings; they're too small for vegetables or other provisions from a street market; you see, there's no green head of leek peeping out of the basket, no telltale bunch of carrots,” Justine proposed. “No, she's clearly a servant; she's just come back from market and she's stopped to talk to another servant on her way back to her mistress's house to give her an account of what she's bought for the family meal. Look at the way she's dressed; look at the other group on the left; you see the difference?” And they went on. Carpentier was more interested in the disproportionate amount of space occupied by the clouds in the canvas, like tapestries in other Vermeer paintings.

On other evenings, in other apartments, studios, or student rooms, the exchanges were about the philosopher's lecture at the university in the woods that week, or the movie they had seen earlier. The discussions and arguments went late into the night.

Carpentier is blissful; he is pushing forward and fully understands when Nabil tells him one afternoon on their way to the movies that he wishes his name were “Pierre” or “Jean-Pierre,” which Nabil pronounces with a scrupulously Parisian accent, telling him that he wishes he could just be sitting on this bus, or anywhere, a café terrace, a library, a restaurant, or just walking in the streets, that he could just be *a-no-nyme*, Nabil carefully pronouncing each and every syllable for emphasis, with his usual ironic touch. He doesn't say, "Instead of clearly not being from here," but he does continue by saying, "It would be wonderful, wouldn't it, if I could just be doing what I'm doing, just another Parisian, not having to deal *with the rest of it*, as you say? If I could just be buying some bread or sitting in a bus, without the rest of it? Without anyone even thinking of asking me what I'm doing here?"

Knowing that he cannot always go unnoticed in that place and time sometimes leads Nabil to push the limits, to goad those around him: the very polite, too polite, lady at the *boulangerie*, the polite policeman who stops him in the metro to ask for his papers, the vehement ticket seller at the movie house who refuses to believe that his student card is not a fake. "You probably just wash dishes at the university," she says. Nabil just pays the full ticket price and, smiling all the while, calls her an imbecile who will remain displayed behind her glass partition like an animal in a zoo till the end of her days.

Carpentier and Nabil are on their way to the movies once again, this time to see a film by a young German director already making a name for himself, but they realize they won't make it through the show without having eaten something. In a grungy café in the Marais, as the two of them are quickly swallowing their sandwiches, Nabil does something that makes Carpentier wish he were miles away. They're standing at the counter and, for the third or fourth time, Nabil has asked the man behind the counter for a glass of water, but his several requests seem to have vanished somewhere. The man is busy serving a glass of wine to another customer, the man is busy washing glasses in a plastic tub filled with gray water, or leaving his spot behind the counter, serving at one of the tables, anything but acknowledging the request for a glass of water from

Nabil, who, with no warning, without a word, casually lifts a half-filled carafe standing on the counter, raises it a few inches above his tilted head, pours an arc of water into his open mouth, and swallows several times, belching loudly when he is finished. Carpentier feels exposed; he wants to disappear. At any moment, the man behind the counter will grab something, maybe a club, or a bottle from the shelves, and hit Nabil in the face, shattering the carafe, putting a sudden stop to the pouring of water into his mouth; blood and shards everywhere. The man is just a few feet away across from them, behind the counter, but he seems not to notice anything and meticulously goes on polishing a wineglass with a rag. After placing the carafe back on the counter, Nabil slowly and delicately wipes his mouth with the thin paper napkin lying on the remains of his sandwich, leaves some coins on the counter, and exits the café, with Carpentier in tow. Nabil is already talking about the movie they're about to see. Carpentier feels they've just escaped something terrible.

Carpentier has moved out of his room at the Maison du Maroc. He has found translation work to supplement his scholarship and now shares an apartment with two other students, but none of the Greeks he now seldom sees, including Nikos, who remains in a room at the Maison du Maroc, intent on obtaining his degree in computer science and returning home as quickly as he can. "I'm here because I had to come, Robert; it's time for me to go back," he offers, almost like an apology. Nikos is already in his last year at the university and will leave for Greece the following summer; Konstantinos will also be returning home. The surprise to all of them is Yannis, the anointed best-dressed anarchist of the campus, an early target of the junta, who could have gone back home once the dictatorship was over,

Yannis, who, after a short two weeks in Athens, returned to Paris to take up a teaching position at a university. When they run into each other in the streets over the following years, Carpentier and Yannis are barely cordial; they exchange a few words and then go on their way. The girl from Berlin who chose Carpentier over Yannis and the girl from the Polaroids that Yannis spread before his friends like a croupier's cards linger between them like ghosts.

Reminders of the life Carpentier wanted to leave behind continued to come to him in Paris as he remained there well beyond the three years of his scholarship. His mother's letters, his brother's letters arrived regularly, his mother, as usual, wishing him well, telling him how the winters in New York were getting colder, about the friends and relatives who came to visit, the meals they had, how they all missed him. His brother's letters were very short, less reserved, even reproachful as time went by: "Write to them more often at least; you could at least come for a visit or ask them to come." The pull of past and clan. His father, he would find out later, seemed content with his son's being alive and well: "Let him stay there if that's what he wants."

He stayed there. The year he started his research on Chardin in earnest, he understood he could not delay his parents' visit any longer unless he stopped communicating with them entirely. Even in his impairment, he knew this was a step he was not ready to take. He wrote to his mother in the spring, "If you and Papa can manage it, you should come to Paris for a week in June or July. I'll be able to take some time off then." He picked them up at the airport in the old Renault. In the arrival hall at Orly, as his parents came through the glass doors with their suitcases, his father's first words were somewhere between command and reproach, a cover for his shyness and reserve. "You need a haircut." Meanwhile, his mother embraced him. His father, too, unable to prevent himself, held him, his elder son, his boy, whom he hadn't wanted to see killed somewhere in a war on the other side of the world. Carpentier felt he was being reclaimed, but he dutifully went through the motions of the reunion.

While he was driving his parents to their hotel in Paris, the Renault began to wobble, and they had to stop. By the side of the highway, father and son looked at the damage. One of the tires was completely flat; all four tires were bald; even the spare looked like it would last only a short while. They put on the spare together, his father much more capable at this than he was. They drove on to Paris; on the way, his father asked him, "Where do they sell tires in this country?" and later he bought his son four new ones. "If you're going to take us around a bit, I'd like us to be safe."

They visited Paris. His father wanted to see the Invalides, Napoleon's tomb; his mother wanted to go to Notre Dame. "I'd like to light a candle." He took them around to all the places they wanted to see; they walked down the Champs-Élysées and visited the Louvre; they walked through gardens and stopped at cafés for cold drinks and sandwiches. After two days, he took them to the Loire Valley; they visited châteaux, stopped at inns. His father wanted to see the D-day beaches; he drove his parents to Normandy. It rained steadily on the way, but, once they reached the coast, the sun came out from behind the low, leaden cloud cover and one could see quite far along the arc of beaches and villages on either side of the already bustling town of Arromanches on this Saturday morning; French families, groups of ancient American tourists in raincoats, some wearing military caps, decorations, their wives holding on to them, old soldiers and their wives cautiously stepping out of buses, waiting in line at the town's war museum.

The twisted remains of rusted metal bridges built by the Allied forces decades before protruded from the ocean; the sun shone on the water, on the wide sandy beach, and on concrete bunkers overgrown with grass. "So many young men," his father said, "but Hitler and his Nazis had to be stopped; a just war, that one." Left unsaid, Carpentier knew, *not like the other one they wanted to send you to.* Carpentier remained silent; he would not revisit their discussion in the kitchen on the evening he left for Paris years ago.

They drove back to Paris, arriving in the late evening. Carpentier's parents were leaving for Italy the next day to complete their first and only "European tour." They would then go back to their life in New York, unsuspecting innocents, sacrifices to his attempt at *getting beyond already traced channels.* He would stay away—as long as he could; indefinitely; forever.

His scholarship ran out; he found other ways to make money; he taught private lessons, English to some, French to others; he translated articles, even a book on the history of diplomatic relations between the United States and Poland. He lasted. Now that he had graduated from the Institute and completed all his coursework at the Sorbonne, the writing on Chardin took up most of his time. When he presented his dissertation topic to a committee at the Sorbonne—"The old Sorbonne, the real one," as one of his professors had pointedly informed him when he first started his studies there, "not that new place they built so quickly after May '68"—his choice of Jean-Baptiste-Siméon Chardin's paintings, especially his proposed approach, his focus on Chardin's still lifes, seemed peculiar to some of the faculty, the younger ones especially, who expected other affinities from this particular student. One of them suggested that he could "*at least* look into the historical implications of Chardin's work; the larger picture, damn it!" The young professor was turning red; he seemed on the verge of some sort of attack, but he continued, his voice getting louder. "The patronage system of the Old Regime, the plunder of global wealth that made such work possible—and these are only two possibilities! After all, Chardin was the son of a cabinetmaker!" Impervious, Robert Carpentier remained who he was. Those younger professors, some only a few years older than he was, seemed so smug, so assertive in their advice. No, what interested him in Chardin's work, what he wanted to pursue and hold on to, was in the paintings: light and surface, flatness and foreshortening, harmony and color. He'd had enough of *everything else*. There, in Chardin's arrangements, he found solace and sanctuary. He held fast to his choice. One of the older faculty agreed to direct his thesis.

At the end of the seventies, Robert Carpentier defended his thesis, with *félicitations du jury*, high honors, in spite of some acerbically formulated divergences during the defense. Members of these juries could always be counted on to settle old scores in public, pursue turf wars among themselves, attack colleagues' protégés while the candidate and the audience looked on. When members of the jury did ask him direct questions, Carpentier answered, explained, justified, committed to some minor revisions. In the end, after the ritual mix of praise and massacre in one of the Sorbonne's ornate auditoriums, there was a celebration at a café on rue des Écoles, the traditional gathering place after a thesis defense. Friends came, Bertrand, Nabil, Justine, Michel, the others, as well as some of the members of the jury; they all drank champagne; they toasted Robert. Two waiters brought out small bowls of tapenade, platters of cheese, thin slices of baguette. An hour later, when the celebrants spilled out onto the street, a smaller group remained together. They would go for dinner; Bertrand was clamoring for onion soup to start. "Something hot, something filling! I think I'm drunk; I have to eat something now." The defense had lasted several hours; it was already nine in the evening, even later, but the sun still hadn't set. On the quays, the windows of buildings were still reflecting warm auburn light; below, the Seine was slowly turning dark. Paris was as stunning as when he had first arrived, but Robert Carpentier could no longer remain there.

There were difficulties, hurdles, the world beyond Chardin's frames, his colors and compositions. University positions were rare enough for French graduates, let alone for this strange, indeterminate interloper who seemed out of touch. Yet he couldn't see himself doing anything else; useless for anything else, he told himself, unable to enter into any other covenant.

Sunday, June 1, 1980—and before, and after

Another violence, still new and potent, lay there, the blood not yet congealed

Carpentier went back to America. There was no other way. He applied for several positions, all on the East Coast, all in New York City or New England. Beyond that particular swath of continent reaching into the Atlantic, the rest appeared far off and inimical—Mississippi, Texas, Idaho, Montana. For him, another violence, still new and potent, lay there, the blood not yet congealed. He would feel exposed.

California might have been a possibility, but there

were no positions in his field advertised in any college out there, on the other side of the country. The offer to visit Wannaford College, in Connecticut, came very quickly after the initial interview at one of the university clubs in Manhattan. The prestige of "the old Sorbonne" was still very much valued in the New World, the academic market so much wider, less prey to connections and fiefdoms than in France; colleges and universities were actually competing for him here, but Wannaford was the first to call him and offer a brunch interview at the Yale Club.

He showed up for his interview wearing a blue blazer, a white shirt, and jeans; he was told by a uniformed concierge at the front desk that "Gentlemen have to wear a tie," and that jeans were not allowed in the club dining room, not even on a Saturday at breakfast time. Robert Carpentier didn't want to make a scene; anything but a scene. He admitted he didn't know; he explained to the man, almost pleading. The man handed him a tie. "Here, you can wear this one." The tie was slightly soiled; he carefully hid the spots behind his now buttoned jacket and went up the steps to the dining room. The interview went well. He was invited to go to the campus to give a talk, to meet with other faculty, with administrators.

He had never been to Connecticut. He took a train from Manhattan, transferred to a bus in Hartford, and there he was, among the hills and lakes, white churches and meadows, the fields and the drystone walls. Then came the people through the landscape, unfolding like figures from another time, one with which he was already familiar but had never encountered in three dimensions before: the old professor with a German accent, chair of the Department of Art History, who moved cautiously in his wood-paneled living room, mixed martinis, and seemed so satisfied with Carpentier's view of Chardin after his presentation, introducing him to other colleagues but always keeping him close by, offering his own views, shuffling around but expertly handling the shaker and pouring drinks: "I only have one a day; I've been doing it for a long time, but only one before dinner; that's the secret, only one"; the square-jawed, gray-haired dean in his tweed jacket who asked Carpentier whether he had questions about the college's *research funds for junior faculty*; the specialist in Italian primitives, wrapped in the folds of her black poncho, offering to help him find housing, if, of course, the position was offered and if, of course, he accepted. All of them smiling, benevolent, all of them in this landscape of hills and lakes, white churches and meadows that seemed a stage set from another time. If the position was offered, he would accept it. Here was fine; here was a harbor. He wouldn't pursue any of the other advertised positions.

He went to see his parents and brother a full week after returning to New York. They were all living in a two-family house on Long Island now, just a few minutes from the beaches where he used to go swimming in the summer. His brother had married a girl whose family had known his from before they all came to their new country; they now had two children, a boy not quite a year old and a girl. "She's five; she's starting school this year," his sister-in-law offered. He already knew this from the letters; he was being told some things once again. Carpentier glanced at his brother; they used to be so close, so complicitous, the two of them; now he seemed so established and compliant. *He has remained*, he thought. They were all sitting in the living room. His brother's wife was holding the boy on her lap, his brother was sitting on the couch between their parents, and the little girl was somewhere upstairs. Carpentier told them about the campus visit; his brother and sister-in-law told him about their jobs, the children; his parents reminisced about their time with him in France.

"It seems like a long time ago; it *is* a long time ago; it's been four years!"

"Is that car still around?"

"Yes, but I had to let it go at one point; I couldn't afford to keep it. I gave it to a friend. I have to thank you again for those tires."

"I wanted to see just one thing outside of Paris, the D-day beaches; that car got us there."

. . .

"So, when are you leaving for Connecticut?" (His brother, as always, got to the point.)

"Tomorrow. I'm taking a train from Penn Station."

"We're taking the train into the city tomorrow; work beckons. We're not professors, you know. We could drive you to the station; we leave the car there."

"Thanks, but my train is early; I'm sleeping at a friend's in Manhattan. I'm not a professor yet, you know."

"You mean you're not staying with us tonight? You just got back! I've made your favorite—meatballs in sauce, wrapped in sweet plantains, the way your grandmother used to make them!"

"I can't; I really have to leave early from Manhattan; my train's at seven-twenty."

. . .

"Well, let's eat. I like that dish, too. You only make it for your son; you neglect your old husband."

. . .

He left after dinner. His brother drove him to the station. The following day, he took the train and then a bus to the Wannaford campus. The position was offered two days after his visit—a phone call from the chair of the department, the mixer of martinis. He accepted the offer without any discussion. He took the train back to Connecticut the day after the offer was made; he found a cottage by a lake with the help of the specialist of Italian primitives, who took him around in her car.

Robert Carpentier settled in at Wannaford. He bought a car—there was no other way to get around in the bucolic landscape; he moved the furniture around in the cottage; he lived in the theater set of rolling hills, drystone walls, flaming maples in the fall, frozen lakes in the winter. He taught the classes in the redbrick buildings; he wrote the articles for scholarly journals and attended professional conferences in the heartland; he gave the talks he was invited to give and almost never ventured beyond campus or conference hotel on those trips to other cities or other colleges in the middle of nowhere. He made an exception once and ventured far from the safe confines of colloquium or campus library: He rented a car in Tucson and drove out *to see the wide-open spaces of America.* Throughout the short trip, in the motels, in the bars and restaurants, in the streets of small towns, something oppressive lingered, the feeling of being extraneous, uninvited. Driving on the highways was an exception, especially in the desert; there, alone, contained, and safe in the air-conditioned car, with the music blasting, he could see the magnificent landscape pass by like a dream of movies from childhood.

The thesis on Chardin would be turned into a book; he worked slowly, steadily. He would be granted tenure, and promoted to the rank of associate professor. He was beginning to be interested in Watteau. He was drawn by the painter's meticulously rendered gestures, the fluidity of his brushwork, the pastels, the glazed pinks and yellows of landscapes, clothing, and faces, his enigmatic and wistful figures set in places that could never be, unless in a dream. Carpentier bypassed the war scenes that had first made Watteau famous throughout eighteenth-century Europe and focused instead on the painter's gatherings and processions of carefree, lavish, yet delicate figures and landscapes; he was particularly attracted to Watteau's figures from the commedia dell'arte, busy plotting, performing, or suspended in uncertain stances, swathed in the lustrous folds of their costumes. There, once again, as he had with Chardin, Carpentier found what he was looking for, an unspecified place *far from everything else.*

At first, only the boy notices the men's sudden appearance on the veranda, and he wonders why no one is reacting as the walking and flying men fill the veranda, then the inside of the house, taking up all the room in the wedge of light. The one who seems to be the leader unfastens his wings and orders the young aunt to take off all her clothes. She complies; she's crying. Some of the other men use their rifle butts or their guns to break the teeth of all those sitting at the table; they do this casually, as if they were arranging glasses on a shelf

or tidying up a closet; yet another one takes out a machete and begins to slash repeatedly at the two boys' small necks in determined arcs, cutting deep bright red strips.

He worked slowly, steadily, at his office and at the cottage. He bought food at the supermarket in the nearest town, stopped at the farmers' markets for fruit and vegetables, corn and apples in the fall, asparagus and blueberries in the spring and summer. He bought books at the college co-op and at bookstores in Manhattan when he drove there for an opera or a movie that would never play near Wannaford. He usually cooked for himself and sometimes ate at the Chinese restaurant across from campus or at the Crossroads, a diner a few minutes away by car. With its leatherette booths, chrome stools, polished soda fountain, and yellowing menus, the Crossroads seemed even more preserved from another time than the rest of the theater—or movie—set in which Carpentier saw himself living. A place where he could continue to leave everything behind, build a pristine, unencumbered life.

Although he could easily drive down to New London and take the ferry across the Sound, he very rarely went to the two-family house on Long Island. He almost always managed to find a reason not to: He was attending a colloquium; he was traveling to Atlanta, or Miami, or Saint Paul; an article had to be revised and sent to journal editors this week and no later; he had a cold. He could feel his mother's disappointment on the phone, her incomprehension, her sadness. She never asked him any questions, saying instead, "I understand; we'll see you next week. I'll make your favorite dish. Your father says hello."

At about the time Carpentier started teaching at

Wannaford, an aging Hollywood actor with a still thick head of hair and bright red cheeks the color of crushed beets was elected president of the United States; two years later, an opinion piece in a British newspaper would mention "the braying of the Yuppies" (a newly coined word) after a woman with a brassy helmet of hair won a second term as prime minister. From somewhere, far away it seemed, the AIDS crisis, as it was called in that place and time, was just beginning, and gaining momentum. The epidemic had generated new rules; many panicked, even in the northeast corner of the small state, far from the "urban areas where the mysterious illness primarily infected gay men," as Carpentier read one morning in *The New York Times*, delivered every day to his office at Wannaford College.

He hardly noticed who was in power, in the United States or elsewhere, but he abided by the new rules that regulated bodies encountering other bodies in those early years of the epidemic in his time and place. He had run into a colleague at the farmers' market in the fall of his first year at Wannaford, an associate professor from the school of business, a married woman a few years older than he was, who had asked, quite matter-of-factly, holding her paper bag full of vegetables, looking straight at him, "Robert, what *do* you do with yourself all alone in that cottage?" They saw each other with regularity in the afternoons after that, until the summer.

In the fall of his second year at Wannaford, Carpentier met another colleague, this time an assistant professor from the linguistics department. Her name was Erika and she was from Hungary; he saw her for quite some time, even after the colleague from the school of business and Carpentier started meeting each other again at the cottage, and Erika knew about it. "We're all adults," she said, adding something about all of them finding the "not so circuitous routes to fulfillment in the age of safe sex." She spoke like that; she played games with the expression "safe sex," its various possible meanings and permutations; she told Carpentier about a philosopher who'd written a book called *How to Do Things with Words*.

Erika had come to the United States from Hungary as an adolescent, but unlike many of her fellow Hungarians, who wanted nothing to do with the old country anymore, who wanted to leave everything behind, forget, make another life entirely, she went back regularly. "To see relatives, to see my friends, the ones still over there," she told Carpentier, but also because she just *wanted* to do it. "You know, Robert, there are things you can't get rid of; there are smells, details, places; maybe you think you can leave them behind? I don't think so." Carpentier looked at her and volunteered no answer of his own. He admired her; he envied her. There was a whiff of an accent in her very American English. "I kept it on purpose," she admitted to him. They continued to see each other well into the decade; Erika continued to consider their encounters "philosophically," as she put it.

There were no *entanglements* or *imbroglios* (again, Erika's words). The three of them, Carpentier, Erika, and the colleague from the school of business, all behaved "philosophically," even if this was not the way the colleague from the school of business put it; she was less abstract in her description of the situation.

No, there were no entanglements, no imbroglios, but, for Carpentier, the rules that regulated bodies encountering other bodies in those early years of the epidemic gave a clinical tinge to sex. In the age of AIDS, people seemed to have a posture, something akin to a method, a manner at once rapacious and calculated, that sapped his exultation; he was slightly repulsed by the soft and globular coldness of used condoms, a stain on the framed carnal scenes. At different times, either immediately preceding or well before their encounters, Carpentier and Erika, or Carpentier and the colleague from the school of business, asked each other, either point-blank (never Carpentier's manner) or offhandedly, about *other partners*. The attempt to at least prune the arabesque of encounters, to contain it somehow by at least knowing or pretending to know, was a new ritual in the age of AIDS, even if no one was ever completely sure. At least in that uncertainty there was room for something artless; *Liebestraum*, Erika the linguist called it, playing with the German she had learned in Hungary as a child and which had become one of the main languages of her research. "*Liebestraum*, Robert, a dream of love or, let's play with words a bit, *Liebensraum*, a vital space for love." She had to explain to him; he already knew about Hitler and *Lebensraum*, having had to read so much about it during his years at the Institute in Paris; and he enjoyed Erika's ability, as she explained it, to sidestep the obvious, the serious, to follow her own bent, her own pleasures. She was playing with words, as always.

It was all done with clean hands, in clean underwear, with intelligent phrases, among people whose awareness and capacity for self-preservation could be taken for granted. Life went on easily, pleasantly, and even decorously for Carpentier; he was far away from that other life and that other past, free of clan, blood, grief; he was in his element, in spite of his aversion to condoms and his knowing without knowing that something was only being deferred in this life among the rolling hills, the lakes, among the white steeples and the brick buildings. He plodded on, immersed himself in the colors and compositions, precariously holding on to another life *away from everything else*. Meeting Eve would take him further in his undertaking. Years afterward, it would also contribute to his devastation.

MONDAY, AUGUST 1, 1988—AND BEFORE, AND AFTER

They made their pact

The first time he saw Eve, she was reading on the same pine-scented beach he had gone to with Konstantinos years before, his first year in Europe, his first time in Greece. The return to that beach the summer he met her was both fate and pilgrimage: He was already in Europe and had gone to Greece because, once again, Nikos had invited him. "My mother passed away this year; I would really like it if you came to visit; it's been a long time. I'm still in the same apartment you know on Dorileou; come when you're through in Vienna; we'll catch up."

He had gone to Austria to research an article on Giuseppe Arcimboldo. He had arrived in Vienna in early July and now, as the month was ending, he had accomplished everything he had hoped for, gathered all the material he needed. He had seen the paintings by Arcimboldo in the Kunsthistorisches Museum; he'd struggled with this mouthful, but the taxi driver who took him there had deciphered it very quickly, used to outsiders slaughtering his language. In Innsbruck, "Habsburg Schloss Ambras" was easier to say; there, he had seen more Arcimboldos. He was only interested in the composite heads. By the end of July, he had seen and taken notes on all the paintings he needed to see in Austria. He was ready to continue work on the long article he'd wanted to write since seeing the painter's four seasons, four composite heads, for the first time at the Wannaford library while looking for another book. Not at all his field, but he couldn't stay away; the ordered opulence, the aloof weirdness of these faces made of everything under the sun beckoned to him. He would take a break from the long book on Watteau without really leaving it; the same thing attracted him in both painters, something he saw as their disregard for anything outside of their frames, and their analogous focus on their work as something removed from the real world; a work of color, light, composition, an art that took from the world what it absolutely needed and then stood alone: unconcerned, flawless, unassailable. Now, Carpentier was finished gathering. Now, his own head filled with Arcimboldo's assemblages, he was ready to leave. He had everything he needed for his article; it was time.

And so once again he'd accepted Nikos's invitation and gone to Athens. Not driving this time, as he had done in that old Renault years before; just a three-hour trip by plane, and there he was, the bright sun startling after the days of gray and drizzle in Vienna. The apartment on Dorileou was exactly as he remembered it; Nikos had left everything the way it was when his mother was alive; there were more books on new shelves in Nikos's former bedroom, now his study, where Carpentier would sleep.

They speak in French, the language of their student days. They talk about their days in Paris, that summer in Greece, the last summer of the colonels' dictatorship; how Nikos had left Paris as soon as he had completed his studies and could return to Greece; how Carpentier had remained.

"You stayed on, Robert, and look at you now, a professor."

"You're not doing too badly, either, Niko—Monsieur le Directeur at the Department of Education."

"You know that Yannis is a professor, too, in Paris, at Jussieu?"

"Yes; I ran into him a few times after you had all left."

"He comes to Greece every summer, with his French wife."

"Can you believe it, *the best-dressed anarchist of the entire campus*, Yannis the skirt-chaser is married!"

"How about you, Robert? Anyone?

"No, no one. You?"

"There's someone at work—Eleni; I'd like you to meet her."

. . . (A Greek woman, of course. He has *returned home*.)

And they go on. As will old friends who haven't seen each other in years. The following day, a weekday, Nikos has to go to work at the department and leaves early. "I'll be back around six this afternoon and we'll leave for the taverna around nine. I left you the keys on the small table in the hall. You have the apartment keys and the car keys. I don't need the car to go to work; it's parked right on Dorileou, across the street. Why don't you go to the beach after all this time in Austrian libraries and museums?" Nikos, as attentive as ever. Carpentier is glad he accepted his friend's invitation. "How will I recognize the car?" he asks as Nikos is about to close the entrance door behind him. "A Peugeot, Robert, the only one on the street; same model, but it's not the old one that you knew; I've moved up in the world!"

Carpentier makes himself coffee and takes out the desk chair to the terrace adjoining Nikos's old bedroom. Below, he can see the kiosk where he bought gum years ago, using that perfectly pronounced Greek sentence. He never made it to the islands that summer. Maybe this time around. For today, he'll just go back to that pine-scented beach a few miles away, one of the only two places he knows on the coast. He remains on the terrace, drinking his coffee; he has a second cup; he watches people walk up and down Dorileou, coming up the hill or going down to the main avenue below, mostly schoolchildren and old people. After a while it gets too hot on the terrace and he goes into the apartment to take a shower and get ready for the beach.

The Peugeot is parked right across the street. It gleams in the sun. The inside of the car is steaming; the seat and the steering wheel are burning hot. He leaves the door open for a few minutes, then gets back in and turns the car on. At first, he uses the beach towel to hold on to the steering wheel; he drives the car down Dorileou to the main avenue and manages not to get lost on his way to the road leading out of Athens. After a few miles of crossing through the immediate suburbs, the road takes an uphill turn and the sea appears down below. The beaches closest to Athens are crowded; tourists, Athenians having a swim during the long midday break from work. *A happy people*, Robert Carpentier says to himself; the years of the dictatorship are now far behind. A few minutes after the uphill climb, the road slopes down again, and he begins to recognize the area and even finds the dirt road to the pine-scented beach. The pebbly sand, the clusters of pines and tamarisks, the calm, clear water, all the same as he remembered. But there are no old people bobbing in the water today. It's the middle of the day; they come early in the morning or in the late afternoon, grandfathers, grandmothers, old aunts coming to the beach with babies and children; they count the number of "sea baths" they take over the summer, storing up health for the winter, Carpentier remembers; a happy people. Today there are quite a few high school kids and a group of a dozen or so young men and women, too old to be high school students, gathered under one of the clusters of pine and tamarisk.

Three young women have splintered off from the group, opting to stay in the sun; all three are lying down on the sand, their towels folded into pillows; all three are reading books held at arm's length, creating bounded and momentary shade between their faces and the dazzling sky.

Carpentier doesn't know how he finds himself near them, near enough to hear one of them say something to him in Greek; he doesn't know which one. After his reply, in Greek, quickly followed by the unavoidable discovery that his Greek is nonexistent, names are exchanged in English for his sake.

"Daphne."

"Anastasia."

"Evie."

"I'm happy to meet you, Daphne, Anastasia, Eve."

Carpentier's shadow falls on the three young women sitting up in the sand, adding a layer of shade between them and the sun at his back.

"No, not *Eve*, E-vie, short for Evangeline."

She says this even if she is obviously not unhappy with *Eve*, but from the instant she said her name, Carpentier either misheard the syllables or willfully (teasingly?)

dismissed the second one; to him, she was already Eve, only Eve, and he would continue to call her that throughout the summer and throughout the fall in New York, and still two years later, when they were married, she would always be Eve, the one and only Eve, the girl, the woman he could not bear to be without. There simply would be no possibility of going on without her. *I will die if I am not with her, I will die.*

On the pine-scented beach that morning, the sun pouring from above, it is perhaps not yet too late for him, his blindness not yet irreparable, not too late to put an end to his impairment and his misdirected flight forward, the result, in part, of an old brutality, of having seen what people can do to one another, even if he had emerged intact in body, not too late, on that pine-scented beach that morning, for him to see that there can be no complete and undamaged separation between the life imagined and the life lived. It is perhaps not too late because, for the first time in his still young life, he is being overwhelmed by a rapturous anguish that leaves no room for calculation or control, for he is out of his depth, defenseless, unable to feign or evaluate; he cannot but be here, now, on this pine-scented beach with the sun pouring from above, neither slayer nor victim, artless, wholly here, and now, just seconds after the exchange of names, and the initial and apparent lightness of *I'm happy to meet you, Daphne, Anastasia, Eve*, he is unable to move, only able to conjure up the most fatuous of phrases for the young woman leaning on one elbow, her sunglasses pushed up to her forehead, a hand held up, opened against the glare, placating and imperially pushing back at the same time, it seems, as she looks at Carpentier standing between her and the sun, riveted to the warm pebbled sand, seeing only her. In other words, as some in his time and place say—though he himself never would, certain as he always is of being lucid, controlled, even duplicitous—he is *falling in love.*

The three of them are looking at him from below. There is nothing left for him but to continue on his way to swim. As he heads for the water, he hears her say, "Maybe we'll see you tomorrow?"

Of course, he is there the next day. She has come alone. After a few cursory exchanges—"Would you like to be in the shade? Would you like to be in the sun? How about here?"—they swim out together, as far as he had years before with Konstantinos. They stop heading for the horizon at the same time and face each other, the sea vast around them, their hands and legs moving just enough to keep afloat in the deep, calm water; then she comes to him and kisses him, her legs around his waist, her arms around his neck and his shoulders, the floating left up to him as she pushes down his swimsuit with her feet and toes; the kissing stops as he slightly nudges her backward, just enough to remove the bottom of her bikini, his head going underwater for a few seconds as he slips the bottom piece down her legs, off her feet, and when he emerges to the surface again, she is quickly around him, and he is quickly inside her as they float together like a single animal, some limbs tightly stuck to its body, other limbs fluttering and keeping it afloat, an amphibian breathing in short gasps, its double head precariously close to the surface of the water, the rest of its body submerged. This only lasts a moment; they cannot find their rhythm and now frantically seek a fulcrum, but quickly have to concede; they separate and look at each other once more before swimming back to the thin line of the beach.

When they reach their towels, she stands still, her feet

planted firmly in the sand, her legs slightly apart in a stiff and geometric warrior stance; then she suddenly bends, pushes out her shoulders and her chest in an abrupt perpendicular thrust above her waist, and shakes the water from her hair in rapid, repeated, and twisted surges of her head and neck, her hips remaining the immobile center of this flurry while the salt water whips out in cold drops from her hair, repeatedly and violently spreading in dark, wet strands, like the tentacles of a squid being hit against a rock. He sits on his towel in contemplation. After the flurry of motion, she serenely gathers her hair in a rubber band and sits next to him. They both stretch out on the towels, their faces open to the sun; she speaks as if to the sky, to no one in particular. She can only stay until lunchtime, and then she has to go back to a house on the hill on the other side of the road, her parents' summer house. "We always come here, every summer; we've never missed a single summer. Summers are precious. So, tell me about you."

He speaks; she listens. This is his first summer back in Greece since he was there in the early seventies; a friend had invited him; he tells her about the scholarship to Paris, his departure from New York, the years in Paris, the Greek friends he made there. He tells her all this in a continuous flow, as if unburdening himself, the confession of a boy murmuring to a priest in a dark church smelling of incense, rather than a man, here, with the sun pouring from above. "More," she says. "Tell me more; tell me everything." And so he tells her about his parents, his brother, the first years in New York, Chardin and the Sorbonne and the Institute, and still she wants to know more; he then tells her about his childhood, the bliss and the brutality, a shorter version of this last part; he wants to take his leave from that memory in his headlong rush, to retain no room for it in the newness of her. He tells her about the first departure, the new life in New York, the discovery of ice in the streets. "Now I'm teaching at a college in Connecticut—Wannaford; I've been living in Connecticut since I went back to the United States." He's come full circle.

When he stops, she begins—a tacit agreement between them, the way they had both stopped swimming at one point in the sea. "I don't know where to start," she begins, and then she tells him about her grandfather's departure from a small mountain village on an island in the middle of the Aegean, a boy leaving the only life he had ever known, finding his way to New York all alone, with only a cousin's address folded in his other pair of socks in the cardboard suitcase. Thousands, hundreds of thousands leaving behind countryside and pastures, farms and villages already left by others making their way to promised lands, beckoned by tales of magnificent cities, Rome and Athens, Timbuktu and Cairo, New York and Paris, all part of the massive migratory movements on the planet from the very beginning, hundreds of thousands, millions, at first on foot, camelback, horseback, muleback, aboard rafts, ships, airplanes, this particular pilgrim a boy still in the early part of the century going through his own enactment of the ancient undertaking, in his own time the cargo ship, the harbor lights of Manhattan, the shames and mortifications of triage—"Cough; cough again; bend down; are you an anarchist?"—but also the lucky encounters and the kindnesses, this particular boy wise well beyond his years and with the energy of the young and desperate managing to shorten the customary time between arrival and settled life, or arrival and departure, yes, in his case between arrival and departure, this pilgrim actually opting to leave the Land of Opportunity, but with a wealth accumulated through double and triple shifts working in factories, construction sites, the systematically saved salaries, meals eaten in the restaurants where he also worked, the purchase of one and then two dilapidated apartments in Hell's Kitchen, New York, USA, first renovated and then rented out to two Irish families, the encounter with Bill Davies, the third- or fourth- or fifth-generation American from a mining family in Wales, now one of the men to contend with on Wall Street, Bill Davies in his expensive double-breasted suit, his hair parted in the middle, Bill Davies, who took to this boy serving him his steak—"Make it rare; leave out the potato"—after his usual two bootleg martinis, "What's your name?" and then the ensuing recognition of the young man's humility, keen intelligence, energy, and apparent disregard for remaining in the Land of Opportunity—five years after the processing at Ellis Island—now yearning to return to home, place, and clan, to the clear nights of the Aegean and the smell of thyme, fig, salt air, Bill Davies, who, taken by the combination of humility, desire, and disdain for the place that made the realization of the craziest dreams possible, introduced him to that disembodied way of making money: "You have to understand how to let money make money for you." The young man from the island in the middle of the Aegean was a quick learner and understood, even before the end of the meal he had served, that this portly, expensively dressed man wanted nothing from him, that this was an offering that should not be refused, and so the two small apartments in Hell's Kitchen were sold within weeks, following Davies's advice, "Still, you have to start with something; I can front you a bit, but you have to bring something to the game; the more you bring, the higher the returns," followed by the offer of an advance here and now, that night at the restaurant where Eve's grandfather was serving out his second shift; the offer conquered any reticence he might have had; in fact, there was no reticence, only the immediate recognition that this was a whim, a gift from someone who wanted nothing in return, and three years after their first encounter in the restaurant, in spite of Davies's earnest encouragement to *remain in the game*, "You'll see, you'll multiply it tenfold in a year or two," the young man from the rocky island in the middle of the Aegean booked a private cabin aboard the luxury liner RMS *Mauretania* and disembarked in Europe at the wheel of his brand-new Model T just weeks before the Wall Street crash. *Some people go back, and they're happy to be back*, Carpentier tells himself as Eve stops the flow of her story for a few seconds.

"In a way, our family is still living on what he brought back with him; he married a Greek girl from Smyrna; you know what happened to the Greeks in Smyrna in 1922, the great catastrophe?" Carpentier has only a vague knowledge of these events, and she tells him about the razing of Smyrna by Mustafa Kemal's forces, the great fire, the tens of thousands of dead Greeks and Armenians. "My grandfather married my grandmother after his return from New York, and he decided never to go back to the United States; he stayed in Athens; he bought apartments and land in Athens and nearby; he never invested in the market again." Eve's grandfather never *let money make money* for him again, something he distrusted, the peasant in him who felt he had gotten away with murder, and there had also been the crash to remind him of how lucky he had been. The only bad investment he ever made, the wrong choice, if the idea had been to make money, was made in the suburbs of Athens. "Two towns from this one; there was nothing there back then, or here, either; just sheep and a few fishermen," Eve tells Robert Carpentier. His only bad choice was where he chose to buy a big swath away from the beach because of his bees; the salt air was no good for his bees, or there were fewer flowers for them to gather their precious nectar. "You can imagine what that would be worth today; shipowners built their villas there in the '50s; my parents moved to New York around that time and, of course, I moved with them; they continued the tradition, you know, Greeks leaving for the United States, and staying there; my grandfather was the exception; he went, and he came back; we didn't come back; we've stayed, but we spend every summer here; summers are precious." Again, Carpentier thinks, that yearning to return home, so strange and foreign to him.

Two days later, the departure *for the islands*, as Nikos had predicted years ago. Eve has arranged for them to meet at Piraeus to board the 8:00 A.M. ferry. "The ferry is called the *Miaoulis*," she tells him. "Buy the cheapest ticket at Piraeus, a deck ticket. There are booths there; it's written in English, T-I-C-K-E-T-S. Meet me on the top deck, near the lifeboats." He wakes up at dawn in the apartment on Dorileou Street. He packed the night before and now quietly leaves the dark apartment, where Nikos is still sleeping. Alone once again in the streets of Athens but carefully following Nikos's directions, he doesn't get lost this time; the Athens metro is simple enough. He gets to Piraeus, purchases his ticket, and finds Eve on the top deck of the *Miaoulis*, already there a half hour before the ferry leaves port; she has a knapsack and two sleeping bags. She's bought thin crowns of sesame-encrusted bread from one of the vendors walking through the boarding crowds. "Waking up early always makes me hungry; I also have some peaches." The ferry pulls out of Piraeus packed with tourists; it seems as if all the carefree blondness of Northern Europe has descended on these islands for the summer. Carpentier thinks of the young Lebanese guy in the train compartment all those years ago on his way to Amsterdam in the middle of winter, turning the pages of his leather-bound binder full of pictures of golden beaches, olive groves, blue skies.

A cool breeze from the sea wafts through the ferryboat's upper deck. The morning is still fresh, the sun not yet hot. "But, you'll see," Eve tells him. They manage to find a shady spot under one of the lifeboats and remain on the top deck for the full journey. The crossing is calm; sun pours from above. Small, uninhabited, rocky islands pass by like rough shields of bull's hide on the calm sea; the ferry leaves a stream of foamy white in its wake. This is no place for old people, the young in one another's arms, seagulls diving for pieces of bread thrown overboard, Carpentier and Eve looking out to the horizon, reading, falling asleep in the shade.

Hours later, the *Miaoulis*'s anchor is lowered. Two small boats come to carry passengers from the ferry to the island's port; as the crowd disembarks, old women in black are holding up cardboard signs for rooms to let. Carpentier follows Eve, who has to pull him along several times, rapt as he is by everything around him, she having been there before, knowing, and hurrying to where she wants to take him, first a bus and then another small boat with a few of the young men and women from the ferry, each handing out coins to a man casually holding out one hand to help them come aboard and the other to receive payment. Another boat ride follows, this one short, with the island's rocky coastline always close by, then a sudden break in the coastline and the boat veers toward land as the water gradually changes from dark blue to a transparent turquoise and the beach comes into view.

"It's beautiful."

. . .

There are about thirty or forty young people, maybe more; it's hard to tell, as they are either swimming or gathered in groups on the beach, most of them reading, some wearing glasses that look odd against their nakedness.

. . .

"Yes; it's like that here; some of them have been here since June, since May even. You see that place a bit farther back there, behind all the rows of bamboo? It's a taverna; the owner has showers in the back. We have the sleeping bags; we have everything we need."

. . .

That evening, Carpentier and Eve are sitting at several large tables with most of the people who were on the beach earlier. Everyone is drinking beer and cold piney wine in frosty bottles from the taverna's ancient humming refrigerator. Carpentier is gulping down the wine like ice water. A bearded young man has taken out a guitar and starts singing, only American songs; it seems like a scene from a decade before, frozen in time. Eve says hello to a few people she knows; he is introduced: "My friend Robert." Greek, Italian, French, Scandinavian, only a few Americans sprinkled in there. After they eat, Eve and Carpentier quickly leave; the voices and the music recede as they walk away from the taverna's bare bulbs glowing under the night sky. The sea is scarcely visible as they unfold their sleeping bags at a spot on the sand away from the voices and the lights. The moon rises bloodred behind the hills on one side of the bay, poised to begin its night-to-dawn journey, red to orange to yellow to white, then going through the same shades in reverse before setting red again at dawn on the other side of the bay. This time, Carpentier and Eve find their fulcrum and rhythm on the still warm sand, from red moon to red moon. They live on the beach for two weeks.

Carpentier is in a state of recovered bliss, deep in an enchantment he has not known for many years. Eve is a sumptuous and foreign landscape he is discovering with all the wonderment of a navigator stepping ashore after years at sea. The two of them and the young people on the beach live in a cycle governed by sunrise and sunset. They are all sleeping on the beach; they are awakened by the heat and light a few hours after sunrise, then make their way to the two showers behind the taverna before feeding on fruit and roughly cut slices of bread set by the owner with small pots of butter and honey on the large tables in the shade of his taverna's bamboo canopy. Their days are spent swimming, walking, reading, all those bodies in the perfection of their youth lying naked in the sun. One day, Carpentier sees on the beach someone who seems to have just arrived, an older man, Scandinavian or German, perhaps? He is already badly sunburned, his skin crimson and raw, but he sits there, by himself on the beach, naked like all the others, supremely at ease, his legs open, his penis buried in the folds of his pink scrotum, which sags in the sand. Carpentier quickly closes his eyes and only reopens them when he has changed the direction of his gaze, and, when he has, he lingers for a long time on a couple hitting a ball back and forth to each other with rounded wooden rackets on the strip of wet sand between the beach and the blue water; he thinks of Chardin's *Girl with a Racket*, but, in the waning late-afternoon sun, as bodies are becoming dark silhouettes against the sea and sky, this image is replaced by the lithe brick-colored bodies of leaping, dancing, cup-bearing figures of Minoan frescoes, inhabitants of a world far away from the older man's sagging scrotum.

Then there is the rest of the summer, other islands, short stays in Athens in between. During the day, Carpentier has the apartment on Dorileou Street to himself, since Nikos leaves early for the Department of Education. Eve comes to meet him at the apartment. She rings the buzzer in the late morning; he has seen her walking up the narrow street; he gives her time to get to the building, buzzes her in, and waits a few seconds before opening the apartment door to the coolness of the marble-floored stairwell. She is standing there, once again. She fills the apartment. He is faint with desire. She brings him still warm crusty cheese pies wrapped in paper; she also brings bread. In the small bedroom, they leave the glass sliding door open and also pull up the slatted shutter to let air in; now only a thin flowered curtain stands between them and the terrace and the street below—passing cars, horns honking, people late for work, passersby walking and talking, the sun already hot. A fan is turning above Carpentier and Eve, its quiet whir a counterpoint to the life outside. They feed on each other; the sheets are heavy with sweat. They emerge as the heat of the day fills the small room. They walk to the kitchen, the marble floor cool beneath their feet. They make salads—tomatoes, cucumbers, olives; they soak up the olive oil and vinegar from the bottom of the bowl with chunks of bread; they eat cold slices of watermelon, including the seeds. They go back to the shade of the bedroom; the thin flowered curtain hangs motionless in the heat of the day. They begin again.

Suddenly it's the end of the summer. They are having dinner in Athens, at one of a dozen tavernas set on a steep street leading to the Acropolis. The hum of hundreds of people talking and eating; the tinkle of cutlery against plates; bottles being uncorked; the smoke from the grilling of meats rising to the sky overhead. A glass breaks on the street's flagstones, and a waiter quickly sweeps it up. Eve and Carpentier are sitting at a table under one of the olive trees that border the street on one side; the tree trunks are painted white. Eve has been telling him about the wine festival at Daphni, a few kilometers from Athens; there is also an ouzo festival somewhere. He can't stop looking at her. *A wine festival, an ouzo festival, gatherings under a cloudless sky: celebrations of a carefree people; her people, her country, even if the family now lives in New York; it does not rain in the summer here, or hardly ever, and even then, only for a few minutes. Another country.*

The remains of their meal lie on the table; the waiters are in no hurry to clean up; soon they will bring watermelon, or cantaloupe, push plates aside to make room on the small, cluttered table. Eve has stopped talking about the wine festival, the ouzo festival. "You have to meet my parents; they want to know who their daughter has been going to the islands with all summer; they want to know who she's been going to see in Athens." He is to come for coffee; after the hot afternoon, right before sunset. The family, again, but under a different guise this time, not his family and thus new, thrilling, and unscathed. Of course he will meet them.

The following day he drives to the house located on the other side of the road that leads to the pine-scented beach. Eve is waiting for him in the street when he arrives; she is wearing a long cotton skirt and a man's shirt, a thick leather belt, sandals; she is dark and golden; once again, he is stunned.

She leads him into the house, through the living room, where a few children and adolescents are gathered. "My cousins," she says. They're playing board games or watching television and barely raise their heads as Eve takes him to the veranda, where the adults are sitting: the parents, grandparents, aunts and uncles, a gathering that takes him back to his childhood, before the brutality, Sunday afternoons in the waning heat of the day, before the quick coming of the dark. *I'm far from home; I'm home again.* Now the conversation is in English and Greek; Eve and her parents are translating for the others and for him. One of Eve's aunts brings out small cups of dark coffee. "Don't drink the bottom. Have some water; have a *loukoumi.*" Advice, encouragements, questions in Greek, in English: "How do you like Greece?" "Is this your first time?" "Eve tells us you teach in Connecticut." He does his best to understand, acquiesce, comply. After the coffee and the *loukoumi* and the cold glasses of water, the farewells, in Greek and in English. "It was nice to meet you."

"They seem to like you," she tells him once they're outside again. "That's a bad sign; we'll have to stop seeing each other." Again, that ache in his chest; he is still too fragile for such lightness. *Hit her? Embrace her?* She sees his surprise, his gravity, and bursts out laughing before putting her arms around him and kissing him. "I'm going to miss you; it's too bad you already have to get back." The following day, he takes the plane to New York, with a connecting flight to Connecticut.

It's only the second weekend of September, but

the weather has already shifted; the air is cool, brisk; early-morning and late-afternoon skies are the clear, deep blue of fall. Carpentier and Eve are now both in New York. Eve arrived from Athens in the late afternoon, and he drove from Connecticut to meet her at JFK. Here she is, coming out from behind the frosted-glass partition, pushing a carriage; she's wearing a cream-colored long-sleeved blouse, a gray skirt, and derbies—he thinks that's what they're called, these laced shoes with short heels. All this gives her an oddly Victorian look, but her hair, now cut short, and her suntan quickly wipe away the impression. Carpentier has no words. She kisses him; he picks up her suitcases from the carriage and they drive back to her apartment in Chelsea. They don't remain there; she wants them to see the city together, immediately, to show him her neighborhood. She is eager to start this new life. "Let's go to the river; let's just walk. Let's get something to eat; I'm starving." They leave her luggage in the apartment and go back out into the bright streets. Carpentier is dazed. To be here, with her, even in this city he wanted to leave behind, to be with her and not have to leave her after a few weeks is a gift that cannot be refused.

Eve takes him through her neighborhood. Mostly brownstones, a few more recent buildings. "This must be one of the last shoe-repair shops in Manhattan," she tells him as they walk by a small store; behind the smudged glass front, an old man is hammering away at a boot; then she leads him down a few steps to a restaurant that seems to be an Italian place. Eve orders a pasta dish. "They say starch is good for jet lag." She orders a bottle of Sancerre; he can't eat a thing, but he gratefully drinks several glasses of the wine; she eats her pasta as well as the small salad he's ordered for himself to keep her company. They return to the apartment, where Eve's luggage lies on the living room floor; they go into the bedroom. It's only been a week since they were together in Greece, but their appetite is endless. Suddenly it's deep summer again. When they emerge, she proposes a pact: They will do this every day, every single day, with no exceptions at all. "No squeamishness," she adds, challenging him. "Every single day through the fall, the winter, and the spring, until we leave for Greece for the summer."

"That isn't even a complete year." (Carpentier, so sure of his desire, of his body, now provoking her a bit, now a bit brash.)

"No squeamishness, yes? No skipping of any days, including—"

"Why don't we say a full year, three hundred and sixty-five days?"

. . .

"A year, then?"

"Yes, three hundred and sixty-five days."

He is enthralled; he holds on to her like a desperate man. *I will die if I'm not with her.* The promise of yet another life, even another country, further removed from the past. The pact is implemented.

She asked him to leave the cottage in Connecticut, to move in with her, even if he was still teaching at the college, even if he'd made a life for himself in the northeast corner of the small state, among its hills and lakes, white church steeples and meadows. He didn't even try to explain to her why Wannaford College, with its students and faculty who still looked like they'd emerged straight from the fifties, its redbrick buildings from even further back, why this landscape with its red maples in the fall and thick snow in the winter were fitting, yes, that was the word, fitting for what he wanted, away from everything else. He knew that any attempt at explaining to her why he wanted to remain there would eliminate even the possibility of the second chance he thought he saw hovering on the edge of a new life with her. She herself made it seem inevitable, fated. “You already have a car; you can easily drive there; you can rent something for one or two nights up there, but we’ll be together, here in the city. Besides, I do have a job, you know.” She told him about her work at UNICEF, how she loved to walk to the UN building on the East Side in the morning. She was taking him into her realm; he was helpless in her wake. Beyond this new life with her, he also saw the possibility of another landscape, another country. He left the cottage by the lake in Connecticut and moved in with her in Manhattan. Her apartment in Chelsea was large enough for the two of them. “Easily,” she said. “You can even have your own office here.” He lived with Eve in her apartment in Chelsea like a patient recovering from a long illness, basking in health regained but still fearful of a relapse. He wanted to see no one else, as if prolonged contact with the outside world would break the spell and take him back. Eve understood his reserve, even if she found it peculiar sometimes. At the beginning, after their first summer in Greece, after a few months in the apartment in Chelsea, she was the one to ask to meet his parents. “Don’t you think I should? I think it would be the right thing; I’d like to.” The immediate tautness, almost a hostility in him, was not visible to her. *Why does she want to complicate things by bringing them in? She has no idea.* “Okay, I’ll take you to see them.”

The leader is spread over the young aunt and the boy can see that his belt is undone and his pants pulled down to his knees; the others are also watching. The grandfather says between his broken teeth, "All men are lecherous," but he's smiling, and the ones wearing sunglasses are all saying in unison, their voices becoming unbearably loud, "Let me have a go at it" and "The one with the earrings, too!" pointing to the boy's mother. Then the boy has lost too much blood and begins to cry; he pulls on his younger brother's hand in an attempt to leave.

He drove Eve to the two-family house on Long Island. She brought a box of Greek pastries and a bouquet of flowers; he brought a bottle of wine. He noticed Eve's immediate affinity with his father; she found the still robust man's shyness endearing; his mother took the young woman in her arms and kissed her. Carpentier's brother and sister-in-law came down with their two children; the little girl sat on Eve's lap. "You're lucky, Eve. She refuses to sit on my lap; she thinks she's too old," his brother's wife said. The little boy sat on his mother's lap, but his eyes were fixed on Eve. They were all taken with her. Carpentier could not wait to leave. Something acquired over years was at risk, dissipating in the conversation, in their even being here, in the house with three generations of his family, something being reset like a trap, taut and threatening, ready to snap him back.

They didn't linger very long on the steps of the house when they said their good-byes. It was early December; some of the houses were already decorated with Christmas lights. The lawns of the quiet neighborhood were covered with frost. Before he got onto the highway, Eve asked him to park the car on a dimly lit street bordering a school; white empty playing fields, the dark mass of the school in the distance, and not a single passerby on this cold night. While she lifted her dress to her waist and slipped off her underwear, she asked him to push back his seat, and straddled him.

On the drive back to the city, she dozed off for a while. "I think I've had too much wine," she told him, and relaxed into her seat. They were nearing Manhattan; the city's buildings were brightly lit against the dark winter sky when she woke up and turned to him. "You looked so sullen at your parents'. Why? They're all so nice. Your father's so shy; your mother adores you." He reached out and held her hand. "I adore her, too." He said nothing else. She looked at him, at his impassive profile, as he continued driving; she thought she detected something askew, something she sensed but could not place. She knew she could not be without him, not now. They were deep in the sumptuousness of their pact.

She watched him leave for Wannaford and come back two, at most three days later, anxious to be with her again. She enjoyed listening to him tell her about his work, so different from hers. At the very beginning of their life together, he was, as he told her, "still recovering from the book on Chardin, taking a break from Watteau," and was writing a long article on Giuseppe Arcimboldo. The Renaissance Italian painter was well outside of Carpentier's field, but, he told her, he couldn't resist those composite faces made of fruit, vegetables, fish, flowers, animals, trees, plants, sheaves of wheat, as if the painter had wanted to funnel everything under the sun in his works, gathering and shaping all of nature into those strange, luxuriant portraits. "Remember? This is what I was researching last summer, before I went to Greece?" With her sitting next to him on the couch in the living room in Chelsea, he leafed through glossy reproductions in a thick, oversize album. He was especially fascinated by *Water*; he pointed to the head in the album, tracing its outline for her with his index finger: the pensive and sinister head, a tight but meticulously delineated patchwork of gray fish, sea snakes, eels, shells, crabs, worms, an octopus, a turtle, even a frog; the orange-red lacquer of a lobster, and of a piece of branch coral, along with the body of a langoustine and its tendrils emerging from the back of the man's head were the only bright patches of color in the somber swarm.

"You see how the octopus is reduced in size on the shoulder, and the way the lobster, the turtle, and the crab over there, part of his chest, are the same size as the octopus? Arcimboldo just wanted all of this to *fit* together; he didn't care about proportions. And look at this. The man is wearing a pearl necklace, and a pearl earring; his ear is a shell; his entire cheek, almost half his face is a ray. . . . " Eve took the book on her lap and began to turn the pages herself; as one luxurious portrait followed another, cheeks of peach, eyebrows of straw, a peacock chest, a cabbage shoulder, he told her about Arcimboldo's career as court painter, designer of stained-glass windows, frescoes, tapestries, and even festival costumes for the Habsburgs in Vienna, in Prague. She joined him in his fascination for the ornate and static past; she admired his perseverance, his apparent detachment from his surroundings, the world's upheaval, its political disarray and injustices, its cataclysms. She felt that he lived in another sphere; she sensed something amiss but could not identify it; his aloofness drew her in.

Well before Eve met Carpentier, she had been hired as a bilingual assistant in the Latin America Offices of UNICEF. She had just graduated from college; her Spanish was excellent; her French passed muster; sometimes, she was asked to help in the Africa Section. Four years after she started working at UNICEF, having had several promotions, she was asked to participate in the agency's campaigns, to become its global video distribution manager. This involved a fair amount of traveling; she scouted locations and went on filming missions with the videographers; she saw children in open-air schools, in hospitals, in orphanages. When she met Robert Carpentier in Greece that summer, she was coming from Sudan.

After they'd been living in Chelsea for two years, Eve suggested they get married. "I really don't care; this would really be for my parents; maybe for yours, too?" Carpentier's father had said something to him about "respecting these people's daughter; you don't want to be a . . ." He could find no word in any language to continue; a man of other times, other ways of behaving; to him, there was something indecent about his son living "this way" with Eve, "this young woman who seems so nice." Carpentier saw no reason not to get married; so much easier to comply.

He didn't want to offend, to hurt. If this was the way to avoid any disturbance, to salvage his distance, he would do it; but he reduced it to a cheerless, almost vacant modicum.

Eve's father had wanted a "big wedding," with the entire family, on both sides, many friends; some of his close friends were restaurant owners; there could be an elegant reception with a fine meal, many courses, and music, especially since there was to be no religious ceremony; "a real feast to celebrate our daughter's wedding." All this, Eve's father had told her, and she conveyed it to Carpentier.

"He's really counting on this to be something special. He's like that, my father; he wants to dance and drink, invite all his old friends, meet new people."

He hesitated before saying, "I don't think it's a good idea. You know how complicated these things get. And all these people I don't want to see."

"Robert, please do this for me, for all of us."

"I think we should keep this small, intimate, just a few people. Please."

A tinge of something vicious about to erupt in the living room, where their exchange was taking place. She was stunned by the discovery. Neither one was screaming; no tangible threat in the quiet room, but she understood that to go any further would cause an irreparable breach between them. She was still drawn by his remoteness, understood his reserve, and still wanted to shield him, even as she was discovering the limits of her tolerance. She put her hand on his cheek and said, "Okay, I'll let my father know; I'll let everyone know."

They had a city hall wedding. In fact, the ceremony, such as it was, took place two blocks from city hall, at the city clerk's office. It was the middle of the week, near lunchtime, and it was over very quickly. Their parents attended. No one else was invited, not even Carpentier's brother; nothing was said, but his brother understood and stayed away.

After the contract was signed at the city clerk's office, Eve, Carpentier, and the four parents went to a French restaurant downtown. Eve's father had insisted on choosing the restaurant and on paying the bill. "At least let us do this, your mother and me." He said this with no bitterness at all; Eve's parents were fond of Carpentier; they, too, respected his separateness, his seriousness, and they could see how much their independent and volatile daughter was taken with him. Carpentier's father was already familiar with what he called his son's "strangeness," and he enjoyed the celebratory meal. Carpentier's mother was happy that her son was back and was now married to "such a kind and beautiful young woman"; she asked for no more.

Even in its reduced form, the marriage was something of a sign for Carpentier, a sense of something beginning again. He had never asked Eve about anyone she knew before him. The shadowy figures of horny high school boys, or later encounters, closer to the time he met her that summer. Their life together started on that pine-scented beach, he told himself. And it was starting again after this ceremony. No use asking about the past.

They spoke only once about having children. At first lightly, almost jokingly. It seemed like something far away, a vanishing point they could both take for granted, but Eve did make it clear that "this was not like that city hall marriage"; this was not something she would do for her parents, or for his. "At one point, I want to have your child, Robert; I don't care if that sounds like a line from a movie." At the end of their conversation that day, his words seemed strange to her: "I wouldn't want to extend the surface through which I can be hurt." At once heartfelt and hollow; put in such an odd way; a strange thought; or maybe a strange way of expressing something simple? She was used to his way of talking; it was one of the things that had attracted her, but, once again, she felt she was encountering something obdurate, unpleasant even; she didn't ask him to explain. She already knew and had accepted his reluctance to see his parents, to gratify her own father's desire for a "feast of a wedding," but this was different.

Even if Carpentier's mother rarely saw him, she patiently awaited the child of her firstborn. There was no question in her mind that Eve and her son would have children. In spite of her invitations to dinner, or lunch, "any day, anytime you can come," regularly repeated on the phone, and Eve's encouragement, Carpentier almost never went to the two-family house on Long Island. "I just don't get it, Robert; you should try. It makes her so happy to see us both, especially you; your father doesn't show it, but it's obvious he'd like to see you more." The visits to the house on Long Island remained rare—the holidays, a birthday, just what would suffice to avoid confrontations, unpleasantness.

A few days before the marriage, at the house on Long Island, where Eve had been visiting while Carpentier was still at Wannaford, his mother had handed Eve a compact, heavy package and invited her to unwrap it on the dining room table. "Here, I'll make some room. Open it. Don't worry, you can tear up the paper; I'll put it all in a shopping bag for you afterward." She'd stood back a bit while Eve slowly separated layers of richly embroidered sheets, pillowcases, a tablecloth, dinner napkins. "These have been in the family for many generations," she told Eve. "These were my wedding sheets; and my mother's, too; I think her mother gave them to her." Eve then opened a smaller package that had been wrapped separately. "This is Robert's baptismal dress; you see how fine the linen is? How delicate? Don't tell him I gave it to you." Eve was almost in tears; she hugged Robert's mother, and promised she would not tell him. "I'll take everything else with me, but I'll leave this here with you; we'll take it when the time comes."

Still, for a long time, Eve was content. Carpentier waited for her to come back from work, from that still impressive UN building on the East River, or back from Sudan, Colombia, Peru. She waited for him to come back from Wannaford.

Since meeting on that pine-scented beach, they have spent a long stretch of every single summer in Greece. His teaching ends in early May, and he could travel on his own, but he remains in Manhattan, waiting for Eve, for her to return from somewhere out there in the world, Bolivia, Ecuador, Chad, so that they can leave for Greece together. He has no interest in going anywhere else. Eve always manages to take at least four continuous weeks off, usually in August. They spend the first week at her parents' summer house, and then leave for one of the Cycladic islands, where they rent rooms or houses on the smaller ones, away from the crowds.

Since that summer when he first met Eve, the summer she took him to the Cyclades for the first time, those islands in the Aegean have become a fixation for Carpentier, the possibility of another place, the setting of an ultimate severing. In this stark golden landscape suspended between blue sea and sky, he has found another country; there he knows no one but Eve, and he does not want to meet anyone, not the friends she has made over the many summers she has spent in Greece with her parents, not vacationers from Germany or Belgium, Sweden or France, the United States; he does not want to know anything about *the long history* of those islands, the Ottoman or Venetian presence on some of them over decades or centuries, the civilization that produced the marble figurines of musicians, cupbearers, and fertility goddesses, the role this island or that island played in antiquity or the war of independence from the Turks, the remains of this or that Neolithic settlement, the origin or the purpose of the drystone walls that wind their way through the rocky landscape among low bushes of dried thyme, sage, asphodel, and the powdery silver of olive trees. This landscape, this other country is unattached to anything he has known, and he wants it to remain so: untainted, impregnable.

The drystone walls remind him of the ones in Connecticut, but here in the dryness and wind and sea of the islands, the lakes and ponds of Connecticut, all that sweet water, the maples and oaks of the lush green hills have all vanished. "The scars of the islands," he tells Eve. Sometimes those walls emerge from the middle of nowhere, not a house or a farm or a settlement for miles; he thinks of them as senseless and beautiful remnants of a madman's harried passage, traces of someone relentlessly, fixedly piling and artfully fitting rocks into stone strips that cut through the russet hills. He does not consider once that the stones that were used to build these walls were painstakingly gathered and removed by the populations of entire villages over months of labor, often under the hot sun, to expose rare arable land, men, women, children gathered in this task of communal survival in the dry, taxing landscape, or that they were used to delimit property, more secure dividing lines than simple wire fences that could be surreptitiously moved during the night to extend one farmer's land, one family's property, one shepherd's land inherited over generations and reduce another's. "Stone walls can't move so easily overnight" is a common saying on those islands. "The rocks fit together the way the fish and other marine creatures fit together in that Arcimboldo head," Carpentier proclaims, and to him the Cycladic figurines are "enigmatic, like characters in a Watteau painting." The daily life of the islands, the waiters in tavernas, families at the beach, the fruit and vegetables he and Eve bring back from the markets are laid out in his mind like Chardin's framed scenes, intimate gatherings of people set in indeterminate rooms, plush colors and ornate arrangements of cheeses, lobsters, oysters, hams, flowers, and fruit gathered on the thick folds of tablecloths. At times, Eve loses patience with his inability to be in the present, to acknowledge the people and things around him, here and now. "They're Greeks, real people, Robert; this young guy serving us our meal could be a law student making some money for school in the fall. And take a bite of this watermelon; I'm sure it tastes nothing like any of Chardin's fruit." She even sounds slightly exasperated. He picks up one of the cold pieces of watermelon with his fork and chews on it slowly, hoping she will stop, but she continues. "You told me so much about that Arcimboldo, his life, all the politics and intrigue around his work, but you don't want to do the same for all these people around us. . . ." The waiter is back and Carpentier quickly asks for the check, a way of putting an end to the conversation.

It was a light lunch, a salad and some grilled fish, but the heat of the day and the half liter of wine have made them both drowsy; they head back to their rented house nearby in the town; they close the bedroom shutters against the bright light and will not emerge until the heat of the day has ebbed.

Carpentier wishes they could spend more of the summer here, in the dry Cyclades, where everything is so clearly drawn, sparse, and ordered. *Away from everything else.* This is where he would like to live with Eve, beyond the summer months, when everything is pared down by the sun. He wishes they could stay here into the fall, watch the weather change, the first rains, as houses, hills, trees, bushes take on color and volume. They've looked for a place to buy, maybe a small house. "Maybe a house in ruins, that we could renovate?" Eve proposes. "It's easier that way, with building permits, the whole bureaucracy." He suggests they could perhaps buy a piece of land, "Then we could build a house exactly how we want it."

Quite by accident, during one of their long walks on an island where they had disembarked after a long ferry ride from Athens, they stumbled on something that seemed perfect to him. They had driven up a curved road to the hilly northern part of the island and then taken a footpath leading to the church of an abandoned village. There was something oppressive about the narrow path; goat droppings strewn about, their smell rising from the confined path bordered on one side by the ruins of the village's abandoned stone houses and, on the other, by a tall mass of rock that seemed as if it was closing in on them. They hurried up, but once they reached a small church at the end of the path, they suddenly emerged on a luminous open landscape that had been hidden from the path by the tall mass of rock. There was no transition from the restricted, stifling path to the wide, rounded expanse that spread out before Eve and Carpentier: a succession of hills gently sloping to the surrounding sea, which seemed immobile in the far distance; before the blue of the sea, there were rectangular plots of cultivated fields enclosed either by drystone walls or lines of tall reeds, the gold of the summer wheat broken by green patches of olive and fig trees or ordered rows of planted vegetables. Out there, in the distance, the elongated shapes of other islands lay on the sea like placidly grazing brontosaurs. As the sun started its descent into the sea, the breeze that had appeared the moment they'd emerged from the path carried to them the mingled smell of sage, thyme, and the faint remains of the day's heat. Carpentier felt fulfilled, unassailable. From a house built here, from such a house, here, in this place on a hill, you would be able to see people approaching from a long way off, moving quickly or slowly, depending on the time of day, advancing figures making their way between the low bushes of gorse, thyme, and wild rosemary. You would have time to call for help, flee even; then again, how could they come *all the way here*?

Summers on those islands, like slices of still and flawless time. If Eve and Carpentier have rented a house rather than just a room, they sometimes cook their meals. In the morning in a town on a hill, or at a port, they buy vegetables, fish, cheese, bread; on the way back from the market, they might stop for breakfast, or they continue to the house with their purchases before the sun gets too hot. Often, in silent agreement, one leads the other back to bed, or they find each other in a hall, on a chair, unable to wait, in the kitchen, where Eve is reading the newspaper she insists they buy every day. He says he "would gladly not know what's going on out there." "Why don't we just forget about everything while we're here?" he asks Eve, meanwhile slowly pushing down with his index finger the newspaper she is reading. "The world will wait for us," he continues as he leads her back to bed. Afterward, Eve begins to read the paper again, from where she stopped: a black teenager named Yusef Hawkins was shot and killed in the white working-class neighborhood of Bensonhurst, Brooklyn, USA; two million people in the Baltic states made a human chain to demand independence from the Soviet Union; R.D. Laing died of a heart attack at 61.

They go to different islands every summer. They drive every day to one of the many beaches or walk to one of the more isolated coves. He swims very far out; Eve goes along with him but always stops at the point when the turquoise water turns a deep, almost purple blue. In late August or early September, they return to New York, Eve like a bar of copper, Carpentier a deep nut brown. Once, at the airport in Paris, during a layover between Athens and New York, his passport is politely but firmly withheld from him, and he is led to a small windowless office, where two men question him for an hour. When he joins Eve again in the waiting area, with the gate about to be closed, he tells her, "It was the usual bureaucracy. Let's hurry up; we don't want to miss our flight on top of it." During the long flight back to New York, Eve tries to find out more, but his reluctant answers remain variations on what he's already told her: overzealous border officials; mistaken identity, probably; they told him nothing specific. "Let's just forget about it." The men, their questions in the stuffy room are a temporary nuisance, a disagreeable interlude to be left behind and expunged. Why linger on the disagreeable?

The rhythm of seasons. A good part of Carpentier's life is parceled out like a schoolboy's; vast summers released from regularity and obligation, followed by the return to school in the fall, the New England fall, in his case, a season richly extended for him since the colder weather and the change of colors reach Manhattan only weeks later. "I get to have two falls," he tells Eve. Winter is broken up by the break from teaching at Wannaford, but the cold months are the most difficult for Carpentier, who increasingly lives in nostalgia for Cycladic summers, a longing appeased only by the coming of spring and the prospect of returning to the spare, ordered islands, *away from all the rest of it*. Progressively, his life in the United States, the drives back and forth from Manhattan to Wannaford, all become a digression. His work on the article on Arcimboldo, the book on Watteau, the teaching, and the conferences provide a semblance of stability, but only serve to fill the time before he's back on those islands in the Aegean with Eve, always with Eve, and, since their accidental discovery, always to that particular island, to that particular hill between sea and sky where the wind carries the mingled smell of sage, thyme, and the faint remains of the day's heat. He is torn between remembrance and anticipation.

Eve is puzzled by his reluctance. She loves Manhattan. "Robert, anything you can want in the world is on this island where we live; you can't take this with you." When she's not traveling with the UNICEF videographers, she goes to work every morning in the United Nations building on the East River. If it's not too cold or raining, she walks from Chelsea to the East Side. She savors early-morning Manhattan; she walks slowly, unlike the others around her rushing out from diners after a quick breakfast, or carrying it in paper bags to their offices, fried egg on a roll, toasted bagel and cream cheese, coffee, cream, black, no sugar. From Chelsea to the East Side, she walks through the Garment District; the sidewalks are taken up by men unloading trucks, piling cartons onto dollies, pushing hand trucks or racks of dresses, suits, coats under their plastic coverings; in the middle of the block a meter maid is writing up a ticket. All those people moving about, the traffic at a standstill, drivers leaning out of car windows, opening their doors, a few stepping out of their cars, stretching their necks, attempting to make out the cause of the obstruction, looking to the end of the block like sailors looking for land from a ship's mast, others just honking their horns, all this in the still, fresh morning, but already so busy; Eve loves Manhattan at this time of morning, the rush and flow of her fellow New Yorkers, all of them.

When she is not away on a trip for UNICEF, Eve sees her parents every week and always asks Carpentier to go with her to their apartment near the Metropolitan. He finds these visits uncomplicated, and usually complies. He even goes with Eve and her parents to the Greek Orthodox Easter Mass, the one day of the year when he enters a church. Not his family, not his tribe, not his church; he doesn't have a church; that was such a long time ago, and so different from now, on this Easter evening after all the lights in the church have been turned off, all the service candles snuffed out, now in the complete darkness, as the priest emerges from behind the altar at exactly midnight with the light of "He who is risen" cupped in his hand, using his candle to light other candles held out by the worshippers, each lighting another candle in turn, the gathering candlelight at first slowly and then completely brightening the church, the faces and bodies of the crowd of worshippers, the church's walls, the icons, all that gold and polished wood, as Carpentier smells the cloying smell of burning incense and can only think of Byzantium, far from here, removed in a magnificent amber-colored past.

Food follows; all are invited to the church basement

for the traditional Easter soup, whose main ingredient is the lamb offal that Eve chews on with relish; she swallows the rich granular broth, closing her eyes in delight, while Carpentier reluctantly puts a small spoonful into his mouth, a slight tang of faintly scented urine on his palate. This is their third or fourth Easter Mass, their third or fourth Easter soup in the church's basement, and Eve has now abandoned any attempt to get him to finish the soup that takes her back to family, tradition, home.

Afterward, the men go back to the jeeps and cars, the winged men leading the way, floating silently above the ones walking and taking longer to get back to the jeeps and cars. They stop in front of the gate of the Montrosier house; then the jeeps and cars stop in front of the gate of Cécile's house; they make the rounds throughout the entire town in the hills. The procession is endless.

It was the first and only time he yelled at her

It was about a trip to Brazil, when Eve was set upon by a group of boys as she was walking home alone after what she described to Carpentier as "one of those long, boring UNICEF dinners." Four, five of them approached her as she was nearing her hotel. "Just boys, the oldest was maybe thirteen, fourteen years old." It happened in one of the dark stretches of the street; a cluster of almond trees blocked the light from a streetlamp. One of the boys asked her in English to hand over her bag; he pointed at the same time to make sure he was understood; there was something delicate about his voice, almost pleading. Eve replied in Spanish, trying to play for time, to pacify; they all looked at her; the tallest one, the one who had spoken, reached for her bag, while another one standing behind him showed her a small knife; he held it up, as if displaying a prize; she struggled very briefly with the tall one, and managed to hold on to her bag. "My passport was in there; I didn't panic; I could see the hotel steps from where I was; the doorman was right outside." Before they could decide what to do, before the next step in this quick, silent, almost orchestrated series of movements and gestures that had been taking place forever, she opened her bag, took out her wallet, and held out to them all the bills it contained. A supplicant in an ancient scene. "The tall one just snatched the money and they all ran away."

Carpentier couldn't contain himself; his heart was beating fast, and he could feel his temples throbbing. She had just returned from the airport; her suitcase was still in the hall; he had taken a bottle of Sancerre, her favorite, from the freezer—Eve liked her white wine very cold, almost icy—and instead of sitting down together and finding each other once again after one of her absences, she was telling him *this* story. She didn't seem to understand the story she was telling; she was asking him to pour her a glass of the wine, while he was seeing images she was stubbornly ignoring, refusing to acknowledge his agitation.

"Do you realize what could have happened?"

"Robert, they were just boys. Nothing happened; pour me some wine."

"What do you mean, 'nothing happened'? What if they had cut you, left you bleeding there on the sidewalk in *fucking Bra-si-lia*? Why do you have to go to those places anyway? Can't you find something else to do? Can't they give you something that would keep you in New York?" He was now screaming.

"Robert, Robert, it turned out just fine; this never happens; this was the first time. And it was my fault; I should have taken a taxi or walked with someone else back to the hotel, but it was so close to the restaurant."

. . .

Carpentier could go no further. He just wanted this *not to have happened. Doesn't she see that that it was rash? No, worse than rash; stupid, reckless, blind. Something in her that comes from having always been sheltered. She seems so serene sitting there; so lovely and whole*. Eve leaned forward from the couch where the two were sitting and poured the cold wine into the glasses he had set on the coffee table. *My strange husband*. She lifted her glass to him and took a deep swallow. "Here's to us; this is what I needed. Let's not argue." Carpentier drank his wine, too, more slowly. Now he also wanted to leave the other conversation behind; he didn't know what he'd do if it continued. He would be driving to Connecticut early the next day and needed his sleep; besides, there was no more he could say. Now he just wanted to talk about something else. He told her he'd gone to the Metropolitan in the afternoon, "to see an Arcimboldo on loan from a museum in Sweden." Eve continued to look at him as she drank, inviting him to continue. "Vertumnus, the god of seasons, of change; but it's really supposed to be Rudolf the Second, Arcimboldo's patron; usually, you would have to go all the way to Stockholm to see this painting." He got up from the couch to get the album from a shelf and opened it to the painting. Eve poured herself a second glass of the wine. She had the fleeting urge to throw the glass at his talking face.

When he finally stopped telling her about the painting, she asked him what he'd done the rest of the day. "I prepared my classes for tomorrow. I walked around and did some grocery shopping." "Anything else?" she asked, as if prodding him on. He complied, grasping at anything to leave the other conversation behind. "I saw a sign outside that corner bodega, where you get coffee sometimes? 'Egg whites, turkey sausage, on whole-wheat pita. $3.95'; that guy's really trying anything and everything to get customers, but it sounds very healthy." Eve poured herself a third glass of wine and raised it to him again. "It doesn't sound very appetizing, does it?" She added something about people taking such good care of their bodies, how very careful they'd become.

They finished the bottle and drank half of a second one; she began to unbutton his shirt and didn't ask him to draw the living room curtains to block out anyone who might be observing the two half-dressed bodies slowly and then frantically moving on the couch. Later, Eve awoke in their bedroom, thirsty and restless; maybe the first pangs of jet lag, although there was only a two-hour time difference between New York and Brasilia; probably just the long trip, and maybe Robert was right: Maybe that incident with those boys had left some traces, even if she'd managed to avoid being harmed. Before going to the kitchen to pour herself a cold glass of water, she took a long look at her husband sleeping next to her, a steady, ruffled snore humming out of him. She thought that he should move beyond what she called his "safe triangle," New York–Connecticut–the Cycladic islands, a rare trip to Paris, where he still had some friends from his student days, a city he knew, a place he could go back to safely, easily. As he'd told her, even when he did have to travel for a talk, a colloquium, or for a research trip, he rarely left the vicinity of the campus or the hotel. *He looks diminished and weak lying there.* She left the bedroom very quietly.

Eve had been up for two hours when Carpentier awoke; she'd made coffee and offered to toast some bread. "Or you could have some cereal? Have to eat healthy!" Carpentier was too absorbed in the morning haste and getting to Wannaford to notice the sarcasm simmering beneath her words. He opted for coffee and toast. As they were having breakfast, she reminded him that Yann and Adelaide were coming for dinner later on in the week. "I told them Thursday night, and it works for them. I also asked Sebastian to come."

Sebastian, the childhood friend; oddly handsome; lithe and muscular Sebastian; all that compact leanness, something almost reptilian about him, if you didn't know his warmth and generosity; playful Sebastian, completely and immediately at ease with anyone. Maybe it was something intrinsic to his calling. Sebastian was an actor, a struggling actor, like so many in Manhattan—waiters, office workers, store clerks, even bicycle messengers, waiting for that big break, or, short of that, the steady gig. But Sebastian was different; he was possessed, and he knew it was only a matter of time. Eve had introduced Carpentier to her dear friend Sebastian years before, in September, when he had just moved into Eve's apartment. After a few drinks at the Dublin House, an Irish bar conveniently located next to the Oriental Lamp Shade Company, where Sebastian worked three days a week, he looked at Carpentier over the rim of his third or fourth martini and said with an exaggeratedly complicit wink, "What you need, Robert, is one good fuck with a guy, and that'll set you straight . . . so to speak." This was said loudly enough that several students drinking beer at the bar turned around. Carpentier wished Sebastian would not speak so loudly, make a scene; he felt he was being tested by this brash young man so serenely at ease in his body, basking in his friendship with Eve, pushing the limits. He lifted his martini glass to both Eve and Sebastian and spoke as clearly as his own fog would allow. "You know, Sebastian, I have no qualms at all; it's just that that time has passed for me, a long time ago." He had found just the words that would do, to grant and dodge at the same time. Sebastian laughed, almost spilling what was left of his martini on the bar. Eve was sipping on her own martini, enjoying the small scene being played out by these two men she loved; she wanted so much for them to get along. Carpentier slowly put his glass back on the bar and signaled for another round.

After the martinis, they went for dinner at Café Luxembourg, a nearby French bistro that Sebastian really liked but where he could rarely afford to eat. That evening he was Eve and Robert's guest, and they were celebrating. Sebastian and Eve shared an appetizer of blood sausage and apple compote; Carpentier winced and ordered a green bean salad with slivers of Parmesan; they would all have fish afterward. Sebastian ordered the wine—"I know, I know, I know, we should have red with the boudin, but we'll have a bottle of Sancerre, because that's what Eve would like. Right, Eve? And to hell with it!" He flirted with the waiter throughout the meal, a young man who looked like he was from somewhere in the Midwest, probably another struggling actor, who didn't seem to mind at all, although he blushed once in a while at something Sebastian whispered as he bent to fill a glass or to place a plate on the table, his redness flaring against his starched white shirt. Eve was in all her glory, flushed after the martinis, her skin still glowing from the summer; she was being attended to by these two men she had brought together, two parts of her life converging here, in this restaurant with its plush velvet-upholstered booths, white linen tablecloths and dinner napkins, plates of food and bottles of wine carried by aproned waiters. She was sitting between Sebastian and Robert at a booth far from the entrance; the jumble of other conversations, the chinking of cutlery, the crowded restaurant's resonant hum seemed to stop somewhere at a line separating them from all others that evening.

After the fish was served, Sebastian told Eve and Robert about his upcoming tour; the play was a hit in New York and the small company had now been invited to perform on the West Coast. "I only have a tiny part, but it's a juicy one—a bad guy, a traitor, a betrayer." Eve, who had seen the play, agreed. "I'm sure you'll steal the show, Sebastian; you already did here. You should have seen him, Robert; you wouldn't think such evil could ooze out of him." Carpentier hadn't seen the play; Eve had only managed to get tickets on a day when he was in Connecticut. He couldn't stop looking at her; her hair was cut short, the way he liked it, barely reaching her jaw; he felt grateful, invulnerable. The only unpleasantness for him that evening was Eve's insistence on smoking two or three of Sebastian's Dunhill cigarettes, delicately taking them from the gold-and-red pack Sebastian held out to her throughout the evening, a private ceremony in which he played no part—something of her life before him.

They saw Sebastian as much as Eve's travels to faraway places and Carpentier's regular trips to Connecticut allowed. They went to see as many of Sebastian's performances as they could; small theaters, unknown playwrights, almost no audiences sometimes. Once they were the only two in the audience until, right before the lights went out, a group of about half a dozen young men came and sat in the front row of the minuscule theater. Sebastian shined once again that evening, an outstanding, subtle performance in a miserably bad play. The other actors gravitated toward him.

Sometimes, after a performance, they went out for drinks, or, if he succeeded in persuading them, Sebastian took them out to dance. "Why do you want to go home? It's still early, come on! It's not even eleven yet, but there'll be enough of a crowd." And he added, like an afterthought, "Even if it's just not the same anymore." Now that they'd both agreed to keep going, to stretch the evening, Sebastian didn't want to spoil the mood, but as they were walking arm in arm, the three of them, he reminded Eve about their outings to Crisco Disco, the old warehouse turned into a club where no one would arrive before midnight and they would dance until daylight. "Remember that gorgeous bartender?" Sebastian asked, turning to Eve. "He looked like an angel, with his blond curls and two shiny hearts taped to his nipples. . . . That kid was no angel." Eve told Carpentier that the place was now closed. "But Sebastian knows all the new places that have sprung up." Carpentier and Eve usually left the clubs not too long after one, waving good-bye to Sebastian, still on the dance floor or having yet another drink at the bar with someone he'd just met.

At Eve and Carpentier's apartment one evening, the three of them were sitting in the living room. Carpentier had made dinner; they were now having coffee; Carpentier had also served them small glasses of rum, "as a digestif."

Sebastian looked around the apartment, at the prints and paintings on the walls, the shelves of books, the furniture, the lamps. His words were like a lament. "Why can't I just stay home like you two? Just stay home and read, sit in an armchair like this one? What drags me out there, even now?"

Carpentier and Sebastian also saw each other when Eve was away; they went to the movies, museums; they crisscrossed the city on foot. Sebastian told Carpentier about Eve's life before she met him. They'd known each other since grammar school; they'd gone to the same high school on the Upper East Side. "I had a scholarship; they called me their 'Little Thespian'; such a bunch of uptight assholes." Eve and Sebastian had kept in touch throughout the college years; Sebastian had even gone to Greece two summers in a row; he got along with Eve's parents; he was like a brother to their daughter. "They really like you, Robert." Carpentier told Sebastian about his work at Wannaford, his years in Paris, the time before that. They talked about Eve. "You know, Robert, I think she was waiting for you—like a meal waiting to be served."

There were other people, other friends, over the years, David and Carmen, Yann and Adelaide, and the outer circle, usually colleagues of Eve's from UNICEF. Carpentier increasingly preferred to be alone with Eve, and now with Sebastian, but he did sometimes enjoy the outings with the others, an unattached tribe living on this island on the edge of America, people with no children, with old or ailing parents in California, Florida, Arizona, only seen at Thanksgiving, other holidays. Carpentier was grateful for what he saw as their buoyant, carefree lives.

On the day Eve and Carpentier had their city hall marriage, Sebastian was in Italy, where he had a substantial part in a big-budget film, a Western. "Playing a villain, of course," he told Eve and Robert. "I seem to have found my niche; *they* seem to have found my niche." During the two years since that dinner at the Luxembourg, his career had taken off; now he had an agent and was even refusing parts. When he returned from filming in Italy, he could afford to leave his cramped studio in Hell's Kitchen, with its peeling layers of linoleum and its bathtub in the kitchen. Eve had found him a large one-bedroom on the top floor of a brownstone in Chelsea, just two blocks from where she and Carpentier lived. As Eve was helping her friend settle in, both of them sitting on the floor, sorting through Sebastian's meager belongings piled up in the middle of the living room, she said, "You have to come for dinner at least once a week, on a day when Robert is in town, so we can all be together as often as possible." Sebastian was moved by his friend's offer; he could now afford to eat at any restaurant he chose; he was out almost every night, late into the night, often not back home until well after dawn, after having danced all night in some club, a beautiful young man in tow. The prospect of meals cooked by Eve or Robert, or both, of quiet evenings spent with them in their apartment seemed like a sanctuary. He didn't want them to detect any emotion in his reply. "Yes, regular dinners on an evening when we're all in town, *chère* Evangeline."

Three years after he moved into his new apartment, Sebastian began to lose weight—noticeably, even on his lean frame. "No, Robert," he said to Carpentier at the beginning of that winter, "I just can't go on that shoot." They were sitting in the living room of Eve and Robert's apartment, where Sebastian, contrary to habit, had come without calling; Eve was away with the videographers, and he was telling Carpentier about a project his very excited agent had called him about in the afternoon. "This would be my first starring role; can you imagine? Of course, a villain again; well, not really a villain, but, yeah, a duplicitous character; he has an affair with his best friend's wife; it doesn't end well." But he wouldn't be accepting the role; he was dreading having to tell his agent, but there was no way he could accept. "I'm just too tired, Robert; I'm so tired every day. . . ."

"You know what's going on, don't you? You understand? You see how much weight I've lost?"

. . .

Carpentier knew, Carpentier understood, but he didn't say anything immediately. As long as he didn't say anything, a chance remained that what Sebastian was telling him was not possible. There were years and years left of going on as before. They were all unscathed, intact.

"Are you sure?"

"Yes, I'm sure; I did the test, all the blood work. I'm sure."

. . .

"I wanted to tell you before Eve comes back from her trip. Where did she go this time?"

"Bolivia. She's coming back tomorrow, but I'll be in Connecticut. I'm leaving in the morning."

. . .

"I just don't have the strength, Robert. Fuck! Fuck! Why now? Why ever, Robert?"

. . .

It was a face Carpentier had never seen before, not even when Sebastian was onstage. Eve's childhood friend had been pacing around the living room, unable to sit or stay still; now he was standing in the middle of the room, not defiant, not imploring, just waiting. Carpentier remained on the couch, where the two of them had been earlier. Carpentier felt trapped; anything to stop the conversation; anything to delay *this*. "Why don't we get together, the three of us, after Eve gets back and I'm in New York again. Thursday?" he offered. Sebastian was not waiting anymore; the moment had passed. "Okay, Robert, Thursday. Maybe you can make us one of your delicious dinners; apparently, I have to eat, keep up my weight. I'll bring some Sancerre," he said as he headed for the hall closet to get his coat. Carpentier was relieved. There was something about embracing Sebastian even briefly that he found unseemly, an acknowledgment he could not take back; something of the perfection of their camaraderie, as he saw it, as he wanted to keep it, its blithe flawlessness, their conversations and outings throughout the city, with Eve, and, afterward, without her, all this would be irremediably damaged.

With his offer of bringing something to dinner, Sebastian himself had provided a way out, and Carpentier only had to reply, "Don't bring wine; don't bring anything. I'll take care of everything." Words about wine, about dinner, and getting together, everything was as it had been, as it should be. Sebastian was suddenly worn-out; he needed to go home, rest, sleep, if he could manage it. Carpentier walked him to the door. By the time Sebastian made it to the stairwell, Carpentier had shut the door. He then went to the kitchen, put ice cubes in a tumbler, poured himself a large rum, and turned on the television.

When he called Eve before driving to Connecticut early the following day, Carpentier told her it was very cold in New York; he told her that Sebastian had dropped by, and then he told her what she already knew. Mercifully, there was no muffled sobbing, no anxious questioning at the other end. She already knew; she was hoping, but she knew. He was afraid of a scene, of having to comfort her over the phone, of having to say the things people say in these moments. He saw himself from a distance, speaking to Eve on the phone, he in Manhattan, she in some hotel in Bolivia. He wished it were summer again and they were swimming far out, where the water turned a deep blue, almost a dark purple. Away from everything else. On the phone, Eve seemed to be close by, taking charge.

"My flight is on time; I'll be in New York around five. I'll call him; I'll see him. Oh, Robert."

. . .

"You told me he was coming for dinner tomorrow?"

"Yes. I told him not to bring anything."

. . .

"I'll be home early enough to take care of everything."

Over the next two years, Sebastian came to the apartment several times a week. Carpentier cooked; Eve cooked. They watched movies on television, sitting next to one another on the couch. Sebastian wanted to stay as long as possible; he dreaded going back to his empty apartment. At one point, he had to use a cane. "Don't I look like some flaneur? All I need is the cape and hat." Eve hugged her friend, passed her hand over his cheek, pushed back a thick lock from his forehead. "You're as dashing as ever, Sebastian."

Carpentier felt snared. He wondered at Eve's capacity to embrace *these new circumstances* with such resolve and tenderness. That at least was something, he told himself, something whole and beautiful about the woman who embodied so much for him. He wished they could stop seeing Sebastian completely.

Sometimes, when Eve was just overwhelmed with

work, he reluctantly walked Sebastian back to his place alone, always leaving him at the bottom of the brownstone steps. One evening, Sebastian turned to him as they reached the steps and asked, "Would you mind helping me up the stairs, Robert? I don't think I can make it tonight." Carpentier looked at him distractedly; he searched for a way out. He had to get up very early the next day, and there was the long drive to Wannaford, a class to prepare tonight. He had to leave Manhattan early, before the traffic got bad, but then he realized the feebleness of any of these justifications. *Better go through with it, not make a scene.* "Sure; here, let me take your stick, and you can hold on to the rail; I'll be right behind you." It was only two flights of steps, but it took a long time; on the first landing, Sebastian was already out of breath. "Robert, can you help me take off my coat?" He supported himself on the handrail to lift one arm, then the other as Carpentier slipped off his coat; the lining was wet and dark with sweat. Carpentier made sure to fold it on his arm on the dry side and continued to follow Sebastian's slow climb. They finally made it to the third floor. "Here, Robert, take the key; open the door for me, please."

Sebastian's shirt was now drenched; he was still muscular under the wet shirt, but so thin. As he unbuttoned his shirt in the kitchen, the closest room to the apartment entrance, he suddenly began to sob. From where he stood, reluctant to go to Sebastian, Carpentier noticed the spittle gathered in the corners of his mouth. Sebastian managed to take off the shirt by himself and was only able to let it fall to the floor. "Would you like some water?" Carpentier asked him. Sebastian only nodded. He poured him a glass of water from the faucet and then went to the bathroom to get a towel. By the time he came back, Sebastian had managed to take off his sneakers and to slip off his pants; he was in his underwear, sitting on one of the kitchen chairs, his hands resting on his knees, his head bent forward. Carpentier briefly thought of Rodin's *The Thinker*, but now he wanted to leave; he'd done enough. Sebastian's voice was low, a moan from far away. Sensing he was about to be left alone, he said, "Don't go yet, Robert; here, sit on this chair." Sebastian was not ready to tell Eve about what he called *all the gory details*; he wouldn't, not yet, but maybe Robert could *break it to her easily*, give her all this detailed information, how this thing was progressing, "Can you believe it, Robert, *progressin*g?" As he continued, Carpentier handed him the towel, sat on a kitchen chair across from him, and listened. Swollen lymph nodes, candida, low T-cell count, weekly visits to the doctor, scouring newspapers, magazines for new developments, a possible cure, hope, a mother in the bus wrenching her toddler from the seat next to him, the chills, the fevers, Sebastian's daily routine and specialized vocabulary, knowledge now shared between them, taking Carpentier somewhere he did not want to go. "I'm not at that stage yet, Robert; but this is what's going on." Carpentier helped him get into bed; there was no way around that. "We'll see you tomorrow, Sebastian. Do you want me to turn off the lights?" "Yes, Robert, please; just leave my bedside lamp on." Carpentier quickly walked through the dark, quiet apartment and ran down the three flights of steps; once outside, he deeply breathed in the cold night air.

Days in Connecticut were like another life, far from New York and Sebastian and having to attend to him, especially when Eve was away on a trip. When she was home, Carpentier was relieved and relinquished all that he could.

By the time the first lesions appeared on Sebastian's chest, two smaller ones on his face, there was no longer any need for an intercessor or restraint. He told Eve and Robert that he applied makeup to the marks on his body that could be seen by others. "They cringe when they see you; they think just passing by will get them sick." And he added, "I'm speckled by death." Eve took hold of her friend's hand. Carpentier was stunned by the words; he wished Sebastian hadn't said anything. *He could have waited. Why say this now? There's talk about a cure; there's this AZT everyone is talking about.*

The night Sebastian had to be hospitalized, Eve and Carpentier were having dinner with some of her colleagues from UNICEF. Before the main dishes were served, Eve had excused herself from the table to call her friend, "just to check up on him, to make sure he doesn't need anything; I'll be right back." Carpentier thought she was pointlessly interrupting this gathering of friends around a meal, but there was no stopping her. When Eve returned to the table a few minutes later, her face was livid. "I'm sorry, we have to leave now. He has to be taken to the hospital, Robert; let's get a cab." Carpentier halfheartedly pushed back his chair and asked, "Are you sure we shouldn't just call an ambulance to get him and go straight to the hospital?" Eve looked at him. He wondered if it was surprise on her face or disdain. "No, let's go now," she said, and, turning to the others, she added, "I'm sorry, guys; we really have to go. Please take care of the check, I'll see you at work tomorrow."

It was a cold night; the streets were empty. Eve managed to wave down a cab speeding by just as they came out of the restaurant. During the short ride to Sebastian's apartment, Carpentier reached out to his wife, who was looking out the window; she'd withdrawn her hand, maybe to look for something in her purse. He couldn't tell in the dark. Neither one talked. When they arrived, Eve asked the driver to wait.

They climbed the steps to Sebastian's floor; he was waiting for them, one hand on the door handle, the other leaning on his cane. Eve hugged him softly, her head resting a few seconds on her friend's chest; he looked like he could break. Carpentier focused on his sallow skin, his hair sticking together, a strand plastered on his sweating forehead. Eve led her friend back into the apartment. "Come, Sebastian; we have to hurry. Did you pack something?" Sebastian seemed lost in his own living room, and could only drop himself on the sofa, drained. His cane fell to the floor; Carpentier picked it up and handed it back to him. Eve went into the bedroom, quickly gathering what she could—T-shirts, underwear, a pair of pajama pants; she couldn't find a small suitcase anywhere and instead put everything in a plastic bag. She came out of the bedroom, moving fast. "Any medications I have to pack, Sebastian?" He pointed her back to the bedroom, and could only whisper, "On my night table." Eve called out from the bedroom, "Robert, could you just get his toothbrush from the bathroom, his brush, whatever you think he'll need?"

They were ready to leave. Carpentier got Sebastian's coat from the hall closet and helped him put it on, one sleeve, slowly, then, just as slowly, the other, pulling up the collar, straightening out the coat on his meager shoulders. Sebastian seemed swallowed up in the dark coat. *An effigy*, Carpentier thought. Sebastian suddenly pulled out a wool cap from one of the pockets and brought it down low on his forehead in a surprisingly capable gesture. Again, the whisper: "Can't catch a cold, you know." Eve turned off the last light in the apartment and took Sebastian's arm as she spoke to her husband. "Here, Robert, take the bag. Go tell the driver we're coming down." Carpentier, relieved not to have to take the steps one by one, hurried down. Sebastian leaned on Eve going down the flights of stairs. "Don't rush, Sebastian; we have all the time in the world." After their slow descent past the three landings, as she let go of him to open the brownstone's door, she turned to him. "Hold on to the rail, Sebastian, just a second," but as she moved from him to open the door, he grabbed her arm and looked at her, his eyes bright under his wool cap, and whispered, "It's so beautiful; I want to die under the stars." Something from their past, from one of their two summers in Greece when they had camped on a beach.

Eve visited Sebastian at the hospital every day for the next few weeks; she'd managed to avoid any trips for UNICEF. Sometimes, Carpentier accompanied his wife, but his teaching at Wannaford couldn't be avoided, or he had to be away for a talk or a colloquium. "I can't just cancel tomorrow's classes," he told Eve on the phone; she'd just asked him to replace her at the hospital the next day, when she had to attend an evening meeting. "Robert, please make an effort. He was asking about you today; he says he misses his walks in the city with you; he misses you." Carpentier relented. "I'll ask one of the graduate students to fill in for me tomorrow; I should be in New York by two or three, so you can go to your meeting." "Thank you, Robert." Eve was at once grateful, saddened, and riled. Since Sebastian's illness, it was as if the pieces of a puzzle were fitting themselves together, with no effort on her part; pieces, moments from the past: Robert's reluctance to visit his parents, his avoidance of any conversation about having a child; more recent pieces: the time he screamed at her after she'd told him what had happened in Brasilia, even the way he spoke about the painters whose work he admired, and, the most distressing piece, his reaction to Sebastian's illness, the most recent and illuminating fragment of a picture that had been coming into focus steadily but always shrouded by the overwhelming appeal she had felt initially. Now their meeting on that pine-scented beach, their pact that September years ago, when the weather had turned to fall so suddenly, seemed like a scene from another life. Now she sometimes felt she was living with a troubling stranger.

When Carpentier dutifully showed up at the hospital the following evening, there were two visitors on Sebastian's side of the double room: a robust red-haired young man wearing a plaid shirt, jeans, and work boots standing at the foot of Sebastian's bed; he seemed bursting with health; there was also Adelaide, sitting in a chair at Sebastian's bedside. She seemed about to cry; once again, and as always, Carpentier told himself that she seemed to feed on that sort of thing, to feel responsible for everything in the world.

The curtain separating the two sides of the room had been left open. Sebastian had been introducing the man lying in the other bed for several weeks as "my roommate, Alfonso." Alfonso was hardly moving today; he was entirely covered, except for an unbearably thin arm resting on his lap, and his head, which seemed too large for the slender shape under the white sheet. Sebastian raised himself slightly from the bed to welcome, to officiate. "Well, hello, Robert; you know my roommate, and you know Adelaide, but I don't think you know Michael. Michael, this is Robert; Robert, this is Michael." Carpentier shook hands with the red-haired young man and nodded to Alfonso and Adelaide. They'd all been talking about how bad the food was at the hospital, and how mild the winter had been. "It's almost spring; you can already smell it in the air," Michael of the plaid shirt said to no one in particular. "Well, you won't have to eat the hospital food tonight," Carpentier said to Sebastian. "I've brought you some prosciutto, very thinly sliced, the way you like it, and some bread from Rafi's Bakery; he asked about you." Sebastian smiled at this and told Robert to put everything in the small refrigerator in the corner. "All my victuals in one place; have to keep up that weight!" Sometimes, he seemed to regain his energy, his playfulness, but his eyes were set deeper, his nose seemed more pointed, and his thick hair was now cut to a gray stubble on his skull. His smile was as mordant and generous as ever. Carpentier was grateful for the others in the room, even Alfonso. He managed a few questions for Adelaide and for Michael, who asked him about Eve; Carpentier was surprised at this. "Yeah, we met here a few times; I usually come to visit Sebastian on Thursdays, and she's always here in the evenings." When Carpentier left a half hour later, Michael was standing at the foot of the bed; Adelaide, with her tragic face, was still sitting in the chair; Alfonso had turned toward his side of the room and closed his eyes.

Alfonso died a few days later. "When I saw him last week, I asked him what I could get him, and you know what he asked for, Robert? Ben and Jerry's ice cream." Eve was on the phone with her husband, who was at his office in Wannaford. "And when I asked him what flavor he would like, he said 'Cherry Garcia.' I had no idea, Robert, 'Cherry Garcia'; I didn't even know that flavor existed, but they had it in that bodega on Second Avenue; I took it up to him; poor Alfonso." Carpentier barely remembered Alfonso's name.

Sebastian died in May. Six people were in the hospital room with him: Eve, Carpentier, who could not avoid showing up on that day, Michael, Adelaide, Yann, and Sebastian's mother. She was a surprisingly small and delicate woman, not at all like her muscular son, her only child, her boy; she had come from Arizona; she hadn't seen him in two years.

Michael and Eve were on opposite sides of the bed as Sebastian was dying, each holding one of his hands. From far below, the clamor of the streets and avenues of Manhattan drifted upward, but the blasting car horns, the sirens of ambulances, police cars, fire trucks were now only faint echoes in the room. Carpentier listened to the hum from below; another life down there, all those people walking around, enjoying the first warm days of the season. He wished he could be in that anonymous crowd, but here, in the closeness of the hospital room, he was fixated on Sebastian's eyes, wide open over the oxygen mask covering the rest of his face; the mask fogged up and then cleared up again. Sebastian's breathing seemed so strong, even if it sounded like there was something stuck in his throat. Carpentier felt like he was the only one thinking, *He can't be dying. We should not let him know that he's dying. He can't be dying. He's dying. He's not going to be here anymore. He can't be conscious of this; we can't let him know.* When he looked away from the eyes, Carpentier saw Sebastian's body laid out. *He's like a long bird under the sheets, pared down. There is nothing left, but we can't tell him anything.* When Eve began to say, softly and over and over again, "Let go, Sebastian; it's okay; let go," Carpentier was shocked. *Why doesn't anyone tell her to stop?* he wondered. Eve tried to have him hold on to Sebastian's hand, but he kept his hands away. Eve couldn't bear to look at her husband; she continued to hold her friend's hand, and to murmur, "It's okay, Sebastian; let go; it's okay." Carpentier was appalled. *Such tenderness, such love, such cruelty. Why tell him this? Why tell him such a frightening thing?* No one was trying to stop Eve from saying this; they all seemed to agree, and he couldn't stop Eve from speaking. He wanted to ask her why she was telling Sebastain this; he wanted to tell her not to tell him this, to let him be. Yet Carpentier couldn't stop his own tears from flowing. He hadn't cried in such a long time, not since he was a child. When Sebastian stopped breathing, Yann went into the hall to find someone.

Carpentier drove Sebastian's mother to the airport the day after the cremation. When he left her at the terminal, she was holding her small suitcase and pressing against her chest the urn that contained her son's ashes. Her voice was feeble but steady as she spoke to Carpentier. "He wanted to stay; he wanted another life here in New York. Frank and I couldn't take the cold anymore, and he was on his own anyway. You were more his family than us out there in Arizona, especially after Frank died. He often called, but you were his real family." She was thankful to Eve, to Robert, to all her son's friends in New York. "I knew it would be like this; I knew I'd have to come to get him one day, like this." She seemed even smaller than before; Carpentier didn't know what to say, and he told her that her flight was being called for boarding. He enjoyed being alone as he drove back to Manhattan.

Summer came very quickly; the trees turned green overnight, it seemed. Carpentier was grateful to Sebastian for having died when he did instead of in the middle of summer. He was ready to go to Greece. He was looking forward to leaving New York more than ever this year. He'd bought some linen shirts, shorts, swimming goggles. He was showing Eve his purchases before they sat down to dinner; he'd taken out the swimming goggles from a bag. "Well, you certainly seem all ready to go."

"These things don't last from one summer to the next; the rubber gets moldy; it shrinks, and the water seeps in."

"Do you need *three* pairs?"

"You know this is basic equipment for me; I use them every day."

. . . (They both remain silent, until Eve seems to give up.)

"I saw your mother on Tuesday; she says hello; she'd like us to come out for dinner before we leave."

. . .

"Can you promise me you won't swim out so far?"

. . .

"I think you'll end up alone one day, like that old man with the little dog in that movie."

. . . (Such finality; the pronouncement of a stern oracle.)

. . .

Robert and Eve had seen the movie a week before, the story of an old man in postwar Italy who had nothing left but a little dog; the dog's name was Flag, Carpentier remembered. He put the three pairs of goggles back in the bag and placed the bag on the coffee table.

That summer, Eve didn't mention Sebastian at all, and Carpentier was relieved. He preferred to at least pretend for a while, to let time pass a bit; a reprieve of sorts, a way of not spoiling the fullness of the long summer days, away from everything; as if Sebastian had been left in

New York, or was away, in Italy or France somewhere, for a film shoot, and they would resume their dinners at the apartment again once they were all back in the city; fall in Manhattan, walks with Sebastian, going to see him in one of those movies he'd been in these past few years, Sebastian taking them to yet another club where he would remain chatting with this or that young guy at the bar, waving a quick good-bye to Eve and Carpentier as they left the crowded, raucous place.

That summer, Carpentier swam "like a beast," as he put it. He and Eve went back to the hill on the island where they'd talked about buying a piece of land. They rented a small house in the main town. For the first time since they had started coming to Greece together, Eve wanted to go straight from the airport to Piraeus to catch the ferry for the island; they would not stop at her family's summer house, and, at the end of their stay, she would go back there on her own and wait for him; he could spend a few days on the island on his own, and then they would return to New York together. "I'll see Mom and Dad and the others; they'll all be there from New York and Athens the same week at the end of August; you don't need to come; this way, you can have some time on your own." Carpentier felt he was being left out of something, but he didn't insist. Maybe if he went along, didn't challenge, didn't ask for any explanation, it would all go away, and they could be as before—before Sebastian's illness, before he started to perceive the signs of her drawing away from him. He agreed with her proposition. "Yes, I'll make some headway on the book."

It was windy on their first night on the island. "Very unusual," they were told by the woman who owned the house they had rented. "It's windy everywhere, not only up there in the hills but on the beaches, too, and even here in town; it's been blowing since yesterday." It felt more like October than the middle of summer. Eve and Carpentier were both tired from the long trip; the taxi from Chelsea to JFK, the plane to Athens with a layover in Paris, another taxi from the airport in Greece to Piraeus, the ferry crossing, and, finally, almost twenty-four hours after they'd left New York, the lights of the small port as the ferry slowly approached the island. The owner of the house was waiting for them among a group of women brandishing rough cardboard signs and shouting, "Rooms! Rooms!" The house was only a few minutes away. They took a short walk after dinner at one of the tavernas that lined the port and went to bed early.

When Carpentier awoke, feeling refreshed, the room was completely dark; he reached over, but the bed was empty next to him. He got up and opened two of the shutters; dazzling white sunlight filled the room; the crumpled sheets, the open suitcases on the floor, the clothes spilling out, the dark icons and framed watercolors on the white walls were all suddenly whole and bright. He picked up his watch from the bedside table and had to turn away from the light to make out the numbers; already past ten! He'd slept twelve hours. As he headed for the bathroom, he heard something like a baby or maybe even an animal noise coming from the kitchen; he began to enter the kitchen and saw that Eve was sobbing; he headed for the bathroom very quietly, brushed his teeth, shaved, took a shower, and got dressed. When he entered the kitchen, Eve turned to him. Her eyes were dry; she was smiling.

"Good morning. You really slept."

"Good morning. Yeah, I was done for; I needed this. Did you have breakfast?"

"Not yet. Look, she's left us a few things."

Milk, butter, bread, honey. Eve had laid them out on the wooden table: milk in a glass pitcher, honey glowing in an unlabeled jar, a mound of butter, and thick slices of bread on clay plates. Eve was wearing a long, loose robe; she reigned over the table; she had all the time in the world. An ache in his chest; he could stay in this room forever, with her, in this kitchen from another time. Sebastian's hospital room, his body like a thin, long bird on the hospital bed belonged to another place. No decay for him; his mother had left with an urn filled with her son's ashes. The splendor of Eve, here, now. *Away from all the rest of it.*

"Here, sit, I'll pour you some coffee."

"So, should we go for a swim before it gets too hot? Last year an Australian guy told me about a beach in the south. No wind ever."

"If you'd like."

"Yes, of course, let's go. Come on, this is our first day! Let's not miss any days."

. . .

"We should also ask about that piece of land on the hill."

. . .

"Don't you think?"

"We don't even know that it's for sale, Robert."

"But we could ask around, no?"

"Who? We haven't seen anyone around there."

"I don't know, maybe go back up there, or go to one of those real estate places? I noticed one in town last year." He felt her reluctance but couldn't stop himself.

Their summer life, the one he yearned for during the year—to be here with Eve, *away from all the rest of it.*

Days at the beach, without missing a single day; the sun always shining, pouring down. Eve usually went with him to the beach in the early afternoon. Sometimes she prepared a salad for lunch if they happened to be at the house; the main meal was in the evening. She watched him swim far out; he came back to her. He never asked about her crying in the kitchen that first morning. Why now, when everything around them was flawless? He was finding her again; she seemed to be coming back to him after weeks of distance.

Early afternoon at one of the family beaches; deck chairs and umbrellas for rent, children running around; Eve and Carpentier swam out together to a raft. When they reached it, he hoisted himself up and helped her climb. The sun would not set for quite a long time; Eve lay down on the raft; he let his head sink back onto her lap; the sky was full in his eyes, all blue and gold, and he could feel her stomach rising and falling under his head. That evening, when they were in bed, Carpentier began to kiss her, first her mouth and then her breasts; for the first time since Sebastian's death in the spring, Eve didn't stop him.

Long hours at the beach; he worked on his book on Watteau in the mornings; Eve sometimes went for an early swim; she came back with fruit, cheese, tomatoes, bread. He'd lost count of the days. He did manage to get her to go to the small real estate agency he'd noticed in the center of town the summer before. The young woman who was alone in the office and spoke English quite well told them that she didn't know of this property but that she would "inquire among her clients." She reassured them: "I'm sure I'll get you some information; it's a small island." Once outside, Eve seemed relieved and told Carpentier that they probably wouldn't hear from her. She didn't wait for him to reply, and proposed a drive to a taverna in a village in the south of the island. "They have great fish there." She took his arm and they walked back to the car.

When she left for Athens a few days later, Carpentier accompanied her to the ferry; on their way to the port, she didn't once mention the land up in the hills. He walked beside her, carrying her suitcase; they got to the departing ferry just in time. He kissed her on the lips before she stepped onto the passenger bridge; trucks, cars, and motorcycles were also entering, faster and faster as departure neared. Eve squeezed his arm, "Work well, Robert. See you soon—at the airport. I'll say hello to everyone for you." She walked quickly up the ramp and didn't turn back.

During the few days Carpentier spent on the island on his own, he found himself unable to do any of the work he had planned to do on the book and spent all the remaining days at the beach. He swam to the point of exhaustion; he collapsed on his towel and fell asleep in the middle of the day, then awoke a few minutes later, burning from the sun pouring down directly from above. He went back in the water and swam again. The days passed; he remained at the beach until sunset. Going back to the house, showering, getting dressed used up some more of his time alone. In the evenings, he drank several small carafes of that cold piney wine at dinner down in the port. Unable to fall asleep, he read late into the night, discovering a murderer's identity, following the complicated and treacherous back-and-forth of spies in London, in Paris, in Eastern European capitals of another time. Carpentier appreciated the polished symmetry of this type of book: people and events pared down to a fine, fanciful, and resolved narrative.

He was up at dawn; the book he'd been reading had

fallen to the floor. Throughout his time alone on the island, the incipient thought of something owed to him made its way, a blind expectation being denied, the possibility of another life escaping him. The one night they'd *had sex* since Sebastian's death was an exception in all the weeks he'd felt Eve withdrawing. During his time alone on the island, he felt he'd been granted permission to do something, anything, to reclaim something for himself and feel whole again, so that he could be invincible in their pact again. *Eve my love, my country.*

Early September, a few days after their return from Greece. Carpentier has just finished teaching his first class of the fall semester at Wannaford, a senior seminar; he is gathering his books and papers and hasn't noticed Emma Zhao, a student who was in one of his classes the previous spring; she usually sat in one of the back rows. Now she's come up to his desk. They are alone in the empty classroom. "You're bronzed; you look like a bronze statue wearing pants and a jacket." Her voice is deep for someone her age; her abundant hair is loosely held up by a tortoiseshell comb. She's half joking, half serious; she's testing the waters. He knows he should put a stop to *this* immediately. They leave the classroom together.

Over coffee in that place across from campus, half burger joint, half café, he mentions "Greek statues, Greek temples painted all kinds of bright colors back then." She obviously already knows all of this; she seems to know more about Greek statuary than he does. She tells him about two bronze warriors found in the sea off the coast of a small town in Italy. "You didn't know about them?" she continues in that voice too deep for someone her age.

"I went to that town with some friends in August—Reggio Calabria. No one ever went there before those two statues were displayed in the tiny museum; now thousands of tourists go there. I'm surprised you didn't know about this." While he tells her that this is not at all his field, she sips her coffee; she hardly seems to be listening and asks him where he lives in Connecticut. "You don't drive back to New York the same day, do you?" "No," he replies. He is unable to stop himself. "I rent a room in a big house in Winfield, about ten minutes from campus; two colleagues of mine live there; the house is so big, we don't always know who's home, who's not; they call the part they rent me the 'scholar suite'; it's convenient." Carpentier knows he's saying too much; she seems so sure of herself, so composed. "Why don't we just leave?" she offers. He stumbles into this like a blind man. "Yes, let's leave."

He drives Emma Zhao to the house in Winfield. It's the middle of the afternoon; the big house is empty; there are birds picking at the grass that rolls down beyond the trees to a lake below. She follows him to his room on the second floor. Afterward, he stares up at the ceiling and intones, "'The earth was feverous and did shake.'" Without missing a beat, her head on his chest, her long black hair spread over his torso, she murmurs, "I think 'La Belle Dame Sans Merci thee hath in thrall.'" He is defenseless. He takes her to his room in the big house throughout the fall and into the early spring. At first, she waits for him after class and they drive to Winfield. In the spring, when she is no longer in any of his classes, he picks her up at her dorm or at the burger joint–café place across from campus. A few weeks into the semester, she begins to mention obligations; she can't make it this week because of a concert she has to attend or a visit home; at one point, she says something about a boyfriend, "someone I just met." Very early on, Carpentier knew he would have to let her take the lead; he is like a king without real power; he can only wait for her to return to her life. After spring break, Emma Zhao stops coming to his office. By then, he is appeased, thankful. Life can continue as before.

Monday, April 10, 1995—and before, and after

Light is fading over the city on this early spring evening; the long days have returned. Light is still receding in gathering shadows across Central Park, on the other side of Fifth Avenue. Robert Carpentier is standing in the living room of a penthouse apartment with his wife and about fifty other people at a reception held for the emissary from across the Atlantic who has come to plead the case of Sarajevo, the besieged city. Carpentier has seen snippets on television, but what exactly is happening over there remains vague to him; there are rules and restrictions for the news in this country, in the United States of America, an unspoken consensus governing the amount of death and blood the general audience is allowed to see—blurred bodies and faces, the edited aftermath of shootings and explosions. He gives a wide berth to certain events, but, like most people, he has seen the photos of emaciated men behind barbed wire on the covers of magazines and on the evening news, the rare times he watches. Other images are about to be projected onto one of the white walls of this vast living room where dozens of sturdy folding chairs have been placed in neat rows by two uniformed maids and the bartender, who has been enlisted by the lady of the house to assist in that task. "Harry, could you please help them set up? Could you also draw the curtains in a few minutes? I'll let you know when. Thank you." The lady of the house—for an alarming few seconds, Carpentier doesn't remember her name—is wearing a long black dress; the rich folds of a gray-and-tan shawl are spread over her shoulders; her husband is wearing a tuxedo, as are a few of the other men. For once, Carpentier is wearing a suit, his only suit, bought for him by his wife, who likes to see her husband out of his usual *professor clothes*.

"You look good in your suit; you academics always look a bit messy, especially the old ones, with spots on their cardigans and corduroys; there's no reason; my father always tells me that as you get older you have to take care, make an extra effort."

. . .

"Well, you do look good in your suit; you should have worn a tie."

"No, he looks fine just like this, and we appreciate the effort. Thank you, Robert. Thank you so much for coming." (Now her name comes back to him: Nancy, Nancy Smythe. How could he have forgotten?)

"How is the book on Watteau coming along?"

"It's going well, Nancy. I should be done this summer."

"Well, you make sure Steven and I get a copy. He's crazy about Watteau; always wished he could buy one."

"Even if there were any of the good ones for sale, dear, I'm sure the Frenchies wouldn't let them out of their country." The starched, slightly cambered front of Steven Smythe's white shirt gleams like armor against his black tuxedo jacket; he is loosely holding a tumbler filled with much scotch and little soda; his already ruddy face leans close to Carpentier's shoulder, and he does a mock gangster routine, maybe Peter Lorre in *Casablanca* asking

Humphrey Bogart to save him. “Robert, Robert, help me! Maybe you could put in a good word for me with the Frenchies?”

. . .

“Mrs. Smythe, we’re ready to begin.”

“Thank you, Harry. Dear, could you make yourself useful and get their attention?”

Steven Smythe picks up a small fork from one of the tables covered with geometrically aligned hors d’oeuvres and proceeds to tap it repeatedly against his tumbler, a flurry of small crystalline strokes on the glass; he is clearly enjoying this call to order and just keeps on hitting the little fork against his tumbler until his wife places her hand on his wrist to stop him.

In the now quiet living room, Nancy Smythe stands in front of the bare section of white wall from which a large gilt-framed painting has been unfastened and taken somewhere in the apartment’s outer reaches. Nancy Smythe holds a flute of champagne and introduces the man standing next to her. “Our guest who has come to alert us, more than ever, more urgently than ever, to the plight of Sarajevo . . . And so, dear friends, will you please join me in giving a warm welcome to Salko Dudakovic.” Some of the guests have already been approaching the rows of chairs; others are already seated. They all find spots—tables, their laps, the thickly carpeted floor—on which to rest their drinks momentarily, and applaud vigorously; they applaud their hostess and the man who has now joined her in the space between the first row of chairs and the expanse of white wall, their tall, smiling hostess in her long black dress, her gray-and-tan shawl, and the Yugoslav, as they have been referring to him. He seems quietly at ease standing there; about him the air of someone who wishes he were somewhere else rather than standing next to Nancy Smythe in the bright rectangle of light from the projector, their two black silhouettes running into each other on the white wall. He seems both courtly and vital, his dark and gray hair thick and cropped short, like that of a soldier, or an artisan from another time. His own voice is deep and subdued as he quickly thanks "Mrs. Nancy Smythe and her husband, Steven, who have been very kind, very generous," and he thanks their friends who have come here this evening, "I am not good at speaking in English; I prefer to just let you watch the pieces of film I have brought with me; you say *pieces*, yes?"

. . .

"Yes."

"Yes, yes!"

Apprehension and curiosity in the spacious living room; they are about to see something most people don't see. More applause follows as the bartender and the two maids dim the lights.

The scenes projected on the wall take place in winter. People are desperately rushing around, their coattails flung about them; men and women wearing wool caps or hats or scarves are running, some carrying dead or wounded bodies. A man thought dead is still alive; his left hand is moving, but when his body, facing the concrete, is turned over by three other men, you can see that the back of his trousers has been burned off; there is a purplish red blur where his back, buttocks, and thighs should be. Children are carried in their mothers' arms, in their fathers' arms, some too old to be carried, but being carried nonetheless, their dangling feet scraping the sidewalks and the cobblestone streets covered in ashes, debris. The juddering camera stops on an old woman: The tops of the stockings on her thin thighs are revealed under her raised skirt as she is lifted off the ground by two young men. A young woman, thumbs and palms under her ears, her fingers spread to her forehead, is pushing back her hair; she is crying; her mouth is twisted; she's been looking at what is happening on the streets and sidewalks but is now looking up at people dangling from the windows of a burning building; they've slung out ropes, sheets, and are attempting to climb down. Below the burning building, people are running, in the hope that they won't be hit by a sniper's bullet; they run fast, as fast as they can, with the useless efficiency of the desperate: purposeful, arms bent, sprinters nearing the finish line, stooping in the hope that the bullets will not find them, like rushing pedestrians caught in sudden rain pretending that this small, crooked gesture will get them less wet.

Things happen quickly after the last images of dark fumes spewing out of buildings, broken glass, pools of blood, ambulances, hospital rooms, amputees laid out on gurneys lining hospital halls. The ornate chandelier, quietly turned back on, is now sparkling over the living room; the table lamps are all lit again; the night is dark and serene outside the penthouse apartment on Fifth Avenue overlooking Central Park. No one is applauding in the large living room now. The guests are turning to one another, worshippers after Mass enjoined by the officiating cleric to greet one another. In the lingering silence, the Yugoslav walks back to the front of the rows of chairs, his hand held by Nancy Smythe, whose voice now seems inordinately clear, her words sharply outlined in the aftermath of the film's frenzied sounds. "As Steven and I have, please open your hearts, and your wallets, and give generously;

let's let the world know that we will not stand by while this massacre is taking place."

The two uniformed maids pass among the guests once again, this time with trays of miniature pastries, followed by a last round of drinks before the guests begin to stream out of the brightly illuminated penthouse into the night. For a long while, Carpentier doesn't see his wife among the groups that have formed one last time, but then he finds her speaking with Nancy Smythe and two other women near the entrance hall. They exchange the complicit nod that means "Yes, let's leave," followed by the thanks and farewells to Nancy Smythe, but not to Steven Smythe, who seems to have disappeared somewhere far in the depths of the apartment. The Yugoslav is surrounded by several women, some holding checks.

Carpentier and Eve take the elevator with a few other people, exit the lobby, and emerge into the chilly spring evening. They stand in front of the building as the doorman, who had stayed out for a few seconds, retreats to his spot behind the glass and copper doors.

"That guy was laying it on thick, no?"

"Who?"

"Who else? The Yugoslav, the honored guest; he seemed so smug. How did he get to New York anyway? And all these cozy people buying into it. 'Open your hearts and your wallets'; I mean, really."

"I think he's here for a reason, Robert. Why can't you see that? Did you see the people in the film? You know what's going on over there; you of all people should understand."

. . . (They both seem stranded, with immeasurable space and time between them.)

"Should we get something to eat around here before I leave?"

"I'm not very hungry after all those shrimp things and the pastries. Are you? You have a long drive. Why don't you just leave from here now and I'll take a cab home."

"Are you sure? It'll only take me a few minutes to drive you home."

"No need to go back all the way home and up again; I'll be fine."

"Really?"

. . .

"Okay, then. I'll leave from here."

They kiss on the sidewalk; he hails a cab for his wife and opens the door for her. He kisses her again before she steps into the cab. "I'll see you on Wednesday," he says. "Drive carefully; don't speed. I know you," she replies as he slowly closes the door. She seems so solicitous, but she doesn't ask him to call her when he gets to Connecticut, as she always does. The bright rectangular sign on top of the taxi goes off; there will be no sudden change of heart; the anonymous driver, now ruthless and hurried executioner, steers the car away as Carpentier looks at the red taillights of the yellow cab rushing down Fifth Avenue.

After looking around a good ten minutes and finally finding his car two blocks from where he thought he had left it, he drives across Central Park and enters the West Side Highway at the Ninety-sixth Street ramp. A few minutes later, he passes the George Washington Bridge, glowing in the night, and crosses into what he thinks of as the Land of Bucolic Names: Riverdale, Lakeview, Saw Mill River Parkway, and then for a long while he will be in the narrow and comforting confines of the Merritt Parkway, arriving in Connecticut late in the evening, months or years away from Manhattan. Not quite a two-and-a-half-hour trip.

He enjoys the drives on the Merritt Parkway at night, the stillness of being alone with music or listening to the unrolling plot of a book read by a well-trained voice. On either side of the road, the same unfurling of trees, windows of houses either television gray or a warm orange, bright against the dark; once in a while he passes under a stone bridge or drives by the lit oasis of a service station. The gas tank is full and he won't have to stop anywhere until he reaches his colleagues' house, where he's rented a room for the one or two nights when he's in Connecticut, in the "scholar suite."

Tonight, he's thinking of his wife's remoteness. Interfering images appear to him: the young woman in the Yugoslav's film, with her thumbs and palms under her ears, her fingers spread to her forehead, pushing back her hair; her crying eyes, her twisted mouth; all those people writhing in the debris and the blood. The evening chill is suddenly noticeable inside the car as he heads farther north; he quickly dismisses these scenes from faraway Sarajevo, adjusts the heat, and turns up the volume on the radio.

He usually leaves without a second thought. He likes to think of these weekly trips to Connecticut, these regular absences, as recurring departures from Ithaca, returning to Eve, returning home after days that stand in for heroic years and adventures. He's repeated a phrase like a mantra or a motto to himself, and even to others in moments of giddiness brought on by an extra glass of wine, or probably more by the need to maintain an allusive and perhaps absolving accuracy, a few words whose alliteration makes him smile: "Odysseus stops for sexy sea nymphs and nubile Nausicaa but always sets sail for Ithaca." The framed poster of a mosaic hangs on a wall of his office at Wannaford College. The mosaic is from a museum in Carthage and depicts Odysseus tied to the mast of his ship, listening to the sirens' song; the poster was a gift from the couple he stays with in Connecticut; they brought it back for him after a trip to Tunisia. On the poster's framed glass covering, Carpentier has taped a thin paper strip from a fortune cookie, the yellowing remnant of a meal at the Chinese restaurant across the campus where he often eats on those nights away from Manhattan. "You are deeply attached to your family and home," it reads. The pithy rendering of Chinese characters seems to no longer tell fortunes, but to make pronouncements. In his case, the fortune cookie is wrong anyway. The only home, the only family, the only country he is attached to is Eve; if it were made just for him, for him only and for no one else, the fortune cookie's thin strip of paper would decree *You are mad about Eve. You will die if you are not with her.*

The jeeps and cars come to a standstill in front of the main gate of the house in the hills right after nightfall, but the sun seems to still be shining brightly in the sky, round and white and malevolent. Men in denim or shirts and pants, or suits, all wearing sunglasses, all carrying rifles, pistols, machine guns, emerge from the cars and jeeps. They are all tall and lean. Some of them have wings that unfold and shed a few feathers as they emerge from the cars and jeeps; some are also holding silver tridents; some are smoking cigarettes whose orange tips glimmer in the weird dusk. The smell of cigarette smoke, incense, and rose petals fills

the bright darkness. From the gate, the house looks like a lantern filled with the glow of candles, like the churches and cathedrals built during the Christmas season by the same boys who build kites during the windy weeks of Lent. As they approach, the armed men, the winged men can see silhouettes moving about inside the vast lantern; music is playing in there, a woman's voice accompanied by a full orchestra and an accordion; the men move impossibly slowly and impossibly quickly through the gate and fan out into the gardens, some flying between the trees, others walking, and, as they all reach the main veranda at the same time, the silhouettes in the wedge of light inside the house take on sudden density and color: The young aunt, sitting in a wheelchair, is playing cards with her two nephews in a corner while, in another corner, the grandfather, his wife, his eldest daughter and her husband, his two sons, and several gardeners and maids are sitting and talking at a table that could also be the desk where the grandfather registers new arrivals; the people at the table are playing cards and having an animated conversation about the water in the pool, whether it is too chlorinated and whether the thick layer of rose petals covering the water should be cleared; they're being served club sandwiches and champagne by a servant wearing black pants, a white shirt, and a black bow tie. At first only the boy notices the men's sudden appearance on the veranda, and he wonders why no one is reacting as the walking and flying men fill the veranda, then the inside of the house, taking up all the room in the wedge of light. The one who seems to be the leader unfastens his wings and orders the young aunt to take off all her clothes. She complies. She's crying. Some of the other men use their rifle butts or their guns to break the teeth of all those sitting at the table; they do this casually, as if they were arranging glasses on a shelf or tidying up a closet; yet another one takes out a machete and begins to slash repeatedly at the two boys' small necks in determined arcs, cutting deep bright red strips. The leader is spread over the young aunt and the boy can see that his belt is undone and his pants pulled down to his knees; the others are also watching; the grandfather says between his broken teeth, "All men are lecherous," but he's smiling, and the ones wearing sunglasses are all saying in unison, their voices becoming unbearably loud, "Let me have a go at it" and "The one with the earrings, too!" pointing to the boy's mother. Then the boy has lost too much blood and begins to cry; he pulls on his younger brother's hand in an attempt to leave. Afterward, the men go back to the jeeps and cars, the winged men leading the way, floating silently above the ones walking and taking longer to get back to the jeeps and cars. They stop in front of the gate of the Montrosier house; then the jeeps and cars stop in front of the gate of Cécile's house; they make the rounds throughout the entire town in the hills. The procession is endless.

THURSDAY, APRIL 20, 1995

Salko Dudakovic is on the subway, traveling from Brooklyn to Manhattan, where he is going to meet Eve Carpentier in an apartment on the Upper West Side loaned by a friend of his. "You can bring her here while I'm at work; I don't get home until late, never before eight. There's beer and even a bottle of champagne in the fridge; there's a bottle of vodka in the freezer; there's food. I've left you sheets and towels."

The apartment is on Riverside Drive. Eve Carpentier will arrive soon. Dudakovic is still alone there; he looks out the windows. The sun is still far from setting between the recently blooming trees; dark barges slowly float by on the wide river below. After the lottery of living and dying in Sarajevo, the besieged, crumbling city, after the explosions, the mangled bodies, the people running to collect water, scrambling to and from fountains while snipers are firing from the hills above, people filling up glass bottles and plastic jerry cans with precious water, anyone could be hit, blood trickling from under bodies just hit by a bullet fired from the hills above, after the weeks and months of dark nights suddenly lit by flares in the sky, this apartment with its view of barges leisurely passing by on the Hudson below, this apartment, with its quiet lobby, its uniformed doorman, its punctiliously recorded, regularly billed, and regularly paid utilities, is another world.

They've been in bed for hours, passionately and pornographically, sometimes even lovingly as the yellow light of afternoon turns into dusk and then into dark. "I have to leave now; let me leave now," she says as she begins to get dressed, but, in the dark this time, they go back to the bed and start all over again, like adolescents in the throes of discovery.

Dudakovic has been in New York for just over a week now and has met Eve Carpentier twice in this apartment since his arrival. He will be leaving soon, going back to the besieged city; he will go back home once he has done his work here on behalf of those he feels he has left behind.

Friday, May 19, 1995

A Friday, early evening. It's noisy in the restaurant in SoHo; the usual packed crowd of those who have come for drinks at the bar and those who have come for an early dinner, two waves of customers blending in that indeterminate late-afternoon, early-evening shift, like a storm before the calm. Eve and Carpentier are sitting at a table near the sliding doors now left open onto the narrow street; the past few evenings have been warm enough to do this. Eve has come straight from work; she had asked him to meet her here for dinner. They've been talking about her day at work in the UN building, his research in that beautiful room at the Forty-second Street library. Even after a whole day at UNICEF, Eve looks like a woman who has just left her house for a meal with friends. They've been drinking the Sancerre she likes so much. He is weak with desire for her. Suddenly, she's crying. Yes, she's sobbing; he doesn't understand why she's sobbing. At first, he thinks that she isn't feeling well, that she is choking. He may be wrong; he may not be hearing her in the din. A waiter is pulling cutlery out of a drawer in a cupboard right next to their table. The music, all these people talking, it's difficult to make out what she's saying; he doesn't want to understand what she's saying; it's impossible that she could be saying what she's saying. There's been a mistake. "I don't think we can go on, Robert." Or "I'm leaving you, Robert." Phrases like a softly delivered verdict. She's unable to contain herself; she is sobbing. He can hardly make out what she's saying to him, but he thinks he also hears her say something about Sarajevo, maybe something about going to Sarajevo?

Epilogue

You know or should know. Or perhaps once these things have happened, we do not realise that we knew they were going to happen and that this was precisely how it would turn out. And isn't it true that, deep down, we are not as surprised as we pretend to others and, above all, to ourselves, and that we then see the logic of it all and recognise and even remember the unheeded warnings that some layer of our unconscious mind did, nevertheless, pick up?

—Javier Marías, *Your Face Tomorrow*

SUNDAY, JUNE 4, 1995—AND BEFORE, AND AFTER

The humid summer heat seems to have started early in Connecticut this year. The air is still, the surrounding trees oppressive; even the grass seems hostile. Robert Carpentier has to turn on the air conditioner to its maximum level as he drives from the "scholar suite" at his colleagues' house in Winfield, where he has been staying once again after having moved out of the apartment in Manhattan, no longer their apartment but, once again, only Eve's. He is going to catch the ferry at Bridgeport and then it's only a short drive to his parents' house on Long Island. Today is his mother's seventieth birthday and there is to be a party for her. "Come, Robert; please; it's a special day for me; it'll only be the family," she had told him on the phone during their last conversation, two weeks ago. Carpentier knows what that means; counting her brothers and sisters, their children, all those cousins he's never met, or hardly, and the friends who've been coming to his parents' successive homes over the years, there will be at least thirty or forty guests at that gathering. Carpentier knows this, he knows his mother's loving guile, he knows what she will resort to when it comes to seeing her elder son, who has remained so far from her for so long, and, still, he would have found a reason not to say yes. But he seems to have lost that ability.

Eve remained silent on the day he packed to leave for Connecticut. There was no more crying; she was spent. She remained sitting in the living room mostly while he gathered what he could around the apartment: clothes, shoes, a few books. Throughout, Eve was either not in the same room or remained so quiet and so still when they were in the same room that she seemed unreal. He went through the motions of opening closet doors, picking books from shelves, filling up two suitcases. He was having a nightmare. When she walked him to the door, he could not restrain himself and began to cry. He dropped the suitcases he was carrying and held on to her, now sobbing, unable to stop. She held him for a few seconds and then gently released him, softly pushed him away. He felt he was being slayed. He managed to pick up the suitcases again and to walk out the door. He continued sobbing in the street; people were turning around to look at him.

Eve hadn't told him when she would be leaving. He called her parents a few days later and Eve's mother told him that she "left for Europe; we don't know when she'll be back." He managed a few more words, and Eve's mother replied, "Yes, of course, Robert, you can visit us anytime."

A few days after that conversation, he attempted to keep working on the book on Watteau. Despite the steady rain, he drove to Hartford, took an early-morning train to Penn Station, and, since the rain had relented by the time he'd arrived, he walked over to the Forty-second Street library, where he'd put a few books on reserve in the Arts and Architecture Collection. He'd discovered Room 300 at the time of his continuing research on Chardin, and he'd been returning to that quiet room for years now. It was much smaller than the library's main reading room and, usually, almost empty. The quiet opulence of Room 300: a dozen or so large tables of thick, richly polished wood, each with eight finely designed oval-backed chairs; solid, beautiful tables gleaming like honey in the room bordered on all sides by two main tiers of shelves separated by an elevated wrought-iron walkway that also circled the room; shelves filled with oversize art books, catalogs, files; two brass reading lamps permanently placed on each of the tables, always on, as were the overhead lamps that lined the ornate ceiling, since there were no windows. A serene place that smelled of varnish and paper, an oasis in the midst of bustling, noisy midtown Manhattan. Unlike the main reading room, Room 300 was air-conditioned, which made it even more separate from the outside. A place to work. A place away from everything.

That morning, Carpentier was the first to arrive; his books were brought over by one of the students employed at the library for the summer. *Maybe a college student, since it's a bit early for the high school year to be over,* Carpentier thought as the young man smiled at him and deftly placed the stack of books on the table in front of him.

After a while—it was hard to tell how long, absorbed as he was in his attempt at reading or taking notes—a man who smelled of wet tobacco was standing near him, not quite hovering, not at all threatening, but strangely solicitous. Carpentier raised his head and looked at him, surprised, uncomprehending, and relieved at the same time. The man was wearing glasses; the lenses were very thick; he had a large, melancholy skull and nicotine-stained fingers; he was wearing a lumpy sweater against the air-conditioned cold of Room 300. "Having trouble?" the man said matter-of-factly, not in a whisper, as one tended to do in libraries, churches, museums, but in a normal voice, not caring about being overheard; in any case, they were the only two in the spacious room, bathing in its golden light, isolated from the gray drizzle outside. "Psychotic?" the man continued. "I know. I am." Carpentier had no specific idea what the man was referring to, but he was intensely grateful for the bizarre interruption. An apparition, a savior, someone come to rescue him. Now he realized he'd done nothing for the past hour, two hours, more? The man must have been observing him for a while, something in Carpentier's face, his stillness sitting at the polished table with a stack of books and papers just lying in front of him. He could only mumble incoherently, "No, there's nothing." "Are you sure? You okay?" "I think I just need to go home," Carpentier replied, more distinctly now. "I just need to go home. Thank you." He smiled at the man, gathered his papers, his pen, left the pile of books on the table, and headed for the exit. He felt the man looking at him as he walked out.

After that morning in Room 300, Robert Carpentier

understands he won't be able to do any work at all. The summer stretches out before him, vacant. He hasn't been in Connecticut in the month of June, well after the end of the semester, since he moved to Eve's apartment that brisk September when the weather had suddenly changed from summer to fall. In the past, the semester at Wannaford would be over, as it is now, but he would be waiting for Eve, working on the book on Chardin, or some article, but already preparing to leave for Greece with her, to that other life away from everything.

The Connecticut landscape in June; all that overbearing green, all those lakes and hills. He is alone in the big house; the two colleagues have left for the summer—for Tunisia, or was it Morocco? He lives on bread, cheese, and eggs he eats straight from the pan; some of the cheese has gone bad in the refrigerator; sometimes he drives to the Chinese place to get something to take back to the house. On some days, he is so incapacitated, he even thinks of going to look for her in Sarajevo. This is where she must be. To go over there and bring her back. The uselessness of that thought, the impossibility of it. The impossibility of her having left. The impossibility of her not being in their apartment, with him, now. He closes his eyes. *I must be having a nightmare*. He feels he is drowning. The madness of the relinquished, the discarded.

And so, here he is, driving to his mother's seventieth birthday celebration.

When he arrives, he has to park some distance from the house; the driveway is full; the street is already lined with parked cars on both sides. The front door of the house is ajar; he goes in. The house is quiet; everyone has gathered in the garden. There are several foil-wrapped pans on the oven; a multilayered chocolate cake bristling with unlit candles reigns on the kitchen table. Through the open sliding doors of the living room, he can see that quite a few small tables have been set up in the spacious garden. Some groups are standing; others are seated. His mother is standing and talking with several women he doesn't know; she is holding out a tray of asparagus sandwiches; even from the living room, he recognizes those sandwiches, a staple of birthday parties, wedding receptions, and First Communions when he was growing up. All his mother's brothers and sisters seem to be there; all those faces that look like one another—the quality of a smile, the eyes, noses, necks, the shape of a head. The family.

His father is sitting with several men in the shade of an enormous oak in a corner of the garden; they're having drinks. As usual, the people gathered around his father are intently listening to what he's saying; he's probably talking about what's going on *over there;* still, after all the years. There is only one woman in that group in the shade of the oak; she is sitting next to a tall man whose hand she is holding. Among the kids running around, Carpentier recognizes only his brother's son and daughter, but there are quite a few more children and adolescents; again, the faces, familiar and unexpected. The family. For a few seconds he thinks he might leave, but the thought of returning to Connecticut, to be alone again in that house, is unbearable. He places on the kitchen table the bottle of wine he has brought and walks out into the garden.

His mother is the first to see him; she hands over the tray of sandwiches to his brother's wife and quickly comes to him; she holds him in her arms and kisses him on both cheeks. "My son, my son. Look at you; you've lost weight!" "Happy birthday, Mama. I'm sorry, I didn't get a chance to buy you a gift; I will." "Don't worry about it; what does an old lady like me need? I have everything I need; I've received so many gifts. Come." He tries to protest, but she's already taken his arm and begins to take him around. Uncles and aunts he hasn't seen in a long time, friends he doesn't know; it seems endless. Then his mother stops. "I'll let you go say hello to your father over there. Look at him; he can't help himself, and they're all listening to him." The tenderness in her voice is palpable.

Carpentier walks to the far end of the garden, to his father in that circle of guests under the giant oak. He goes straight to him, bends down, and kisses him on one cheek as his father remains seated, lightly tapping with both hands on his son's shoulders in response. Carpentier raises his head from the embrace to meet the faces of the others who have been listening so intently. A quick general greeting will do. As he begins to smile and say the few words that will release him, the tall man and the woman sitting so close to him and holding his hand stand out from all the others in the group. Carpentier's recognition is so sharp that nothing else remains; there is no one else at this gathering to celebrate his mother's seventieth birthday on this day in early June, on this quiet street of a small town on Long Island, New York, USA. He is shocked by those two faces marked by a suffering that has survived all the years since he was first introduced to them and thought they had been *scooped out from within*, the faces of the deeply stricken, the faces of people *who have lost everything.* And yet, here they are, sitting among other people who are laughing, having drinks before a meal, having come to celebrate with them an old friend's birthday. Carpentier can only blurt out his sentence, the polite words of greeting—"Hello, everyone; good to see you all," or something like that—before turning around and heading back to try to lose himself in the compact gathering of other guests. *Their daughter, old enough to bleed, old enough to be slaughtered. And the baby who would be a young man now.* His mind is finally beginning to work, as if time, brutality, and blood have finally forged a path through his thoughts. Here they are again, after all these years, the tall, imposing man and the striking woman, among the other guests.

His mother's voice rises like a song in the early afternoon. "Time to eat! Please, everyone, go serve yourselves in the dining room, and come back outside!" The man and the woman are among the others responding to his mother's beckoning; they rise with difficulty from their chairs. After all the time that has passed, there is still something stately about them, but the raw glare of their grief remains and strikes him to the core. They are the same age as his parents but seem immeasurably older, and unable to be without each other. As they wait in the line that has formed, they continue to hold hands; they whisper to each other. They steady each other. They persevere. They, too, will partake of the celebratory meal with friends.

Robert Carpentier can't take his eyes off them. From the vanishing point of his future, throughout the years of the idealized life he had been living and that had leveled what came before, distilled it of pain and belonging, a vague reticence in him had sometimes surfaced, faint but persistent warnings that he had blindly disregarded, engaged as he was in avoiding the return of something that had lain fallow throughout the years. He had allowed no sorrow to touch him, steering recklessly toward a deceptive radiance.

Looking at the old couple, still impressive, still

striking, in spite of what happened to them, standing in line for a celebratory meal in this serene suburban garden, so much older than their years, damaged, but persevering, he understood that he was like all those others he had scorned for their complacency, for the privileged comforts they enjoy, seemingly unaware of the dangers and sufferings of other lives, and yet he was just like them; even worse, he had been a figure in events that took place a long time ago, but today he knew he was merely the barren bearer of a memory he had blindly elevated to the value of a loftier knowledge, a useless, misleading knowledge, for there was no second chance, no possibility of a life emptied of damage, and now he understood how he had failed Eve, why her passion, then her distance, had turned to disappointment and contempt, why she had left for a place where bodies were being destroyed by a conflict that belonged to the realm of death and decay as much as the disease that had killed Sebastian.

Now that he could see clearly, he stood there in the suburban garden, facing the terrible emptiness of his life. Ashes.

Again, he thinks of leaving and, again, the thought of being alone in that house in Connecticut overwhelms him. He can't bring himself to leave the garden; he can't go to Sarajevo.

Illustrations

(listed in order of appearance)

Acknowledgements

Encouragement is particularly precious for a debut novel. Precious encouragement was generously offered, and thanks are offered here to trusted readers without whose balm this beast just might have stopped in its tracks: Esther Allen, Cassandra Celestin, Patrick Celestin, Maryse Condé, Peter Constantine, Mona de Pracontal, Henry Gifford, Jackie Loss, Donna Masini, Karen Van Dyck. Colum McCann's reading and comments made for equally precious balm at a later stage.

Debut novel, debut voyage: thank you to Jennifer Lyons, my adventurous agent, and to Erika Goldman, editor extraordinaire.

Bellevue Literary Press is devoted to publishing literary fiction and nonfiction at the intersection of the arts and sciences because we believe that science and the humanities are natural companions for understanding the human experience. We feature exceptional literature that explores the nature of consciousness, embodiment, and the underpinnings of the social contract. With each book we publish, our goal is to foster a rich, interdisciplinary dialogue that will forge new tools for thinking and engaging with the world.

To support our press and its mission, and for our full catalogue of published titles, please visit us at blpress.org.

Bellevue Literary Press
New York